# Under the Mountain

Clarissa L. Ross

Cover Art by Sherry Zaat

ISBN 978-0-578-00547-8

*For My Heroine*

*To the Woman that held off her today*
*So that I could have a better now*
*For the Lady that sacrificed for the moment*
*In hopes of a better tomorrow*
*Who taught me never to give up*
*Whatever the circumstance*

*Mom, for going*
*Under Your Own Mountains*
*And showing me what*
*Love is*
*I dedicate this book to You*

# Chapter One

Blue lights alternated with red ones causing a surreal atmosphere to take over the small living room. The rapid pulse flashed off picture frames on either side of the red brick fireplace making the poses of two growing boys difficult to see. In the large mirror over the mantle the reflection was blinding. Two brass lamps in the crowded space were not enough to blot out the cycling of car top lights parked in the driveway and street. Between the sofa directly in front of the fireplace, two wing backed chairs on either side of the picture window and a beige recliner off in one corner there were plenty of seats for everyone. But only two of the four people in the room were sitting. Others were wandering through the rest of the house with rubber gloves and flashlights.

This was the sort of thing one watched on television. It could not really be happening to them. Any moment the heavy wooden front door would bang open and school bags would be dropped next to jackets. Dirt would land in small clumps on the gray rug. White socks would scatter the dried mud at least three feet off the small rectangular carpet onto the dark wood floor. Keys would clunk into the white basin on the hall table as loud voices would cry out impending starvation.

But that was not to be. Deep inside she knew it. The police officers searching her home for clues were proof of that. So many questions had been asked over the last few hours that she began to feel more like a suspect than a grieving mother. Her boys were never late for dinner. Where could they be? How could three boys just disappear in broad daylight and someone not see something? What had happened to them? Though her eyes had been staring straight ahead for what seemed like hours, she had no idea at what she was looking.

School had been out for nearly six hours. They were supposed to come directly home. Of course it had been one of those beautiful days just meant to spend in the sunshine. Daylight had faded two hours ago. Why hadn't they at least called? Though it was still early fall, the temperature was known to drop several degrees overnight. What if they were still outside? Ryan always caught a bad cold when he got chilled.

Why were these police officers just standing around instead of searching for her boys? Didn't they know how dangerous it could be for them? Fatigue was beginning to sap her strength and her ability to think clearly. Tears threatened once more so she automatically tipped her head to her left side.

Just as always the broad shoulder of her husband was there to give her strength. A long arm went behind her back drawing her close to his side. Words weren't necessary. He was hurting just as much as she. Without looking at him she knew what the expression on his face would be. His vibrant blue eyes would be staring straight ahead, the life behind them all but gone. Deep creases would be across his wide forehead and between his eyes. She suddenly felt him shift slightly as he looked up at one of the officers asking yet another question for the hundredth time.

"Are you having any family problems? Any problems in your marriage that might drive the boys to run away from home?" Large sausage like fingers gripped his pen tighter over the small notepad. This seasoned officer was clearly suspicious of their situation as he glared down on them waiting for one of them to crack.

As she distantly heard her husband's voice she thought about the answer to that question. They had had the usual ups and downs any other couple would have faced over the years as well as some unusual circumstances to overcome. When he had been about seventeen he had suffered some sort of trauma and could remember nothing about his past. He had been discovered by hunters in the foothills of Kentucky sleeping in tattered clothes and many cuts and scrapes covered his body. Doctors at the nearby hospitals were baffled by his case and sent him to other medical facilities for help. In the end no answers were found and his picture plastered all over the country had resulted in nothing.

That was how she had met him. Her father had wanted her to do some work in a hospital to see if she really wanted to be a nurse. So she volunteered to deliver books and magazines to patients. It had not been the most exciting work; in fact it got downright boring much of the time. But the second she laid eyes on him everything changed; including her desire to be a nurse. From the moment she learned that he couldn't remember how to read she became a teacher. She loved every minute of her time with him and quickly fell in love with him. So yes, they had their issues, sorting out the workload around the house had been the most difficult because she had had to teach him how to do many of those tasks. But then who didn't have a few issues in marriage?

"...there's been a little strain between the boys since we took in Andrew. Ryan liked the idea well enough to begin with but it has come to make him feel odd man out. Handling issues with Andrew has caused us more than one disagreement but we faced those head on worked them out and moved on."

"And what about your older son, Mr. Sauntage, uh sorry, Smith? How was he dealing with his friend turned brother of sorts?" Dark eyes bored into the strained face of the tall man seated before him. Something about this case tore at his gut. It wasn't adding up on the surface. So far they had turned up nothing. No plausible explanation for these disappearances.

"Don't worry about it. People mix up my name all the time. Charlie hasn't had a problem with Drew that I know of. In fact, he rather enjoyed having someone his own age to hang out with." Sauntage gave his wife's thick waist a gentle squeeze of support and comfort and then rose to his full height of six foot two inches. "It's Ryan that has the short end of the stick you might say. Instead of having two big brothers like he was counting on, he got a team of teasers. They did a fair amount of picking on him I'm afraid."

A thoughtful frown came to the officer's wide face. "Do you think he had had enough and took revenge?"

Before Sauntage could respond his wife jumped off the couch and flared, "NO! And they would never do anything to hurt Ryan either! Why aren't you out there looking for them?" She pointed at the large window facing the street.

"Maureen, darling, they are doing everything they can." Tenderly he enfolded her against his chest, rocking back and forth on his feet as though he were comforting a child.

"You say that Andrew Carson, age 13, came to live with you a few months ago?" Once more the pencil was poised for any new facts.

"Yes, it's been about four months now. He moved in just before school let out in May." Sauntage answered quietly.

A frown came to the officer's mouth as he wondered, "How is it that he came to live here? You're not a blood relative are you?"

"No." His head shook back and forth as he turned to face the blue uniformed man. "Andrew has been friends with Charlie for many years. When he was a toddler his parents were killed in a car accident and he came to live with his Grandmother just down the street. About seven months ago she discovered that she had cancer and decided against treatment because it was at an advanced stage. She came to us and asked us if we would take him in when she got too sick to care for him properly. We are in the process of legally adopting him."

"Is this Grandmother still living down the street?" As much as he tried to make his voice gentle, the officer knew that he had failed when Mrs. Smith responded.

"No. She passed away in the hospital just two weeks after Drew moved in with us." Fresh tears were swiped at before she went on to add, "Anna Carson was such a dear lady."

Thoughtfully the officer looked around the room. No help was forthcoming from his co-workers. He was in charge and at the moment they were more than happy to let him be. "Are there any other relatives or friends that he might have tried to go see? Maybe your sons went with him?"

"Andrew didn't have any family left to speak of. Just a cousin or two on his Mother's side. And neither do we for that matter. I think that was why we were so close to Anna and Drew. As for friends, there aren't any that we haven't tried to call already. We gave Officer Miller a list of their names and telephone numbers." Sauntage could feel the strength melting from his wife, so he turned to draw her into his chest.

"Now let's see, Mrs. Smith, you are a teacher at Lincoln High and, Mr. Smith, you work for a company by the name of..." He paused to go back through his notepad, "Ruffwell Corp. Is there anyone that you work with that might have a grudge against you?"

Keeping his arm around Maureen's shoulders he turned to reply, "Most of my time is spent on the road with my partner, but we don't talk very much. Usually he drives the truck and I load the trash into the hopper and crush it. And everyone loves Maureen at the school. She is tough with the grades, but she also knows how to show the kids how much she cares."

The front door came to life seconds later and they turned around with hopeful expectation. Her heart dropped back to the pit of her stomach making her legs weak. Once more she sat on the edge of the green floral sofa at the insistence of her husband's strong hand. Tears burned painfully taking clarity from her sight, but her ears were unhampered when the officers just coming into the house drew closer.

They spoke softly with their superior officer for several seconds. As the three of them quietly conferred their gazes went back and forth between the bereaved couple. One of them produced a small plastic bag from inside his jacket and held it out for the older man to examine. There seemed to be a large piece of gold jewelry sealed inside. Finally, the man in charge of the investigation held it out to the man and woman now seated side by side holding tightly to one another's hands.

"This was found in the bushes just outside the front door. Do either of you recognize it?" His brown eyes studied the parents' reaction carefully. The woman he noted wiped her eyes harshly and then took the baggie in her grasp. It was harder to make out the man's response. After one quick glance as his wife examined it, he seemed to dismiss the item, but not quite.

Maureen could feel her fingers shaking as she held the cool plastic in her hand. To her amazement there was a large medallion that appeared to be made of gold. There were several letters engraved along the outer edges of the round disk, but the scrolling of the font made it impossible for her to decipher. Towards the center there were intricate lines of a strange animal face. To her it resembled a large cat with curly hair. On the back side of the disk were several lines of curly cued letters in the center. Shaking her head wearily she passed the baggie to her husband saying tearfully, "I've never seen this before. Or anything like it. I know that gangs sometimes have symbols they paint when they commit a crime. Does it belong to some gang?"

"We don't know for sure, Mrs. Smith, there is no one here that has seen this image before tonight. Even if it does, though, it is no proof that a gang has had anything to do with your sons' disappearances. Maybe we can get fingerprints or some other information from this and have a lead to work from in a few hours." He reached for Mr. Smith's outstretched hand to take back the medallion. "What about you? Do you have any idea where this came from?"

His face suddenly hardened and he reached out to pull his wife against his aching chest. His head lowered to the top of his wife's head and he shook it, saying, "I've never seen that before." A glaze fell over his eyes as his thoughts turned inward.

Another two hours ticked off the clock before the last of them left. Sauntage encouraged Maureen to go upstairs and get some rest while he kept watch for the boys. Reluctantly, she had dragged herself up the creaky narrow staircase.

For awhile Sauntage paced back and forth in front of the fireplace. His thoughts seemed to be distracted because he tripped on the multi-colored braided rug under his feet three times and rammed into to the coffee table twice with his shins. Rubbing his lower leg absently he sat on the sofa to grapple with whatever was on his mind.

Slowly, he began to walk around the rooms on the first floor seeming to look for any clues that the police might have missed. The crowded living room muffled his footsteps fairly well, but the dining room with the rectangular table and matching wooden chairs echoed his every movement. Nothing was out of place. Pictures were all level and straight while the heavy, dark blue drapes rested in their usual place. Maureen's papers were still scattered across the surface. Pushing the lower button on the wall plate near the kitchen doorway, Sauntage darkened the family's eating area.

In the kitchen he went to the light yellow cabinet over the sink and pulled out a black mug. Next to the left side of the gas stove, was a gray laminate countertop just big enough for the coffee machine. As carefully as his tired hands could they poured a large measure into his waiting mug. Leaning his hip against the sink he looked to his left towards the refrigerator and saw nothing out of the ordinary. On his right side a small portion of window's glass peeked out from the white ruffled curtain. Behind him Sauntage had already observed the raw chicken waiting to be cooked. Nothing was out of place.

More time slipped away as he appeared to be wrestling with his thoughts. His mind went over everything. Suddenly, he moved into action.

No more tears were left in her eyes. She was sure that it would be impossible for her body to produce any more moisture when her heart kept bleeding painfully in her chest. The empty rooms down the hall had caused frightened chills to run up and down her spine.

Ryan's was smaller but because he was not sharing space with anyone he had more room to spread out his things. He certainly took every opportunity to do so. It was difficult to determine which clothes on the floor were clean and which were dirty. The gray carpet that matched the front hall rug was only visible in a few small spots. Cars made of metal were scattered in front of the closet door, building blocks of colored plastic were arranged under the window and little green army men were lined up on the bed ready to take out the stuffed toys across from them. There was one bear exempt from the impending battle. He was sitting on the dresser next to the door. Absently, Maureen picked him up and left the room.

Charlie and Andrew were a bit better about their clothes, but because there were two of them it did not seem that way. When Andrew had first moved in they had simply moved a second twin sized bed into this room. The boys really had made an effort to make room for each other. In the end though they realized a new arrangement had to be made. With some of the money Anna had left for Andrew they purchased two loft beds for the thirteen year olds. Only three months separated them and like twins they were similar.

Both boys liked sports a great deal. Charlie followed football while Andrew enjoyed baseball. On these facts alone it was easy to tell that Charlie slept next to the door and Andrew next to the window. One bed was covered in helmets and goalposts. The other had wooden bats crossed on the fabric.

Their dressers were tucked beneath the frames of the beds. On Andrew's there were books with stories of dragon's and knights. He loved tales of adventure and history.

Charlie liked to read too, but not as much as Andrew. His favorite things to read were about space or football. It was more interesting to him to learn facts about something than to read a made up story.

Each of the boys had a few trophies on his dresser to commemorate his time on various sports teams. A couple of posters adorned the walls with sports superstars in action.

She had stepped back into the hall unable to close the door behind her. It had now been more than eight hours since she had come home from work to find her boys missing. Deep down she knew the odds of finding Charlie, Ryan and Andrew safe and unharmed were slim. Her stomach lurched at the realization as her heart rallied against the negative current with hope. Maybe, just maybe there was a chance.

Sitting on the side of the queen size bed hugging Ryan's dark brown teddy bear she looked as if she were in a catatonic state. But she wasn't. In her mind she was reliving each moment since she had come home from work, in slow motion. Had she missed anything important?

After parking her car in the small garage she had picked up her bulging leather briefcase and equally heavy purse and then headed for the wide door behind the small blue Escort. Her steps halted when she heard the fabric of her full brown skirt giving way. The hem of the new outfit was caught in the door. With a tired moan she opened the car door once more. Hopefully she would be able to repair the damage and not have to turn the expensive garment into a rag.

Without taking time to look at the damage she swung her purse and briefcase up on her shoulder so that she would have one hand free to close the dark gray garage door. Small stones along the driveway crunched under her light weight black leather boots.

When she had unlocked the back door and lowered her things on the kitchen floor in front of the white refrigerator she lifted the hem of her skirt. Much to her dismay she found a gaping hole in the lowest 'ruffle' of her tiered skirt. There was no way to fix that.

Giving her purse and briefcase a harsh shove with her heeled boot she made way for the appliance door to swing open. The chicken she had pulled out of the freezer that morning was nearly defrosted so she moved to set the package next to the sink for a few minutes.

It was then that she noticed that the sink was free of dishes. A wry grimace crossed her lips as if she knew something was going on with the boys. They must want something because they never took care of their after school snack dishes without being told several times. Whatever it was it must be expensive. Probably going to ask for Karate lessons again, she thought to herself.

With a shake of her head at their persistence she went upstairs to change her clothes and say hello. When she passed into the tiny foyer and saw no shoes or bags lying about she had only a momentary twinge of concern. They probably went home from school with some friends and left a message on the answering machine.

Once she had pulled a casual sweater in lime green as well as a pair of jeans from the closet, she clicked a button on the small black box on her dresser. While she switched outfits a stream of recordings from various companies trying to sell her products that she did not need or want played in the background. One quick tap on another button erased the tape.

A frown lowered the corners of her wide lips as she descended the stairs. Perhaps there had been an after school activity that she had forgotten. Her pace quickened as she decided to check the calendar on the refrigerator. There was nothing listed.

At first she wanted to give into the sense of urgency that threatened to overtake her, but with a deep breath she resisted the urge to react. She was over reacting as usual she told herself. Business was the best thing to calm her crazy thoughts so she sat at the dining room table with a large stack of papers to grade. Red ink flowed more freely than usual though it was some time before she realized that she was taking out her frustrations on innocent high school students. With a sigh she vowed to go back over those first papers using a less critical eye next time.

Not long afterwards the rattle of Sauntage's truck could be heard coming up the driveway. Anxiously, she got up from the table to greet her husband.

By the time she had walked around the table and through the kitchen, he was closing the door. An easy smile came to his lips as he looked up at her. "Hello, Beautiful." As quickly as he could Sauntage stripped his outer layer of clothing off and tossed it down the flight of steps to his right.

"Sau, the boys aren't home yet." Her eyes darted back and forth over his weary face.

"Oh, they probably went to one of their friends' houses and lost track of the time." His hands kneaded the tight muscles of her shoulders as he bent to kiss her soundly. When he stepped back and saw how worried she was he asked, "Have you tried calling any of their friends?"

She shook her head back and forth, "No, I haven't..."

"Well, why don't you try doing that while I remove as much of the sanitary landfill off my body as I can? If you haven't figured out what friend they are hanging out with by then I'll take over for you."

Her lips had lifted in a weak smile as she quietly agreed to his plan and watched him leave the room. He always had a way with problems that didn't necessarily solve them, but brought them into a manageable size. His plan had been good and true to his word when he had cleansed away the scent of garbage, Sauntage took over the telephone. The only thing was none of the boys' friends had seen them since school had let out at three-thirty.

Now hours later Maureen sat questioning every move she had made that day. Even going as far as berating herself for going back to work when Ryan had begun school; if she had been at home where she belonged then she might have been able to stop it.

The light on the night stand to her left softly illuminated her side of the bed. In front of her was a low dresser with a mirror over it. No light was visible from the window next to it. Besides the fact that it was so late and faced the backyard, the window was covered with heavy drapes in a yellow rose pattern. Under her was a matching coverlet. Normally these roses cheered her and the room was bright. She knew the darkness she felt right now had very little to do with the sun being gone for the day.

Footsteps coming up the stairs caused her to tighten her hold on the stuffed toy in her lap. Part of her wished that he would get to yelling at her. He had to blame her for what had happened. If she had started making those calls right away they wouldn't have lost so much precious time.

Instead of raising his voice Sauntage stood in front of her with his hands pushed deeply into his pockets as he softly said, "Maureen, Honey, I love you so much." His hands trembled at his sides as he removed them and looked down on her frozen form.

"I love you, too." She answered hoarsely and then went on to add, "I'm so sorry, Sau. This is all my fault. If only...."

With some force he took her by the shoulders. In a whisper he admitted, "Mo, we need to talk."

"Now, Sau? I can't even think straight. I keep thinking if I'd been home..." Her face crumpled as hoarse gasps of pain escaped.

"This was not your fault, Darling..." He tried to assure her.

"But..."

Forcefully, he took her face in his hands and declared firmly, "There was nothing you could've done to stop this."

With confusion Maureen looked at him and wondered, "How can you say that for sure? I should have been here." She pulled her face back from his hand and dropped it into her palms.

Biting his lip Sauntage took a deep breath to admit; with his head lowered shamefully, "Because I know where the boys are."

Maureen snapped her head up so fast for a moment she was dizzy. "What?"

"This is my fault, Mo, not yours." His voice shook with emotion.

Fear walked boldly up and down her spine. The rhythm of her heart sped up unmercifully. "What are you talking about?" There was something about the look in his eyes that was haunting.

"That medallion the police found..." He paused to gain control of his voice, "I know where it came from."

"You do!" Like lightening she came off the bed sending the bear head first into the dresser. "Did you call the police already?" When she saw the slight shake of his head she cried, "Why not?"

Slowly he licked his lips and breathed deeply.

"Sauntage!" Excitement, confusion, fear and hope now raced through her heart painfully. "We have to tell them right away."

"Sit down..." Tenderly he pushed against her shoulders to encourage her, but she did not budge.

Every instinct in her prickled, "We don't have time for this now.

We have to let the police know right away. The sooner they know where you have seen that medallion the sooner they can find the boys."

"It comes from my homeland, Maureen." His voice was raspy with unshed tears. He watched the muscles around her eyes tighten and relax several times.

"You've regained some memories after all these years?" A strange wave of joy washed through her whole body as she threw her arms around his neck and kissed his cheek. "Sauntage, that's wonderful!" The implications of his statement hit her a few seconds later causing her to pull back from his embrace. "Where are our sons?"

"There is a great deal for me to explain and it will take some time." Much to his relief she sank slowly to the mattress to listen. "Maureen, I don't have amnesia..."

Excitedly she squeezed his warm fingers crying, "I know. We've waited so long for this day. I thought it would never come."

"...and I never did have amnesia." Sauntage finished lamely with his eyes averted from hers.

"What?" Confusion wrinkled her eyes and forehead.

"The truth is I remember my childhood perfectly." A heavy sigh left him.

"How is that possible? You could hardly speak let alone read when we met. And your picture was on every television station and in every newspaper. No one came forward with any credible knowledge about you." Maureen could feel her head shaking back and forth but her strained eyes never left his tense face.

"Yes, I know." He answered quietly.

"Is your family dead? Or do they live under a rock? Is your past so horrible that you couldn't share it with me?" Maureen wanted to scream but just could not find the strength to do more than whisper hoarsely. This was some kind of nightmare. In shock she heard a soft chuckle come from him and felt her blood pressure rise. He thought this was funny!

His head wagged back and forth briefly. "No, as far as I know most of my family is still living. And in a strange sense they do in fact live in a place that can only be reached by crawling under rocks."

Horror rounded her wide mouth and flashing eyes. "Is your family some kind of Mafia, Sau? Oh, my...what is your real name? I should have known something was up when you insisted on calling yourself by such an unusual name!"

"My birth name was Sauntage Vadelum I added Smith here because where I was born we don't have middle names."

The calmness in his voice was unnerving. Raising her hands in an effort to regain some control over her raging thoughts she stood to pace along the end of the bed. After a few moments she cried, "And what has your lie got to do with my sons?"

"That medallion has the picture of an aragaff, an animal that is the symbol for my family. Tonight was the first time I have seen that medallion since I left home..."

"Are you part of the witness protection program?" Somewhere deep inside; her body found water because tears were able to flood once more into her eyes.

"No, Darling..."

Rage rose from the pit of her stomach, "Don't you dare call me that! Where are my sons!" She screamed at him and then gaped at him openly. This man was a total stranger to her. What was she going to do?

"I believe they are being taken to my birth land." Sauntage swallowed hard

"You're not an American?" Her breath was coming in heated gasps. Tremors had overtaken her arms and were quickly advancing through her entire body.

Sauntage lowered his eyes to the worn carpet on the floor.

"So let me guess, you only married me so you could stay here legally...good grief! You're a spy!" Panic seized her as she started to back away from him.

"I married you because I love you with all my heart, Maureen." He pleaded with his eyes for her to listen to him. "And no I am not a spy."

"Then why didn't you tell me all this before now?" Something in her began to tear. And her heart was beginning to rend under the struggle.

With a deep breath he straightened to his full height and took a step closer to her. "Because I know how crazy this all sounds. And I had no intention of forcing you or the boys to make the journey back with me..."

"But you have gone back haven't you?" With all her being she wanted him to be able to deny it.

"Yes. Every year I make the journey to my homeland." A slow nod accompanied his answer.

Understanding dawned in her eyes as she realized what he was saying, "All those fishing trips were a lie!" Her teeth clenched together as her fingers laced through her shoulder length auburn hair.

"Not entirely. I went fishing, just not where you thought I did." Once again he moved closer and took her by the shoulders as he spoke urgently, "Please, listen to me, Maureen, time is of the utmost importance. If I am to have any chance of getting the boys before they cross into my homeland, I have to start my journey before morning and there is a great deal that has to be done between now and then." He saw the minute dip of her chin and then drew her back to the bed so they could sit. Once he had lowered his weight to the mattress he patted the space next to him.

Her head jerked from side to side as she said, "This can't be happening. You're trying to make me think I'm going crazy..."

"I am the eldest son in my family." He began his tale softly. "I have an older sister, Raijika and a younger one named, Didwalra. Tagurah is my brother. He is just a year and nine months behind me. When I left home they were all well. Raijika had married a year before and the others were completing their training as I was. We all were so close in age to one another that our birth order meant very little to us. In our land, however, the order of the children is important. It dictates our position in society, what job we will hold or whom we may choose to marry. As the eldest son I was expected to someday take my Father's place. So childhood was short for me. There were always lessons and training sessions. I never minded the learning, but the truth is my Father is a great man and I was overwhelmed with the thought of taking his place when he retired or died. I could never be the kind of man he is or was..."

"He died?" Despite her desire not to be affected by his tale, Maureen felt herself being drawn in against her will.

"I don't know for sure. You have to understand how much my

coming to live here affected my life there..." For some reason he held back. "I wasn't even given the option to go back to my homeland permanently. My parents disowned me, Maureen. In their eyes I guess I committed the gravest act of betrayal against my people and its land."

"I think I can one up them on that." There was a sneer on her lips as she leaned her right shoulder against the curtains.

Nodding Sauntage went on to add, "Yes, I have managed to hurt everyone that I love through all of this. But I never imagined something like this ever happening. I made my choice years ago and have never regretted it..."

"So have you told your parents all of this during one of your 'fishing' trips?" Some of the initial shock was wearing off.

"No." He answered and then lowered his chin.

Maureen jumped when he came off the bed with clenched fists. Was he going to hurt her? Every nerve and muscle of her body was preparing to flee.

"One of the things I was naturally required to learn was our history. For the most part I didn't mind because I found it interesting. One thing I uncovered was a long forgotten legend about the road to another place. I spent almost two years looking for clues about this place. I saw it as a way I might be able to have adventures of my own choosing before having my life dictated by my position. Most of what I learned turned out to be bunk, but there really was a way out. My brother and I talked about this many times and he knew how I felt about my future so he kept my secret when I started using the path.

"I made many trips back and forth and learned a great deal about life here before I slipped up. Getting that close to people was a mistake and I knew it. When I stopped to rest I honestly thought I was far enough away from them to be discovered.

"Once those hunters found me I had no choice but to stay. I couldn't risk someone following me on the journey back." A soft smile came to his lips as he stopped pacing in front of her and tenderly drew the fingers of his right hand down the side of her cheek. "Oh, but then I met you. I wanted so much to take you to my family."

For a full minute he said nothing and she simply stared at him.

Then he began to pace once more. "The first time I went back was when you went camping with your parents. On my way to my parents' home I met my brother. I couldn't wait to tell him about you. Tagurah was genuinely happy for me. Apparently our parents weren't home but traveling on business so I came back here at his insistence. I agreed to let him speak to our Father because he told me Father was livid over my leaving and he knew my time was short. He said that our parents had practically dragged my whereabouts from him. We made arrangements to meet at The Gateway two weeks later and that time Tagurah told me my Father was sending word through him that I was dead to them and he no longer wished to call me son.

"Since that time I have secretly met with my brother once a year at the gate of my homeland and we learn of each other's lives. Every year it has been the same, the second weekend in July. Last year though you remember how I was late coming home from my yearly fishing trip? Well, my brother was not there when I arrived and I waited an extra day for him. I felt it was odd because there was evidence that he had been there since our previous meeting. I still don't know exactly what this means except that I am certain the boys are with him. Tagurah is the only one I talked to about The Gateway and my travels as well as you and the boys. Something tells me that the boys are not in any immediate danger from him. Maybe he told my Father that I had children and Father sent Tagurah to find them."

"Why wouldn't he just come to you then?" Maureen puzzled aloud. "Why would he steal our sons away?"

A heavy sigh lowered his shoulders as he admitted quietly, "I have no idea. You're right; none of this really makes any sense. All I know is that I am sure the boys are with Tagurah."

Silence filled the room for sometime before she pushed her tired frame away from the window saying, "Sau, we have to tell the police. They can help us..."

"No, they can't, Mo."

"Well, why not?" She cried with exasperation.

A heavy sigh left him. "Because no one on earth knows of this path but me. And no one else can know about it. If people here learned of it they would come to explore it and destroy it. No, I must do this alone."

"No, I'm coming with you." From the way that his frame stiffened she knew he was going to protest. "They are my sons too, Sau."

Sauntage slowly drew close to her and gently placed his hands on her shoulders as he vowed solemnly, "I will bring our sons home to you, Maureen."

Fiercely she slapped his hands away. In horror she hissed at him, "After what you told me you expect me to trust you? No, Sau, I will be by your side every step of the way. Until my sons are home safe and sound you will not be out of my sight."

For a moment he looked at her without making a sound. Then he started to fold his arms around her back. Her words caused him to jerk as if he had received blows from a prize fighter.

"Don't touch me! You have no right. Together we will bring our sons home, but that is all." When she saw the blue of his eyes begin to move like waves Maureen screeched at him, "You've betrayed me, Sauntage Vadelum Smith, and nothing you can do will make up for that!" When she saw his nod of resignation she went on to ask, "Do I need to pack my passport?"

"No, you don't need a passport." He replied quietly. "Maureen, I understand how you feel about me, but you must understand also how difficult this journey is."

She saw his gaze going over her body with concern. "You think I'm too fat to handle it?" Her eyes flared briefly then narrowed on him in rage. "My weight has never been an issue before. Are you ashamed to be seen with me in your homeland?" In tears she rushed past him to leave the room.

"No!" Sauntage yelled as he reached for her forearm and forced her to face him. "You are wrong. This journey is hard. Even with all the physical demands of my job, I have trouble making it."

"Then you have under estimated the will of a mother to reach her children." Wrenching her arm free from his grip, Maureen headed for her dresser. "Now where exactly are we going? I need to know what to pack."

"Liguesis. It should be pleasant this time of the year, but you will have very little room to carry extra clothing." His words were measured very carefully.

"Liguesis? I've never heard of it. Is that some little town in

Canada?" Her lip was curled comically as she stood trying to recall the name from an atlas or globe.

With hesitation he cleared his throat to answer, "No, it is not in Canada. Liguesis is not on any map." The pause in her movement told him that he again had her undivided attention. "It is a world apart from this one."

"Are you asking me to believe that you come from outer space?" In disgust she slammed the drawers shut and quickly walked around the end of the bed past her husband. "I'm going to go call the police myself."

In a flash he caught her in the doorway. "Maureen, no. If you do that I won't have a chance of getting to the boys." His fingers clamped over her upper arms. "Listen, if you don't trust me fine, just give me a two hour head start, please."

As she studied his tense cheek muscles and wrinkled eyebrows she debated. What choice did she really have? Stay here risking the possibility of him taking her sons away or go with him to some unknown place where he could do whatever he wanted to her.

With weary resignation she asked, "Okay, what do we do now?"

"Let's go downstairs to the table. We need to make a list. There is a lot to do and we can't afford to forget anything."

Her briefcase had been shoved into Ryan's place at the table with a large pile of loose papers on top of it. Each of them had a sheet of note book paper with detailed lists on it. Maureen pressed her palm into her forehead and sighed with exhaustion. "I don't like the idea of lying to the police, Sau. It's just not right."

"Yeah, I know, but there isn't any other way. No one can trace our steps. That's critical." His finger tapped firmly on the smooth wooden surface. "Liguesis would be destroyed if anyone followed us."

"Yes, I understand but I still don't like it." Her plump arm dropped to the table with a light slap. Inside she was panicking. What should she do? He was insane. For the moment she decided to play along with him. Perhaps if he were appeased long enough she could figure out what had really happened to her sons.

"Well, don't worry about it. I'll handle talking to the police. They have to believe that the boys are back home safe and sound. I feel funny that the entire department is out looking for them now when I know that they won't find them. And the fewer eyes on us when we leave tomorrow the better off we are."

She pulled her page closer and read though it as she said, "So tomorrow we both call in to work and say we're not coming in because the boys were missing half of the night. And we call the schools with the same story. Then we drive off to Kentucky..."

"We'll need some supplies before we leave town. I don't want to stop anywhere along the way if we can help it."

As he spoke she felt a chill settle over her heart. His explanation for everything made sense, well, except for this crazy notion of another world. She felt trapped. If she trusted him it could mean untold danger for her. But if she didn't at least pretend to go along with this plan she might miss her only chance to help her children.

"...it's time we got some sleep." The narrowing of her puffy eyes revealed her thoughts. "Maureen, at some point you have to remember the last seventeen years. When I've promised something haven't I got a decent record of following through? I promise not to leave without you."

Her lips curled and pursed for a few seconds. Then looking directly into his steady blue eyes she confessed, "And after tonight why should I believe you, Sau?"

"Because I realize now that despite my reservations and concerns that I can't bring the boys back without help. I need you, Mo." His voice faltered as he went on to add, "And we both need to get as much rest as we possibly can."

"Fine. Let's go to bed." In rushed movements she leapt from her chair nearly knocking it into the wall.

Carefully Sauntage collected their notes and coffee cups. When he came to his feet a heavy sigh loudly left him. Behind him he could hear Maureen straightening her papers.

The chicken on the countertop caught his eye as she entered the room. Lifting the package carefully he held it out towards her. "Is this going to be any good?"

"I won't risk it. Just throw it in the garbage." Maureen shrugged at him as if it were no big deal.

"No, we can't do that. We have to make things look like we went on vacation. Nothing can be out of the ordinary or out of place."

Tiredly she snapped, "Well, what are we supposed to do with it then? I'm not going to eat it."

Looking around the room he then went to peek inside the refrigerator as he replied, "We'll pack everything that will spoil within a day or two and find a dumpster to drop it in when we go pick up our supplies." The appliance door closed with a dull thud just before he went on to add, "Come on let's get some sleep."

Reluctantly, Maureen preceded him up the creaky stairs. At the top she turned with longing to the doors on her right side. Tears welled up as she couldn't help thinking that maybe he was wrong.

"We're going to find them, Mo." His large hands came to rest on her shoulders and gently guided her to their bedroom.

"How can you be so sure? What if you're wrong and this brother of yours didn't take them? That gold disk could have been there for months or maybe even years." She turned to him with near panic in her eyes as her chin wavered.

With a nod he encouraged her to go into the bathroom. As the two of them prepared for sleep he explained, "Do you remember how I told you that birth order was very important? It determines to a large extent what career options one has. My brother was the second son, but the third child so that meant he could choose to learn metal work, mining or go into the military. Part of our education was to experience each of the trades to find what you were best suited for. Tagurah chose to work in the mines though he was very adept at working with metals of all kinds."

While he brushed his teeth she watched him closely. His frame was heavy though not with fat. Sauntage was all bone and muscle. Once his teeth were rinsed he splashed water on his face rubbing it through the black stubble.

"What has that got to do with when the medallion was dropped?"

"On the outer edge there were some etchings..."

"Yes, I saw them. They looked a bit like letters."

He nodded briskly as he switched off the light and moved toward the bed. "That's exactly what they were. It was a bit strange but it was clearly a message from Tagurah to me."

With her hand poised over the coverlet, Maureen observed, "But you hardly glanced at it."

"I suppose it's like riding a bike. Everything came back in a flash." He gave a shrug as he slipped under the covers.

"What did it say, Sau?" Her voice was hesitant. Did she really want to know?

"It is a bit cryptic in nature, but it said, 'time to train in Liguesis'. Career training actually begins at fourteen and he knows how old Charles is so that's what makes it all confusing to me." Sauntage explained with a tired sigh then reached over his head to turn out the brass lamp on the night stand.

"Sau?"

"Yeah?"

"Are you sure the boys aren't in danger with him?"

"I don't believe they are." He answered emotionally.

"I wish I could believe you." Maureen whispered sadly under her breath as she pulled the covers up to her chin and allowed silent tears to wet her temples.

# Chapter Two

The sun was shining brightly when Maureen opened her eyes. It was nearly a minute before everything came rushing back at her. A cry broke from her lips as she noted the empty space next to her. Angrily, she punched her pillow. Despite her resolve she had fallen asleep.

Heavy foot falls up the stairs caused her to look up at the door with wide eyes. Seconds later Sauntage appeared fully dressed and breathing deeply.

"Are you all right?" When he saw her eyes flick to the floor beside the bed he went on to say, "You thought I left without you?" Gently he sat on the end of his section of the mattress. "I was wrong to keep everything from you all these years. Don't feel bad about not trusting me. Can't say that I would trust me if I were in your shoes. Maybe someday, somehow I can earn your trust once more."

Flipping the covers off her legs she snapped bitterly, "You betrayed my trust. How can I not question everything you say or do? I can't help but wonder what else you have lied about."

To this he said nothing but simply nodded. Slowly he got to his feet and walked out of the room with his shoulders hunched.

When she had finished getting dressed a few minutes later Maureen found her husband seated at the table making marks on their lists from the previous night. "How long have you been up?"

"A couple of hours." Sauntage replied after quickly looking at the clock on the wall.

"Why didn't you wake me?" She slipped into her chair and glanced down at his notes.

"You needed the rest. This journey will be torture on our bodies and you have never made the trip." Referring to the paper before him with his pencil he said, "I've called the police, schools and my dispatch office."

Her eyes flared wide. "Wow, you've been busy this morning!"

"I just had to get up and do something. This waiting game is beginning to wear on my nerves." He admitted quietly.

"Me too! Why don't we just go? The sooner we leave..." Impatiently she rose from her seat.

With his hand he reached out to take hold of her forearm as he explained, "We have to be careful, Mo. There can't be any questions when we come back. Everything must look as though we took an extended vacation. Otherwise there could be an investigation into our disappearances. It will be hard enough for us to explain a sudden vacation, but if we don't cover our tracks now..."

"I understand. Now what is next on the list?" She nodded her head towards the papers he had been studying. He sounded even more determined to go on this crazy venture than he had the previous night.

"We need to go through the house and prepare it for us to be gone. You know, unplug the TV in case of storms put a few lights on a timer so that it looks like someone is home and clear out any food that might spoil." He paused momentarily. "The other thing we must do is pack suitcases for all of us."

"What do we pack? I mean where is our imaginary vacation going to take place?" There was a note of sarcasm in her voice as she raised her right eyebrow at him. This was insane.

"Oh, gosh, that's a really good point. We all need to take similar clothing. Let's go with something tropical, so we won't have as much to worry about."

"Fine, I'll start with Ryan's things so if you need me that's where I'll be." Quickly Maureen charged up to the second floor and went straight to the hall closet. From the floor she pulled out an eclectic collection of suitcases. Snatching one of the smaller ones, she went to her eight year old son's room.

It was so hard looking at his things waiting for him and not giving in to the overwhelming sense of loss. She resisted the urge to pick up his toys and clothes. There wasn't enough time for that.

As she zipped the top down Maureen remembered her husband's work clothes in the basement. If this really had to look like a pleasure trip then she had to do something with Sauntage's smelly wardrobe. Hoping to jar him with the only piece of logic he seemed to have missed, she went racing down the stairs startling her husband as she went. "Your work clothes need to be washed. They could stink up the whole house by the time we get back." Her words caused him to look at his watch.

"Good thinking. We ought to have time to finish a load of laundry before we drive out of town. Go ahead and start it, hopefully it will be ready for the dryer when we go dump the trash and pick up our supplies." He called loudly after her and turned to finish setting the light timer he had in his hands.

Less than an hour later they were sitting side by side in his old truck. Large patches of the orange-red paint had been replaced by rust, but this did not effect how well the engine ran. This was not the case for the shocks, every crack and divot in the road felt like a deep pit.

Bouncing on the seat next to her husband, Maureen stared out the windshield in a daze. Her head was whirling with all the things they had to do before they went after her sons. Sauntage had told her very little about the journey itself, except that it involved a great deal of hiking.

First on their list of places to stop was a sporting goods store. Most of the items she would need were apparently found there. Within an hour they had selected hiking boots, gloves, a backpack, rope, repelling harness and all the other equipment to go with it, a hard hat with a halogen lamp on it and batteries. Most of their purchases were chosen by Sauntage because she had no idea what she really needed.

After cramming the bags and boxes in the back of the large cab they then drove to the grocery store. Here they chose some canned foods but most of their choices were jerked meats, nuts and dried fruits. Also added were freeze dried packets that they could just add water in order to dine. Soup was not among Maureen's favorite menu selections so that was reluctantly put in the cart.

By the time the two of them reached the checkout she began to question how they were going to manage carrying all this stuff. There was no way it would fit in her new backpack. And even if by some miracle it could be jammed into it, she would never be able to haul it. She was about to ask him about this part of the plan when he seemed to sense her puzzlement.

"I have a hiking pack in the garage that I use for this journey each year." When he saw her nod her admission of this making sense, Sauntage went on to add, "Of course we have to take more food with us than I usually take because there are two of us. When we reach the interior of the cave we will be able to drop some of it for our return trip which means even more food because the boys will be with us." Gently he stretched his right hand over her left one to give it a squeeze. Seconds later she pulled her hand into her lap, keeping her gaze averted from his probing eyes.

Back at the house they sorted through all the purchases, trying to organize all of it as quickly as possible. Sauntage wanted to be on the highway before rush hour traffic. In the end she all but threw stuff in the pack that was spread out on the bed. It took a lot of pushing and prodding to encourage all of it to squeeze. Proudly Maureen dragged it down the stairs, bumping it against the walls as she went outside to his truck.

Time was short so Sauntage did not take the time to check over her supplies. Instead he asked, "Were you able to get it all in here?"

"Yes, it's all there." She lifted her chin slightly as if to say, 'of course I did. Why wouldn't I?'

"Good let's go through the house one last time to make sure we didn't miss anything. Then we need to get going." With a mind of its own his arm draped over her shoulder as they walked side by side to the back door.

Once the latch clicked behind them Maureen gave his hand a shove and turned in his direction to free herself. "Maybe it's okay for you to simply forget what you've done, but I can't and won't do that." Her heart pounded fiercely with concern that she might do or say something that would provoke him. After what he had told her she was frightened that she did not know what he was capable of doing.

A soft moan escaped her lips as her head thumped against the truck door. Groaning she rubbed the ache near her temple and then sat up straight. At first she was disoriented and then panic seized her. She braced her hands on the dashboard as she stared in horror at the windshield.

Outside the truck it was pitch black except for the small patch of illumination from the head lights. What she saw nearly drove a scream through her gaping mouth.

There were trees everywhere! Growing very close together. And even though Sauntage was driving very slowly they still came within a fraction of an inch of too many of the tall slender trunks.

"Sau? Where are we?" She gasped as low branches rushed at her face.

"Not too far from the place where we'll ditch the truck and start hoofing it." His fingers tightened over the black leather steering wheel grip.

Flicking her saucer like green eyes to his face she could not help but notice the change in his face. Muscles around his eyes and mouth twitched with tension. There was a hardening of all the planes on his angular face, though not an angry change, just extremely determined.

Maureen thought the truck would never stop. For ten minutes it kept bounding forward at Sauntage's direction. The tires had no trouble finding each and every patch of uneven ground. Her head and neck started to ache with the constant jarring and snapping motion. Just when she thought she couldn't possibly take it anymore it stopped.

A sigh of relief left her. They had made it through the first leg of the journey. Suddenly, it occurred to her that she had no idea how many legs there actually were. In silence she tilted her chin upwards. With all of her being she hoped that this trip could not be compared to a centipede.

"It's about two miles from here to the mouth of the cave." He said twisting the ignition and door keys of the heavy ring in his hand. Without looking at her he seemed to know the questions running through her mind. "I can't risk parking any closer. If by some outside chance anyone stumbles across the truck, I don't want them to be able to easily trace our steps to the cave." Wearily Sauntage leaned over to open the glove box. Out of it he pulled the owner's manual and into it he placed the ring of keys. Again he took a second to explain, "If I cover up the VIN number and take off the license plate it might slow someone down in finding out the truck is registered to me.

And I'll lock the glove box for the same reason."

Grimly she nodded as she watched him open the door and get out of the truck. Her tongue slipped over her dry lips as the twinge of fear crept over her. This was so risky on her part. Not a soul knew there was anything amiss in their family. No one knew where they really were. Not even her! For all she knew Sauntage could have lied to her about everything and simply wanted to get her out of his way. Fear had rattled her so much that when he opened the door next to her she jumped. Maureen dumbly watched as he shoved the thin metal plate into the tiny compartment and turned the key in the glove box lock. Then as he walked around the front end of the truck he stuffed the key into the front pocket of his jeans.

Knowing that forward was the only possible way for her to find out what had happened to her sons caused tears to form and cling to her lashes. In all her life Maureen had never felt so hopeless. How she wished her parents were still alive! Dad had never steered her wrong. He would have known just what to do.

But they weren't alive, so she had to trust her own judgment. Despite the mistake she had already made in her marriage, she chose to take the chance. With trembling fingers she followed his lead and got out of the truck.

Sauntage was already yanking his pack from the backseat. As quickly as she could, Maureen did the same. Somehow it had gained fifty pounds on the trip here and it had become more bulky. Several strong tugs finally brought it free. Looking towards her husband she tried to mimic his actions to get the heavy contraption on her back.

Using the tailgate of the truck to hold the weight he carefully enfolded himself in the straps. Then he took a few moments to adjust the length of them so that it was as comfortable as possible. When he was finished with his own load he came to help Maureen with hers.

"I know this is unbearably heavy, but as soon as we reach the mouth of the cave we should be able to leave a good portion of the canned goods."

"Should be able to?" She questioned sharply.

"Well, if there are any signs that someone followed Tagurah, then I'm not sure what we'll do." Once the pack was securely attached to her, he reached out to take her face in his hands. "I love you,

Maureen."

Great tears rushed into her eyes and splashed down over his fingers against her will. Reluctantly, she admitted in a pained whisper, "My heart rages against my mind. Though my head tells me I shouldn't, I still love you, Sau." Her face crumpled as she backed away from him. "But I can't trust you."

"I understand, Darling." He nodded solemnly and then changed the subject, "We need to get moving. There's a lot of ground to cover before we stop to rest for the night and some of it is tricky."

Using flashlights to light their way and a compass to guide them, they headed off in a north easterly direction. Because his legs were a bit longer Sauntage was able to cross the uneven ground at a much faster pace. Many times he would pause at the top of small ravines or gullies to watch her progress.

Maureen was uncomfortable from the first step she took. Even though her boots were the correct size they were stiff in their newness. She was used to wearing low heeled pumps to work each day so these heavy, thick leather clunkers that wrapped over her ankle made it difficult to maneuver. Her world was for the most part level walking surfaces not slippery leaves in differing depths.

It was not long before her legs began to ache and she found her feet sliding out from underneath her. The weight of the pack made it hard to keep her balance. Not long after they left the truck Maureen found herself on her hands and knees in the midst of damp maple leaves.

Though the decent was rapid the landing was not as bad as she would have thought because the natural cushion was quite thick. A few seconds were lost as she located her flashlight and got back on her feet. This, as it turned out, was much harder than she thought it would be. In fact it took her three attempts to regain her footing because of the extra weight on her back.

Once she was upright she took a moment to look around for Sauntage. The trees surrounding her all looked virtually the same. Slender ash brown trunks, that rose in dizzying heights above her head. Even her heavy duty flashlight failed to reach beyond the lowest branches. Muffled footsteps startled her as she looked up, causing her to take a step backward.

"Are you okay, Mo?" Sauntage looked down from the edge of the little ravine.

"Yeah, I think so." She admitted and then quickly scrambled up to stand next to him.

"I'm sorry. I'll try to slow down some." He tightened the muscles around his eyes.

Maureen could see the debate on his face. Determination hardened her features as she snapped, "Just because I have extra pounds on me doesn't mean I can't do this!"

A sigh softly left his lips as he responded, "It's not a matter of whether you can do this or not. I just wish we would have had more time to prepare for this." As he turned to move on he paused to look at her. "That is the second time in the last twenty-four hours you have mentioned your weight being an issue. I kept a secret about my heritage; if I had wanted out of our marriage I would have called a lawyer. If you are unhappy about the way you look then by all means change what you will. But don't ever do something like that thinking it would change how I see you." His eyes purposely walked over her body.

Seeing the slow smile form on his face and watching his chest heave caused a strange fluttering in her stomach. Slowly she followed him through the dark forest keeping her eyes carefully trained on the ground so that she wouldn't fall again. Layered on top of the colorful leaves was the look on his face. It was so intense and she had seen it many times over the years. Wonder washed over her in great waves as she began to think maybe he was telling her the truth. Perhaps there really was a world under this mountain.

Rational thought quickly returned, however. That idea was crazy. No one could walk into a cave entrance and pass out the other side into some other world. It wasn't possible. With this in mind she tried to think of a reason for why Sauntage was doing this.

There was no logical explanation for any of this.

If it had been daylight Maureen was sure that she would have loved this wood. But darkness as deep as this made a chill go through her bones despite the mild temperature. Every once in awhile the moon peeked through the clouds and filtered down passed the trees causing eerie shadows to fall across their path. In the distance they occasionally heard the rustle of some forest creature making evening rounds of its territory. Gritting her teeth Maureen hoped that they were not going to cross any animal tracks.

Her breath halted as she wondered what kinds of creatures might inhabit the area. Were there possibly bears out here? What about wild cats of any sort? A muffled whine escaped before she could stop it. Snakes! Might there be reptiles squirming under foot?

Sauntage turned back to look at her using his flashlight to see her. In the dim yellowish beam she appeared pale. "Mo, is something wrong?"

Tremors ran through her from head to toe as she came up next to him. Her voice came out no louder than a whisper, "Have you ever run into unpleasant..."

"Animals? No, not really. They can hear us coming a mile or more away and stay clear. Hang in there, Darling, we only have another mile or so to go before we reach the cave." He gave her upper arm a gentle squeeze of encouragement. "You're doing great."

"And once we reach this cave there aren't any animals to worry about?" As she looked up at him her eyes seemed to begging him to give the proper response. He didn't.

"Uh, well, at the mouth of the cave there isn't likely to be critters of any kind that will stick around after we arrive. However, when we pass into some of the inner caverns we will probably find bats..."

"Bats!" She shrieked. "Please, tell me that you are kidding."

Slowly he began to move forward. They had so much ground to cover he had to keep her moving. "I'm afraid not. It is a natural environment for them. Very dark for them to sleep during the day as well as being a regular temperature all year long. Don't worry though I always try to go through those areas during the day when they are tired and less likely to get close."

"Very reassuring, thanks." Maureen curled her lip in disgust.

Five minutes after their exchange she stubbed the toe of her heavyweight boots on something and went head long to the ground. She had lost count of the number of slips she had taken in the last hour. This fall was different, however. Instead of landing in a bed of autumn leaves she felt the jagged edges of rock beneath her right knee.

Sharp pain raced up and down her tired limb. Nausea overwhelmed her momentarily. Her vision blurred for twenty seconds.

For a full minute Maureen remained on the ground balancing on her hands and left knee. The moisture from the few leaves underneath her began to seep through the denim legs of her jeans. Immediately she realized how grateful she was for the thick leather covering on her fingers and palms. Without them she would have been a bloody mess.

"Do you need some help?"

His voice came from somewhere over her head. Shaking her head vigorously Maureen replied, "I need a bit more time here. My kneecap just took on a rock and lost." Because of her position and the fact that she had lost her grip on her flashlight which was now several feet to her right, she could not see the look on Sauntage's face.

Without another word he went to retrieve the flashlight for her. By the time he had turned around with it in his hand she was working at a slow pace. Tenderly he took hold of her upper arms to offer her added strength and stability. "Are you feeling dizzy at all?"

"No, I didn't hit my head just smashed my right knee." She had automatically wrapped her fingers around his thick forearms.

"Give it a minute and then try to put some weight on it." His jaw muscles worked overtime.

Dutifully she did as he asked. Biting down on her lip helped her to stifle the cry that rose in her mouth. The blood throbbed through her entire leg. Very slowly she was able to put most of her weight on the stiffened joint. As long as she didn't try to bend it too much she would be able to walk on it. "It hurts, but I can go on now."

"You sure?" Sauntage asked and then accepted her nod. "Okay. From here the terrain gets a little rougher. We've made good time getting this far so take your time. We won't be moving from the entrance of the cave until morning which leaves us plenty of time to rest."

His brief warning about the changes in the landscape was accurate. There was a definite incline to their path and it was littered with rocks of all sizes. The trees were a bit thinner and a few scrubby bushes cropped up next to the larger boulders. Moonlight was able to filter through the canopy making their way a bit easier to see.

Suddenly, without any  warning a black wall rose up in front of them. It was a little over eight feet tall and about six feet wide. Maureen felt her eyes widen at its presence. One moment they were in the middle of the woods with towering trees all around them, and then the next they were standing in front of this. A damp draft met their warm faces.

It was not until Sauntage moved forward again that she figured out that this was the cave entrance. Relief flooded over her in great waves. She could finally take the pack off her back! Until this moment she had not realized how much her body ached from the extra weight. Her momentary joy stalled as she heard her husband speak.

"Mo, I want to go in and check things out. Wait here for me." Without waiting for her to respond he melted the blackness with a small circle of light from his flashlight.

In her weariness it did not occur to her to wonder what exactly he was 'checking'. At least it did not right away. But as she stood at the mouth of the cave doubt started to creep up on her.

What if he were going on without her? Maybe leaving her here in the middle of nowhere had been his plan all along. Was he trying to make her think she was crazy? Or himself? Perhaps he was having some sort of mental breakdown. The trauma of the boys' disappearances might have caused some part of his brain to snap. It made sense. Heaven knew she wasn't herself. Good grief she was standing out in the woods looking like a hiking enthusiast! A shopping mall was much more to her liking.

Tears pricked her eyes as panic seized her chest. What on earth was she going to do? How on earth had she allowed herself to end up like this? This was insane! Had she lost her mind? Her eyes darted all around her as if the stones at her feet or trees overhead might give her an answer.

"Well, there are signs of the boys but..." The loud screech of his wife startled him. "Hey, it's me, Mo. What is it?"

Great sobs rose against her will and threatened to send her to the ground in convulsions.

Sometime later, she didn't know how much later, Maureen

regained her senses. They were standing just inside the opening of the cave, his arms were not touching her, but the equipment that was strapped on her back. Cautiously, she drew away from his outstretched arms pulling off her dirty gloves as she did so. Wiping the streaks from her cheeks with the palm of her hand she tried to focus on their surroundings.

Warm light from the flashlight sent weird shadows dancing on the rough walls. From where they stood she could only see a bit of the wall on her left and a small section of the ceiling just a few feet overhead. The reddish-brown color seemed to absorb the light making the illuminated area even dimmer. Under her feet was the same colored stone though it was much smoother than the walls. A few pieces of trash were scattered on the far side of the circle of yellow. Most of it appeared to be from candy bars.

"You okay now?" His chin tilted to one side as he tried to assess her state of mind.

"Yeah, I think so." She responded dully as she strained to see more of the cavern. "What were you checking for?"

Sauntage pressed his lips together for a moment and then said, "Let's get these packs off first." After he saw her nod absently he hooked his thumbs under the straps tightly pressed against his chest. A low grunt left his throat as he removed the heavy bag.

As soon as his pack hit the dirt he reached out to help Maureen out of hers. She was leaning this way and that trying to get the weighted bag to come off her shoulders. Her smaller bag hit the ground next to his with a thud and then leaned crazily unto its side.

It was so painful to have the straps lifted that she cried out loudly. The echoes bouncing off the walls and ceiling startled both of them. In amazement they listened hardly daring to make a noise.

Gently he began to rub the muscles of her neck, upper back and shoulders. "I was hoping to find something that would tell me for certain the boys had been here and maybe how long ago."

"And did you?" Her attempts at looking over her shoulder at him were so uncomfortable that she took a few steps forward and then turned to face him.

"Well, there are a bunch of candy wrappers on the ground, which tells me that they were probably here not too long ago. But it is too late for us to go on. We're better off waiting until morning to keep going." Stiffly he bent down to retrieve the flashlights. After handing one to her he walked farther into the large room. "They are scattered everywhere."

Maureen saw in shock what her husband meant. Dozens of papers were strewn across the area in which they were standing. As her beam of light waved back and forth there was the feeling that she was looking at something very important to their quest. But for the life of her she could not figure out what it was.

All she saw were papers of every color tossed here and there. Some were crumpled, a few were folded and still others looked as though they had been dropped as soon as the prize inside had been removed. It appeared someone had gone on a gluttonous candy raid. Not only were there chocolate bars of several varieties, but chewy fruit treats, suckers and caramels as well.

Just thinking about the contents of these packages made her stomach roll. Tearing her eyes from the scene before her she decided to investigate the rest of her surroundings. Fifteen steps brought her back to the entrance of the room. Slowly she turned around in the doorway counter-clock-wise so that she was once again facing her husband's direction. On her right there was no wall space of which to speak.

Ceiling and floor met at waist height ten feet away from where she was standing. If she were to walk in that direction the floor would have sloped upwards sharply at the same time the ceiling lowered at a lesser angle. This part of the 'wall' was about eight foot long at which point it made a dramatic twist to the left with the ceiling soaring too high for her to judge the distance. Along this far wall there was a narrow opening that reminded her of a staircase. The steps, however, were made for a giant because the second one she was able to see was higher than her knees.

Six feet to the left of the stairs the wall grew in height even more and it seemed to angle a bit farther back. Although there were a few sharp rocks jutting out here and there this part of the wall made a wide arc around to end at the entrance. So part of the room where Sauntage was now studying the trash was almost circular.

As she watched him come to his full height she asked, "Do you see something?"

He sighed with frustration as he admitted, "No, not really. It's just wishful thinking I guess. I keep looking at this feeling like there is a message."

"I felt exactly the same way." Maureen shared as she drew closer to the papers once more. "Where would they get all of this stuff anyway?" Her eyebrows drew tightly together as her arms wrapped around her torso with a shiver.

Sauntage caught the motion out of the corner of his eye. "I think I know. I'll tell you my theory about it after we get a fire going." From the side of his backpack he pulled out a small hatchet as he explained, "There is enough draw in here between the door and a few cracks up in the ceiling for us to have a fire. This will be the only place for one for a few days. On the hike in I saw a couple of fallen trees; I'll go see if I can't turn some of it into firewood." He did not wait for her to respond but walked quickly to the entrance. Before he disappeared into the darkness he said, "While I am gone could you see about unpacking all canned food we brought? We can leave all of that here for our journey home."

Only a few seconds past before she moved into action. Trying to kneel next to his pack was too painful for her knee so she sat on her bottom to carefully unzip the main compartment. Much to her surprise it was neatly organized without an inch of wasted space and the weight was evenly distributed. He really knew what he was doing. Somehow this realization caused a chill to settle in her heart.

All the years she had known him Sauntage had always been fairly neat. She had often wondered if that had something to do with his trauma. That somehow his brain could not handle chaos well because of what happened to him. Now as she sat there pulling one can after the other from the bag she realized that he had let her believe that lie! Angry tears welled up in her eyes.

When she had emptied all the cans she shifted her weight so that she could reach her own pack. If she was lucky she would have time to reorganize the stuff in hers so that he would never know what a poor job she had done. And maybe the darn thing wouldn't be so hard to carry in the morning.

Luck was not on her side, however. Just as she removed the last items he came back in with an armload of wood. Heat rushed into her cheeks as she dipped her chin away from his line of sight.

"You're one step ahead of me I see." The wood dropped to the ground with a loud echo.

"What do you mean?" She snapped at him, still not looking in his direction.

For a moment he simply stared at her. It was such a rare thing to have her speak to him like that out of the blue. "With all the cans out of my pack we can move some of your stuff into mine. I think a couple more loads of wood ought to be enough for tonight, but I'll bring back a few more than that. What we don't use tonight we can use to hide the cans from possible visitors. Could you lay out the wood for me? I should have some newspaper in one of those side pockets."

Silence filled the cave for sometime before she jerked his pack closer. As he had said a few sheets of newspaper carefully folded to fit the small zippered pouch were waiting for her. They had been folded into four separate packets; each packet contained enough paper for one fire. Leaving three packets where they were she slowly rose to her feet.

After sitting for even that short time all of her muscles had begun to tighten. She hadn't hurt this much since she had tried aerobics for the first and only time. But she could not let on to Sauntage how much pain she was in because he might not let her go on with him if she did. It might kill her but she was determined to do everything she could to find her children.

By the time he returned with another load of wood she was nearly finished. He did not comment out loud about her efforts, but looked over the placement of the paper and wood with a nod of approval. "Matches are on the other side of the pack. You'll find them in a plastic baggie. Be sure to seal it tightly when you've taken what you need."

Sauntage was out the doorway before she could say a word. With a heavy sigh she went to get the matches. Every cell in her body was in protest. At least she was able to read her pulse without any difficulty because each time her heart beat it throbbed through all her extremities.

The fire was crackling loudly through the chamber and she was sitting before it with a glazed expression, when he returned. Her frame shuttered wildly when the logs he dropped on the ground clattered against one another. Absently, Maureen lifted her gaze to his dirty face and stared blankly at him.

"Almost done with this wood just a couple of more trips ought to do it. Once the fire dies down a bit we can warm a few of those cans for dinner. Would you like to choose what's on the menu and prepare it for heating?"

Confusion knit her brow as she stared at him asking, "Prepare it? How? I didn't see any pots and pans packed?"

A soft chuckle left his lips as he squatted in front of his bag. As he opened yet another section he explained, "No, we didn't bring pans. They are too bulky not to mention the fact that they are heavy. I have a can opener here so we will be able to heat our dinner right over the coals without worrying about an explosion."

"Sounds simple enough." She admitted with a shrug.

"Yeah, heating the food isn't a big deal. Not burning it; that is the real trick." His eyebrows lifted with sarcasm as he left her alone once more.

None of the labels looked very appealing to her. Food was not what she wanted. It was her sons, a warm bath and sleep that she was craving. Still they needed to eat something so she chose a couple varieties of beef stew. Using the sharp point of the can opener Maureen removed the red and white labels and as much of the glue as she could.

She left the food a few feet away from the fire and crawled to her backpack without putting any weight on her right knee. It suddenly registered in her brain how tight her jeans were over the tender joint. As soon as he left for the next round of wood she would take a peek at it and assess the damage. Not believing she had enough time to properly examine it before he came she decided to see if she could arrange her backpack in a more orderly fashion.

Food was grouped together, as was the hiking equipment and a change of clothes. There were a few toiletries and a tiny first aid kit; not nearly enough if anything serious happened. As for the other things, they were not really related to each other, with the exception of the bright yellow hard hat and batteries.

Her dry lips were moistened with her tongue as she looked at the small collection of unrelated items. A picture of her family, a diamond pendent necklace, a diary, and leather bound Bible. This she picked up and hugged close to her chest. Just holding it brought her comfort. It had belonged to her father. Swallowing with difficulty she remembered the day he had received it.

He had been in the hospital for a week going through tests of all kinds. Her mother had sat by his side nearly every minute. Maureen had done her best as their only child to support them in whatever way she could. For the most part she simply ran errands so that her mother did not have to leave her father's bedside.

Sauntage had been absolutely wonderful. He had taken charge of things around the house and with the boys. Without batting an eye he had arranged for Anna Carson to watch four year old Ryan while he was at work and she was at the hospital. Then in the evenings he made dinner for himself and the boys.

A middle aged man had come into the small hospital room as the three of them sat wearily waiting for word from the doctor. At first they thought he was there to give the reports so they straightened in their chairs and clasped hands for strength.

As it turned out he was not there for a health check but he said he was there for a spiritual one. Actually, he had done very little talking at first. After asking a number of questions and listening intently to their answers, he told them about Jesus. In the midst of tremendous pain her parents had hung onto this man's every word.

The story was certainly compelling. A great king that left his kingdom and all his glory just to be able call people to live with him. What kind of person did that sort of thing? It was too good to be true she told herself. But her father had felt very differently about the matter. Without question he accepted the words of this stranger and never looked back.

His time after that meeting had been very short. Weeks later he peacefully died at home somehow confident that he was going to heaven. So much about his outlook had changed in that time. Her mother angrily questioned the suffering her husband endured for awhile, but eventually she must have gotten acceptable answers that she wanted because she became devoted to God.

Maureen had had a difficult time with their sudden conversion. Part of her had worried that these caring people might not be what they seemed. Perhaps they were running some sort of scam to get her parents' money.

When her mother died from a heart attack less than two years later her worst fears were realized. The last will and testament declared half of the property and money belonging to her mother was to go to the church she had been attending. It was not the money Maureen cared about, but the apparent lies with which her parents had been brainwashed.

Heaviness settled in her chest as she now understood how easy it was to want to believe in something. All of her being wanted to believe that her sons were alive. Her gut ached to have the imagination to believe this other world was possible. She felt the pressure in her chest as her heart longed to believe in her husband. Oh, how much she loved him, but how could she trust him now?

Not wanting to have him catch her in tears again she drew in a deep breath and wiped the moisture from beneath her lower lashes. A damp coolness in the air was starting to make her uncomfortable. Taking the pictures and the Bible she went to sit near the fire.

Despite the short time that her parents had owned the Bible, the cover was worn and several pages were bent. Curiosity niggled at her causing her to wonder what they had found so fascinating about this large book. So she opened to one of the folded pages. Some of the names at the top edges of the guilt papers were familiar to her. Psalms, Proverbs, Genesis, Matthew, Mark, Luke and John. There were many more that she didn't know. This one was labeled Proverbs and several verses were highlighted with yellow ink. The first to draw her attention read, 'Trust in the LORD with all your heart, and do not lean on your own understanding.'

Though more words were actually marked she curled her lips with disgust and stopped reading. How could she trust in a God she could not see when she could not even trust her husband anymore? It was just a little too much to ask of her at the moment she reasoned.

Maybe once her sons were safe and sound in her arms she could consider the matter seriously.

Sauntage came in quietly and dropped his burden with a heaving sigh. "Fire looks really good, Mo. We should be able to put the food in soon. I'll be back with the last of the wood in a few minutes and then I'll get some water from the nearby stream."

"I don't remember crossing any water." She frowned with suspicion.

"We didn't. We came in from the south-west; the stream is a little east of here. Be back in a few minutes." His eyes settled on her face briefly and then he turned to leave.

Once he was gone Maureen scrambled to her feet with the flashlight in her hand and went to the point of the curved wall that was farthest from the entrance. As quickly as she could she unzipped her pants. Sliding them down past her knees proved to be a bit harder than she thought for she now realized her skin was raw from the constant movement of the last few hours. The cool air of the cave felt good on the burning cells.

Bending over she carefully examined her aching joint. It was certainly swollen, though not so much that she had trouble bending it because of that fact. She still had nearly the full range of motion. Just below the center of her kneecap there was a smear of blood where the skin had torn on the rock. Underneath the little patch of blood she could see other unnatural colors developing. In the end she decided that it was going to hurt for awhile but she could probably deal with the pain without too much difficulty.

When Sauntage returned she was back in front of the fire as though she had never moved. His voice was airy with exertion as he warned gently, "Your muscles aren't used to this kind of workout, Maureen. They will stiffen quickly. You might want to get up every few minutes and walk around a bit."

"I will, Sau." She promised softly. Then when she saw his stern expression she got to her feet once more. As she shifted her weight she thought of something and asked, "Is there a safe place around here to go to the bathroom?"

"Yeah, come on. You can go a little ways downstream." Without pausing he held out his hand to her. It was not until she hesitated in taking hold of his fingers that he realized he had done it.

They walked slowly side by side along the uneven ground. The air was growing colder but it did not really seem that way because of the temperature in the cave. It was also much fresher out among the trees. If the disappearances of their sons had not been the reason for them being there, Maureen might have found this place romantic.

Only the soft crunching of leaves under the thick soles of their boots could be heard. Once in a while she thought she could hear the distant hoot of an owl.

Without warning he came to a halt, just steps from a tiny trickle of water. A thoughtful look came to his eyes as he stared at the ground.

"Is something wrong, Sau?" Her fingers clutched onto his arm tighter while she used her flashlight to study his face more closely.

"No, I don't think so." He shook his head and pointed to the stream as he went on to say, "The water level is much lower than I have ever seen it. I've never made the journey this time of year. Maybe this won't be as hard as I thought."

Relief flooded over her. With a raspy giggle she commented, "That's the best news we've had all day." Releasing his upper arm she sighed, "Can I go anywhere around here or is there a special spot?"

"Oh, no just make sure you are some distance from the stream because...well, for obvious reasons." He responded with a tilt to his head and a shrug of his shoulders.

When they reached the cave safely minutes later the fire had warmed it considerably. It was almost ready to use for heating their meal. As they sat to watch the flames die down a bit more she turned to him and said, "You said earlier that you had some idea where all that candy had come from."

"Yes, I did. I think my brother probably bought it for them." Sauntage stared into the fire intently with his knees tucked into his chest.

Her eyes narrowed on him as she challenged, "So this place that no one knows about sells the same kind of candy as we do?"

"No, of course not. We have sweets in Liguesis, but nothing refined and packaged like candy bars." Moving towards the cans she had prepared he declared, "I think this fire is ready." Carefully he set the cans in the embers then sat back to wait. "When I met my brother each year we talked a lot about what life was like here. Tagurah always seemed fascinated by the idea, but afraid to come here himself. All that time he was apparently gathering the information he needed to come here." In frustration he pounded his fist into the palm of the other hand. "We talked about everything. I even managed to get a US road map through The Gateway and showed him how to read it. Oh, now I know why the ancients hid all knowledge of The Gateway and warned strongly against its use."

"So you told your brother about life here. That still doesn't explain how he got all that stuff. How would he have gotten the money to pay for all of it?" Maureen countered harshly.

Another shrug and shake of his head left him as he admitted, "I don't know, Mo. Perhaps he didn't buy any of it. If he would kidnap the boys then it wouldn't be a big stretch to think he stole all that junk."

"What else do you think he is capable of, Sau?" Her voice sank low with worry and fright.

After a moment of thoughtful silence he said, "Something tells me that the boys aren't in any real danger with Tagurah. I think it's me he's after."

Under her breath she whispered, "Oh, I wish I could believe you."

# *Chapter Three*

Hours later she woke with a start. Something had disturbed her while she slept. There was no way to determine what time it was because the fire Sauntage built up after dinner had gone out completely.

Shifting on the ground was so hard. Each and every muscle was complaining. To tighten any of them she had to clench her teeth to keep from crying loudly. Next to her Sauntage was softly snoring.

When he had told her that they would have to share the one blanket she had been furious. They could have easily carried another one. But now she had to admit she was glad. His warmth had been soothing and comforting which was a big help in falling asleep.

Now in the darkness Maureen frowned, wondering why she was awake. It was not as though she felt rested she thought as she stifled a yawn. Her eyes clamped shut to go back to sleep and get the rest for which she ached.

Suddenly, she knew what had awakened her. The candy wrappers! Of course it was so simple. Why hadn't she picked up on it right away?

As much as she wanted to jump up from her place and examine the floor closely, she couldn't get her body to move very well. With a good deal of twisting she was finally able to reach almost her full height. She took a few blind steps forward before she snapped on the flashlight to see where she was going.

Once she reached the other side of the room she stood still carefully looking over the mess. A cry ripped from her excitedly when she saw that she might be onto something. Sauntage was already stirring when she turned to wake him, "Sau, Sau! I think I..."

"Mo? Mo, where are you? What's wrong?" He leapt to his feet turning this way and that to locate her.

"I'm over here." She waited for him to draw closer with his light before she said, "There is something with the candy wrappers."

A frown pulled his brows together at a downward slope.

"Just listen to me, I'm not going crazy or sleep walking."

Exasperation came out in a heavy sigh. When she saw him nod slightly Maureen turned back to face the trash. "Okay, if you look on the left side the papers are a bit closer together and more of them are crumpled."

His frown lessened for a moment then tightened once more as he said slowly, "Yeah..."

"Now look at the middle and the right side. They are spread out more..."

"You're right. And not as many are in tight little balls. But that doesn't really tell us anything."

With growing excitement she explained her idea, "No, you're right it doesn't. At least not by itself. If you look carefully though you'll see that between the middle and right side there are more packages that were left alone after they were opened. Sau, there are different brands and kinds candy in each area."

"Okay, I see that, but I'm afraid it doesn't mean anything to me." His head shook back and forth as he spoke.

She smiled at him as she revealed, "It means two or three different people left those wrappers. The one on the left was smaller than the other two; he couldn't throw as far..."

"Ryan," Sauntage breathed softly.

"Yes, and see how nearly every one of his wrappers is wadded up? Well, he doesn't have preferences with sweets, he likes almost any candy." She paused to walk closer to a flat wrapper on the left. "But he definitely does not like malt chocolate."

Flaring his eyes widely he gasped loudly, "You're right! And Charlie must have sat in the middle. All the stuff with peanuts in it is flat."

"Drew, hates chewy, gummy fruit stuff. It's all been eaten though." Maureen puzzled quietly. "Do you suppose some animal came in and ate what the boys left?"

"I have no idea. Maybe they shared with each other and there weren't any leftovers." A shrug lifted his shoulders as he dropped to one knee and picked up a wrapper from a peanut encrusted bar.

Shaking her head sadly she tried to keep tears from over flowing. "I guess I was wrong. There really wasn't any deeper meaning in this."

"Look, Maureen!" Sauntage held out the paper to her. "You were absolutely right! Charlie must have used some dirt from the floor along with some moisture, probably saliva, and wrote on it."

With trembling she snatched it and put it under her flashlight. "It looks like a date."

"The date they were brought here perhaps." He thought aloud as he reached for a crumpled wrapper which ended up containing no clues.

"This was two days ago when they were taken." She realized. "What else did they tell us?" Forgetting the aches and pains especially her knee, Maureen sorted through Ryan's trash while Sauntage started with Andrew's wrappers.

Several minutes later Sauntage paused. "There is no way I can go back to sleep now. You keep looking while I get us a fire going." Silently he received her nod and got up to build a fire to make them a bite to eat and to warm themselves.

Soon they were seated before a roaring fire with three small piles between them. One by one they examined the marks on the inside. Only a small handful had anything discernable written on them.

"Let's see what we have so far." Sauntage cleared his throat. "Okay, this one has the date."

"And this one looks like a time. Six-thirty I believe." She held out the fruit rollup package for him to take.

"That would be about right if they were picked up as soon as they came home. Without backpacks and other stuff to haul around; you can make the trek here much faster than we did."

"Wait a minute. How can that be? We had your truck so how did they get from our house here faster than we did?" A flutter of worry rolled in her stomach. For every question it seemed he had a quick and ready answer. This could all be part of some sinister plan to get her alone and... Shivers went up and down her spine.

His hand rubbed down the rough skin of his face. "I wish I knew. One thing is clear though, Tagurah lied about coming through the passage. Obviously he has done so many times because of how this was done." A frown puckered his lips as he tried to make out a clue from Andrew. "They must have written these things in the dark. All I can make out on this one is '4 me', the rest is all gibberish."

Maureen received the sticky wrapper from him and studied it briefly. Excitedly she cried, "Four men. He is telling us there are four men with them."

"You really think that is what it says? Great. Then we're seriously outnumbered. We'll have to go to my Father right away. Hopefully, he is still alive and will be willing to help his grandsons, despite his anger towards their father." As quickly as he could Sauntage got to his feet saying, "We need to pack up and get going. See what you can decipher off of these while I get our breakfast and the bags."

"Let's see, Ryan loves us. And the next one says he misses us." The third one broke her heart and made speaking difficult. "I scare. They mean. His last one says 'feel sick'."

Pausing, he glanced at his wife and commented, "It's no wonder. All that candy is bound to make anyone ill. At least we shouldn't have trouble keeping them away from sweets for awhile." He was relieved to see the slightest lift of the corners of her full lips.

"Besides the date Charlie says legs tied, hands tied walk, scared, and care Ryan. I can't imagine what made them think to do something like this." Her eyes blinked back tears as she looked up to check her husband's progress.

Shaking his head as he zipped the last compartment on his bag and turned to hers, he admitted, "It was a stroke of genius there is no question about that. This information could be very valuable to us."

Maureen lifted her eyebrows with some apprehension and glanced down at Andrew's words. For a moment she simply stared. "I see what you mean, Sau. Andrew wrote '4 men', '1 tall', '3 short', big knife and no guns."

"That is incredible! We know exactly what we're dealing with. Hope abounds where there is knowledge." Sauntage came back to the fire with energized steps. "It's really early will you be all right with so little sleep?"

"Yes, I'll be fine." A firm nod of her head accompanied her words. "How long before we can get going?"

Softly he cleared his throat and then he said, "About a half an hour I should say. We need to make breakfast and eat when the fire dies down a bit." Again he saw the determined dip of her chin and then he turned away.

Close to an hour actually went by before they were on their feet, packs on their backs and hard hats instead of flashlights. The first few minutes with the backpack were agony. It was like her muscles all knew what it meant and cried out for mercy.

Once they climbed the high narrow stairs leading out of the rear of the cave there was a wide somewhat level tunnel. She was grateful for this because it gave her some time to adjust to the damp musty odor and chilly temperatures.

The walls and ceiling were more or less an arch spread over the pathway. Varying degrees of rusty brown was the only way to describe the color. Some horizontal ribbons of color indicated times of flooding. After they had been walking for about five minutes the wall on their right began to veer away from them. Sauntage kept his steps close to the left wall so Maureen did the same. She was about to ask him why he did not move more to the center of the path when the floor next to her feet suddenly disappeared. Now on her right side there was a deep pit with which the light on top of her head could not reach its bottom.

Her eyes immediately drifted to the ceiling and she was amazed to see that it soared much higher than it had been just a moment earlier. With confusion her eyes squinted at the rock above her head because it appeared to be moving. Then much to her surprise a piece of it had fallen away and was dropping right over her head.

Instinctively her arms drew up to cover her head as a scream left her lips. As she waited for the impending impact Maureen lowered her face, squeezing her eyes tightly shut. Once more she was confused because as she waited all she felt was a slight rustling of the air around her wrists. Lifting her gaze slowly she heard the long sustained cry leave her mouth a second before she even realized what was happening.

Bats! There were bats flying right at her! At the same moment her brain comprehended this fact Maureen felt a tug on her hair. One was caught in the thick plait down the center of her scalp.

Somehow her hard hat had slipped off her head. Light from her helmet danced crazily along the walls, floor and in places it could reach, the ceiling as she jumped in terror. Those sharp little feet felt like they were pulling her hair out by the roots as the leathery wings beat against the sides of her head.

A loud yell finally broke through her wild panic, "Hold still, Mo! Stop it. He's just as frightened as you are." Sauntage firmly grabbed her head just behind her ears and waited for her uncontrolled wails to pause.

Pressure from his gloved fingers was somewhat reassuring, but she could not help the loud whimpers that escaped, "Get it off! Sau, please, get rid of it." Her feet were still shuffling back and forth under her.

"I will just relax. Take a deep breath." When that did not work he quickly slid his hands to the crown of her head to grasp her assailant. The dark wings flapped loudly against his thick brown gloves as he worked to untangle the tiny feet. Only a few seconds past before the bat was able to race down the corridor from which they had just come.

If it had not been for the fact that her husband was holding her fast, she would have darted back the way she had come. Surely there had to be an easier way to reach her boys!

Neither of them spoke for a long time. She stood in front her husband's chest sobbing harshly. It was not until she felt him rub her upper arms and step away that she realized how dark their surroundings had become. In the midst of the struggle he too had lost his helmet.

When he had leaned over to pick them up he commented, "Maybe we'd better use the chin straps now. Up 'til now it's only been me so I don't usually bother with it until further on in the tunnels."

All she could do was nod in an uneven jerky pattern as she took her light back from him. Moments later they were walking once more. Not a word was said about the incident, they moved on as though nothing had happened.

It was quite a long time before Maureen's heart rate returned to normal. She carefully kept her eyes trained on her husband's backpack. As long as she did not see those evil creatures maybe she could pretend they did not exist. That was much easier said than done she discovered as they traveled into narrower areas with smaller caverns appearing on either side of the path. Much to her relief they never entered those areas.

For quite a long time they walked in silence with the echoing of their heavy boots on the rocky floor the only sound. It became monotonous and was beginning to drive Maureen nuts. Because the size and color of the tunnels were the same it felt as if she were on a treadmill of sorts. Even their pace was obnoxious for her ears. She was ready to push her gloved fingers into her ears just to change the noise a little. Just when she thought she couldn't stand it anymore Sauntage's voice scared her.

"Watch your step. The trail slopes for a ways. It is pretty steep in a couple of places." His headlamp turned in her direction briefly.

Blinking rapidly from the harsh light in her eyes she nodded. "I'll be careful."

"At the bottom we will rest in a large domed room." He placed his hands on either side of the wall and moved ahead slowly.

"Sounds good to me." She followed his example by pressing her gloved palms against the cool stone. Seconds later she was thankful that she had because her toes suddenly pointed downward causing a shift of her weight. There was a moment that Maureen thought she would fall into her husband's back and keep right on rolling. If she had to guess she would have said the slope was more than forty-five degrees. This would have been no big deal without the bag strapped to her back.

A few yards later the pitch lessened, but the walls grew farther apart; which meant that she only had one hand able to stabilize her if she lost her balance. Sounds in this part of the tunnel changed too. The reverberating echoes diminished in intensity. It no longer felt as though she was in the middle of a drum.

Time ceased to be a factor for them. Without the sun to tell them whether it was daylight or dark they had to rely somewhat by how they felt. Pain intensified in her calves from the constant downward slope. Her heels grew tired of trying to grip the rock and keep from running head long into the darkness. Every couple of minutes the sleeve of her gray sweatshirt snagged on the rough surface of the cool rock causing a wide patch of the fabric to wear out. She could feel her skin underneath becoming raw from the constant contact.

When they reached the wide open dome at the bottom of the long passage her breath caught in her chest. It was beautiful. Soft plinking sounds drew her attention to the right side of the doorway they had just come through. The light on her hardhat reflected off rock formations above her head that were coated in various minerals. Stalactites shimmered like icicles. In an uneven chorus small water droplets fell into a pool several feet below the floor where they stood.

More stalactites and stalagmites were scattered throughout the dome. Wonder widened Maureen's eyes as she turned with amazement to see as much at one time as possible. A gasp of awe left her lungs slowly, "Oh, how magnificent!"

"Isn't it beautiful?" Sau agreed. "Just watch your step, there is some water here and there on the ground that makes it slippery. We can rest here for a couple of hours."

"Hours? Shouldn't we keep going? With more people in their group wouldn't they move slower than us? Maybe we can reach them before they cross..."

His head shook fiercely causing her words to slowly come to a halt. "They outnumber us, Mo. Plus they are armed. If we tried to confront them here we would almost surely lose."

"Okay, I get it." A heavy weight in her chest made the rest of her body hunch dejectedly.

"Here let me help you get your pack off and then you can have a seat. It is a good idea to stretch your muscles a bit." Gently he lifted the weight off her shoulders cringing as he heard the hiss of pain cross her lips. "I know that hurts, doesn't it? Hang in there darling, in just a little over two days we will be done with the rock climbing equipment and then we can leave some of it for the journey home."

"Will it be safe? Might someone steal it?" Her wide eyes turned to look at him over her shoulder.

Sauntage tenderly rubbed the muscles along her neck as he replied, "To my knowledge no one has ever touched the things I have left over the years. I have a special place to store this stuff."

A shutter went through her and she started to walk aimlessly around the dome. There was something ominous about the thought of going that far below the surface of the earth. As she walked Maureen saw two other passages leaving the area. "Is there any other way out of here?"

"Yes, there is." The pack from his back hit the ground next to hers with a dull thud. "And I hate to admit it, but it is a much easier way. However, the tunnel entrance is in a more populated place so it is harder to get here unnoticed. That is how I got caught by those hunters."

She found a thick pillar to lean against. Wearily her head rested on its mineral encrusted surface. Her eyes wandered over the floor and walls nearby. Along the rock face in front of her Maureen could see that letters had been etched by previous visitors. Using her finger tips she examined the rock behind her and found the same type of indentations. Swallowing the lump of worry in her throat she asked, "Sau, how can you be so sure this is where your brother has brought the boys? This place looks like it is visited frequently from the marks on the walls. Couldn't they have taken any number of paths we passed along the way?"

"I suppose they could have made a wrong turn along the way, but I don't think so. In order to take our boys like this he must have made this journey many times. Tagurah knows exactly where he is going."

Catching her lip for a moment she moved her eyes around the room. After a brief silence she wondered aloud, "Do you think the boys might have left us a message here?"

"As much as I'd like to believe so, I doubt it. And even if they did we would probably spend hours looking for it." His chin lowered in sorrow.

"How far is it to your homeland, Sau?"

"I can't give you a distance because I've never measured it. But it takes me three days to get to the place we call The Gateway. It will take us a bit longer than that to make the trip." He sat on the ground moving his arms and legs in various positions.

Maureen tipped her head from side to side following his example. "You're going slower because of me." Bitterness ate her words. When she saw his head dip slightly she snapped, "Don't do that on my account. Whatever pace you pick I'll find a way to keep up."

Slowly he crawled to the place where she sat. Then he took her face in his gloved hand. "I can't do that to you. This journey is hard enough at the pace we are going. Speed would bring even more pain and injury."

"We are talking about the lives of our sons. I don't care about any pain..." Determination hardened the soft contours of her face.

"But I do, Maureen. My heart can't bear the guilt of the pain you are in now. We will get our sons back." Tears swam in his eyes.

Her gaze narrowed on his face as she spat, "I don't know why this pain should be a big deal for you. You've had no trouble whatsoever lying to me all these years. That hurts far more than my body ever could."

Silence dropped between them like wall. With a downcast gaze he crept back to the wall next to their backpacks. Closing his eyes and resting his head against the cold rock Sauntage tried to go to sleep.

For a long time Maureen simply sat staring at the water collecting and dripping off the ends of the stalactites on the ceiling. An intense ache filled her chest as she went through all the events of the last few days. Good grief four days ago life was normal!

Against her will her eyes drifted to Sauntage's form. She knew that he was having trouble sleeping because of what she had said to him. Well, at the moment she didn't give a hoot. He deserved it and a whole lot more!

It was not long before her eyes grew heavy. Lifting her weighted lids became too much of a chore. Her last waking thought was that her husband had fallen asleep and he was snoring.

Surprisingly she was warm when sleep began to lift from her mind. A few seconds went by before she realized that the reason she was warm was the blanket covering her. Regret for the loss of blissful slumber brought a sigh from her lips and stirring on her right side. Sauntage had come to sit next to her after she had fallen asleep.

He shifted slowly so that she could come fully awake without too much disturbance. In a quiet voice he spoke, "Hope you were able to get a little rest."

"Yes, I think I did." Croaked her throat as her gaze moved on him and she saw that he had been up for some time; up reading the Bible that had belonged to her parents.

"What are you doing with that?" She snapped harshly reaching for the leather volume.

"Sorry." His hands rose up on either side of his stunned face. "I didn't want to wake you so I read it to keep still and quiet.

"Why didn't you just wake me up? We could already be moving." As quickly as possible she got to her feet, though it was not smooth and looked like she would tumble forward onto her face.

Sauntage grasped her upper arm with one hand while the other went to the other side of her body. "Because I knew you needed the rest." When he saw the scathing look in her eyes and felt her pull against his hands, he sighed heavily. His lips pressed together tightly for a brief moment before he released her to speak, "Darling, getting into Liguesis is only our first step here. I have no idea where Tagurah has taken them. And if what the boys wrote to us is true, we are outnumbered. We must have help. Finding our help could take us some time. Liguesis is not a small land. So you see a couple of extra hours here makes little change in our overall time table."

In shock her jaws gaped silently. Nothing in his demeanor suggested that he was joking. By small degrees she closed the gap to speak, "How far will we have to hike before we reach a car?"

"Uh, we won't." His eyes shifted uncomfortably to the floor.

"Thank goodness. At least I won't slow us down..." A sigh of relief brought her words to an airy end.

Clearing his throat Sauntage said carefully, "Actually what I meant was that we won't have a car in Liguesis." He cringed when he saw the heated storm in her green eyes. "That kind of technology doesn't exist there."

"What kind of technology does then?" Maureen demanded softly through clenched teeth.

"To compare it to earth I suppose you might say that it is a bit in the dark ages. We do have a few mechanical advances like printing presses, but they are run on horse power or by a water wheel. As far as I know there aren't any engines or motors of any kind."

All she could do for a long time was stare at him. After what seemed like an eternity she realized that he was not about to amend his comments. As the facts started to add up in her mind she awkwardly lowered her frame to the ground. "Would it be safe to assume that there are no hotels in Liguesis?"

"Yes, when people travel they stay in each other's homes or if necessary, build a kaveta." Squatting next to their packs he started to pull several baggies of dried food out for them to eat.

She received the packet in silence and then wondered, "What does kaveta mean?"

"Oh, a kaveta is a sort of hovel I guess you could say. It is a simple structure that is not always stable. People will throw a kaveta together if they are caught in bad weather. It is not usually needed for very long and it is more work than it is worth to carry the pieces with you..."

"So they are left for the next unfortunate soul to be trapped by a storm." Maureen ended for him with a nod of understanding. Her lower lip rolled between her teeth for a moment as she thought. "Are we likely to cross paths with many people in Liguesis?"

He shrugged absently as he finished a mouthful of nuts and then answered, "We are most likely going to find Tagurah in an unpopulated area, but we have to find some help before we confront him."

"Perhaps you had better tell me more about this place and its language." Although her voice was calm there was a warning charge in her eyes. She saw a thoughtful nod with satisfaction and fastened her eyes on his face to begin a crash course.

At first Maureen had seemed interested in learning only what she needed to survive in his world, but then something had changed during their conversation. She had become so interested in what he was telling her, that she forgot to ask questions about the actions he was taking to pack their bags.

As they maneuvered through the maze of passages she paid little attention to their surroundings. Her eyes focused on her husband's back while her ears listened intently to the sound of his voice. At first she had simply wanted to have some idea what she was getting into, but then she recalled his statements about needing help. If he planned on seeking the help of his parents, then it would not be long before she met her in-laws. She was desperate to make a good impression with them. The boys' lives could depend on her fitting into Sauntage's world.

Though she could not say when that compulsion changed Maureen recognized later that her curiosity had gotten the best of her. Soon there was an anxiousness to not only reach their children, but to see with her own eyes the land of her husband's words.

Conversation really helped the time to pass more quickly. For this she was grateful because the constant darkness and closed in spaces were beginning to get to her once more. Despite her desire to know how much longer they would be in this cold damp dungeon, she was afraid to ask because the answer might be more than she could stand.

Learning bits and pieces of his native language also helped to draw her mind away from the pain that she felt; except when she stubbed her toes on the uneven floor. Then every ache cried loudly for her to stop. Though her pack was considerably lighter than when they had begun this trip, the strap had worn her skin away and bruised the bones beneath. Her new boots were broken in now, but so was the tender flesh on her heels and toes. Countless blisters had formed inside the stiff leather boots. The tired muscles in her neck, back and legs announced every beat of her heart. She could almost hear the pain in her ears.

They had been walking for a couple of hours when Sauntage halted in the middle of a tight spot in the corridor. "We'll get a short break in here. This is as wide as it gets for quite a ways. In one place the ceiling drops about three feet."

"So we'll have to crawl a bit." That did not sound so bad.

"It isn't that simple I'm afraid. You see we have to take off our packs and drag them along because the passage isn't wide enough for us to face forward." As he spoke Sauntage removed his pack and set it between them. "We have to shuffle sideways in order to make it."

She reluctantly followed his example and then turned her head so that her lamp shone on his dirty face. "How long do we have to do this?"

"I don't have any way to tell the distance, but it usually takes me a little over an hour to get through. What you have to keep in mind though is the fact that there are two places where we will be able to rest somewhat comfortably. One is after the ceiling lowers about three feet for about nine yards or so. And the other is a small section where it widens into a room for us to stretch a bit and there is a pool of water where we can get a drink."

With a deep sigh she nodded her head firmly. "Okay, I'm ready to get this over."

He smiled wryly with a warning, "Be sure to keep a tight hold on your pack because it is hard to turn your head in some spots."

"Got it." Her arm went through the strap and hooked it firmly.

"Here goes then." His light turned to the right and his pack scraped along the ground at a slow pace.

Maureen waited a few seconds and then took a sliding step to the right. It came as a bit of a shock when she didn't feel the intense pain in her calves and thighs. This relief was short lived, however, for as soon as she yanked with her left arm it all came back. Gritting her teeth she repeated this action and felt the wall behind her close in a bit. Each step it continued to grow narrower.

A feeling of darkness settled around her, though it had nothing to do with the lack of light. Her heart rate began to increase with each movement. Was there enough oxygen for them down here? Even though Sauntage was quite a bit taller than she was, Maureen knew that he was thinner. Would she be able to fit through this corridor without getting stuck? Drawing a deep breath of air into her lungs she pushed back her fears.

The damp smell grew stronger and she even felt moisture seeping through her gloves. Once in a while her boots squished in small puddles on the floor. As she pulled her pack through a deeper one she called out to her husband, "Sau, what about the stuff in the bottom of our packs, it's getting all wet?"

His voice came drifting back at her with an eerie echo, "Yeah, a few things might get wet. That's the reason I used all those baggies back in the dome. Most of the stuff in the bottom of our bags is sealed now, but I don't have enough baggies to do everything now. We can't afford to waste any more of them for this part of the journey."

A thoughtful frown came to her brow as she questioned, "What do you mean by that?"

"Before we reach Liguesis everything left in them that is not sealed in a baggie will be soaked. That is why I made sure to put the Bible and blanket at the top of our bags for the time being." Sauntage tried to look back at her but couldn't without knocking off his hard hat. "There is a river we must swim in order to reach The Gateway."

She was about to respond and then decided against it. At this point she couldn't handle any more information. Her head was already swimming with new words, basic laws and social practices. How was she ever going to remember all this stuff? It felt as though she were sleep walking in the middle of someone else's nightmare.

Suddenly, her right foot hit the side of his bag. When she tipped her chin down to look at it Maureen felt her helmet slipping and found that there was barely room to use her right hand to put it back in place.

"Here it is. Now go slow and watch your feet. Don't move too fast or you'll lose your backpack. You hook your toes through the strap and keep your ankle at a ninety degree angle. Bend your knees as far as you can and put your arms over your head. Then slowly lie down in the tunnel. Use your hands to pull yourself along. There is a little wiggle room for you to bend your knees and push yourself forward, but don't let go of your bag." With a deep breath his frame dropped close to the floor.

Closing her eyes for a moment she tried to keep her tears at bay. Once she no longer felt his supplies against her boot she reached out the toe of her left boot. It was a real trick to bend her knees after having them straight for so long. Slowly her arms stretched up and she tilted her torso into the straw-like tube. Within seconds she regretted being inside this tiny space. All she could see was the rock inches from her eyes because when she tried to tilt her chin up toward her hands her hard hat slid from the top of her head.

There were small bumps on the ground that she was able to use to inch forward which was a big help. But they were a curse too because the rest of her body had to be dragged over them. One sharp point caught on the backpack nearly pulling it from her ridged foot.

Moans escaped her dry lips as she strained to gain ground. Her elbows and knees hit the walls every few seconds causing large holes in her sweatshirt and jeans. Sweat was pouring from her brow despite the cool temperature. She ceased to hear noise from Sauntage because every move she made rang back in her ears in deafening volume.

Panic seized her. Whatever it took she had to get out of this deathtrap. Briefly she thought about letting that bag go. It was heavy and it was slowing down her movement. Her toes had just relaxed a tiny bit when her fingers touched something much softer than rock. His voice cheered her onward.

"Great job, Mo! Hang in there, Honey, you're almost home free. Just a few more inches and you can start to get up." He paused to allow her to reach the mouth of the straw. "Now you should be able to use your arms to help you rise off the floor. There is a little more room on this end so it should be easier to stand up."

Words were impossible for her dry throat. Through her clenched teeth sobs of frustration and fear echoed into the tunnels. She could feel the dirty trails of moisture on her cheeks. Soon she would be able to dry them with her filthy sleeves. It brought a wry grimace to her lips to realize that she was joyfully looking forward to that moment.

When it finally came five minutes later she almost couldn't believe that she had made it. The pressure of Sauntage's gloved hand over hers brought it into reality. Tearfully she croaked, "I did it!"

"You sure did!" He cried loudly.

A sarcastic glare crossed her features as she snarled lightly, "This isn't exactly what I would call comfortable, Sau."

His lips lifted as a loud chuckle left him. "Well, it's all relative, Mo. Compared to that tiny pipe this is paradise."

"You do have a point." She felt a tightening over the fingers on her right hand.

"If you can hold on just a little longer there is a tiny cavern we can really relax in for a bit."

"Great, I say we get to it." Gently she pushed against his side and reached her left arm down for her backpack.

Leading the way once more Sauntage picked up his pace. Maureen heard a weary sigh come from her husband but didn't think much of it. They were both exhausted beyond belief. She was beginning to think that she couldn't take another sideways step. If only this path was wide enough to turn forward. Inside she whined about each ache and pain. At first the cool rock against her heated skin had felt good, now it felt as though her body was one big scab.

Without warning their surroundings changed. While the air was not exactly fresh it had the ability to circulate which improved its quality tremendously. Once more she could hear the plink of water dripping into a small pool; though at the moment she could not see it. Water plopped onto her hardhat causing her to tilt her head back.

The view over her was staggering. Hundreds of spikes in a rainbow of colors were growing so close together that they resembled the spires of an upside down castle. Splash! One cool drop landed on her cheek. A girlish giggle rose from her throat. "Ooohhh. It's soooo..."

He watched her awestruck face.

"I've never seen so many colors at one time." She gushed.

Sauntage lifted his gaze to the familiar view. This was something he saw twice a year. As he looked at all the different rock and mineral formations he recalled, "'How lovely is your dwelling place, O LORD of hosts!'"

"Huh?" Maureen lowered her head so that she could see him.

"I was just reminded of something I read from that Bible. It was from the book of Psalms I think. You know I've made this journey so many times and even from the very first one I have looked past these dark passages to the goal. Either Liguesis or Earth was my focus. This has always been the nether place without much significance in and of itself. But watching you view this makes me realize how much I have missed."

Her lip curled up at him and then she moved to the small pool of water in the corner. As she walked across the seven foot by ten foot space she noted the slant of the rock beneath her feet. That explained why the whole floor wasn't flooded. All the stalactites moisture trickled to the lowest point in the room. "You've missed much more than these rocks, Sau."

"Be careful, Darling, that water is much deeper than it looks." He warned as he stood over her and watched her scoop some water in her hands and splash it in her face.

It was much cooler than she thought it would be. And it was unbelievably refreshing. After making sure her hands were as clean as possible she dipped her hands once more to get a drink.

Sauntage squatted next to her. He was deep in thought so his actions were slow. In the moments after she got back up and started stretching her back and legs he stared at his wavering reflection. Finally, he rose to his feet and asked, "Maureen, if I had told you everything when we first met would you have believed me?"

For a long while she stared at the streaked wall. In a quiet voice she admitted, "I don't know. To be completely honest, Sau, if it weren't for the boys I certainly wouldn't be here now."

A steady nod preceded his response, "Trust me I know how crazy this must sound to you. But do you think I would carry a lie this far just to keep you away from our sons?"

Her eyes narrowed on him as she challenged gently, "I have no idea what to make of you. Never in all my wildest dreams would I have thought the man I married could lie to me. But the man I married doesn't exist." Tears flowed over her cheeks onto her tattered shirt. "He never did."

"You have no idea how much I wish I could go back in time." A sigh left him as he came to his full height. "We have another short jaunt through a tight passage. It shouldn't take very long to get on the other side."

"When do we leave earth and reach Liguesis?" Her voice had a sarcastic edge.

"I can't answer that. All my research never revealed 'how' this passage works. It just does." He paused to move his pack to the other side of the little room. "From here there are three major hurdles for us to pass. The first one is a high wall we have to climb over..."

"Is that what the harnesses are for?" She followed in his footsteps.

"Yeah, it's a climb, straight up so the rope and harnesses are necessary to be safe. Once we are up on the wall we have another long walk, but it's nothing like this. Most of it is in wide open caverns. Then we swim in the river." His voice was echoing once again as they shuffled along.

Maureen gasped as her toe hit an outcrop in the rock. When she felt the wave of pain pass, she asked, "How big is the river?"

"Not very big at all really. If I had to guess I'd say at Its wldest point it is about ten feet."

"That doesn't sound so bad." She said with relief, but then something occurred to her, "It must be pretty deep then if you are concerned about it."

Chuckling loudly he shook his head until his helmet hit the wall and nearly fell off. "The depth is not usually a big deal. But the thing is that we are not going to be crossing the river we have to travel through it."

"I don't understand. Why don't we walk along the shoreline?" She too whacked her hard hat because she moved her head too much.

A sigh left him before he answered, "Except for the place where this path meets the river there is no shoreline. It's really more of a wide tunnel that is filled with water."

"I see." Her volume dropped as she began to consider his description. Everything up to this point could easily have been staged for her benefit. The boys' disappearing, the medallion and the candy wrappers all might have been a cover for some sinister plot Sauntage was carrying out against her. This didn't make sense if he was out to harm her. There were any number of places they had passed where he could have left her and no one would ever have found out about it. But what else could they be doing there?

To consider his ludicrous story of another world was out of the question. It was crazy! She was out of her mind to be here learning some weird made up language and talking about non-existent relatives. 'Get a grip Maureen!' Her thoughts churned in many directions but always ended up in the same place. Hope of seeing her sons again lay with her husband.

Just a few minutes later the walls started to recede slowly. Each step brought more breathing room between them and the rock. It was not long before they were able to hoist their packs onto their backs and move facing forward.

This change was harder than Maureen thought it would be. Because her neck muscles had been stretched in one position for so long they were in agony as she put the weight over her shoulders and started to walk. Her legs had not fared much better. They were stiff and weak, ready to stumble over any object larger than a pea.

The chamber they were walking through was wide but the ceiling was much lower than the previous rooms the two of them had gone through. Color was much less of a factor in inspiring awe here. Not more than three or four shades of brown-red existed on the walls, floor or ceiling. All of the surfaces appeared smooth as if someone had chiseled away any sharp edges. Several arches opened up along the walls making her wonder how many other entrances to the surface there might be.

As if reading her thoughts Sauntage spoke, "Though I haven't taken the time to go in all of these tunnels those that I have gone though are either dead ends or loop back here. This place has quite a few entries in our historical journals, but I never found evidence that it was used by thieves from Earth or the lawless from Liguesis."

"Are any of them supposed to lead to the surface?" Her eyes darted back and forth looking briefly into each empty black hole as they walked past it.

"Nope. According to all of our records there are only three entrances. The one we came in, the one from the more populated area of Kentucky and the one from Liguesis. About a half mile or so ahead is the wall we will climb." His gaze rested on her face and he noted the fatigue drop on her with the mere mention of the wall. "Let's plan on sleeping for the 'night' as it were when we get there. We can't have a fire of course, but we can stretch out under the blanket and give our muscles a much deserved rest."

"Sounds good to me." She responded breathlessly. In her mind she pictured her soft bed with the yellow roses sprayed over the coverlet. It seemed like a far away dream in the middle of this barren rockiness. Right now she would be happy to stop walking and close her eyes until the sun shone down here at the end of time.

When the two of them quit walking that is what Maureen did. She took barely three handfuls of dried fruits and nuts and before she had swallowed them all she leaned against her damp backpack to rest. Within seconds she was sound asleep and didn't even stir when Sauntage knelt beside her to massage her overtaxed muscles. As soon as he had done all he could for her comfort he rubbed out his own tired limbs. Nearly two hours passed from the time they stopped until the moment he lay next to her practically sleeping before his head hit the floor.

# *Chapter Four*

Sleep lifted slowly hours later. Stiffness and pain registered after a few attempts to move closer to the source of warmth beside her. She felt cold despite the blanket wrapped around her. Hours of lying still after so much physical exertion had wreaked havoc on her body. Her thoughts did not remain on the many aches crying out for mercy because she felt the strong arms of her husband drawing her close to him. His warmth soothed the chill and a soft sigh of relief left her lips. In the midst of her sleepy awareness his lips sought hers. At first there was no thought of resistance, it felt good to be held. By the time full awareness had come to her there was a battle between her heart and her mind. Something in her response to him must have changed because he firmly held her by the shoulders and pulled back.

It was not until this moment that she realized they were in the dark. This was unlike any darkness she had experienced before. There were no shadows no differences in what her eyes saw in any direction. Everything was exactly the same. Black.

In a soft breathless voice she leaned toward his body and said, "Sau, it's all right." Suddenly, his presence was gone. If she hadn't heard his boots shuffling along the ground she might have been afraid he had vanished.

"No, Maureen, it isn't." Sauntage answered firmly. "Your helmet is somewhere on your left side. Watch your eyes I'm turning mine on now."

"But I'm telling you it's okay. I'm willing, Sau." Her arm swung in front of her face with the blinding appearance of his light.

He waited until her eyes had adjusted and she could look at him. Then he gently informed her, "No, I do not have your trust, Darling." His eyes left her face slowly and he then announced, "I need to take a short walk. I'll be down the first tunnel on the right. Feel free to eat and explore some of the tunnels around here for a bit to loosen up your muscles for the day."

Before she could say anything he had walked through an arch to her right and left her sitting once more in the dark. Fumbling around on the rock next to where she had slept Maureen was able to locate her hard hat and switch on the bulb. Sorrow settled over her heart. Just days ago life had been going along as planned. How could everything have gotten so mixed up?

Although she knew that her husband was right, she needed to prepare her body for whatever came next, Maureen couldn't seem to move. She found a baggie filled with trail mix and sat eating it in silence. When the first bag of food was gone she reached into her pack for another one. Instead of food, however, she found the Bible.

As she flipped the pages open she recalled the look in Sauntage's eyes when he had turned from her a few minutes before. It was not anger that she saw, but a resolve; a determination for something. What for she could not quite figure out, but guessed he was out to have her trust once more. Could she let him have it? In some sense she felt he already had her trust. Just being in this deep pit under the mountain with him was proof of that. There was a quiet thought gently pressing to the forefront of her mind. It was not because of trust that she was in this God forsaken place.

By the light of her helmet Maureen found the New Testament. She knew that the first four books of the New Testament were called the gospels and that meant something about good news. Well, she could certainly use some good news right about now. And so she began to read the book of Matthew. After about the fourth or fifth name she started to skim past the first chapter. Near the end of the chapter things got a little interesting. A visit from an angel! Wouldn't that be something? Oh, she wished she could have an angel tell her whether she could trust her husband or not.

Several pages had been turned by the time he returned. He made no comment about the fact that she was in virtually the same place as when he left. His only words were, "I'm hungry. I can't wait to be able to catch a fish and cook it over a campfire. It will feel so good to get out of this dungeon."

Her chin nodded in agreement as she awkwardly made it to her feet. "I think I'm ready to take that walk now. Hope I can find my way back here."

"You won't have any trouble. Just don't go very far. If you think you're turned around then shut off your light. I'm not going anywhere and you'd be surprised how far this light will carry in these caverns." Sauntage pulled out his breakfast and prepared to dine quietly.

Turning to her left Maureen headed to the largest of four openings clumped together on one side of the narrow path that had brought them here. The door was almost a six foot square cut into a much higher wall. Like the rest of this area the brown red theme prevailed. Until she had come here it never occurred to her that there were so many hues of one color.

Small cracks ran along the walls of this passage. A pile of rock was close to the left side. When she got closer she could see that it had been removed from the wall with some kind of tool because there were deep scrapes and gouges all bearing a likeness to each other. It was not clear what the purpose of this spot was so with a puzzled frown she continued further down the path.

More twists and turns were ahead that made her unsure of her direction. After a short time she was ready to turn back because it all looked the same to her. Walls, floor and ceiling; all brown. The rough surfaces seemed to repeat wherever she went. They resembled a huge paper bag that had been crumpled up and then reopened in various degrees. She paused to go to the bathroom next to the pile of rubble and then quickened her steps back to their mini campsite.

Curiosity got the better of her and for a brief moment she switched off her head lamp. Darkness rushed upon her like a tidal wave, but it quickly receded with the faint glow of her husband's light. One small spark could really change how much someone was able to see under these extreme conditions.

By the time she drew close to where they had spent the night she could see Sauntage arranging ropes and hooks. Without a word she lowered her frame to the ground across from him to watch what he was doing. In confident strokes he was tying knots in one rope and then carefully winding it into a circle.

"This is for you to use if you are having trouble with foot holds on the wall." He explained as he finished the last two knots.

"What about you? What do you use?" Her brows drew together tightly as she looked for another rope.

"I will be using my feet and the rock." His answer was brief though not nasty or rude. "I will take the lead. Hopefully I will be able to drive in a few of these anchors along the way to make this a bit safer for us."

She looked over the yards of nylon, pile of metal anchors and carabiners with a feeling of dread. Clearing her throat she nodded toward the equipment and suggested, "I don't know the first thing about rock climbing. Maybe you better go over this a few times before we actually try it."

"It's not as bad as you think, Mo. Since I come through here every year I have a pretty good path already marked. Believe it or not there are lots of deep cracks and crevices to use as hand holds and footholds. We have about five stories to reach the top..."

"That's more than fifty feet!" She cried loudly as she felt the color drain from her face.

"Yes, I know. And I know how much you hate heights, Darling, but this is the only way to reach the boys. Listen; in no time at all we will be celebrating at the top." He reached out to cover her hand. "All you have to remember is to keep looking up and to take your time."

Minutes later Sauntage was checking her harness for the third time. To her the contraption didn't look strong enough to hold someone half her weight. With a nod he handed her the end of the longest piece of rope and waited for her to wrap it around her waist and right foot. Then he stretched his arms above his head and grasped the wall.

In silence she watched him inch his way up the sheer rock face. None of his actions showed a lack of knowledge. There was no doubt that Sauntage was experienced. So when he paused to call that it was her turn there was only a moment's hesitation.

A deep breath and clenched teeth were the escorts that saw her hands to the cold brown stone in front of her. As she stuck her toe in the first space and pushed her body upwards she was grateful that there was almost nothing left in the pack on her back. This fact made a huge difference in keeping her balance.

Each time she pulled herself a little higher her muscles quivered weakly. Soft words begging for the strength to do this were mumbled between her tightly closed jaws. One more step she kept telling herself. She could make it one more step. That one turned into fifteen. Then the tears pooled In her eyes because she saw her next move was two feet to her right and almost three feet up.

His deep voice called out in the surrounding darkness, "Hang in there, Mo. You're doing great. Rest where you are for a few minutes; while I go a bit further and place the next few anchors."

"Sure thing." Maureen called in a hoarse voice. Both of her hands held onto the wall for dear life. With soft pants she leaned her head into the wall until her helmet tapped against it loudly. The scraping sounds of her husband's equipment made her nervous. One wrong move and both of them could plunge to the floor of the cavern.

It was not long before curiosity overwhelmed her. Tilting her neck back slowly Maureen observed the progress of her husband. He was more than two stories higher than she was and all that she could see was his shadowed form tightly clinging to the rock face. His right hand left the cold stone briefly to grasp at something near his waist. Seconds later she heard metallic pinging as if metal were striking metal.

"I've set another anchor, Mo. Think you can manage a few more feet?" He seemed to be out of breath from the exertion.

At first she only nodded, but then it occurred to her that he could not really see her either. "Ready." Her eyes stared at her next goal sternly. She could reach that spot if she stood on her tip toes and stretched with all her might. Sweat trickled down her spine and off her forehead. It seemed as if time had slowed down, almost came to a complete halt as she continued to stare. Then suddenly, somehow, it sped up once more with her now standing one step higher.

A sense of power washed over her. She had done it! Her confidence grew with this accomplishment and her progress went on at a much faster rate. It was not long before her gloved fingers hit something other than rock. Sauntage's words distracted her from immediately figuring out what she had touched.

"Hold on there, Darling. You must be close to the next anchor. Let me move up a bit farther." He made a couple of adjustments in his position and then hoisted himself up the cliff.

To Maureen this part of the climb seemed to take longer. Perhaps it was because of how tired she was getting. A yawn crept up from her lungs. No matter how exhausted she was, she had to keep moving. The lives of her boys depended on it.

"I'm nearly to the top. About ten feet to go. My legs are tired though. Why don't you go for a bit?" Air was gasping in and out of his chest at a rapid pace.

Without hesitation she reached for the next logical place to hold. It was a nice cut into the face of the rock giving her plenty of room to spread out her fingers. As she pulled her weight up with her arms her right foot lifted several inches looking for the next step. Just as her boot made contact with it her hand slipped.

A loud cry escaped as she felt herself sliding along the stone face. In the distance of her mind she could hear Sauntage screaming at her. Although she didn't fully comprehend his words she understood what he wanted her to do.

The knots bit into the flesh of her hands and legs, but the rope he tossed down to her helped her stop the rapid descent. Silence filled the dark space for some time. "Maureen? Maureen, are you all right?" His voice was strained.

Forcing the petrified sobs back into her throat she answered as loud as she could, "I'm okay, Sau." She closed her eyes and concentrated on holding the lifeline. There was no way she was going to let go.

Time passed without knowledge for either of them. Sauntage took many deep breaths. "Darling, you have to go back to the rock to climb."

Tearfully she admitted, "I don't think I can. I'm so scared, Sauntage. You go ahead and I'll use this rope to get up."

"Mo, I can't move until you go back to the rock. That rope is tied to my harness." The strain in his voice was growing.

Horror rounded her eyes and lips as she frantically looked for someplace to grab. Any place. Once she was clinging to the rock again she allowed some of the tears to slide down her cheeks.

Determination would not allow her to stay where she was for very long. Soon she was back to the place where she had fallen from and ready to move past it as quickly as possible. Step by agonizing step she reached the next wall anchor.

While she rested in place her mind relived the fall. A shudder went through her and she lowered her chin to her chest. When she did so she saw with amazement just how far up she was. The ground was not even visible to her anymore. To combat the dizziness that threatened to overwhelm her, she looked up to watch her husband's progress. Small clumps of dirt showered down into her face as he hoisted himself over the rim of the wall.

"Keep on coming, Mo. I'll see if I can anchor this rope off and pull you up." His light faded back from view though shadows shifted faintly above her head.

In the end she had to complete the climb on her own because there was no place for him to tie the knotted rope off and lift her safely. As soon as she reached the lip of the cliff he grabbed her by the wrists and dragged her ten feet from the edge. Maureen did not stand up on her feet. Sauntage pulled her up from the ground into his arms, backpack and all. His large trembling hands wrapped around the back of her helmet and pressed her tightly against his heaving chest. Great sobs convulsed her frame as she cried hysterically into his dirty shirt.

Neither of them spoke for a long time and both knew without saying a word that something between them had changed. When they drifted apart each of them quietly removed their backpack and they sat next to each other.

"We ought to press on." Sauntage finally broke the silence in a quiet voice, but regardless of his volume the cave echoed the sound loudly.

She nodded thoughtfully and for the first time looked around to see what that might mean. They were sitting along one wall of a tunnel that twisted away to their left and ended at the cliff on their right. No major changes had occurred in the surrounding color. Everything was still some variation of reddish brown. While much of the ceiling was invisible to their lights there were a few spikes slowly growing towards the floor.

A deep frown puckered her lips and eyes as something struck her mind. "Sau?"

"Yeah?" He responded getting to his feet and then turned to help her rise.

Maureen looked past his proffered hand to ask, "Do you really believe that the boys were brought through here?"

"Yes. Why?" His hand slowly withdrew as his knees folded

underneath him.

"Since we started walking through the caverns and tunnels I have seen no sign that anyone has been here in years." Her throat audibly constricted when she swallowed the bile in her esophagus. "How could that be; if four men and three boys traveled through here just days ago?"

A sigh left him as his dirty hand rubbed over his tired face and thickening beard. "It is hard to tell, but there have been a few signs. During my walk through the tunnels below I found the place they used for a bathroom. I'm sorry I guess I should have said something. Whatever his reasons for taking our sons and drawing me back to Liguesis, Tagurah planned this well. He knows the danger of someone following this path. That is probably why there are four of them. One man for each of the boys and one to cover their tracks."

"Do you really think the boys could've made it up that wall? Especially Ryan?" Her eyes were blinking back fresh tears as her teeth clenched together to hide the building sobs.

"I don't know how they managed any of this trip, Mo. The boys certainly wouldn't have come to this point quietly or without a struggle of some sort. In my heart though I know this is where they are." His head dropped to his chest in sorrow. "Until I see something that tells me different I have to believe that they are alive."

With a nod Maureen obeyed his silent signal to rise. Then she picked up her much lighter bag wondering, "What about us? Shouldn't we take the ropes, clips and anchors with us?"

"I can't get the anchors or clips until we go home, it would have been too dangerous to have you try to pull them out as we went. The ropes are tied to the outside of my pack." He turned it around so that she could see.

"Shouldn't we take off the harnesses?" As she spoke she reached for the buckle at her waist only to discover that it was gone.

Pressing his lips together momentarily Sauntage replied tenderly, "That fall shook you even more than I realized. Darling, I helped you out of that just before we sat down.

"But it's not in my bag." She countered looking on the ground for it.

"I put it in my pack, Maureen. I have plenty of room for It and my back is used to this sort of thing." His glove came off and his warm fingers cupped her cheek lovingly.

As they moved around the first of many bends in the corridor she lightly brushed her glove along her skin where he had touched her. The heat from his caress was burned into her memory. This was certainly not the first time he had touched her like that, so why did she feel so overwhelmed by it? He was right that fall on the rock climb must have really rattled her.

When she pulled herself from these thoughts she realized that her husband was several paces ahead of her. It took quite a few jogging steps to catch up to him. Once she caught her breath Maureen renewed her quest for answers, "Tell me about your parents, Sau."

At first he was silent as if he had not heard her request, but after a moment or two he started talking, "Well, I haven't seen them in seventeen years so things could be different. Father is a bold man, not afraid to make a decision. He takes his responsibilities as husband, father and good citizen of Liguesis very seriously. Though he's not exactly a harsh man he tends to sound that way because of his big booming voice. He is not a man to be crossed or taken lightly."

"Do you think he will help us? Would he choose our sons over your brother?" Her lip curled under her teeth in worry.

"Not for my sake he wouldn't. But if Mother asked him, he would come to our aid."

"What is she like?" Though she could not see it Maureen could hear the smile on his lips.

"Beautiful. Mother is a beautiful lady. She is wise and knows how to 'turn' Father's will as he would say. There aren't any women like her in Liguesis. You see, like earth's younger years Liguesian people have put men and women into their roles."

"You mean a submissive one for the women don't you?" Her fingers tightened into fists at her sides.

He nodded, "I'm afraid so. Though there are some differences. For example they are not viewed as property. They are never forced to marry a man if they do not wish it. A woman is seen as treasure, to have a wife is a gift to a Liguesian man. His reliance on her is never questioned. He works at his profession to provide for her needs, but she makes it possible for him to live."

"Sounds a bit like Utopia." Maureen commented as they turned yet another corner.

"Oh, it is far from perfect I assure you." Sauntage chuckled. "Perhaps you recall how I told you that one's birth order determined what profession you could join and whom you were allowed to marry?"

"Yes, I vaguely remember that."

"Well, if there is not a woman of his class who wishes to marry him a man must remain single for the rest of his life. Though that doesn't happen often it does happen occasionally."

Thoughtfully she considered his description then said, "Hmm, I guess that puts everyone on their best behavior."

A heavy sigh left him as he confessed, "Yeah, it tends to put a false front on some people. Always having to worry about what others think. It gets to be a heavy burden." He fell silent.

Watching his slumped shoulders Maureen saw how much this fact affected him. Then in wonder she thought about how this kind of society had molded her husband. This explained so much about how he treated her and why. A lump filled her throat for a long time. There was no doubt that he loved her. But could she really trust him?

Shortly after he fell silent the path began to take a downward slope. She lost all track of direction because of the many turns and twists. In fact she began to wonder whether or not they had even left the area by the cliff. It was almost like walking on a spiral staircase except the curve was irregular and sometimes went in the opposite direction.

Time ceased to be something she could measure. The constant darkness was making her crazy yet again. She wanted desperately to see daylight, any light other than the ones on their heads. When there was a sudden change in the slope at her feet she broke the silence, "Sau, I thought we were headed out of here. We're not moving upward at all."

"You're right on both counts. We are much closer to the end of this cave than you realize. If you remember I told you we have an underground river to navigate. That's where we are headed now. The river is really our way out of here." His voice had lightened considerably and he sounded almost happy.

"What happens when we get out of the river?" Maureen asked slowly licking her lips nervously.

He stopped walking to look at her with his head cocked to the side. A sad look washed onto his face as he studied her. "I can't say for sure, Darling. I have no idea if Tagurah is waiting for me at The Gateway or not. Something tells me he isn't. He's probably taken the boys somewhere else, but I honestly don't know where that could be. My hope is that he will have left a message of some kind."

"So this whole trip could be wasted!" She cried out hysterically. Her fists balled in the air wanting to hurt him the way that he was tormenting her.

Sauntage shouted back at her, "No, it's not! If our sons are not at The Gateway and there is not message either, then we go to my Father for help." Determination turned his deep blue eyes to steel. "One way or another I will find my sons and punish Tagurah for this pain if I can. He will wish he'd never been born when I am through with him."

Without another word he turned around and began to walk once more. This time, however, he only remained silent for a short while before he began to tell her about some of the festivals and holidays that were celebrated in Liguesis.

Soon his words were working their magic. As his voice echoed along the corridors her mind was transported to somewhere else. Excitement rose in her chest to see some of the things he talked about. Large gatherings to show off the labors and skills of the people sounded a lot like a rodeo or county fair. There were a couple of more formal ceremonies that he talked about that seemed very solemn and important to their culture. One was a wedding and the other was a tree planting that took place soon after a marriage.

Before she knew it Sauntage was stopping. She didn't have to ask what was happening because the sound of water filled her ears. It was not rushing as she had expected, but a slow gurgle that lapped against the walls of the cavern on either side of them. Maureen gaped at the dark flowing water. This was much smaller than she expected. A smile of relief came to her face.

"We'll rest here for a few hours and then head up the river to our left." His pack slid to the ground ten feet from the water's edge.

"Let's keep going. You said this was the end." Her eyes sparkled with hope that daylight was just a few minutes away.

"It is. And it isn't a long distance compared to how far we have already come. If I had to guess I'd say we're a mile or two from The Gateway now." He brought his gloves gently to her shoulders and slowly lowered the straps.

Looking into her husband's serious gaze she felt a weight drop into the pit of her stomach. What wasn't he telling her? "Sau, why are we stopping if we are so close? My sons could be less than a mile away." She stubbornly pushed his hands away from her pack.

"Mo, it is possible and if they are there we have to be ready. I can't face a kitten let alone four grown men if I am tired. This last mile is grueling."

Color drained from her face and she felt faint as the meaning of his words absorbed. Slowly she sank to the ground in quiet tears. To be this close and be made to wait was torture to her soul.

Squatting before her he tried to explain, "For several hundred feet it isn't difficult at all. In fact the water will feel wonderful. A little chilly perhaps, but all this dirt and grime simply soaks away. After that first stretch the ceiling drops almost to the top of the water which is only three feet at low tide. We have to go through parts on our hands and knees..."

"And the others?" Maureen asked hoarsely.

"The others we must swim through." He could see the panic in her eyes as he spoke.

Taking a deep breath he leaned forward to lightly brush his lips over hers. In a whisper he suggested against her cheeks, "Maybe we ought to turn out our lamps and rest for awhile. There was no argument from her as he reached between them with his right hand to extinguish the bulbs on their hard hats.

Once the darkness enfolded them she leaned into his frame for comfort. What choice did she have but to follow his every whim? It was pointless to think of turning back and going forward alone seemed more suicidal than waiting for him to move. A few tears splashed on her cheeks but not many because she realized that she was tired of the battle. All she wanted was for Sautage to get this over with whatever that might mean. At this moment she was too tired and sore to care.

Awareness did not come easily. Dreams fought with reality for some time before Maureen opened her eyes. A small circle of light was creating shadows from behind her. Moving onto her back caused spasms to run through her legs. She turned her chin to the right to see where the light was coming from.

Sauntage was seated near their packs. In his lap her Bible lay open and he held one of the flashlights above the pages to read. On the ground in front of him was a large pile of zippered plastic bags. Many of them held the items from their backpacks that could be damaged by water.

He must have seen her move because he looked up at her. There was a thoughtful expression on his brow as he asked, "How much of this have you read?"

"Not much." She shrugged as she shifted to a seated position. "I can't even remember putting it into the pack honestly. Why do you ask?"

"Some of this is like the books I read in the library in Liguesis and it is very much like the teaching of my parents. Of course the language was different but the ideas and stories were the same. Now I wish I'd listened to your parents when they tried to talk about it."

"Do you think there is something in there that is significant to us finding the boys?"  Was he okay? Or had this situation started chipping away at his sanity?

With a shake of his head Sauntage closed the book. For a second he held it in his lap and then pulled one of the large baggies close. "No, it's just interesting to think that we have some similar writings between our worlds."

"You said you read that this path was known to your people. So somebody must have used it long ago. Why wouldn't someone come from this world to share the gospel?" It surprised her how easily that answer had come to her and how natural the explanation sounded.

"Good point, Mo." His fingers pressed as much air from the baggie as possible and then carefully closed the zipper. "This is the last of the stuff to protect. So I say we get a bite to eat and prepare to go."

As they opened bags of dried fruits and nuts Maureen asked,

"What do you mean prepare? Don't we just start walking?"

"Not quite, Darling. First we need to put our climbing harnesses back on. They will help us get through the deeper places. Then we'll use that knotted rope and tie it between us. There will be four places along the way where we will have to swim between air pockets." Cautiously he looked at her. "I also have a couple pair of knee pads for us to wear since we'll have to crawl for a while."

A wry grin came to her lips as she commented sarcastically, "Could've used those in the woods."

"That fall on the rock hurt a lot more than you let on. We should've taken a look at it days ago." Creases formed around his eyes and lips.

"I checked it out that night. It was a bit puffy with a small cut and bruise. Nothing to worry about at least not compared to everything else that hurts now." Her shoulders drew close to her head in a deep shrug.

"Remind me about it when we get to The Gateway. I'll get something to ease the pain and swelling." After one last check of their bags he got stiffly to his feet to put on his climbing harness.

Minutes later they stepped into the cold water. It was quite a shock to her already chilly system. Maureen's breath came in huge gasps as she adjusted to the frigid liquid. In between her breaths she could hear her husband drawing in oxygen with a loud hiss through his teeth.

Their head lamps reflected off of the choppy surface of the river causing dancing shadows overhead and along the walls. As soon as they had taken four or five steps the waterline was just above their knees which made it hard to walk. Instantly the weight of their boots and pants felt like it tripled. It was not long before the water temperature was forgotten due to the amount of effort they had to put into moving forward. Between the sound of water sloshing and the strain it was to get enough air they hardly spoke.

When the ceiling began to drop Maureen kept an eye on her husband's every move. If there was any way to prepare for the next step she wanted to be ready. She had seen more than she ever wanted to in caves. The sooner the two of them got into fresh air the better as far as she was concerned.

Her thoughts were just starting to run a bit wild when Sauntage lightly touched her arm. Gently he said, "This is where our headroom disappears. From now on we'll have to go on our knees. As far as I can tell the depth is okay, we should be able to go through each of the four under water passages without worrying about the tide."

"Will our head lamps work under there?" She asked nervously biting on her lower lip.

"They are supposed to be water proof, but we have to go on knowing we could go into total darkness at any time. That's part of the reason we are wearing the rope."

"Part of the reason? What's the rest?" Though they could not be seen, she had her hands firmly planted on her hips.

His body lowered into the shallow water as he dropped to his padded knees. "These under water air pockets are spaced some distance apart from each other. So I will swim ahead to find them and when I get there I will tug on the rope three times to let you know I made it. Then all you have to do is follow the rope."

With a rapid nod she let him know she understood the plan. Gritting her teeth against the sharp needles of cold she plunged below the surface momentarily and then came to balance on her knees. Suddenly, she felt the press of his fingers on hers as he handed her something. It was heavy and she quickly recognized what it was. A chill having nothing to do with the temperature went from the top of her head to the tips of her toes when Sauntage spoke solemnly.

"If I don't tug on this rope within five minutes then use this to cut yourself free. Go back the way we came and bring one or two people to help you. There is a small leather journal in your pack that will give you all the directions you need as well as the compass. Use diving equipment if you can get it. From The Gateway head due north and tell anyone you meet that you need to get to Sauntago Vadelum. Here is my watch for you to time me." He gave her no time to react as he snapped the watchband around her gloved wrist. "I love you, Maureen."

Worry shocked her beyond words. Her heart pounded harshly in her chest as she stared after him. As she finally got her legs in motion to follow him she called softly, "I love you, too, Sau." If he heard her declaration he gave no indication of it, he simply waddled forward as quickly as he was able.

For some time she wondered if her husband had been mistaken about these under water passages. Perhaps he had snapped from the emotional strain and she had it all wrong. What if he were trying to harm himself? This new concern made her shiver. How could she stop him way down here?

Her mind did not have time to examine the matter because their breathing space was about to disappear. She tried to think of some way to make him stop, but as he sunk below the surface she knew it was too late. As the water swallowed him up she lifted her arm to count the seconds. One by one they ticked off. Out of the blue she tilted her face to the ceiling and cried softly, "God, please, let him be all right." Before the last word left her mouth the rope at her waist was moving.

Taking a deep breath Maureen prepared to follow her husband. The water was amazingly clear. It was such a shock that for a full two seconds she forgot to swim. Her head lamp showed her that this river was much like the passages they had come through except they were submerged. A few more seconds of swimming and she could see Sauntage earnestly searching for her. Maureen knew the precise moment that he saw her coming because he started to do a dance to encourage her to hurry. He didn't need to urge her at all. Her burning lungs were doing that already.

When her head broke the surface his hands covered her almost sending below again. "Watch your head, Darling. You should be able to rest on your knees, the water level isn't that high."

No answer would make it through her gasping lips. There didn't seem to be enough air in this tiny chamber.

"Try to take slow deep breaths. I know it's hard." His hands moved to the sides of her face as he suddenly leaned closer to her cheek and kissed it lightly.

After resting for a couple of minutes; the two of them shuffled along the tunnel. Having the weight off of her feet felt so good, but it was not long before her lower back started to tighten from the position. Her head was beginning to hurt from the light bouncing off the water and reflecting in every direction. It made concentrating on her surroundings difficult so she tried desperately to keep her eyes trained on Sauntage's back pack.

Soon his steps paused. "Here is our second place to swim."

"All right." She once again lifted her arm to keep track of his time with the watch.

There was something in his wife's voice that made him turn to face her. She was licking her lips nervously and her green eyes were wide with fear. A long moment passed before she shifted her gaze to meet his.

Maureen watched the hard lines of determination melt from his face. Replacing those tightened muscles was something she could not quite put into words. There was physical attraction in his study of her face which brought warmth to her cheeks. But she sensed an even deeper emotion behind his rich blue eyes. His words helped to explain what she saw.

"I have never been so proud to call you my wife. You have always been one of the strongest women I have ever known, but this whole thing makes me see how much I underestimated you. I know I said before that I regret not telling you everything years ago. The truth is I am angry at myself because you can't say the same of me." Tenderly he placed a kiss on her cheek and then reluctantly he backed away. "This is the easiest of the swims that we have to make. It should only take about thirty seconds to get through."

Before she could react he was gone. She stared at the space he had been occupying. For the first time since he had told her his story she had to seriously consider the possibility that in some way at least from his perspective he was telling her the truth. Her thoughts went no further because the rope at her waist moved three times.

This time she was prepared for the clarity of the water so she was looking more at the rock around her. At first it seemed to be like the other passages, but then she realized that the slow flowing water had smoothed the walls and corridors.

She remembered to surface slowly so she didn't hit the ceiling. Apparently he was concerned that she would forget because his hands immediately went to her helmet. As soon as she had drawn in a deep breath she noticed his fingers were no longer there. A strange sense of disappointment washed over her.

His eyes carefully avoided hers as he said, "We have a bit of a crawl to the next submerged section. That one is a bit tougher because we have to swim downward more than the others. The path dips quite a bit so you have to watch your head and pack to make sure you don't get caught."

"I'm ready whenever you are, Sau." There was calm in her voice though every other part of her being was on edge.

Slowly the two of them made their way through the cold water. At points along the way Maureen had to tilt her head back in order to keep her mouth above the waterline. She could no longer control the shivers that were convulsing her frame. This cold went deeper than any other she had experienced in her life even bitter snowy blizzards. Her teeth were chattering loudly now and they felt brittle enough to break.

When Sauntage reached the point where he could go no further above the water she did not know whether to rejoice or weep. In the end he did not give her the time for either one.

"Remember to watch your head and backpack." Was all he said before he dove beneath the surface.

Words died on her lips as she watched the ripples slowly level out. "I love you, Sauntage." She whispered softly to the air around her. Then suddenly, she recalled the watch and raised her wrist to keep track of his time.

The second hand seemed to be moving much faster than it should be. Time was adding quickly. He had been under the water for over a minute. Was he all right? With her right hand on the rope she waited for any sign of movement. Almost another minute had ticked off of the watch face. Chewing on her lip she remembered his instructions to give him five minutes before doing anything drastic. In any other situation that amount of time was trivial here it was torture.

Had it just jerked? Every muscle tensed with anticipation. Yes! There it was again. By the time it had been pulled for the third time there were tears streaming down her cheeks.

Not stopping to think about how she was going to manage underwater for that long Maureen took three huge breaths and went. At first she was puzzled because she saw the rope going straight ahead, but after a few strokes of her trembling arms she saw the downward spike. Kicking her feet as hard as she could she pushed herself deeper. Relief flowed through her when she saw that the path turned upwards almost immediately. It was short lived when she realized that the rope went out in front of her for an unknown distance. She couldn't see Sauntage yet!

Her shock had slowed her movements and suddenly her helmet cracked forcefully against the ceiling. Though rattled she doubled her efforts to kicking her feet and pulling herself through the water with her arms.

Pain seared her lungs. It felt like they were going to explode. The pounding of her heart was pressing on her chest muscles. She had to breathe!

Out of the corner of her eye she could see the knots along the rope moving rapidly. Sauntage was trying to help her. Quickly she reached out to take hold of it and felt the gloves shove further onto her hands with the force.

All of a sudden there was air! How she had gotten there she didn't know. But there were great lungfuls of oxygen.

It was a full minute later when she was finally able to see and think clearly. Her husband was watching her closely with his intense blue eyes. Water was still dripping from his thick black hair. "Are you okay, Maureen?" His gaze was moving between her face and the top of her head. "There's a nasty crack in your hard hat."

"Guess that might explain the headache I have." A wry grin formed on her lips as a light snort escaped.

Sauntage quickly drew near to look over the crack. He ran his long fingers along the jagged gap. Concern pressed his lips together and his eyes revealed a debate going through his mind.

She reached up to take hold of his forearms in order to gain his attention as she said, "I was joking, Sau." Her lips spread in a wide grin as her eyebrows lifted humorously at his look of shock. That was the kind of response she might have given a week ago, before all of this had taken place.

"I'm fine. Really." She assured him with a grin still holding his arms.

"Do you remember where we are? Or what we are trying to do?" His hands gently slid to the sides of her face.

"Yes, I know we are under some mountain in Kentucky on our way to finding our sons." Her smile dropped away slowly. "But after everything we've been through these past few days, I'm just so happy to be alive!"

Chuckling quietly he pulled her into his arms. "In a few days this will all be over. We'll be back home making up stories to tell our friends about our family vacation." He felt a twinge go through her and immediately he released her. Sorrow flashed in his eyes and spread across his face as he amended his prediction, "Actually, I will be packing my bags and you'll be calling a lawyer." After a quick sigh he changed the subject. "It's time to move on. Before we get too cold standing here. Now, this is it. When we surface next time we'll be in Liguesis."

"Really?" Maureen asked in a breathless whisper.

"Yes. This underwater section is much longer than the others. So don't be worried if it is more than five minutes before I tug that rope. I will need a minute or two to recover on the other side. And don't worry about not being able to swim that far because I will be hauling this rope in as fast as I can. Just kick as hard as you can and hold that rope." He waited only long enough to see her nod and then he left.

As the water swallowed him up she felt tears pricking her eyes. He talked about ending their marriage so easily as if he would soon get used to the idea. How could he feel that way? She was the one who had been betrayed. Maybe he hadn't told her about his past because he had always wanted a way out. Was that his plan all along?

The doubts were swirling so fast that she tried closing her eyes to push them away. They did not exactly change, but in the midst of them she heard a quiet voice. All that it said was, "Ask Me. Pray."

In confusion she opened her eyes and looked around the small bubble-like space. Who was she supposed to ask? There was no one here but her. God? Was He even real? A moment later she bowed her head as far as she could without putting her face in the water. What could it hurt? She needed all the help she could get sorting out her life.

When Maureen's eyes opened she felt the tug at her waist.

Heaven help her it was time. One. Two. Three deep breaths and she plunged into the water to follow her husband.

This tunnel was much bigger around than the others. If she had wanted to, she could have stood in this passage without fear of bumping her head. It was also much longer just as Sauntage had said. Though she was able to see more than ten feet in front of her each kick brought her no closer to the end.

The rope was tightly in the grip of her left hand while the hatchet was securely in her right. Tiny bubbles escaped her mouth as she tried to lessen the building pressure. That burning sensation was back in her chest and growing more painful by the second.

Suddenly, for no apparent reason the water got warmer. Her eyes began to tear from the intense discomfort all over her body especially her lungs and heart. It felt as if her heart was getting larger and pounding harder. The pulsing of the blood rushing through her ears made her dizzy.

Without warning the rope in her hand yanked her forward. Sauntage had managed to pull in the slack. Maureen was having a hard time hanging on to it. She had lost a good deal of strength in her muscles. A panic came over her as she realized she couldn't make it. There was nothing left with which she could fight. The moment was brief. Everything faded into blackness.

# Chapter Five

There was noise. What was it? A loud roaring; but not very close. Something else was much softer, closer. Was that a song? It was so hard to focus. Everything was hazy and surreal.

Maureen tried several times to lift her eyelids, but they were weighted by lead. For some time she remained still and simply listened. After awhile she decided she did hear a loud roaring though not from an animal. If she had to guess she would have said she was still in the water probably drowning. But then how could she hear that voice singing?

Sauntage! He was the one she could hear. With all of her might she pushed her eyes open. At first she saw nothing that was a surprise to her. Brown rock formed a dome above her head. As she sat up in slow jerky movements, Maureen realized that she had been lying next to a small pool of calm water. Beneath her head had been her husband's lap.

When she turned to face him she was overcome with joy. They were alive! Great sobs rose in her throat as she flew into his arms. His arms wrapped around her back tighter than she imagined possible. It was then that she noticed her backpack was gone and so was his. Water still clung to their clothes and hair.

As the two of them pulled back from the embrace minutes later she looked into his clean face with wonder. Only a second went by before she leaned forward to press her face to his. Her kiss was, she hoped, able to say to him what her vocal chords could not at the moment.

For the life of him he could not find the strength to stop her. Not that he wanted to, but deep down in his gut he felt this was wrong. He was taking advantage of her vulnerable state. Sauntage battled himself to release her.

In the end he found he could not. It was not as though he didn't try to put some distance between them. She was the one who refused to let him go he rationalized with himself that this fact kept him from being the responsible party.

The emotional reaction to the last leg of their underwater adventure finally subsided. With a good deal of shyness Maureen lifted her weight off of her husband's chest. Color flooded into her face as she realized that she had no idea where they were. For all she knew there could be someone else in the room with them.

"Welcome to Liguesis, My Lady Maureen." He said coming to his feet with a stately bow.

Blinking at him with a hundred questions running through her mind she tried to respond, "I - how - where..." Her arms waved crazily as she sought her brain for speech.

A chuckle broke the angles of his face as he moved closer to her. "Darling, I don't know how. I can only tell you that somewhere between that cave entrance in Kentucky and this pool of water is a door passing through space and time. We are now standing along the southern borders of Liguesis."

In wonder she turned away from him and looked more closely at her surroundings. This was similar to the rocks and caverns they had been passing through, but somewhere to her left there was light filtering in to this room. The ceiling seemed to be about ten feet above them with no stalactites growing from the smooth surface. Her eyes drifted to the pool at their feet. Six foot long and four foot wide it looked a bit like a bathtub sitting in the corner. It was filled with the clearest water she had ever seen. From where she stood she could see the tunnel going down and away from where they stood.

Not wanting to startle his wife too much, Sauntage slowly reached out to touch her cheek and said as he did so, "Mo, are you all right?"

Absently, she nodded tearing her gaze from the water. "I can't - it can't be. This is crazy. I'm crazy. That's it. I've gone mad and I'm hallucinating."

"No, you have not lost your mind. It's just being bent and challenged a bit. Come with me. There is a small chamber off to the left there behind you, where Tagurah and I usually meet." Before he could lead her away, she forcefully took him by the arm.

"Sau, I almost didn't make it through that last passage." Her voice paused as tears washed into her eyes. "Charlie and Drew are good swimmers. But Ryan is so..." Instantly his strong arms went about her.

"I know. I've thought about that too." His voice dropped to a raspy whisper as he vowed, "My brother will pay dearly for what he has done."

When Maureen looked up into his determined face she wasn't sure whether to be reassured or frightened. With uncertainty she wiped her tears and walked beside him. Only a few steps were needed to reach this chamber Sauntage talked about sharing with his brother.

It had an opening that was hidden in the shadows and unless you knew exactly where to look you would never find it. He had to stoop to keep from hitting his head but she was able to remain upright. In his hand he held one of the flashlights. From its yellowish beam she could see how different the stone was in here. Instead of the brown tones she had been looking at for days, this was gray.

"Tagurah and I worked together on this chamber. We were concerned that someone might catch us here and so this is where we would hide." With his hand he indicated a place for her to sit.

Slowly lowering her weight to the long bench she looked around the rounded rectangular space. It was six feet wide and eight foot long with a ceiling approximately six feet from the floor. Maureen realized that where she was sitting was actually one of two beds along the length of the room. There was little more than a foot of floor space between these bunks.

To her wonder and amazement Sauntage knelt before the bench in front of her and ran his hand along the upper edge of it. Suddenly, a loud click resounded in her ears as the top of the makeshift bed lifted like a lid. A gasp came from her lips and she leaned forward with anticipation. What was in there?

As he pulled things out from the storage chest he explained them. "Because Liguesis doesn't have technology as we do and we don't want to have to explain things that to most of the people would seem like magic, we have to exchange some of our equipment. Instead of flashlights we'll have to use these lanterns. And we'll have to use spark stones instead of matches. There aren't cotton plants like we have on earth so I keep some leather garments in here."

Maureen reached out to finger the black fabric in his hand. "Oh, it's so soft."

"Believe it or not it is a lot more comfortable than anything on earth I have worn. All I have here is men's attire so one of our first things to do is to find you a proper outfit."

"Is it really that big of a deal?" She asked with a frown as she tried to determine how the item in her hands went on a man's body.

A chuckle shook his frame as he turned to look over his shoulder at her, "No, I guess not. The top and pants will be too big for you though. But, you know, the head covering may work better than a woman's because of your hair."

"What is that supposed to mean?" Her eyes narrowed on him fiercely as she fingered the damp tendrils around her face. "What's the matter with my hair? Why wouldn't a woman's hat work for me?"

"Not a thing." He grinned at her playfully. "But not many women here in Liguesis have hair shorter than their waist."

"You have got to be kidding." Maureen gaped at him.

"Nope. Short hair is unheard of unless there has been an illness or accident where cutting it is absolutely necessary." Once he had pulled what he needed from the chest Sauntage pushed down the lid until he heard a loud click. "Scootch over and let me see what might be in here."

The second bed opened much like the first and she assumed it would hold the same kind of supplies so she didn't pay close attention after the opening click. Her eyes closed in exhaustion for a couple of seconds but flew open when she heard her husband cry out loudly. "What is it, Sau?" With panic she flew off the seat and stood over his trembling shoulders.

"Mo, look." He held up a black rubber mask. "Under these blankets is all kinds of diving equipment. Right down to small oxygen tanks. Six of them."

Tears rushed over her lashes as she cried softly, "Tagurah didn't know about Andrew."

"No, he didn't, Mo, but there were more than enough of them and equipment to get them all through The Gateway. He planned this so carefully. If he went to this much trouble and expense I don't believe he wants to hurt the boys."

Hope flooded through her excitedly, "Then you think they're still alive?"

Letting the lid go he came to his feet with a relieved sigh, "Yes, I honestly believe we're going to find them alive and well. Now let's go get our packs in here and figure out our next steps while we eat."

She nodded happily and then waited for him to leave the tiny chamber first since he was now closer to the door. As she took her first step her smiling gaze went to the storage chest next to her. In wonder she noted that the lid had not closed when he had let it go. Something beneath the pile of masks caught her eye. Though it had been brief she knew she had seen this once before.

Sauntage was nearly out the doorway when he heard scraping sounds behind him. Turning back to look at his wife he was startled to see her leaning deeply into the chest he had left open. Before he could ask her what she was doing she sat up and held up a gold disk for him to see. He took it from her and tipped the flashlight down over it.

"Does it say anything, Sau?" Her eyes danced over his face with hope.

There was a sinking sensation in his stomach as he read the simple words. Could this be right? Would Tagurah really take his sons there? Pressing his lips together he considered the best way to explain this to Maureen.

"Sau, tell me what that medallion says. And don't try to tell me you can't read it." She tucked her hands on her hips as she demanded an answer from him.

"It's the name of a mining region on the eastern border of Liguesis. Shargaunal." His gaze never lifted from the coin as he went on to add, "At the time I left the mining in this region had been closed down because of unsafe conditions. If memory serves it had been shut down for about fifteen years back then. I can't imagine why Tagurah would choose this place except that it is for the most part unpopulated."

"That's good for us. Won't have to worry so much about my hair and clothes." With lifted eyebrows she added, "I can't believe I actually said that."

Her response took him off guard, but made him smile. He curled his index finger and tenderly brushed it under her chin. "There is more to you than you realize." Before she could raise a comment he added, "And I don't mean your weight. Now let's get those bags. I could use a bite to eat and a long nap."

Although she sorely wanted to protest Maureen knew he was right. So following quietly behind him she went to her wet backpack and lifted it over one shoulder. The light shining faintly to her right caused her to slow her steps to ask, "Is that the way out of here?"

"It sure is." He nodded firmly.

"Can't we go outside for even a few minutes before we sleep?" Her voice was tired and whiney as she stubbornly stood in place expecting him to change his mind.

"Mo, we've been underground for a long time. If we go out there right now we'll have terrible migraines inside five minutes. No, it'll be much better for us to wait until after sunset to venture out of here." His expression told her that he knew what she was feeling and wished he had a different answer. "Come on let's get out of these wet clothes."

Soon they were seated side by side on one of the stone bunks with open baggies of food between them. The other bed and nearly every square inch of space on the floor were covered with wet items they hoped would dry while they slept.

Conversation came to a standstill as each of them tried to absorb and process their situation. They ate nuts, dried fruit and jerky without looking at the bags between them on the bench. Staring at the dark material now covering their legs and feet Maureen had to smile. It had taken Sauntage some time to show her how the fabric he pulled out of the built in trunk turned into clothing. He had been right about the comfort of this outfit, but matching the thin strips of leather along the open seams with their proper slots and then knotting them securely took a lot more energy than she would have imagined. Maureen was particularly happy with her new 'boots' because they were much softer which allowed her feet to move with ease.

"Sau? You've said that we need to go to your parents for help, but what about friends? Don't you have some you can call on?" Her leather encased knees bent under her chin giving it someplace to rest.

"Well, it isn't as though I don't have any friends to speak of but it has been so many years that to try to find them would take a long time. At the time I left all of my friends and I were going through our various training. They could be anywhere by now. My Father is really the best for this situation anyway." He dropped a large handful of berries and nuts into his mouth.

"And you honestly think he is going to believe you? That he will take your side over your brother's." Inside her stomach knotted with worry.

Thoughtfully he answered with his gaze trained on the opposite wall, "Well, as soon as he learns his grandsons are in trouble, Father will come to their aid. I don't know that it is necessary to tell him who has taken them."

"I see." Silence fell between them for nearly a minute. "How long will it take to reach your Father?"

"That all depends on where he is. He travels quite a bit for his job. I honestly don't know whether it would be better to seek him out or send him a message through someone." A heavy sigh left him. "If they are at home it will take five days to reach them on horseback."

Her eyes rounded on him as she wondered, "And where would we get horses, Sau?"

"A few miles to the north of here there is a small farming settlement. We shouldn't have any problems obtaining the use of a couple of horses." His eyes squeezed shut as he wrestled with his thoughts. "Maybe it would be best to send word to Father through someone in the settlement. We would reach the boys much faster."

"But what if we are really outnumbered?" She asked with hesitation as she began to see their situation more clearly.

"I don't know, Mo." Thinking through the various scenarios and possibilities was starting to overwhelm him. There were just too many what ifs.

Maureen looked down with sorrow and saw the Bible next to her on the bench. Reaching out a trembling hand she changed the subject, "Sau, what do you think about the Bible? Is it true or just a book of fairy tales?"

Because the question was so far from the track his thoughts had been on, it took him a moment to come up with an answer. "I wish I knew. We sure could use that kind of help right about now. Part of me really wants it to be true but part of me says it's too good to be true. There are writings just like this taught in homes and schools all over Liguesis. My parents are firm believers in Ewaris." He shifted his weight off of the bed and walked carefully through the wet items several times. "I mean the idea that someone created the universe isn't so hard to believe. And the idea that He would have rules for what He made makes sense. But to think He honestly cares about us as individuals is a bit far-fetched in my mind."

She nodded her understanding of his position and then admitted quietly, "I felt the same way." Her eyes lifted to meet his gaze as she went on to say, "Except I'm not sure that I would even have thought a Creator was possible. But now..."

In stunned amazement he came back to sit next to her. "You believe in it?"

"I want so very much to believe in that kind of love. To believe that those kinds of things can really happen and to believe that Dad and Mom weren't deceived." A wide yawn parted her lips. It was growing difficult to keep her eyes open.

Seeing the fatigue washing over her Sauntage decided it was time to turn off the flashlights to get some sleep. With quick motions he closed each of the bags and dropped them on the other bunk. "Perhaps with a little rest the answer will be easier to find."

There was no protest from her. She simply nodded in agreement and then carefully placed the Bible near the food. Her last waking thought was surprise at the comfort of the stone bench.

When she woke up Maureen found the space next to her was empty. It was black as pitch all around her which stirred fear in her chest. Then she slowly sat up on the bench and her fingers hit one of the flashlights. Snapping it on; she tip toed through the stuff on the floor toward the doorway.

Sauntage looked up from the Bible in his lap with relief. He had hoped she would wake up on her own so that he didn't have to disturb her when it was time for them to go. A smirk came to his lips as he observed her tangled mass of curly hair. "Good evening, Fair Lady Maureen."

"Hello." Her dry throat croaked and her hand went to cover it.

"Sounds like you could use a drink." His thumb waved in the direction of the pool. "The air gets dry in that room. It's the povout lining Tagurah used. Works great keeping things warm and seals against leaks, but it absorbs every bit of moisture in the air."

There was a soft moan from her as the cool water washed down her throat. For a brief moment she thought about dunking her entire body, but then remembered that they would be leaving soon. "Is that what the gray stuff is called?"

"Yes, povout. They mine it in the northwest region. Pretty interesting stuff really. You can use it to seal leaks, it naturally holds heat in for long periods of time and it is not as hard and solid as stone."

"So that's why it seemed so comfortable compared to where we have been sleeping." She smiled softly as she guessed, "I don't suppose we will find many kavetas with povout in them."

A sarcastic chuckle rumbled in his chest as he responded, "Uh, no. Povout is also rather expensive."

Her brows lifted with curiosity, "Then your family is well off."

"Tagurah ran those mines for a period of time so he had access to the equipment and as I understand it he pulled most of out it himself." He sighed deeply as he got off the ground. "Enough of that for now. We need to pack our bag and hide what we can't take."

Nodding firmly Maureen took his proffered hand to help her to her full height. They walked side by side to the concealed door where he gently pressed her to go in ahead of him. His voice came over her shoulder unexpectedly.

"I have been up thinking about it for quite some time and I think our best shot at rescuing the boys is to go to the farming settlement that is less than two days north of here. I'm sure we can locate a pair of good horses and trustworthy messenger to send to my Father."

Turning to face him she asked, "And what if he won't come?"

"He'll come. If he is able he will come." There was no doubt on his face or in his voice. "Now let's see how much this stuff dried."

Much to her amazement all of their clothes had dried though they were not really any better than rags. Still she took the time to carefully fold each of the garments. Into the storage bins went the clothing, the climbing harnesses, hard hats batteries, flashlights, and all the plastic baggies.

Sauntage debated about taking the backpacks. He had chosen materials that wouldn't be immediately questioned, but still they were not made in Liguesis. In the end he opted to take the smaller pack that Maureen had used. It could be carried by either of them and if the need arose it could quickly be burned.

For the first part of their journey he said that he would take charge of the bag so she could get used to walking in the unfamiliar clothing. She readily agreed because the over sized outfit was cumbersome. It was made of a dark brown almost black leathery material. There were three pieces in all that wrapped around her body.

The first piece reminded her of chaps that a cowboy would wear except that the material had thin leather ties of the same color along the inside of the leg instead of the back. Over this went a shirt of sorts that tied at her shoulders.

Though it was likely to be warm; Sauntage suggested that she wear the head covering for a bit of protection. "People in this region are more likely than anywhere else to take action before getting information."

"Shoot first ask questions later?" She quoted as she stuffed as much of her hair into the little interior pocket of the stiff head dress. Once it was in place she knelt on the ground before the pool and used the lantern to look at her reflection. Most of her hair was hidden under the funny looking cap. It had a forehead brim similar to a baseball cap, but not as deep. And behind her ears it fell to her shoulders in the form of a pouch that tied in place at the top of her head.

Her eyes rolled sarcastically as she got to her feet. "I'm sure glad they don't have cameras here."

His lips curled up in a wide grin, "We have to find women's clothes for you as soon as possible. You are far too beautiful to pass for a man."

Color flooded into her cheeks and she lowered her face toward the ground. At this moment she felt anything but pretty.

He knew what she was thinking and it caused him to shake his head quietly. In a light tone he said, "If you would care to follow me,

I will introduce you to the evening splendor of Liguesis."

Taking hold of his out stretched hand Maureen walked with him to the small tunnel across the room. When they reached the mouth of the cave he turned the wick on the lantern down and the yellowish glow faded. At first she was puzzled by this, but when he gently tugged on her fingers to pull her into the open air she understood.

Awe stopped her breath and lowered her jaw. Thousands of stars twinkled overhead in light blues, pale yellows, faint pinks and brilliant whites. Their light was more than enough to see the shadowy outlines of the hundreds of plants and trees surrounding them.

Because this was her first breath of fresh air in days she pulled in as much as she could at one time. Her nose started to tingle and burn. Using the back of her fingers she tried to sooth the sensation. "Is that some kind of flower or tree?"

Loud rumbles came from his lips as he explained, "There is very little air pollution here and no manmade chemicals are sprayed on the plants and trees so nothing changes their scent. Most of what you smell right now is weeds."

"It's just so strong. I can't believe it." She turned in a slow circle to get a quick peek at everything before they moved to the north. To the east Maureen was able to see the water that she had been hearing in the cave. "Oh, that's amazing! You don't even see stuff like that in the movies."

Water was cascading over the top of the rocks that formed the cave they had just left. An eight foot wide band dropped from thirty feet above into a wide churning pool more than fifty feet away from where they stood. Even in the dim light it was an amazing sight that left Maureen wondering how it must look in full daylight.

When she turned to look behind her, Maureen met a huge rock face. Its imposing height caused her to take a couple of steps backward. Slowly her gaze went left to right and much to her surprise this mountainous wall went on indefinitely in both directions.

Turning to what she later learned was the north she could see the vast expanse of Liguesis before her. For the most part the terrain appeared to be level, but because of the many scrub trees and bushes it was hard to tell for sure. "This is unreal." She whispered with a hard swallow.

He gave a soft chuckle as he responded, "It's very real I assure you. That's where I fish every year. Well, actually Tagurah and I would follow the stream leading away from the pool for a mile or so." With his finger he indicated the general direction and then he used the palm of his right hand against the small of her back to urge her forward. "This is just the beginning, Darling. Let's keep going."

As they walked along the ground she noted that it was not hard like rock or stone. Beneath their feet was softer moist dirt that shifted slightly under their weight. In the dim light it was difficult to tell whether there was a path to follow. It was not long before she realized that they were forging their own trail amongst the weeds.

She was not bothered by this fact but she did wish that she could see the sources of all the different smells. Some were spicy and caused tingling in her nose and throat. Others were delicate and sweet like a woman's perfume. At one point she was tempted to search for one such plant, it suddenly occurred to her, however, that this idea was not wise. What if she were allergic to it?

After walking for about twenty minutes they finally met up with the winding stream. They each took a long sip from the chilly flow before they followed its course in a somewhat northwesterly direction. A full hour went by before it struck her that she had not seen or heard any birds or other animals since they left the cave. Then it occurred to her that the foliage had changed. Instead of plants, bushes and small trees it looked like everything had been trampled. While this made walking much easier, it caused an uneasy feeling to settle in her stomach.

When Maureen asked him about it he answered thoughtfully, "The wild animals here are leery of humans just as they are on earth. We have probably passed some but they are hiding."

"What do they look like? I mean do any animals resemble those on earth?" Her feet paused as she looked carefully around her. Perhaps there were animals nearby and they had missed them because they were so intent on their mission.

Sauntage stopped next to his wife and briefly checked the ground. Then he lifted his gaze to the sky. "For the most part they do look a lot like the animals in the US. It is a bit strange that we haven't heard or seen anything of a wild animal yet. The ground here looks like a herd of large animals came traipsing through, but there aren't any that are native to this region. There are rodents like groundhogs or gophers, raccoons, porcupines, a few varieties of birds and maybe a snake or two." Without warning he changed the subject, "If I didn't know better I'd say a storm was coming in. But there's no sign of bad weather at all. Let's keep going we're bound to run into a critter or two along the way, but don't worry they're pretty harmless as long as we stay out of their way." With a nod of encouragement in her direction he once again started moving.

About forty-five minutes into their journey they noticed the ground change once more. Grass was no longer lying flat against the ground and bushes were complete; without broken limbs. More trees were visible now which made them wonder if others behind them had been knocked down somehow.

The two of them walked along the river for much of the night. Their stops were brief and as far apart as they could possibly make them. Maureen began to ask him a few questions about the history of Liguesis and he willingly shared all that he could remember. It amazed her that a place so lacking in modern things had been in existence for at least a thousand years. And according to her husband there was evidence of things much older but no written documentation to prove it.

"So the same family has ruled over Liguesis for most of its history?" Her eyes were wide with disbelief.

"I know that from all your experience on earth that doesn't seem possible, but here it is simply the way it is." He stopped to look across the water as he shared, "To rule in this world means a far different thing than what it means on earth. On earth a ruler typically has people under their authority who carry out orders. Here that happens only once in a great while. Our ruler always assesses problems and situations personally. It does tend to slow things down a great deal, but then people are less likely to bring smaller issues to the King. They manage to figure out solutions for themselves."

"Like you sending for your Father instead of the King." She looked at him with an understanding nod. "So if for some reason your Father isn't able to come, then perhaps we could go to the King."

He did not respond to her comments, but turned to continue

walking. As they trudged through mud and weeds he remained lost in his thoughts.

Maureen was not bothered by this in the slightest because as she followed his footsteps she practiced his language softly under her breath. So many new words and phrases were tripping off her tongue that it took her awhile to realize that her husband was no longer quiet. A frown puckered her forehead as she strained to hear his words. Much to her surprise he was actually singing a song quietly to himself.

It was a haunting melody that rose and fell in sad lines she had trouble understanding. If she had to guess she would have said it was a song of mourning. Some of the words she was just beginning to pick up on when he abruptly stopped.

"I think we ought to stop and rest here for the rest of the night. Just another mile or so up the river we leave the dense foliage. From there we have a little more than half a day's walk to the settlement. I'd rather get there well after mid day." Sauntage shifted the pack off his back and set it down a good ten feet from the river bank.

"Why?" She asked sagging onto the ground next to the bag. "What difference does it make as long as it isn't the middle of the night?"

Bending over at the waist to stretch his tight back muscles he replied, "If we arrive in the settlement too early in the day knowledge of our presence would spread rapidly. People would come in from all over the area to greet us and hear news of our journey." When he caught the sarcastic tilt of her chin he added, "Life is simple here, Mo. Anything out of the ordinary is entertainment. So I'd rather not be the side show tomorrow evening."

"I'm all for avoiding that." Her voice rang with more sarcasm.

A groan left him as he slowly sat across from her. "To do that all we have to do is make sure we enter the settlement no more than an hour before dinner. At that time everyone will be far too busy to take too much notice of us. We have to be careful whom we choose to approach because we need to get clothing for you. And without money that could be tricky. The fewer people we come in contact with the better off we will be."

Maureen stifled a yawn with her palm. "Whatever you say, Sau. I just want to get to the boys and rescue them as quickly as possible."

"For now let's finish our nuts and dried berries. Without the baggies any number of critters could smell our stash and come to investigate it while we sleep. In the morning we'll see about catching some fish and building a fire to cook them." As he spoke Sauntage opened a zippered compartment on the backpack and reached in for a handful of food.

Trail mix was not exactly appealing to her but she was hungry. While she chewed she closed her eyes and imagined that she was biting into a thick juicy steak. At first it was a marvelous daydream then her heart had to add the others with which she would want to share this meal. Tears blurred her vision as she shook herself from her wishful thinking.

Sauntage sensed her struggle and ached to be able to put an end to it. In slow halting moves he worked to free the heavy black hide blanket from the backpack. When he had opened it he drew close to his wife and tenderly wrapped it around the two of them. He held her tightly against his chest while she cried herself to sleep. Darkness was melting into dawn as his mind and body finally gave in to the rest he so desperately needed.

# Chapter Six

Sunlight was the first thing Maureen noticed when she awakened. The rays were warm and inviting. As she blinked away sleep as well as the days of continual darkness she was puzzled by the hue of the air around her. From way over her head she saw a bright round orb in a pale green hue. It gave everything around her just a hint of its coloring.

Using her hand to push the hair from her face she caught a glimpse of her skin. Somehow the greenish tint of the atmosphere made the intensity of the freckles diminish.

A soft tapping noise caught her attention and she turned to her left to see what was making it. Much to her surprise a small squirrel sat on its haunches several yards away, chattering madly about their intrusion. She felt the corners of her mouth lift slightly at his angry tirade. With her smile still in place she scanned the horizon and noticed quite a few creatures moving about in the cheery atmosphere.

Once her auburn hair was pushed back into the cap she carefully left Sauntage sleeping on the ground to explore.

At the river she scooped up water to drink. With her face nearly touching the surface of the water she gazed into what she thought were shallow depths and discovered fish moving to and fro beneath her hand. They looked to be just inches from her fingertips but when she stretched out her arm to try to touch them they never got any closer to her. A deep frown rested on her forehead for a minute as she considered what she had just seen. Perhaps it was their silvery purple scales that interfered with her depth perception or the purity of the water. In any case they were not bothered by her presence.

After a few minutes of observing the school of a dozen or so she looked up and down the river bank. Lots of different varieties of plants were growing right up to the water's edge. Most of them were deep green in color and less than three feet in height. Not many nearby had flowers of any sort.

Her first thought was that this could have been a river somewhere on earth. But as she sat quietly observing she felt a difference somehow. It was confusing to her senses to look at surroundings so like what she was used to and yet not like it at all.

Maureen turned to look back at her husband sleeping under the blanket. Not much of him was visible except his black hair. Only the green hint of the sun gave it an iridescent quality that reflected the same color back. The corner of her mouth twisted a bit as she considered waking him. With a tiny shake of her head she opted against that and went instead to find the Bible in the backpack.

She read for quite some time before Sauntage stirred. When she looked down at his bemused expression she smiled softly, "Good morning, sleepy head."

"Good morning." He mumbled back at her, coming to a seated position. When he was fully awake he looked over at her and his movements stalled.

Sensing that something had startled him she looked to either side of her and asked slowly, "What's wrong, Sau? What do you see?"

"It's you, Maureen. In this light you look..."

"Like I have a layer of chalk covering my skin?" She tipped her head to the left studying the strange affect on his facial features. His dark hair and beard were an even bigger contrast to his skin.

Breathlessly he shook his head and then drew closer to her. With his fingertips he gently traced a line down the side of her face as he said, "So different. I've never seen you without freckles."

Despite his serious expression and tone of voice Maureen burst into laughter. "And here I thought something was really wrong. Does my hair look different as well?" As quickly as she could she tugged the cap from her head. The answer he gave her left her blinking.

"Yeah, it's not so red here." Disappointment was written all over his face. With a pout he changed the subject, "You must be hungry. Let's see what we can do about catching some breakfast from the river."

Minutes later they were seated side by side at the river's edge. Beside each of them was a pile of thin reed like leaves that they had pulled from a nearby plant. In quick practiced movements he showed her how to tightly weave the leaves together to form a long chain.

As she worked at this he dug in the dirt a few feet away beneath a large bushy plant. By the time she had created a rope of sorts that was about twelve feet in length; Sauntage had managed to collect a half a dozen pale yellow worms. Her stomach churned as she watched him wind the weed and worm into a tight knot.

Carefully he lowered the fishing line in the water not far from the school of fish that she had been watching earlier. Inch by inch the knotted plant went into the water. Amazement rounded her eyes and opened her mouth as she watched all but three feet sink below the surface. To add to the wonder of the situation there was not a strong current here to pull the line downstream.

Catching a fish for each of them took longer than he had hoped. It was well after noon before they were ready to put their fish in the hot coals of a fire. While they waited for the fire to die down a bit he walked in an ever widening circle around the fire. Every once in a while he plucked leaves from a tree or dug in the dirt.

"Sau, what are you doing?" She snorted at him with a wondering look.

"Collecting some medicinal leaves and roots. They might come in handy along the journey. I don't see a jurop bush yet though." He said with irritation.

"What's a jurop bush for?" Her interest was growing so she left the fire to follow in his wake.

"Jurop leaves are good for a few things actually. The biggest use for them is a paste that can be rubbed into the skin to bring down swelling." His eyes quickly flicked to her knee as he went on to say, "I'm sorry it's taken me so long to get around to this."

"Don't worry about it, Sau. My body must be getting use to this outdoorsy lifestyle because it doesn't hurt quite so much." Her shoulders lifted in a shrug.

"Yeah, I'll bet you're right. Plus I believe the water at The Gateway is special." Sauntage answered thoughtfully as he yanked more leaves.

"Special? Special how? In what way?" She leaned around his back to see which plants he was taking.

Distractedly he replied, "I don't exactly know. But every time I come through that water with an injury I always see a marked improvement in it." Taking a few steps forward he suddenly froze in his tracks. Through clenched teeth he hissed softly, "Mo, as smoothly as you can get back to the fire. No quick motions. Slowly and steadily back up."

His tall frame inched back towards her and she immediately obeyed. As they stepped again she whispered, "Sau, what's wrong?" For a long time he failed to respond so she pressed her hands into his back.

"It's a snake." His head turned back over his shoulder to see where they were headed.

"A snake!" She screeched loudly. Before another thought went through her mind she found herself thrust backwards several feet, hitting the ground so hard her teeth clattered together.

When she recovered a split second later Maureen saw the large body of a reptile literally standing in front of her husband at least three feet off the ground. Its cream colored stomach was weaving back and forth as it rushed forward. The scales of brown, black and gray formed a pattern of interlacing diamonds along its back and were rubbing against each other like sandpaper.

Everything was now moving in slow motion except the snake. Sauntage tried to dodge to his left to avoid the fangs now bared. He was not quick enough.

Instantly he was on the ground wrestling with the powerful creature. His legs flailed in the air trying to capture the beast. Loud cries of pain and exertion ripped from his throat as he desperately worked to free his right arm from its grip.

Maureen watched this from four feet away all the while her mind screamed for her to get in motion. On the ground near her feet was a stone just small enough for her hand. With unbearable slowness she bent over to pick up the stone. Unable to get her body to move as quickly as she wanted; she angrily pressed forward to reach her husband.

Somehow he had gotten the snake's body pressed between his knees and he was squeezing as hard as he possibly could. Sauntage was rolling from one side to the other attempting to pry the fangs from the flesh of his forearm.

There was no time for her to think about what she was doing. She used her left hand to help him hold the reptile's head and then brought the rock down as hard as she could. Though she used every bit of strength she had Maureen was sure it hadn't been enough. When she heard Sauntage's raspy voice she realized that she had closed her eyes.

"Maureen, get the fishing rope. Hurry!"

All her brain registered as she opened her eyes was blood. Lots of it. Fear overwhelmed her. What had she done?

"Now, Maureen!" He shouted at her.

The loud command made her jump into action. Seconds later she rushed back at him with the weed trailing behind her.

His eyes opened with obvious effort and his voice was growing weaker as he instructed, "Tie it at elbow as tight as you can." Licking his lips he continued, "Use hatchet blade. Drain poison. Cover with crushed aukar leaves." Before his eyelids slid down he pushed two wide leaves at her.

Staring at his still form she felt a moment of sheer panic. Now what? Her hands were moving without the full engagement of her brain so she focused on doing what he had asked her to do. Cuts from the thin strip of weed covered the palm of her hands as she struggled to cut off the circulation to his forearm.

With relief it registered that most of the blood covering them was from the snake now writhing sporadically as life left its body. Just seeing the carnage was enough to turn her stomach, but added to that was the smell of blood and venom. It never occurred to her that venom would have a distinct odor; something like rotten eggs but not nearly as strong.

As she raced to the fire to grab the hatchet she drew in great breaths of fresher air. Maureen started to run the sharp blade back to where Sauntage lie, but then she paused to thrust it into the flames for nearly a minute.

By the time she returned to her husband's side his breathing had grown shallow and his skin was clammy. Kicking the still carcass of the snake out of her way she knelt next to his limp arm. She tried to cut his shirt sleeve open with just one small corner of the blade so that the rest could be as sterile as possible when she used it on his arm.

The leather was stronger than she anticipated and the frustration of not being able to get his arm free fast enough caused tears to well up in her eyes. What seemed like hours later the fabric separated far enough for her to cut the flesh around the swollen bite. At first she did not think she could put the blade to his skin but the fear of what might happen if she didn't, spurred her on to try.

Unlike the material covering their bodies Sauntage's wound opened easily. Thick, white-pink fluid oozed from the bite. In just a few minutes time his lower arm had puffed up almost double its usual size. Instinct told her to roll him on his right side so that gravity could work with her. Once she had him positioned with relative certainty that he wasn't going to flop to his back or stomach, Maureen snatched up one of the leaves he had given her.

Carefully she back tracked over the places he had walked through just a short while ago. A cry of victory rose from her lips as she found the bush she needed. With a fistful of the wide leaves her eyes darted around for something she could use to crush them. The bloody stone she used on the snake was not likely to be safe so she glanced frantically for another one. On the other side of the fire she saw just what she needed.

Her feet lost no time now getting her to that rock and then to the river to rinse it off. "Hang in there, Sau. I've almost got it." Her voice rang out with little expectation that he would answer, but it made her feel as if her movements had some focus.

Not knowing what 'crushed' meant when one was talking about a flat leaf she pounded it between the clean rock and the back side of the hatchet until the fluid inside the leaf coated its outer surfaces. When she gently pressed the sticky mess over the wound it was still dripping small amounts of blood and venom.

Now that she completed his instructions she watched his damp face expectantly. Any moment he ought to awaken.

An hour later he had yet to move a muscle. Concern for him was growing by the minute. Every once in a while she put fresh aukar over the hole in his arm and it continued to drain. She became worried that the tight rope up by his elbow may cause further damage so she had loosened its grip on his blood vessels.

As she continued to wait the realization that there could be more snakes in the area hit her. With a sickening sensation in the pit of her stomach she found herself looking around with fear. What was she going to do?

Suddenly, she recalled his direction to her before the snake bit him. He had been telling her to get back to the fire. Glancing to her left she saw the dying embers about fifteen feet away. While she was confident that she could resurrect the flames with a little work, there was doubt in her mind in getting Sauntage close to it. Her insides cringed at the thought of moving around in this place much more, but with a frown of determination she got up to begin a new fire.

First she brought everything over from the other site and then she went in search of more woody plants, bushes and trees that might burn. Once every few minutes she came back to check on her husband. Not much was changing. He was still unconscious and his lower arm was still puffy. It was encouraging to her that the swelling had gone down quite a bit and had not crept further up his limb. His heart rate seemed to be steady, but she was no nurse and had no idea whether it was fast, slow or just right. Compared to her own pulse it was much slower which made logical sense to her.

Another hour past in which she moved their camp and built a new fire. It turned out to be much trickier than she would have guessed to make something burn with his spark stones. Each time she brought the stones together there was a brief flash, but it was never long enough to start something burning. After a couple dozen or so tries she was about ready to give up. Why hadn't she watched him do this more closely?

In frustration she tossed them on the ground by her knees. To her amazement Maureen saw two tiny sparks jump from the stones onto the bare earth she had cleared around the new fire pit. So that was the trick! She excitedly began her venture once more but this time instead of banging them together she scraped them like she would have done with a match.

Soon a fire crackled cheerfully at her from her husband's side. A moment of pride and a sense of accomplishment helped her to relax for a few minutes. With Sauntage's head in her lap she sat staring into the dancing flames for a long time.

She gently rubbed his forehead and cheeks with the back of her hand. It was not long before she noticed the temperature of his skin start to rise. Thinking that this could be due to the flames just a foot and a half away she slowly scooted her bottom further back and as gently as possible moved him with her. When she had waited a few minutes and the only change she could sense seemed to be in the wrong direction she decided that he must have a fever.

Maureen slid out from under his head and neck to see what she could do about his raised temperature. From the backpack she pulled out the blanket and then spread it over his still form. Something about his condition was bothering her though she couldn't quite figure out what it was. As she went to the river with her hat she used it to scoop up water and bring it back to the fire.

In order to spare as much of the cool liquid as possible she had to hold the flexible head covering above the ground with one hand and use the other to cool his face. It occurred to her that maybe she should rinse the bite and then reapply the aukar leaves. When she did this she realized what was bothering her about Sauntage's condition.

He was not moving at all. If one of her boys had a high temperature like this they tossed and turned trying to find relief of any kind. Why wasn't her husband doing the same? The venom must have paralyzed him somehow. Fear walked up and down her spine in shivers.

Time ceased to move forward as she watched each breath he took. Questions raced through her mind in rapid succession. What was she going do? Was there anything more she could do for him? Was his condition permanent? Could one of the plants nearby help him? If so which one? And how would she give it to him?

Tears washed into her eyes as sobs rose in her chest. So much depended on what happened to Sauntage and his well being was solely in her hands. This was a terrifying thought as she considered the facts that she had no idea where she was or where they were ultimately headed and other than a few words and customs she couldn't communicate with the people here. Other than the knowledge that some farmers were north of this place she had no idea where to look for help.

Her face lifted to look out in front of her beyond the fire. In a large shadowy line she could see the top edge of the mountains under which they had passed. In despair she thought about the fact that she had very little chance of getting back to earth without the help of her husband.

Wiping the backs of her hands across her cheeks to clear away the blinding moisture she resolved to make some sort of plan for herself. She knew she had to keep up her strength in order to care for Sauntage so she thought about how she would go about doing that. Maureen pulled the backpack closer to her side to go through it carefully and review what supplies she had to help her.

The first thing her hands landed on was her parent's Bible. A fresh wave of tears threatened as she hugged the leather tightly to her chest. "Oh, how I wish it were real. That there really was a God in heaven that cared whether we lived or died." Her arms dropped weakly in her lap causing the thick book to open over her knees.

Absently, her gaze lowered to the page and read the first words she saw. She felt her jaw slack open and the color drain from her face. It couldn't be. This had to be some kind of a coincidence, nothing more. Once again she read the verses but this time her lips formed the sentences:

"'I lift up my eyes to the hills. From where does my help come? My help comes from the LORD, who made heaven and earth. He will not let your foot be moved; he who keeps you will not slumber. Behold, he who keeps Israel will neither slumber nor sleep. The LORD is your keeper; the LORD is your shade on your right hand. The sun shall not strike you by day, nor the moon by night. The LORD will keep you from all evil; he will keep your life. The LORD will keep your going out and your coming in from this time forth and forevermore.'"

Peace enveloped her like a warm blanket. Somehow she would make it through this horrible nightmare. For now she had to care for Sauntage as best as she could. Anything beyond that she had to take as it came.

From the pit of her stomach she heard rumblings of hunger. Somewhere by the other fire pit were the two fish Sauntage had caught earlier. They might not be any good now, but it was worth it to have a look at them. If she didn't have to hook another fish and attempt to clean it, it would save her a lot of time and energy.

In the end she had no way of telling whether they were safe to eat or not. To her they smelled just as bad as when Sauntage had pulled them from the water. With a heavy sigh she picked up a sturdy stick from the ground and after burning the tip of it slightly she pierced the side of the fish to hold it over the flame.

He still had yet to make a sound or movement other than breathing when she sat next him to eat. Gingerly she touched the black edges of the thick fillet. Though fish of any kind was not on her list of favorite foods she knew that it would be filling and nutritious. As it turned out the filets were so crispy that her taste buds failed to recognize the variety of meat she was eating.

When she finished choking down her dinner Maureen added more fuel to the fire and checked the wound. Much to her relief the swelling was almost gone. With a couple of wide yawns she figured that it was time for her to get some sleep.

Snuggling up to his back she pulled the blanket so that it covered them both. Not a minute past and she was sound asleep.

It was a long night for Maureen. At least once every couple of hours she woke up to check on Sauntage and make sure the fire didn't go out completely. His fever seemed to go down a bit, but it refused to break. She did her best not to panic or lose hope each time she looked at his arm and saw how red the wound was.

Her supply of leaves was nearly gone as dawn was beginning to move across the sky. Using the spark stones she lit the lantern for the first time hoping that she could gather what she needed and turn it off quickly because she had no idea how long it could last or where to get more fuel for it.

By the time she made it back to his side color was slowly washing into the landscape. With relief she turned down the wick and set the lantern near the backpack. He still hadn't moved. Over twelve hours had passed and he had yet to show any signs of improvement. Tears burned in her tired eyes.

A quiet thought came through her discouragement, 'He is no worse.' Somehow this simple fact was comforting and she felt peace once more. Maureen placed a soft kiss on his cheek, curled up next to him and drifted off to sleep again.

Exhaustion finally over rode her instincts as a wife and mother because nearly four hours passed before she woke with a jolt. Something moved. She jerked her body around so fast to look at Sauntage's face that she pulled the blanket off of him. He was still breathing steadily with his face warm and pale.

Gently she tucked the blanket around his wide shoulders. As she did so a soft moan escaped from his lips. Excitement raced through her as she grasped his shoulders and cried, "Sau? Sau, can you hear me?"

Nothing.

It must have been her ears playing tricks on her. With a sigh she got up, took her cap and made her way through the weeds to the river. After splashing some of the refreshing fluid on her face she filled her cap.

Kneeling in front of his chest Maureen carefully peeled off the sticky layer of leaves plastered to his arm. Much to her surprise the redness was diminishing. She felt some part of her relax just a bit as she poured cool water over the bite. There was a hissing sound which startled her. A few heart beats went by before it occurred to her what it was.

Sauntage was reacting to the water. With a cringe she realized that what she was doing was hurting him. "Oh, Sau, I'm so sorry. I know it must hurt terribly."

His face remained flat.

As she pounded fresh leaves Maureen kept flicking her gaze at him looking for any sign of movement. She saw none. Whatever awareness he had a few minutes before was completely gone. That was probably a good thing she thought as she spread his arm with the leaves.

The fire had died away leaving only a few smoldering embers for her to use in rebuilding it. Firewood was running low so she picked up the hatchet to go in search for more. Not many large trees seemed to be growing along this section of the river. For a moment or two she debated which direction she should go in search of larger pieces of firewood. In the end she chose to go back to the south a ways.

To drag the small amount of wood back to their campsite turned out to be much more of a chore than she thought it would be. Sweat was beading up on her forehead as she flopped on the ground next to her husband. A low gurgling sound caused her to snap her head to the left.

"Mmm." His lips trembled with effort.

"Yes, Sauntage, I'm here!" Sobs of joy rose in her throat as she turned over on her hands and knees to lean over him.

"Mmoo." Breathlessly escaped his mouth as his lips grew still once more.

It was difficult not to let disappointment take over. In her mind she knew that it would take time for him to recover, but her heart couldn't stand the idea of having to wait. Swallowing the mixed lump in her throat she got to her feet with renewed energy. He was going to get better and she had to do her part to see that he did. Determination made lines around her eyes and lips as she went to gather more wood.

Maureen knew that besides wood they would need food as well. She hated the thought of tying one of those icky worms to the fishing line they had woven, but she had no choice in the matter. Without his help she had no idea what was safe to eat or how to prepare it. For a full five minutes she stared at the creatures she had unearthed using a long stick. Hunger pangs finally decided the issue.

Her eyes were more closed than open as she picked up the first squirming worm. Although she worked quickly at making knots to hold it in place it managed to wiggle free. On her fourth attempt she finally achieved victory in which she performed a small dance to celebrate.

Celebration soon turned to boredom as she sat waiting for a fish to bite the bait. There were more fish in the school now than there had been the previous day, but apparently none of them were hungry. All of them it seemed had swum up to the worm and then turned away. She even tried moving the weed back and forth to make it look as though the worm was swimming. This finally gained her some measure of success, but it also brought a question to the fore front of her mind. How was she going to 'hook' the fish?

A frown wrinkled her forehead as she tried to recall what Sauntage had done to 'reel' them onto the bank. As she thought about it she could not remember him doing anything special.

When her worm disappeared a moment later into the wide mouth of a fish she slowly brought the weed upwards to be able to replace her bait. To her amazement and wonder the fish remained attached to the weed rope. It struggled against the line but soon she understood that it wasn't fighting to let go of the line, the fish was trying to cut it.

Giggling brightly Maureen carried her spoils back to the campfire, taking care to hold it as far from her body as possible. The fact that it had to be cleaned before it could be cooked escaped her until she picked up her roasting stick from the previous day. A whine sagged her shoulders as she considered what would be involved in preparing this fish to eat.

With the fish still dangling from the rope flopping every few seconds she hunted up another stone. This one was flat on one side and large enough to lay the scaled creature out for butchering. More sweat rolled off of her brow while she figured out how not to fillet a live fish. In the end she had to push down the distaste of touching the slimy scales and hold the jolting body still while she used the hatchet to remove its head.

She was aware that the body would likely continue twitching for awhile longer just as the snake had. A quick glance was spared for the long stiff carcass not far from Sauntage revealed more movement in her husband's lips.

"Sau! It's Maureen. Can you hear me?" Her voice squeaked with excitement as she let go of everything and rushed to his side.

"Yesh." He slurred with effort.

"Oh, Sau, I'm sorry. I don't know what to do to help you." Fresh tears rolled off her cheeks as she scanned his face closely. Was his cheek twitching?

"No-shing." His tongue pushed through the gap of his lips. "Jusht thime." Once again his face went still.

This time she did not feel torn or disheartened, instead she was resolved to keep going. While he continued to sleep she went back to her meal preparations. As she fought the waves of nausea Maureen decided that next time she would catch a bunch of fish so she only had to go through this process one more time.

When Sauntage stirred the next time she was just putting her roasting stick over the flames. Wedging the end of the stick into the ground she scooted to his side. "Sau? Can you move anything?"

"No feeling." He mumbled and then asked softly, "How long?"

"It's been about a day since the snake bit you." Her eyes shifted over his features noting some motion in the muscles around his eyes.

"One more day." Fell from his lips in a whisper and then he was asleep.

Time passed in two ways for Maureen because of the many tasks she had to accomplish and the silence surrounding them. There was not much time to think about being alone now because there were so many things which needed care. Every hour or so Sauntage roused briefly to speak with her. Each time he was able to say more and his speech became clearer.

By the next morning he was able to move his arms and legs though it was difficult, wearing him out within a few brief minutes. She could see that his lack of mobility really bothered him. Especially when he quietly watched her performing all the chores he felt were his responsibility. To the best of her ability she tried not to let him know how exhausted she was.

In the middle of the afternoon there was a marked improvement in his condition. With the help of his wife he was able to eat a few bites of fish and drink some water from her soggy hat.

"I'm sorry there are so many bones and it's burnt." She winced as she held the end of the stick close to his mouth.

"Mo, this is unbelievable. You did this all by yourself." He couldn't help but stare at her.

Color flooded into her cheeks as she listened to the note of pride in his voice. "I just did what had to be done."

His left hand reached out to take hold of her forearm as he said, "You saved my life, Maureen. Thank you."

There was moisture glistening in her eyes as she met his gaze saying, "I love you, Sau. This is all my fault. I'm so sorry I didn't listen to you..."

"No, there was nothing you could have done. I wasn't careful..." A wide yawn halted his words.

"You need to lie down and rest." Maureen gently pressed against his chest to force his back to the ground. "While you're sleeping I'm going to get some more firewood and leaves for your arm."

Weakly he called to her, "Be careful, Darling." Before she traveled ten feet from the fire he was soundly sleeping.

The next time he woke up his arm was itching terribly. It was late into the night according to the stars overhead. His brow furrowed deeply because as hard as he tried he could not move his right arm. Lifting his head off the ground he was surprised to see Maureen's silhouette hovering over him.

Water trickled out of her hat onto his arm in a slow steady stream. She waved the empty cap in the air over his wound in an effort to dry it before she rubbed fresh leaves over it. As his muscles tensed beneath her hands she knew that she had managed to wake him. "I was hoping you would be able to sleep through most of this."

"You should be sleeping. It's been such a long day for you." Strength was clearly returning to his voice as he chastised her.

A wry grin formed on her lips as she commented sarcastically, "Lots of things aren't as they should be right now."

"That is certainly an understatement. This should never have happened." He sighed heavily as he worked himself to a sitting position. "None of this could have happened if I had been truthful from the start."

"No argument there." Her edgy tone was telling of her mistrust and fatigue. At last his skin had dried enough for the sticky fluid to work on the bite. In a much different way she added, "But I do see why you did it. There is no way I would have believed you about this place. Most likely I would have packed you off to some psyche hospital and demanded a competency exam."

Hope rose in his chest as he reached out with his left hand to locate her face. Had she just forgiven him? His features flattened as she pulled her face back from his touch.

"I think you're right we need to go to bed and get some rest." She got to her feet as she explained where she was going, "I'll go get us some water."

With that she drifted quietly away from the warmth of the fire. Seconds later she was back sloshing water down her front as she came. After each of them had a long drink she emptied the cap and the two of them lay down side by side. Almost instantly they fell into a deep dreamless sleep.

Sauntage was already awake when Maureen opened her eyes to the late morning. For a moment she had to think through the events of the last several days to figure out what she was doing. Despite the fact that she had been in Liguesis for a number of days, it still felt more like a dream than reality.

Slowly she moved to a sitting position so that she could see her husband's face as she spoke, "Morning. How are you feeling?"

"Good morning. Much better. I think most of the poison's effects have worn off." To prove his statement he carefully wiggled each part of his body. Then he sat up next to her. "Though I don't think I'll be up for our long trek into the settlement today."

"So after two days the venom just wears off?" She asked with a long catlike stretch.

"Yes, as long as it is treated quickly. The venom from a carkna acts like a potent muscle relaxer in most cases." His eyes transferred to his wound and then rounded in shock.

"In most cases?"

For a moment he seemed not to have heard her, but then he responded, "Yeah, there are factors that can affect the severity. If for instance the person is small or the snake really big." Licking his dry, cracked lips he lifted his head to look at her as he asked, "What happened to the snake? I mean I know you hit it and all, but where is its body?"

"Oh, it's over there, behind you a few feet." She pointed with her index finger to help him narrow down the location. "I kicked it aside and then tried to forget about it." A shiver went through her body.

It was some time before he was able to tear his eyes away from the carcass. When he did his face was a pale paste color. In measured tones he carefully said, "Everything happened so fast that I hardly remember much more than a blur. How did you know what to do?"

"You told me before you conked out, Sau. Is something the matter?" The color of his face was enough to tell her that there was.

"That snake, I mean one that size...I've never heard of a carkna getting that big. One half that size is considered huge...I ought to have died. Unless the poison was drained within minutes. It has a cumulative property where it paralyzes the breathing and heart if it is in the system long enough at a high enough concentration." He sat staring at the fire absorbing the fact that he narrowly cheated death.

Maureen felt the blood drop from her face and sat down next to him so that she wouldn't fall. "I don't remember exactly what you said. Just that the blood flow to the rest of your body had to be stopped, the bite had to be cut to drain the poison and you handed me the aukar leaves and told me they needed to be crushed."

"But how did you know to keep changing it?" He asked with wonder.

Blinking rapidly she met his gaze and admitted, "I don't know. I just...did it."

Silence fell between them for a long time while each of them thought about what had happened over the previous two days. Not knowing the dangers of this land and its creatures had nearly cost her the chance to reach her sons. With a renewed purpose she turned to him and began asking him to tell her more about survival in Liguesis.

He nodded in hearty agreement then lifted his left index finger to point at the carkna carcass. "Well, a good place to begin is that snake. Although too much time has passed and we can't use it for food, we can clean it and skin it. If the venom glands haven't been damaged too much we might be able to use them."

"What on earth for? That monster almost killed you." Distaste twisted her features into angry lines.

"The venom is very potent if it is injected into the body, but if it is carefully measured with water to dilute it, carkna venom is a fantastic local anesthetic. Drag the body over here and let me have a look at it."

She swallowed the moan rising on her lips and stood to do as he asked. "Can I grab it by the tail?"

"Yes, darling, that would be fine." He watched with amusement curling the corners of his mouth upwards. By the time she had managed to bring the bloated body close enough for him to reach; the humor was replaced with respect and pride.

As he examined the damage she had inflicted on the smelly creature Sauntage explained to her everything he saw and was doing.

"I don't think there is enough gland tissue on the left side of its head, but the right ought to work nicely. Okay, the first thing we need to do is skin this stinker and make a water proof pouch out of it. My right hand will be useless for this chore but I should be able to do all the cutting necessary with my left if you can hold it steady."

Without a word she gave him a decisive nod, took a deep breath and moved to get the axe. Maureen could feel the muscles in her arm twitching from exertion and anxiety as she carried the heavy tool back to her husband. It dropped with a dull thud in the dirt to the left of Sauntage as she folded her legs beneath her.

Once again she swallowed her distaste for touching this creature and looked to her husband for directions on where to hold it. Taking a firm hold just below the throat with her right hand and doing the same as far down its belly as possible, she braced herself for what was to come next.

Even though he had warned her about all that she was likely see and smell Maureen was not prepared. The outside of the reptile smelled bad enough, but the inside of it was something beyond description. Her stomach lurched at the wet rubbery noise the wide blade made as it tore through the decaying flesh. Instinctively she turned her nose into her shoulder in an effort to block some of the smell. This did offer some temporary relief for her senses making it possible for her to complete the task.

While Sauntage worked he said nothing. His teeth were tightly clenched with determination. It was not long before he felt tremors along the muscles in his arms. Soon there was a full blown cramp in his biceps. Knowing how valuable this carkna venom could be for their survival, he kept going.

When at last the axe had been able to sever the snake's head from its body he weakly sputtered, "Let's take a break."

Not waiting to be told twice Maureen jumped to her feet and raced to the nearest bush. A full five minutes went by before the violent waves of nausea slowly left.

They had to repeat this process a few more times before there was a piece of skin large enough for the task. While Maureen dragged what was left of the body as far away from their camp as she dared to go, Sauntage searched for leaves amongst the surrounding bushes.

Every few moments he snapped off several small branches and then moved on to the next bush. Once these tasks were finished the two of them went to the river to catch something to eat.

Maureen was thankful that her husband was able to handle the gutting and filleting of the fish. With relief she brought each tool he needed and then quietly turned her eyes away.

As she held the fish over the flames, Sauntage carefully removed the leaves from the branches and set them in a pile next to him. Once the branches were cleared he slowly drew the lower corner of the axe blade down the length of them through the thin bark. She shifted her gaze between the filet on the end of her stick and her husband. A couple of times she had to pull the fish close to her mouth and blow out small flames.

His forehead wrinkled deeply in concentration as he worked to peel each small piece of wood. When he finished each piece, Sauntage took a couple of leaves, split the thick membrane in two and then rubbed the yellow white cream along the outside of the bark. He examined the strip thoroughly and when he was satisfied he coiled the bark loosely around the back of his hand.

It was not long before a sizable pile of small coils grew on his right side. For a few quiet minutes Maureen puzzled over his actions, but then she simply blurted her question, "What are you doing? That doesn't look like a water proof bag at all."

A small tired chuckle left him as he continued to work, "It's not yet. Actually what I am doing right now isn't for the bag. One of these bark strips will be plenty for that. Right now I'm making some extra binding material for the journey. You never know when you might need to tie something together."

"But what good will it be once it dries out?" She frowned deeply at the increasing number of black spots on her dinner.

"The fluid inside this plant is oily and takes a long time to wear off. If it is spread over a surface in a thick enough layer it is water proof. It's almost like flexible polyurethane."

Silence fell between them once more. A few minutes went by before Maureen realized how quiet it had become. Her eyes scanned the landscape in front of her and she released a deep sigh. There was something about this place that could make her feel peaceful at times. Despite what lurked around to threaten them and her boys she suddenly heard herself say, "I wish you would have told me about this years ago."

Sauntage stopped moving his hands and looked at his wife. With surprise he observed the wistful look in her eyes. Sighing quietly he acknowledged to himself that he wished the very same thing. He was discovering that he had grossly underestimated her, but at the same time hope grew that one day they could move forward beyond his mistake.

# Chapter Seven

It was just after midday the following day when they packed up their bag to continue on their way. Maureen swung the pack onto her back without discussion because she knew that he was not strong enough to carry it. Although she felt that they should wait at least one more day before pushing his health, she also wanted to be as far from any more carkna snakes as possible.

She watched his steps closely and each time he began to stumble she claimed fatigue and asked to rest. On the third such instance he turned around to face her as he said defiantly, "I'm not a baby that needs to nap. We have to keep going. Two days were lost because of that snake."

Narrowing her eyes on him as her fists rested on her hips she snapped, "No. You were almost lost because I didn't pay attention to what you told me. I'm here to get my sons and I know I can't do that without you. It is obvious that you are still weak so sit down and rest for a few minutes."

His eyes rounded with surprise and humor. With a slight shake of his dark head he lowered his frame to the ground saying, "I love you, too, Mo."

"Sau, I'm just so scared." Her voice came out in a wavering whisper as she sat next to his right side. She pulled her knees up to her chest and dropped her face on them to sob.

His lips lost all traces of laughter as he suddenly saw how difficult this was becoming for her emotionally. Carefully he scooted to sit on her right side so that he could pull her into his chest. The trembling in her body grew worse when she felt his arm wrap around her shoulders. "Oh, Darling, go ahead let it all out. It's going to be okay. We're going to find the boys."

Pain creased her eyes as she lifted her head to ask harshly, "How can you know that? What makes you so sure?"

"Because in that split second between seeing that snake and knowing he was likely going to strike, I asked for help..."

"All you said was to get back to the fire." Maureen pulled away from him a little more to see his face clearly. Was he remembering hallucinations that he had while under the effects of the venom?

"It was not something I said aloud. I prayed." His voice was so quiet she had to lean closer to hear him as he went on to say, "I told God that if He was real then please take care of you and the boys because I knew that I was about to die."

Silence settled between them as each of them was lost in their out thoughts. Nothing in the quiet was oppressive at all. In fact there was a peace surrounding them that was unlike anything either of them had experienced before. Time stretched out longer than they had planned as they sat huddled together near the river.

"So you think God is real because you are still alive?" She asked in a gentle tone.

"No, not exactly." A deep sigh left his lungs before he went on to explain, "This whole situation...all my life I've been trained to take control of things when they aren't going as I see fit. But with Tagurah taking the boys I haven't been able to do that. How can I take charge of something I know nothing about?"

"By handing it over to some invisible being." The words were not spoken with sarcasm or irreverence, but with thoughtful consideration.

"That's just what I said to myself when I picked up that Bible the first time. It was a nice book of stories to pass the time. Just like the Liguesian version of Ewaris I read as a kid. But the more I read the more real it seemed. Then we reached The Gateway and I figured that I was feeling that way from so much emotional strain and being in darkness for so long." His eyes were trained on the dirt in front of him, but nothing he saw registered with his brain as he tried to put into words what was happening inside his heart. "I expected those thoughts and feelings to go away as we started our journey here."

"Let me guess. They've gotten stronger." Doubt raised the sharpness of her pitch.

"Yes, they have. Instead of forgetting about them as I had anticipated, little bits and pieces of what I had read kept going through my mind. So when that snake came at us I realized that I want to believe what the Bible says; what I was trained in as a child."

She nodded her head slowly with understanding, "Then it was a test to see if God was real."

"Perhaps it was." Sauntage admitted quietly.

"And because you're alive He passed?" While she waited for him to respond Maureen got to her feet.

"It's really more than that." His voice was urgent as he too came to his full height.

"Maybe we should get going." There was the barest hint of strain in her voice. Adjusting the straps on her shoulders she gave him a hard, steady stare to let him know she was serious and didn't want to talk about it anymore.

With a dip of his chin he continued to walk along the river bank. That conversation actually went much better than he had thought it could. After the secrets he had kept hidden and her vow that she would never trust him again, she could have easily torn into him about this. A smile spread across his face as he realized the hope for their future was growing.

Her jaw began to hurt after a bit of walking because she had her teeth clenched together. This idea of God had swallowed up her parents and now threatened to take her husband as well. How could she even consider the possibility? For as much as her mind and heart had been going back and forth over the idea she knew it was crazy. It had to be. Didn't it?

Then a quiet thought dropped into her brain which caused her to look all around her. It was crazy to believe in Liguesis, too. And yet here she was walking through a desert like place with a pale green sun hovering over head. The lush green surroundings were giving way to large patches of dry soil. Right next to the narrowing river bed was the only place green could be seen for some distance.

Shaking herself inwardly Maureen pushed aside the annoying questions for which she would not be able to get answers. Her eyes rolled skyward as she muttered under her breath, "Sorry, God. I just don't see the likelihood of a king leaving his throne to be a peasant in places like Earth or Liguesis."

A puzzled frown settled on her features as she considered what Sauntage had told her earlier. Hadn't he said they were headed to a farming region? This area didn't look like it would grow anything but dust.

She decided to pursue the things for which she was sure she could understand. "I thought you said we were going to see farmers."

"We are." He answered turning his chin back over his shoulder. "Another half a mile downstream we will meet up with a second river that is nearly the same size as this one. Once those two rivers join the landscape changes again though it is not like the weeds we went through. There are green grasses about three feet tall for miles. Not a bush or a tree in sight."

"How many people are in the settlement?" Her steps picked up their pace to walk beside him as they talked.

His lips twisted up this way and that as he tried to recall the answer, "Hmm, as memory serves there are actually eight settlements throughout this farming region. Each of the settlements has about forty to fifty families in it. But you know that was seventeen years ago so it could be different now."

"So you have no idea whether we'll find help or not?" Her shoulders drooped and her eyes were downcast.

"They will help us." His voice held confidence as his shoulders straightened and his feet moved with military precision.

Ten minutes later she started to see the difference he was talking about in the landscape. From a distance it had appeared to be a flat wasteland, but as they walked on the ground had a definite incline to it. Thankfully it was not very steep which made it bearable to their legs. To the east there were a few tree tops visible in the distance giving evidence of the second river her husband had mentioned.

Without warning the top of the hill was reached. In little more than three steps a wide green valley opened before them. It was a breathtaking sight.

As far as she could see to the northwest there was nothing but tall grasses waving in a gentle breeze. Somewhere winding through the vast field was the river gurgling brightly on their right. Trees lined the extreme eastern edge where the two rivers met from the east and south.

It was not until Sauntage spoke that she figured out that she was holding her breath. She released it slowly as he talked and she drank in the view.

"Just another five miles or so to the settlement. I've been thinking it over. We need to look for a farm on the outskirts instead of going directly into the settlement. Something tells me the fewer people here that know of our presence the better." His eyebrow was crinkled with the internal debate.

"But we need help, Sau." Maureen grasped the thick leather covering his biceps. The wild movements of her eyes revealed the panic she was feeling that he would so suddenly change their course without a reason.

"Yes, I know that. But at the moment we need something else even more. We need information. Mo, something doesn't feel right here. Up until we passed through that trampled area there weren't any animals. I can't explain it but even though we've seen lots of animals since then something still feels very wrong." He raised his hands to stall her. "These men till the land, care for animals and hunt throughout these parts. They would know better than anybody what could have caused the wildlife to disappear."

"And how are we supposed to get this information if we don't find a talkative farmer? Or worse, one that simply doesn't know?" She screeched at him.

Licking his lips he gently placed his hands on her shoulders. "Look, I've been thinking about this a lot and honestly I don't know how we go about getting this information. If The Gateway were on any other border we could easily pose as traders from another nation, but the southern border is one long mountain range that is a barren wasteland on the other side." Sauntage slowly released her shoulders and turned away to think out loud. "I think we could try posing as traders from the eastern border. According to that medallion Tagurah left, the boys have been taken to Shargaunal, so our need to travel there would not be questioned."

"Great. That sounds like a plan. Let's go." Maureen started to walk at a brisk pace, but was stopped by the firm grasp of her husband's hand on her upper arm.

"It's not that simple, Darling. We have to have a plausible cover story to tell these people. They're farmers; not stupid. If they don't believe us they will not help us."

In anger her eyes narrowed on him. "Then why don't we just tell them the truth?"

"Because they'll think we're crazy. I told you the ancients buried everything concerning The Gateway. Insanity is not treated any better here than on earth. And contrary to what you might be thinking news can travel quite rapidly here. They have a whole system to spread information from one border to the others in a matter of days. We can't afford to take any risks."

"Okay, if that's true what makes you think some farmer is just going to run off on some wild errand and give away horses? He'd have to be crazy. We'd have a better shot with a larger group. After telling our story once; there's bound to be at least one person willing to help. If we go to only one farmer and he won't help, then we would be wasting more time looking for the next farm."

Calmly he heard her reasoning. Then after briefly considering the matter he said, "All right you've got a point. We'll compromise; if the first farmer we meet won't help us, then we will go into the settlement. But I'm certain we can get all we need in one place."

"As long as it is on the way to the settlement. I don't want to walk miles out of our way for one blind shot." She demanded firmly with her hands on her hips glaring at him.

In response he gave her one quick, firm nod as if to say, "Deal." Then he quickly rattled off the details of their story that he had apparently been working on for some time. Before she had time to react he started walking down the long gentle slope into the valley. There was nothing for her to do but follow at a fast enough pace not to be left behind.

With her gaze carefully trained on his back she had the strangest feeling that he was holding some very important piece of information back from her. A deep sadness welled up in her as she realized that the reason she felt that way was because she didn't trust him. As much as she was emotionally drawn to him she didn't dare let her guard down completely again. Goodness only knew where she'd end up if she did.

To keep from dwelling on the state of their relationship Maureen consciously studied the landscape. The river grew louder as well as wider with the additional source of water flooding into it. Several large stones were plopped in the midst of the flow causing the current to break and foam around them. A bend in the river's bed slowed Its progress slightly and created a narrower place for them to cross.

Cool water rushed over the tops of her borrowed moccasin like boots. It was amazing that a few short days ago her feet had been comfortably slipped into fashionable pumps. No fish were evident to them though they watched carefully. For quite some time after they left the river behind their boots squished and oozed water between their toes.

In a soft voice he drew her attention to a small bump on the horizon. "There it is, Mo. See the cluster of buildings over there? That's where we're going."

Despite the fact that she was excited to have yet another leg of this journey over, Maureen was also scared stiff. With each step her heart pounded harder. What would these people be like? Would she be able to communicate with them? If so, what should she say?

Almost as if he were reading her thoughts Sauntage suggested, "Perhaps it would be best if you let me do the talking. At least beyond a greeting."

"Yeah, okay." She replied in a shaky voice. Her eyes were fixed on the group of buildings growing a little larger with each step.

From their perspective four separate buildings were visible. It was easy to see that the one off to the right all by itself was the house. Though much different than what she was used to it had a warm, inviting look about it that cheered her. Made up of two stories the house was constructed of stone, wood and mud all mixed together in hodge podge layers. There were windows and they appeared to be made of glass, but they were set deep in the walls. Probably the most unusual thing about it was the roof because it was a dome of sorts, but not very professionally designed.

Like the house the other structures had similar roof lines. These buildings did not appear to have windows though. Instead it seemed wherever light was needed there was some kind of a hole simply cut into the wall. As they drew closer she could see some people moving around inside the structures and noticed that the holes were not cut level through the walls but angled in different directions. She was about to ask why that strange practice was done when it occurred to her that it was probably done to keep as much rain as possible from coming in the openings.

"We've been spotted." His head tipped toward the cluster and his steps shortened a bit.

"How do you know that?" Her brows came together in a deep frown as she saw for herself. "Never mind, I see how you knew." A note of disapproval and judgment rang in her words.

Sauntage stopped dead in his tracks to stare at his wife. Then he said with an undercurrent of exasperation, "The women were not ordered back to the house while the men greet us, it was their choice."

"What makes you think so?" Fists were balled up on her hips as she stared him down; daring him to try to come up with a remotely plausible theory.

"Mo, why are you so angry today? Look, I told you that they have their clearly defined roles here. Those women went in the house to prepare for overnight company. Their job is to help the farmer earn his living and they will do it to the best of their ability..." His head was wagging at her in a confused frustration.

"To avoid some kind of punishment." She muttered harshly as she stole a glance at the two men now headed toward them.

"Of course not. They do it to get what they deserve. The highest praise of the men. I know you won't be able to understand most of the words, but listen to their tone of voice when they talk about the women. And then watch how the women respond." For a brief moment he began walking again, but then his forward progress halted. In a quiet tone he commented, "Something isn't right here. They should be waiting by the stable for us to come to them and there should be more men."

"What do you mean?" Maureen could feel her heart squeezing tighter. Part of her wished to ask why they were carrying a pitch fork and shovel but instinctively she knew she would not like the answer.

Licking his dry lips quickly Sauntage replied, "I'm sorry I don't have time to explain everything, but the apprentice system here normally has young men from the age of fourteen to twenty scattered throughout the realm. A farm this size ought to have at least eight such men at various stages of training. I might have to change our cover story so just follow my lead." He cut the conversation short because the distance between the arriving men was growing short.

Maureen could feel her ribs giving way to the pressure under her heartbeat. Never had she been so nervous. Drawing in slow deep breaths she tried to calm herself by taking in details about them. Trickles of sweat ran down her spine despite the fact that she was not terribly warm.

There was clearly a gap in age between the two men. One walked with slow relaxed steps while the other seemed to be holding back energy with each step. Father and son she guessed as she saw very similar brown eyes and hair. The tall lean frames could have belonged to a set of twins. Except for the deeper lines of time and the sun these two could have been siblings. Their clothing was as nondescript as hers; nothing whatsoever fancy or different between them. Just a long leather shirt tied at the shoulder and beneath it long pants tying along the inseam.

When about ten feet separated them the two men stopped abruptly and tipped the ends of their tools in a gesture of warning. Maureen was not prepared for this at all and nervously looked to her husband for comfort. It did not come as she had hoped. In fact his stiffened frame and countenance told her that he was more startled than she was. Slowly his hands came up with backs of them facing outward.

As soon as the elder man opened his mouth to speak her nerves began to tremble. Though his voice was rich and resonated through her, he was clearly not happy about their presence on his property. She tried to match her husband's mannerisms when she opened her mouth in greeting. Her voice clearly startled them because they stiffened slightly and the tools were grasped tighter.

Sauntage quickly spoke again with a great deal of animation that was not like him. With excitement he pointed to his arm apparently sharing the fact that he had been bitten by a gigantic snake. Suddenly, he wrapped his arm around Maureen and drew her tightly to his side and pointed at her.

Heat burned over her cheekbones when she saw the looks of suspicion turn to wonder and then change to short bows of respect. At the moment it seemed Sauntage was praising her efforts to save his life. Lowering her eyes to the ground she waited impatiently for him to finish the story. When would he get on with asking for what they needed?

It was not over as quickly as she would have liked, but finally she ceased to be the center of attention. For another full minute or so Sauntage was the only one to say anything. As he talked she was able to watch the reaction of the two men. Several nods went along with the flow of words. Then suddenly, the elder broke in excitedly and pointed to the younger man who was nodding in agreement. All of their faces were serious. Next to her Sauntage bowed slightly in what appeared to be thanks.

Turning to her he leaned close to her ear and whispered, "Okay, I've told them that you have suffered through some terrible tragedies and that talking is very hard for you. They also believe that you are from a distant country, don't speak Liguesian very well and because the boys were taken you are shy and a bit afraid. So I can speak quietly in your ear without drawing suspicion." He felt her stiff nod and knew she was seething over this. "This is Farmer Master Arvou Trigguard and his eldest son, Arvoa. Arvoa has offered to send a message to my Father and Arvou has offered us a night's lodgings and the use of two horses. There's more, but it will have to wait until I get more details."

Maureen lifted her gaze to the strangers before her. Seeing the hopeful expressions on their faces brought unexpected tears to her eyes. The idea that these men would give so much to perfect strangers they did not trust a few minutes earlier overwhelmed her.

Her tears caused the elder man to take command of the situation and he gave a few orders to the younger man who turned without a word to run back toward the house. Arvou then began to speak to Sauntage in quiet but urgent tones while waving his hand in the direction of the house.

With his arm around her shoulders her husband gently encouraged her to begin walking towards the house. The two men followed closely behind her talking as though they had known each other for many years. Perhaps, they did know one another, she thought to herself.

While they were still some distance away from the house the wide wooden door swung outward. She lost count of the number of children that came pouring out besides the two women and younger man. All of the children were dressed in leather dresses much like her shirt and some kind of a leather sandal on their feet though she couldn't really see its construction because they moved too quickly. Noise was such a new thing to her after so much time alone in the wilderness that she started and took a few steps backward.

Instantly a soft command left the lips of the older woman and the children filed rapidly into the house. Once the children were gone she spoke again. This time it seemed to Maureen that she was welcoming them into their home. Her clothing matched the younger woman except for the jewels that lined the collar of her shirt. There didn't seem to be any rhyme or reason to their placement they were just randomly attached at the neckline of her shirt. It came as a bit of a surprise to Maureen that the shirt was almost identical to the ones the men wore except for the fact that there was a slit tied together down the front that went nearly to their waist. Instead of pants, however, these women had long skirts wrapped around their waists and tied over the shirts. Over their hair was a simple pouch that collected their hair at the back of their heads and then pulled up over their forehead to form a deep brim.

When the woman finished speaking to them Sauntage bowed at the waist to her and gave a short speech. Once he answered the greeting he turned to say in his wife's ear, "Arvou's wife, Narmaka bids us welcome along with her son's wife, Maruti. They will soon have a room prepared for us and soon we will be able to eat. They would like to know if you wish to wash up before dinner or after."

Glancing at the women she felt a tear slip down her cheek. Then she turned her lips to her husband's ear to respond, "Oh, tell them if it's not too much trouble I'd like to clean up first. And thank them, Sau."

A soft smile touched his lips as he tenderly squeezed her fingertips. His voice was clearly emotional as he gave his wife's answer to them with another deep bow.

Narmaka rushed forward to take Maureen by the hand and gently tug her into the house. It took her eyes a couple of moments to adjust to the dim conditions of the interior. Wonderful aromas filled the whole house making her almost regret her choice to wash up first. At least two dozen pair of young eyes were openly staring at her. She tried her best to force her nerves aside and look at each one with a smile.

More light chatter came from Narmaka as she pulled her through a doorway on the other side of the main room. Now it was just the two of them and it seemed that Narmaka was determined to help her break free from her trauma. Guilt chewed at her stomach as she silently railed at her husband for creating this barrier between them. If he had simply told them she was from another country she might have been able to learn how to communicate with Narmaka. As it was she could only stand before this woman stupidly and pretend to be shy and afraid.

The room she had been led to was much smaller and darker than the main room had been. There was one small window in the far corner that gave just enough light for Narmaka to see and light a lantern hanging down in the center of the room. A frown marked Maureen's brow as she wondered why they designed a light like this. Because it was strung so low it literally took up the center of the room. You couldn't walk under it and getting around it looked like it could be a difficult endeavor with stacks of wooden crates along the walls.

Once Narmaka had the flame adjusted to the proper height she turned back to the doorway to grasp a rope tied to a large bent metal pin sticking out of the wall. After pulling on the rope a few times the light had risen to a point just above their heads.

Not wasting a single moment Narmaka went to a stack of crates on the other side of the room which Maureen could now see had writing on them. Each of the boxes had the same lettering and based on what was pulled from them it must have said something like clothing. Several smaller leather garments were set off to one side. Finally, Narmaka found something she thought might work and held it out to Maureen to test it for size.

With a nod she pressed it into Maureen's hands and then turned to shift the boxes around to look for more. The next crate was not nearly as deep as the first one so it took very little time for Narmaka to find a skirt that would fit. After she had put the first two crates in order she turned to face Maureen and as she spoke she made hand gestures at the top of her head. It took a moment for Maureen to understand that her new friend wanted to know how long her hair was. With a slight lift of her lips she used the side of her hand to indicate a place just below her shoulder. This was clearly a surprise to Narmaka because her eyes flared wide just before she gave a sad shake of her head.

In quick steady movements Narmaka also chose garments for Sauntage though she didn't take the time to do any measuring. As soon as she was done she lowered the lantern once more and then led the way to another small room on the first floor. It was already bright and cheery with four smaller lanterns attached to the wall. A large rectangular bathing tub was stationed in the center of the room with steam curling up from its shallow depths.

Joy flooded through her and released in a soft squealing giggle as her hands pressed excitedly together in front of her chest. More words from Narmaka reminded her to be careful with her tongue. They were doing so well with their plans she couldn't screw it up now. Her joy was tempered severely when she realized how deep the longing for real communication was growing.

This lovely woman of about fifty or so had the gentlest blue eyes she had ever seen. Though Maureen could not see a single strand of her hair tucked beneath her bonnet she was sure it was as black as Sauntage's hair. Lines lightly crossed her narrow face and her uneven teeth were just beginning to turn a pale yellow. Sauntage's voice in the doorway drew her attention away from Narmaka.

Each of his hands held a large bucket as did the boy behind him. With ease of practice the slender youth poured the water into the povout lined wooden structure. It was then that she recognized the gray material covering the floor under their feet. When the buckets were empty the boy bowed to them and quickly left the room. His mother followed him a second later closing the door behind her.

For a long time Maureen simply stared at her husband afraid to speak. Finally, she moved to stand right in front of him. "Oh, Sau, why did you have to lie to them? I can't even tell that lovely woman thank you. Why didn't you just tell them I was from a different country and didn't speak your language very well?"

"I did tell them you were from the nation to the east and that our sons have been kidnapped." His hands lifted quickly to stall her coming rant. "Listen to me, Mo. There is a lot I must tell you and we don't have much time because we are expected at the dinner table soon. War is brewing here for the first time in centuries."

"What!" She gasped in horror.

"Shhh! We must be careful. It seems the nation to our eastern border, Galixtorn has suffered terrible atrocities along its border for several years. Even though the King of Liguesis has worked hard to keep good will between their nations, things are rapidly deteriorating. It is the belief of the Liguesian people that a large band of rebels from our northern border is behind everything. This group is growing in numbers and is apparently out to destroy both nations."

"Is your brother part of this group, Sau? Surely he knew of these things before he took the boys." Her eyes hardened with rage at the thought of her sons being held hostage on a potential battlefield.

He sighed heavily with his shoulders dropping forward in grief. "Tagurah must be. It is the only explanation for everything happening. Because of this we must be careful, my family is well known throughout the realm and to suggest this kind of treason would not be a safe thing to do. We would quickly find ourselves in a dungeon."

"So what are we to do now? If there is really some kind of army from the north battering this eastern border we can't expect to simply waltz up and take our sons back." She stared at him almost demanding a quick and ready response.

"Somehow we must reach my parents..." Sauntage thoughtfully turned to pace around the large tub.

"And do what?" Maureen snapped harshly. "Who do you think they are going to believe? Tagurah or their son who walked away years ago and to them is dead?"

Heat smoldered in his eyes as he looked back at her. "Look, I am well aware of what we are up against. No matter what happens between my parents and me, they will help our sons. I'm sure of it."

"How can you be so sure?" She asked crossing her arms over her chest.

"Because Charlie is in line to take my Father's place after me. The well being of our heritage is a very important thing in my Father's eyes. We'd better hurry up they will send someone for us soon."

Her exasperation with him was growing as she tugged at the straps still on her shoulders. "Seems to me that you are placing an awful lot of hope in people you haven't seen in seventeen years."

"Well, maybe I am, but it's still the best shot we have of getting our sons back." He started working at his own laces while he shared, "I've written the letter to my Father and Arvoa is eating a quick meal before he heads out to see it delivered to my Father's agent. Hopefully, the messengers will return with word from my parents and we can meet them along the road to the north and head east across the country to Shargaunal."

"How long will it take to reach your Father?" Her legs were nearly freed from the leggings.

A sigh left him as he admitted, "I'm not sure. It all depends on whether he is home or traveling on business. Either way his agent should be able to get word to us within a few days." He was struggling with the ties over his left shoulder so he leaned over to silently ask her to help him.

Quietly she plucked at the ties on his shirt and then with a sigh of relief turned to get into the warm water. The low whistle of her husband's lips caused her to pause and look at him. She regretted doing so immediately because his eyes were trained on her. Looking down at herself she understood his shock. All of the torturous activity of the last week had changed her body drastically. Many of the excess pounds she had started with had been toned and many of those that hadn't been toned were lost. A warm blush crept into her face that marked both embarrassment and pride. Not since before Ryan had been born had she been this size.

Sauntage leaned over her shoulder to say softly, "These clothes are not suited to you. Beauty should not be hidden entirely." The smirk grew on his lips as he saw the color deepening on her face.

After they had soaked side by side in the wide povout tub for a few minutes he sat up to speak again in low tones, "We will sleep here for the night then early tomorrow morning we will head north towards my parent's home. Until we hear from them we must try to reach them. I know you haven't ever really ridden a horse, so I'll have to teach you the basics here where we can speak somewhat freely."

"Don't you just get up on its back and sit there while it walks along the trail?" Dismay shadowed her eyes.

He chuckled deep in his chest as he clarified, "Only if you are in an old western movie."

Her head dropped back against the side of the tub with a loud groan. "I don't believe it. It goes from bad to worse."

"No, it's not really as bad as all that. All you have to remember are a few simple things to get us a couple of miles away from the farm. After that I can take a bit more time to train you properly." He received her nod as a sign to go ahead so for the next ten minutes he told her all that he thought was critical for her to know.

Fifteen minutes later there was a light tap on the door which Sauntage quietly answered. A few words Maureen could not quite follow were shared and then the doorway was empty. He turned back to her just as she squished the last bit of her wet, red hair into the strange bonnet. "They are ready to eat whenever we are."

"I can't wait. It smells wonderful." She took a deep breath and followed her husband back to the kitchen.

As soon as they entered the room grew respectfully quiet. Arvou stood at the head of the table with his left arm directing them to their seats. With a few simple words of greeting he encouraged them to sit.

Maureen offered a small smile of thanks as she lowered her frame onto a long bench next to her husband. It occurred to her then that not everyone she saw earlier was at the table. Several of the younger children seemed to be missing. For a short time she puzzled over this, but then laughter drifted in through the windows and open front door.

The large pot sitting before Arvou caught her attention as he reached for a long handled ladle and scooped its contents onto a plate. This was the first she had noticed the tall stack of a dozen or so slightly rounded plates in front of their host. He looked to her and then spoke a few words to Sauntage as he handed over the plate.

With a smile and nod he received the dish, and then carefully placed it before Maureen. Leaning into her ear Sauntage whispered, "Arvou offers this to the lovely carkna slayer."

Heat flooded into her cheeks as she met Arvou's gaze with a smile and mumbled thanks. She sensed everyone's eyes upon her guessing that they were waiting for her to taste the meal. Awkwardly, Maureen reached to her right for the spoon next to her plate. There were quite a few different items mixed together in what appeared to be a stew. Taking a few smaller pieces near the edge she brought it to her lips.

As she slowly chewed her eyes closed with pleasure. After so many meals of dried fruit or fish she could not remember tasting anything so wonderful. When the bite had been swallowed she turned to give Narmaka a tearful smile of gratitude.

Narmaka glowed with pride as she took her plate from her husband's hands. Sauntage was the next to be served his meal which he dove into without hesitation. It was at this time that Maureen noticed two of the children waiting just behind Arvou to take plates to the others seated around the table. Slowly, she ate the thick savory stew as she watched and listened.

Once everyone was seated there was some lighthearted conversation to which she heard her husband chuckle many times. Maureen was surprised by the number of words she was able to understand throughout the meal though not enough of them made sense for her to follow the discussion.

A deep melancholy settled on her without warning. As much as she enjoyed the presence and company of this family, Maureen ached to have her sons. She could not help but wonder if the boys had been fed since they left the caves. Were they really safe? Or had Tagurah placed them in harm's way with this rebellion? Her questions might have overtaken her mind if she hadn't felt Sauntage's large frame brush against her side.

With a firm mental shake she moved her focus to their surroundings. The children had all left the table and some of the older girls were cleaning the kitchen while the younger ones went outside to play.

There was an almost instant change in the room. Everything grew quiet and serious as the conversation turned to heavier matters. While she was able to understand much more of this discussion Maureen had to be mindful of her reactions. Things were going too well for her to goof up now.

At first the talking was mostly done by Arvou, but it was not long before Sauntage began asking questions. The more answers he received, it seemed to Maureen, the more tense and uptight he became. She found herself glancing at him with surprise as his edgy tone. Whatever he was learning was not likely to help their cause.

Out of the corner of her eye she saw Narmaka studying her. Their hostess had remained quiet for the most part, but she was certainly involved with the conversation Maureen realized suddenly. Everything the two of them said and did was sure to be analyzed later in the evening. A weight dropped in her stomach as the reality of their precarious position hit her. They could not afford any doubts or suspicion from the Trigguards.

To help with her husband's story about her hearing difficulty she turned her focus to the young girls washing the dishes. It surprised her to see Maruti among them. If she were married and held in higher position than the others, then why was she scrubbing pots? It appeared that this was the normal course of action. Nothing seemed out of the ordinary. Each of them had a particular task and they worked together as a well oiled machine.

This fact impacted her so much that it was the first thing she mentioned to Sauntage when they were finally alone.

"I know this is hard for you to except coming from a culture like ours, but Maruti was working in the kitchen because she wanted to." He explained with a lopsided smile. "In Liguesis certain privileges are earned by your accomplishments. For instance, Arvou is called a Master Farmer because of the number of young men he has trained over the years as well as the fact that his son has reached the age of maturity and works by his side. Besides the honorable name he is now called, he is allowed a higher rank for picking trainees when they are sent. There are other things he has earned, but you get the point.

"Now Maruti is newly married, less than a year, so she hasn't had a chance to earn the privileges granted to Narmaka." He paused to smile widely as he added, "You won't believe what happens to her the day she is able to announce to this family that a child is on the way. That young lady will be treated like a queen for about a year."

"Really?" Maureen felt her eyes widen as she met his gaze over the narrow bed.

His reply began as a firm nod. "Children are regarded highly; as a great treasure or prize so everything is done to ensure their safe arrival." He suddenly grew serious putting his finger to his lips and cocking his head to listen. When he was satisfied he came around to her side of the bed. In an urgent whisper he went on to say, "Mo, we need to talk and you must be careful. It is crucial that you don't make any noise."

Her wide eyes scanned the strained skin around his mouth and eyes with a sinking sensation in her stomach. Tears rose in her eyes without warning, "Sau, what's wrong?"

Taking a deep breath he explained, "When we first arrived here and I introduced myself, I made a mistake. As it turns out it's a really good thing I did."

"What are you talking about? What mistake?" Confusion knitted her arching brows together as she continued to look up at him.

"After using the name of Smith for so many years I naturally used it when we met Arvou. Anyway, I didn't think much of it I mean we were only going to be here for one night and it's not like we were out to hurt this family. But during our conversation tonight I learned many things that affect us.

"First of all, that area of trampled ground we passed through is well known to the settlements around here. It was actually caused by some of them. Apparently the threat of war is greater than I realized and the people of Liguesis are amassing an army to prepare for it. That's why Arvou and his eldest son are the only ones running this farm right now. Everyone else is with the military."

A choked sob rose in her throat as acid rose up through her chest, "No!" She cried harshly under her breath.

His hands came to her shoulders with some pressure to help her brace for the rest of his news. "There is more, Darling. Perhaps you should sit on the bed here." With sorrow he watched her stiffly obey. "I believe Tagurah is leading this rebellion."

Maureen jumped to her feet shaking her head vehemently. She lifted her hands in front of her in an effort to negate his words. This could not be happening.

Sauntage grasped her upper arms and leaned close to her face. "Please, listen to me, Maureen. Arvou told me some of the horrible stories coming from the villages and towns on the Western border of Galixtorn. And they are terrible. Murderous raids, burned homes and businesses, stolen property and all kinds of other evil things. All of these stories have one thing in common."

"What's that?" She asked him tearfully after a long period of silence.

"Sauntage Vadelum." He said simply allowing the information to sink into her mind.

"But...but...that's you!" An angry hiss transformed her features into hard lines and steely angles. "You haven't even been here for more than a few days at a time in more than a decade and a half."

Relief washed into his face and rapidly flowed to the rest of his body. He was not expecting her to receive the news this well. "I know. But Arvou said that is the reported name of this group's leader. It seems that when they commit those atrocious acts the group leaves a mark of some sort that has become the symbol for them."

"So what do we do now?" Maureen sat once more with a heavy sigh.

Joining her on the side of the bed he replied, "I'm honestly not sure. Thank goodness my name is a common one for men my age. No matter what I do now I am putting everyone around me in danger. Either with Tagurah or with the army."

"Sau, what about your parents are they in danger?" Her eyes lifted to his face in concern.

"My Father holds a pretty high ranking position in Liguesis so while there is always some danger for him I am not overly worried. The armies will do their best to protect my parents and siblings." As quietly as he could Sauntage cleared his throat and then reached out to take hold of her trembling right hand. "I think you should stay here, Darling. You'll be safe here with Arvou and his family."

With narrowed eyes and a tense jaw she said, "No. I came here to find my sons. I told you before I am not leaving your side until the boys are out of danger."

"Please, Maureen. Because of what Tagurah has done there won't likely be anyone else that will come to our aid." His lips pressed tightly together as he saw the resolve on his wife's face. That look had crossed her features several times over the last week and he knew what it meant. If he wanted her to stay behind he would have to sneak away in the middle of the night.

"I don't care what the danger is, Sau, my sons are in the middle of it. Promise me you won't go on without me." Maureen glared at him with hardened eyes.

In a hesitant, resigned tone he answered, "I promise." His weight suddenly left the mattress and quietly made his way to the other side of the bed. "Whatever our course of action turns out to be, we need to get some sleep."

When she got up and turned around to face him across the bed, Maureen saw the wavering light playing on his face. Deep lines appeared around the outer edges of his eyes and mouth causing him to look older than he was. For the first time since she had met him in the hospital as a teenager she thought he looked defeated.

Though the borrowed room they were using was sparsely furnished Maureen felt like everything was closing in on them. The four wooden walls had only a window, a door and a row of twelve hooks behind the door, but they all advanced on them like part of a dark army. Besides the small bed there was a little table with the flickering lamp which was fading by the second.

She pulled back the lightweight blanket and sank into the thickly stuffed mattress clothes and all. A couple of tears washed down her temple as the smell of sweet grass filled her nostrils. This bed felt so good. It was such a contrast to everything else in their lives at the moment. Sauntage blew out the nodding flame and quickly joined her. The room was silent for a long time. Each of them was lost in thought, traveling over every detail since he had picked up the phone to call the police.

Suddenly, Maureen found herself whispering aloud, "Dear God in heaven, please help us."

He was not sure what startled him more, her prayer or his own heartfelt response, "Amen."

# Chapter Eight

Sleep was being shaken away from her. Groaning softly she tried to push away from the disturbance. The sound of her name being called urgently caused her eyelids to open groggily. She was disoriented in the darkness. Where was she? It was clearly the middle of the night but this didn't feel like home to her. Sauntage's voice brought her to full consciousness in an instant.

"Maureen, Darling, wake up!" His hands were on each of her shoulders gently pressing her into the mattress.

"Sau? What is it? What's wrong?" With some difficulty she came to a seated position in the middle of the bed.

"Arvoa returned a short time ago. He woke his parents and Maruti. The four of them have been talking in the kitchen below us."

"Do you think they suspect who you are?" Her lower lip folded beneath her upper teeth as she felt around for her missing cap.

Quietly Sauntage pulled out the spark stones to light the lamp. Once he was certain the flame would not go out he turned to his wife. His jaw dropped slightly as he looked at her tumbling hair. "I had no idea how much the sun here really changed your coloring."

"Yeah, or how dirty I must have been when we got into that tub last night." Sarcasm in her voice matched her tense stance at the side of the bed. "So what have you learned? It must be important for you to wake me out of a dead sleep."

"Yes, it is." He nodded at her then drew closer to her as he explained, "Arvoa met another messenger heading south while making his journey for us. This messenger was sent by the king to warn the settlements of this region of the suspected presence of the traitor Sauntage Vadelum in the area."

Maureen felt her eyes widen in the dim light as she wondered, "How could he know you were here?"

"It would seem that Tagurah has spread a web of lies as well as a trap of some sort..."

Frowning at him she questioned, "A trap? What trap? For whom?"

"That's just it; I don't know. All this time I thought this whole thing was about me. But now he's gone and involved the king..."

"Wait a minute. Involved the king? How?" She was beginning to wonder if he had had a bad dream.

"Maureen, the king is on his way here to investigate the situation. We have to get out of here quickly before anyone figures out who I am."

She pressed her fist over her pounding heart. In a trembling voice she asked, "When will he arrive? And how long will we have before he and everyone else here figures out this whole thing?"

With a shake of his head he admitted, "There's no telling. At best I'd say we have a week."

"Worst case would be?" Maureen ventured fearfully.

"Hours. I didn't hear how close this messenger was or where the king is at the moment. Tagurah has timed this and planned it well. Mo, we have to leave now."

Quietly she nodded her understanding and agreement. Then she wondered breathlessly, "Where do we go, Sau?"

"Shargaunal." He replied grimly and then taking a deep breath he reached for her fingers to squeeze them gently. "Let's go see how we can arrange for our departure."

As they soundlessly walked along the narrow upstairs corridor Maureen counted six doorways. Two of them had open doors besides the one they had used. Above their heads about four feet was the highest point of the dome. Across the tops of the walls on either side of the hallway were thick boards which created storage space for items not needed every day.

The stairs were steep but they were also sturdy with a wide railing to hold. They tip toed down the dozen or so risers then turned to their right to go into the large kitchen. Conversation halted with the sound of their footsteps.

When they stepped into the bright light Maureen saw Arvoa come to his feet with his head bowed. He said a few words of which she understood about half. Apparently the young man felt guilty for disturbing their rest.

Sauntage quickly responded in a light tone offering his thanks for what Arvoa had done. It surprised Maureen greatly that she knew what her husband said.

Maruti rose from the table to retrieve two more glasses from the cupboard. After she filled them with a steaming hot herbal brew she brought them to their guests with a smile. In the center of the table there was a small pitcher of cream and dish of a dark granulated mixture Maureen thought must be sugar.

"Thank you." She murmured awkwardly with a smile and a nod. Not knowing what the hot drink would taste like she decided to take a small sip before adding anything to it. As soon as she had touched the cup to her lips Maureen felt everyone's eyes on her. Once the heat left her mouth she understood their shock. This 'tea' was very bitter on its own. Swallowing as hard as she could she did her best not to make a face that would have insulted her hostess.

Narmaka made it for her as she pushed the cream and sugar forward. In a gentle tone she said to Sauntage, "Please, tell your lady how sorry I am to have forgotten that she is not from here."

Before Sauntage could reply Maureen smiled at Narmaka broadly, "It is I who am sorry for not remembering your customs." Words in their language were still awkward to say, but taking her time made it possible for them to understand her.

Loud chuckle escaped from Sauntage as he leaned close to press a kiss to his wife's temple. "I'll bet you are sorry. This stuff has a horrible aftertaste without the cream and sugar."

Color flooded into her face as she heard the chuckles around the table. But it deepened when she heard her husband speak once more.

"I am the one to apologize. Maureen, I should have reminded you about our morning brew." His eyes were lowered to look at the floor.

"All is well, Sau." Her pronunciation was labored, but she sensed a growing respect from this family at her social efforts. A firm grip over the fingers of her left hand told her that her husband was proud as well.

Sauntage turned his gaze on Arvoa and quietly asked after his journey. Over the next few minutes he listened intently to the young man's story. Although most of it he had already heard from the bedroom above, he was glad he had asked because a few new details came to light.

As soon as his son finished speaking Arvou spoke with confidence,

"It is good for you that the king is coming. Now you may rest here for a few days and wait for him. Goodness knows how much you could use it."

"I thank you for your generous offer, Master Arvou, but the king's business in this region is far more important to Liguesis than the kidnapping of my sons." He responded carefully.

"Perhaps that is true, but it may be that he would be able to spare some of his soldiers to aid you in your journey." Arvou insisted as he leaned his crossed forearms on the table.

Silence filled the room for nearly a minute before Sauntage answered his host, "Though I have not lived in Liguesis for many years and my lady is not of Liguesian birth, this is my homeland. And I wish to do all that I can to protect it. The king cannot hope to stop this traitorous rebellion if his resources are split into other objectives. We must leave for Shargaunal immediately. Before war breaks out we must try to reach and rescue our sons."

A quiet nod of understanding came from the father and son. From the two women seated across the table Maureen received compassionate smiles. Narmaka broke the silence with her hands on the table helping her to rise from the bench, "You must have some food and other supplies. We will gather what the horses can handle."

Maruti quickly joined her mother-in-law saying, "I will start on a batch of hard rolls."

It amazed Maureen how quickly these people jumped into action once they were committed to a purpose. Within seconds the men were walking to one of the smaller barns to make preparations, Maruti was pulling a mixing bowl from the cupboard and Narmaka was leading her by the hand into the supply room.

Once the overhead lantern was lit and in place, Narmaka told her to choose another set of large sized clothing for Sauntage. For a few moments she stood still with indecision. Did she dare admit that she could not read? In the end she figured that it actually helped with their cover story so she lowered her eyes to the floor. Her voice was soft and unsure as she asked slowly, "How do I know which ones are large?"

Narmaka paused to look at her with a soft smile. "Please, forgive me Lady Maureen. Of course you haven't had a chance to study our writing. The next two minutes were spent examining the different markings branded into each leather garment.

With some confidence that she knew what to look for, Maureen opened a large crate labeled as clothing for men. Near the bottom of the box she finally found a shirt that would fit Sauntage. Next she moved a stack of crates around so that she could reach the crate holding the pants. It took her a moment to locate the head coverings because the box was much smaller than the others.

When she had an outfit for her husband in her arms she turned toward the door with pride. Her jaw lowered when she saw the pile of items that Narmaka had put together. There was an outfit for her, two blankets, two leather pouches with wooden caps, a lantern and two small jars of what looked to be oil.

"Let's take these things into the kitchen and get everything organized." Scooping up more than half of the pile Narmaka led the way back to the dining table.

Maruti had been collecting cooking utensils as well as silverware and plates. The long table was now loaded with so much stuff that Maureen simply stared at it for thirty seconds.

She was amazed as she watched these two women work side by side. Not many words were spoken due to the early morning hour and the sober nature of their preparations. All of them focused on the fact that this was not a pleasure trip for which they were packing. It was easy to see the love and respect this mother and daughter-in-law had for each other.

By the time they had sorted the clothing into two piles; Maruti was pulling out the first batch of biscuits and putting in another. This second batch was much larger than the first which puzzled Maureen a bit.

With a sigh Narmaka explained, "I'm afraid these hard rolls won't last more than a day or two before they start to rot. Because your husband wants to leave so quickly there isn't time to make something better for your journey. I wish we had more to offer you."

Tears welled up in Maureen's eyes as she looked at the women before her. Her voice trembled emotionally as she responded, "You have given us so much already. I only wish there was some way that we could repay your kindness and generosity." For a long minute she was afraid that she had spoken the wrong words because Narmaka turned away to face the window.

"Two of my sons have gone to serve the king in this battle as have many of our neighbors and their sons." When she forced herself to turn back to her guest tears streaked her plump cheeks and her voice though quiet, was filled with passion. "Arvou and I hear the horrible stories coming from the border. From here there is not much we can do to stop what is happening. But what we can do we will do in the name of our Lord, Ewaris and the king of the land, to hopefully save your sons. Perhaps there are enough Liguesians who feel as we do and can make a real difference in this war."

There was no time for Maureen to respond to the words Narmaka had spoken because the men returned from the barn with large leather pouches. As they all worked to carefully pack the supplies she could sense Sauntage watching her closely.

The more she thought about Narmaka's words Maureen could feel the tension building along her jaw and around her eyes. For the first time since this journey had begun she realized how much others were being affected in this situation. Until this moment the goal had been to rescue her sons and get back home. Suddenly, the realization that things might not be that simple fell on her like a lead brick.

Here before her was another mother whose sons were gone. True they chose to go to battle for their country, but the result was the same. Narmaka longed to see her sons just as much as she wanted Charlie, Andrew and Ryan. Though it was not spoken aloud nor did she fully realize it herself, Maureen vowed to do whatever she could do to repay this family's kindness.

Only an hour and a half had gone by and the sun was just beginning to warm the sky when the six of them prepared to say good bye. Arvou stood holding the reigns in his hands while Arvoa, Maruti and Narmaka wished them well. His eyes widened in surprise at the warm hug Maureen had for his son and daughter-in-law, but felt his jaw slacken at the fierce embrace shared with his wife.

Narmaka whispered into Maureen's ear as she held her close, "Ewaris go before you. May you find your sons quickly and send word to us that we might celebrate with you. Let speed be your friend and safety your brother. Receive counsel from your gut, but always follow your heart."

She did not try to hide the moisture rolling down her cheeks as she answered, "May you be repaid ten times and more what you have given to us. And your sons returned to you quickly. We will celebrate with you on that day." Without further comment she turned to face Arvou. His surprise was comical and she could not help but smile through her tears. Awkwardly she said to him, "No words exist to say how we appreciate all that you have done for us."

He stretched the reigns out to his son, and then gently hugged her to his wide chest as a father might his daughter. "Ewaris bring you favor and shine on all that you do, Carkna Slayer." Was all that he said before quickly releasing her.

As she moved out of the way so that Sauntage could say good bye Maureen turned her eyes to the large animals behind Arvoa. Panic seized her chest. These so called horses were huge dark brown walls!

Now her mind scrambled to remember all that Sauntage had tried to teach her the previous night. Her thoughts went blank. All she could think of was the fact that these horses stood taller than any she had ever seen on earth.

It seemed like only a few seconds had past and Sauntage was turning to help her mount into the saddle. He stepped to the left side of the horse she was to ride and bent down with his fingers laced together. A nod and a small smile of encouragement was all he gave her.

The pounding in her chest made it impossible to do much more than nod stiffly for a few seconds. Taking a deep breath she reached up to grasp the small post at the front of the saddle. Before she was ready Sauntage launched her weight upwards tapping her right foot as a reminder to swing that leg over the horse's back.

Maureen managed to get her right leg to the other side of the horse's body by leaning forward over its neck. It was by no means a smooth mounting, but she was in the saddle. Adjusting her skirt proved to be a little tricky because she had to shift her weight from one side of the saddle to the other which the horse did not appear to appreciate.

Arvou worked quickly to adjust the stirrup on one side while Sauntage did the same on the left. Once she was settled into place Arvoa handed the reins to her with a firm nod.

With ease Sauntage swung onto the back of the other horse and gathered the reigns from the young man. His stirrups had already been adjusted so with a short nod and a soft click to his horse he was moving.

To the best of her ability Maureen copied her husband's actions and sound, but the horse remained still. Color rose in her cheeks as she licked her lips to try again a little louder. Embarrassment washed over her as she watched her husband moving out of the worn grassy yard. What had she forgotten?

Suddenly, there was a light slapping sound and the horse beneath her jolted forward. She nearly went over backwards and would have if she had not been holding onto that post. Several heartbeats went by before she loosened her white knuckled grip. When she did Maureen was nearly caught up to her husband.

As her horse met up with his and they were riding side by side relief flooded over her. Another leg of their journey was completed. A sigh loudly left her lungs as she looked at Sauntage.

"Be careful we aren't out of sight yet. Chances are they will watch us until we reach the far side of that field ahead." His voice was surprisingly quiet for the distance there was now between them and the Trigguards.

Suspicion narrowed her eyes and caused her head to tilt at an odd angle. "What haven't you told me, Sau? There's something odd going on here."

He turned to blink at her when she spoke to him in his own tongue. "I had no idea how much Liguesian you have managed to learn." His eyes drifted forward once more as he responded to her sarcastic glare. "Okay, look when Arvoa talked about his trip he mentioned a couple of settlements. One of them is where the king happened to be at the time the messenger left on his mission. The other was where Arvoa met him."

"So?" Maureen said with some agitation hoping he would soon get to the point.

"The distance the king's messenger had traveled was less than two days from where the two of them met."

Understanding dawned on her causing the blood to drain from her face. "That means the king is only a few days from here."

"Yes, exactly. If we are lucky he is two days behind us." Sauntage remained quiet as they passed into Arvou's grain field. Our best shot to making it to Shargaunal before we are over taken by the king is to ride hard and fast which at the moment we can't do."

It was difficult to move sound through her aching throat, "Well, how long will it take us to get to Shargaunal?"

"About a week from here if we could ride at top speed."

"Thankfully once we pass over this field we can speed up." She said matter of factly.

"No, we can't!" He ground out through his clenched teeth harshly.

"Why not? What's on the other side of that field to worry about?" Her eyes flicked from his hardened jaw line to the landscape before them.

A thin white line surrounded his lips as they pressed tightly together. "There's nothing significant to harm us..."

"Then what is it?" Maureen demanded. When he refused to answer or look at her she went on to screech under her breath, "Sauntage Vadelum, you tell me right now!"

"Mo," Sauntage started slowly. "You've never ridden a horse before..."

"So what? I'm on it now and as long as I can hang on to this post thing I'll be fine..." To demonstrate she took hold of the saddle with both hands.

His head shook sadly back and forth as he explained, "It's not that easy, Darling. Your muscles are going to hurt no matter how fast we travel, but if we push it too far you'll be in agony. You could..."

"I don't care! I told you I would do whatever it took to get to my sons. You said last night that you would teach me what I need to know about riding a horse. So let's get started."

"Maureen, I can't..." He began hoarsely, but then saw the determination in her eyes. If he did not teach her she was going to figure it out on her own.

As their horses plodded slowly through the stalks of grain Sauntage gave her lessons on the names of various parts of the horse. After only a few minutes she became frustrated because none of what he was telling her was going to help them move faster.

When he saw her reaction he gave a series of quick commands at the same time he leaned to his left side which caused his horse to side step to another row of grain. "You have to know about the horse before you can tell him how you want him to move."

With a nod of resignation she let him know that she understood his point. Now as he resumed the lessons she listened carefully to all that he said. She was amazed at the depth of knowledge her husband had. Not that she ever questioned his intelligence, but because they had lived with the lie of amnesia and the fact that he never showed an interest in higher education it did not dawn on her how much he knew on any given subject.

Sauntage was doing his best to draw out the lessons on horse anatomy. It turned his gut to be even the tiniest bit untruthful with Maureen. He reasoned to himself that he had no choice so he strained his memory for every word, phrase or piece of advice that he had ever heard about horses.

They left Arvou's field behind without comment and managed to keep the same speed. Both horses were happy to plod along at a slow pace. For the most part the terrain did not change either. Tall grasses swayed in the cool morning breeze with very few trees visible in any direction. The only change that registered with Maureen was the gentle rise and fall of small hills.

Sauntage knew he could not avoid the issue of their speed for much longer than he already had. So reluctantly he demonstrated how to adjust the body's weight in the saddle to prepare for the more jarring motion of the horse's trot. As he watched her movement he could tell that she had probably been in the saddle long enough for the muscles to stretch past the point of comfort.

Much to his relief there was a small stream running through the valley between the hill on which they were standing and the next one. Nodding his head in that direction he said, "Let's take a break at this stream."

"But it's barely been two hours since we left the Trigguards' farm. Shouldn't we keep going and get as much distance between us and the king?" She questioned gently.

After taking a deep breath he looked at her with tenderness, "Maureen, it is going to take us a small miracle to make it to Shargaunal before we are overtaken by the king. At this point riding hard and fast for as long as we possibly can is the only way. You have to trust me when I tell you that easing into horseback riding is the best chance we have of being able to ride at top speed for the longest period of time and making that miracle happen."

"Trust you." Maureen said quietly under her breath as she gazed down at the water her horse was now drinking.

Another sigh left his lungs as he swung his leg over the saddle to dismount. "Believe me then. Believe what I am telling you."

Her lips twisted up in a scowl as she snapped, "Fine, we'll do it your way." It was harder than she expected to drag her right foot back over the saddle. Once she did Maureen simply slid down the horse's side. As her moccasin like shoes touched the ground she had to stifle a cry of pain by clamping her teeth over her sleeve.

Muscles that she did not know existed burned up the entire length of her legs. No matter how hard she tried she could not straighten her knee joints to walk properly. The only thing that saved her from total embarrassment was the sight of her husband walking stiffly to the water's edge. Taking a deep breath she followed his example and knelt awkwardly to get a drink.

Cool water ran down her forearms soaking her leather sleeves. For more than a minute she contemplated the idea of sitting in the creek bed to soak her aching legs. A deep rumble of laughter from Sauntage drew her attention from the water.

"You do not want to do it, Maureen." His smirk said that he had been reading her thoughts. "That water will feel wonderful on your sore legs and bottom, however, it will cool them down too quickly and when we ride again you will almost certainly tear something."

A rapid nod of her head showed her understanding and willingness to take his word for it. Her eyes went back to the water with longing.

"I don't remember this terrain very well, but I'd bet there'll be another stream or river for us to stop at. If we find one late enough in the afternoon then we'll stop for the night and have a good soak." He gave her a smile of encouragement then came to his feet to walk along the side of the stream with his horse in tow.

"As long as it won't slow us down." Maureen agreed as she too pulled her horse to follow her husband's lead.

Twenty minutes went by before they remounted and rode out of the small valley. Unexpected pulling on the muscles that were stretched out only a short time before caused a grimace to form on her face. Determination helped her fix her gaze straight ahead with the knowledge that her sons were out there waiting for them. Whatever it took she would find her boys.

Sauntage glanced to his right more than once that long morning. Each time he was more proud than the last at the strength of his wife. He had always known her strong will would carry her through difficulties in life, but this went far beyond anything he could have imagined her facing.

Long periods of silence fell between them as the sun rose higher in the sky. Soon it would be at its highest point and shade would be impossible to find. As the air had continued to warm throughout the morning there were times Maureen had wondered about the wisdom of such heavy clothing. Now it was beginning to make sense. Every inch of her skin was directly protected from the sun's burning rays, except for her face which was hidden beneath the wide brim of her unusual hat.

They stopped to rest their legs and backsides shortly after mid day. A couple of Maruti's hard rolls and some apples that had been packed without her knowledge served as their lunch. Though there was not any water at the place they chose, there was still enough water in the leather pouches for them to drink.

After she had replaced the wooden cap and strapped the leather bag back onto the saddle she heard a soft nicker from her horse. A sudden realization caused her to ask, "Do you know the names of these horses?"

"Jeurku is the one you are riding and Dueby is mine." He answered quietly. "They are good horses. From what I saw in his barn these were his best animals."

Gasping loudly she wondered, "Arvou must need good horses to run his farm, why would he give away his very best ones?"

"Because he believes our sons lives to be more important than the amount of money that could be produced from these animals on his farm." Sauntage ran his hand along Dueby's neck with appreciation. "I asked him several times for the smaller pair, but he flat out refused to budge. We should keep moving. If you'd like to we can walk for bit and give our bottoms a break."

Without hesitation she agreed. "That's fine with me. Jeurku certainly lives up to his name."

"What do you mean?" Sauntage asked with a questioning glance.

"He can really 'jerk you' around." She answered with a slight curl to her upper lip.

Light laughter escaped from his mouth as he continued walking forward through the waving grass. It was during this short jaunt that he noticed the change in the grass surrounding them. When they had started out that morning it had been a dark green sea now it resembled the dry sand at the beach. At first it had a bit of a depressing feel, as though it were all shriveling up and dying, but then he began to see little yellow flowers bouncing in the breeze.

Absently, Maureen picked one of the tiny blooms and held it to her nose. The sweet aroma reminded her of a hyacinth flower. Soon her free hand was filled with the long stalks. Once they were ready to get back on the horses she tucked her bouquet into the top of one of the pouches hanging from the back of the saddle.

There was not much difference in the way their afternoon passed. They crossed a larger, slower flowing river but both of them agreed that it was far too early to stop for the day. Once the river was behind them they began to see more trees and fewer hills.

When the sun had dropped behind them and the shadows started to lengthen, Sauntage commented that they should think about where to spend the night. "If I can find a rabbit we would still have plenty of time to roast it before dark."

While the thought of wild game was not all that appealing to her Maureen responded, "As long as it isn't a carkna I don't care."

A few minutes later he startled her when he lifted his hand to point ahead of them. "Look there's got to be water near that line of scrubby bushes. That ought to be as good a place as any to stay for the night. The water might even be deep enough for a good soak."

"Sounds good to me." She smiled in relief that this first day was nearing its end. Only six more days to reach the place her sons had been taken.

Ten minutes later they pulled up at the top of a narrow ravine. Sauntage had been correct about the presence of water near the large population of bushes; the vegetation was anything but scrub, however. From a distance they had only been able to see the tops of the plants. Standing where they were now; they could see that the roots were at least twelve feet lower than they thought.

"This is awfully steep." He said as his eyes scanned from one side to the other. "We should walk up stream a bit and see if we can find a better place to descend."

Without comment she followed him along the edge of the ravine. At the bottom the water gurgled over rocks in a playful, cheery manner. It lifted her spirits to watch the bubbles form along the tree roots. Her eyes shifted to Sauntage's back when suddenly he started to sing a tune quietly to himself. Maureen smiled at him as she picked up Jeurku's speed so that she could ride next to him and hear his song better.

His words faltered a bit when he realized that she was listening and remembered that she had learned enough of his language to understand. Swallowing his feelings of silliness he continued to sing the song he had not heard since he was a little boy. When he finished Sauntage felt heat come to his face as he admitted, "That was a song my Mother sang to us when we were young. There was a river near our home that we would try to visit each time Father returned from a trip."

"Is that how you came to enjoy fishing?" She tried not to giggle at him as she pictured him in her mind sitting at the edge of a stream singing that tune to the fish in the water.

"Well, not the song really, but the time alone as a family, yes." There was a frown on his lips as he heard his wife choking back laughter. "What's so funny? I'll have you know that we caught many meals with that little ditty."

"And is there a dance to go with it?" Her lips curled inward as he looked at her with sarcasm. "You sang, 'come on little fishy dance pretty come on little fishy just like me'." As she saw his face turn back to the water she saw the color rising in his face. "I knew it. There is one. Will you show it to me when we stop for the night?"

"No." Sauntage grumbled at her. "Ask my Mother when you meet her; it was her song."

"All right, Mr. Grumpy, I will ask her. It must be quite a sight to have you so upset." With a lift of her brows she challenged him to deny it.

A sigh left him as he explained, "The whole thing was hokey and silly I admit, but it was my Mother's game. We never knew why but she had this ritual whenever we went to the Kiate River." His words came to a halt as he felt the pressure of her gloved hand on his upper arm.

"Have you communicated with your parents at all since you have lived on earth?" All humor left her as she realized that his lie had cost him more than she had guessed.

"Actually, I have sent them a letter each year. Tagurah delivers it for me and each time the envelope is returned unopened. After Charlie was born I thought for sure they would respond, but even with my brother's pleading they refused to hear from me." An ache in his throat and chest caused him to change the subject. "This place looks good. We can make it down to the water safely here."

Sensing his need to leave the difficult memories behind she followed quietly. Confused emotions washed over her as the image of her husband's grief stricken face played through her mind. Of course she was still upset that he had hidden all of this from her, but now there was a small part of her heart that felt sorry for him.

Water splashed under the horses' hooves drawing her quickly from her revere. Hope sprang to life when she noticed that the stream's depth was perfect for soaking her legs. This spot was even cleaner than the other water sources had been.

Once they were up along the eastern bank Sauntage pulled back on Dueby's reigns, telling him quietly to stop. With a nod of approval he swung out of the saddle saying, "We aren't likely to find a better place to camp out tonight. Let's get the bags and saddles off of the horses so we can picket them under one of these trees."

Jeurku and Dueby seemed pleased to stop for the day. Both munched on the short green grasses growing next to the water's edge. Every once in a while one of them would let out a loud snort and toss their head wildly from side to side.

Maureen was in the process of emptying her water pouch when Sauntage called to her softly. A frown creased her forehead as she looked up at him.

In a whisper he said, "I need you to go along the tree line here and find some stalks with leaves like this one." In his hand he held out a short sprig with a clump of seven leaves. They were pale yellow in color with smooth edges. "Pick as many as you can while I go find us some dinner."

"What do you plan to do with them?" She asked studying the branch closely.

"We'll heat them in one of our pans with some water. The bugs don't like the scent so they should leave us alone for the night. After the water cools we can spread it over the horses to protect them." He gave her a nod of encouragement and then turned to make his way through the tall grasses with a rope and a sharpened stick.

At first she was afraid she would not be able to locate this bush because she had forgotten to ask him where he had found it. Reason soon took over as she realized that he had not gone more than a few feet outside of the circle in which they had planned to camp. Not far from the horses she finally found the plant. A sigh escaped her as she understood immediately why Sauntage had not simply told her about this bush. Only three healthy stalks were actually living.

It felt as though she had walked more than an hour. How hard could it be to find one plant? Apparently it was far more difficult than she imagined because despite searching around every tree and bush none of those stalks were to be found. Maureen considered the idea of crossing the water to walk back along the other side in hopes of finding what she needed, but the steep incline was enough to deter her. At least on this side she had some level areas on which to walk.

Hunger rumbled in her abdomen so she squatted at the water's edge to take a long drink. Looking downstream she had yet to see the leaves they needed. What should she do? For all she knew there could have been more stalks growing up stream from their campsite. Briefly she thought about turning around.

"Which way should I go?" With a sigh Maureen turned to face downstream and began to look once more. "Please, let there be even a few small plants soon."

Less than ten minutes later she came to a bend in the river's flow. When she had taken about three steps past the turn she stopped dead in her tracks. Before her stood the bush she needed. Thankfully this one was huge! Several large stalks were clumped together which made it easy for her to fill her arms.

When she reached the campsite Sauntage was already working to light a small pile of brush. On the ground next to him were thicker branches waiting for just the right moment. "Oh, there you are. I was starting to get worried. These look great. Did you have any trouble finding them?"

"Well, it did take me a long time, but thank God when I did one bush was big enough to fill my arms and then some." She tipped her head upwards to loosen her tight neck muscles as she spoke so she missed the inquisitive look in his eyes as he spoke.

"Yeah, I found myself saying the exact same thing when I hadn't seen any animals that we could eat for nearly a mile. Then suddenly, out of nowhere this gigantic rabbit popped out of the ground and looked right at me." He halted for her gaze to turn on him before he added, "Just after I found myself praying for some kind of meat for our meal."

Maureen felt the hair along her arms lift and prickle as she looked at him. Cautiously she asked, "So you think because you said something into thin air and shortly after a rabbit came into view that the two are somehow related?"

"Sounds kinda stupid, I know, but then..."

Pointing to the bag where her Bible had been tucked away she wondered, "Does God even do stuff like that? Answer a prayer like that I mean."

His shoulders lifted in ignorance as he replied, "I have no idea. Yet." Firmly nodding his head Sauntage declared, "But I aim to find out. If He is real, can hear me and answer my prayers, then I want to know. Maybe we'll get lucky and He'll tell us where the boys are."

"I have a feeling that luck has nothing to do with it, Sau." Her voice held a note of sarcasm but there was no judgment in it. Against her logical mind her heart was starting to cry out that maybe there was something more.

Two hours later they were putting the last of their evening wood on the fire and watching the colors fade from the sky. Jeurku and Dueby had settled down shortly after being rubbed down with their repellent tea. Although steak prepared on a grill was much more to her liking Maureen had had to admit to her husband how good that roasted rabbit had tasted. With her stomach no longer empty and her sore legs finally soothed in the cool water Maureen sat staring tiredly into the fire.

"It's been over a week now, Sau. Do you really think the boys are still alive?" Her voice wavered with tears.

Sauntage did not answer right away. Instead he gathered the leather pouch with their bedding and came to sit next to her. Drawing one of the blankets out; he wrapped it around behind her shoulders pulling her against his side. "Yes, Darling, I do. And while I'm sure Tagurah hasn't rolled out the red carpet for them, I do think he is caring for them." When he saw her questioning eyes turn to look at him he continued, "Because Tagurah knows me well enough to realize that if he doesn't treat my sons well I will kill him without hesitation or regret."

"I hope it doesn't come to that. I just want my boys." A shiver of fear went through her frame causing him to tighten his hold on her.

"Me too." He said quietly. "After they are safe though I'd like to know why Tagurah did all of this." Sauntage felt his breath catch when Maureen cuddled closer into his arms.

"Maybe then we can find a way to clear your name." Silence fell between them for a short time but then a sudden thought caused her to sit up and turn around to face him. "Perhaps these rumors about you are the reason your parents won't speak to you. Arvou said that awful things had been happening at the border for years. If we can get that straightened out..."

A smile tugged at his lips as he reached out with his right hand to caress her cheek. "One thing at a time, Beautiful Carkna Slayer." There had been more that he wanted to say but their eyes met and locked. Time halted. Then Maureen made the barest of movement toward him and then suddenly she was in his arms.

# Chapter Nine

Dawn was just breaking over the eastern horizon when Maureen opened her eyes. Although she was not cold she did miss the warmth of her husband. With some concern she looked around the deep shadows of their campsite to find him. Jeurku and Dueby stood side by side quietly resting with their noses lowered slightly.

A grateful smile came to her lips as she watched them for a moment. They really were amazing animals. In this light the two of them appeared to be solid black in color, but Maureen knew within a few short minutes only their tails and manes would remain so.

As soon as she tried to move she regretted it. Tissue deep inside her thighs felt as though it had separated from the skin and bone surrounding it. Her teeth clamped down over her lower lip in an effort to stifle a loud moan of pain. Tears pricked her eyes as she realized that Sauntage had been right. There was no way for her to learn to ride a horse quickly.

Taking a breath and then holding it she forced her body into a somewhat seated position. A few seconds later she released the air in her lungs as she turned her neck to find Sauntage. He did not seem to be anywhere in sight which made her a little nervous for a moment. When Dueby nickered softly off to her left she instantly relaxed. Sauntage would not have left both horses behind if he were leaving without her. It occurred to her that he must have gone looking for food or some other supply that they needed.

While she waited Maureen watched the sunrise and gently stretched her leg muscles. Inky black soon gave way to rich, velvet green which caused the grass around her to come to life. Moisture on the tall thin blades reflected in her eyes like thousands of tiny emeralds dancing in the light breeze. Soon birds began to call good morning to one another in a loud chorus. There seemed to be four distinct songs being sung at the same time by at least a dozen different voices.

A smile lifted the corners of her lips as she listened. Though the tune was not the same for each species, they all were singing the same thing to Maureen's heart. Hope. It was as though someone had organized this concert just for her. This thought made the smile lessen slightly. Was that possible? Could a God like the one in her parent's Bible do something like that? And if He could why would He take the time?

Question after question rolled through her mind as the sun rose higher in the sky. Now she understood Sauntage's need to find out what that Bible had to say. With cautious movements Maureen went to the leather pouch and retrieved the thick volume.

For a long time she flipped from one book to another unsure of where to start. Then she stumbled across a story that was familiar. At least parts of it were. A young man named, Daniel, was thrown into a den of hungry lions. After being left overnight it was discovered that not only was he still alive, he was completely unharmed. God had closed the lions' mouths and protected Daniel. With excitement Maureen turned back a few pages to figure out what he had done to make God do something like that.

She only had time to read a few verses from the beginning of the book because Sauntage returned from his wanderings. He was still some distance off when she heard him whistling loudly. At first she was puzzled by this but then she realized that he was making his presence known so that he did not frighten her. In his hands he held what looked like a loaf of bread and a packet wrapped with a small piece of string.

When he drew close enough for her to really get a good look at him Maureen saw the dark lines of fatigue around his eyes. Rising to her feet she chided gently, "Where on earth - uh, Liguesis have you been?"

Sauntage laughed at her comment as he handed the oblong loaf to her. "I've been shopping. I woke up in the middle of the night and had trouble going back to sleep. So I tried to count sheep, stars and half a dozen other things, that didn't work. Then I tried to think of nothing which I learned was next to impossible. There was something niggling my mind and I just couldn't figure out what it was..."

"But how and where did you go shopping?" Her eyes were crinkled deeply as she tried to follow his story.

As he continued Sauntage began pulling wood they had set aside the previous night into the fire pit. "Well, I kept laying there thinking there was something significant about this place. After thinking about it for what seemed like hours I finally remembered what it was. According to all the maps I studied growing up there were many small settlements along this river. Once I realized that was what my brain had been trying to tell me, I felt compelled to find a village and see what news I could hear."

"Sau, wasn't that dangerous? What if someone would have figured out who you are?" Her panicked eyes questioned him silently.

"No, no one there realized who I am. Yes, I suppose there was some risk to it, but it was well worth it because I helped with a few chores at a butchers and he gave me a couple of steaks. Cattle here eat different grasses than you're used to but it has to taste more like home than anything else I could get you."

"That was very thoughtful of you..." She started to chastise him lightly.

"Yeah, well don't think anything about it because the information I got from the butcher and his customers was even better than the meat. It seems that several of the smaller villages have banded together and sent out scouting teams to check out the stories from the border. While many of the stories were confirmed, others appear to be completely fabricated. Now I wasn't there long enough to get many details but that certainly is encouraging.

"Anyway one man said that his son went on one of these trips and actually crossed the border and ventured into the capital of Galixtorn. They learned that the army was preparing to cross the border and attack the lawless men of Liguesis. But they are headed further north of here not to Shargaunal."

"Really?" Maureen gasped with rising excitement. "That means the boys aren't being held near the battlefield."

Sauntage was thoughtful for a moment before he answered, "I'm not sure I'd go quite that far with my hope, but it means that the king is less likely to follow our trail. With impending battle to the north that is where he will go. When his scouts reach a village along this river and learn this news he will change his course."

Joy flowed into her eyes as she cried, "Let's hurry up and be on our way then. The sooner we leave this river the better I will feel about everything."

His palm wrapped lightly under her jaw as he smiled at her. "We need to let the fire die down before we can make our breakfast and while we wait for that I'd like to rest a bit I'm exhausted." A stifled yawn escaped him as he lowered his frame to the ground and reached for the blanket.

Several hours later they were plodding along at a slightly faster pace than the previous day. The sun had long since reached its zenith but they had yet to stop for lunch. Other than the tall grass rustling there was not much noise. Once in a while they heard the screech of a large bird of prey just before it swept down along the horizon somewhere seeking out a meal. A few smaller rodents had peeked out of underground dens earlier in the day but now everything grew still except for Sauntage and Maureen.

Silence only lasted a few minutes between them. Curiosity along with boredom caused her to ask him question after question about this seemingly endless land. For hours he did his best to share all that he remembered from his years of study. At one point he was on the verge of going crazy trying to answer the stream flowing from her, but when he turned to ask her to give him a break he felt color rise in his cheeks. In all the years he had spent on earth pestering her for information she rarely lost patience with him; and certainly not within a matter of days.

Somehow she sensed his desire to either talk about something else or stop talking altogether and fell quiet. At first he was pleased to have the peace. It was not long, however, before he too felt the need to break up the monotonous lack of sound. That was how they began discussing the different portions of the Bible that they had read. The more the two of them talked the more curious they became about what else was in that large book.

Nearly four days passed in much the same way. A few hills broke the skyline here and there along with some trees but it was pretty much a sea of grass. There were a few smaller rivers for them to cross that were practically hidden until the horses stepped into the flow of water.

Each time they stopped to rest at least one of them pulled out the

Bible to read. Many times it was spread between them so that they could read at the same time. They had tried to read as they rode, but at the speed they were able to travel at this point it was too difficult.

Maureen was surprised by how quickly her body had become used to the jarring and stretching motion of riding. Whenever they had stopped those first couple of days she thought her legs would literally tear away from her body. Now each time she slipped from Jeurku's back there was only a momentary twinge that would shoot through her muscles. Mornings were a different story, however. Long minutes of stretching were needed every time she woke from more than an hour's worth of sleep.

As the shadows grew longer on that fourth day and wind picked up Maureen was again thankful for her attire. It provided not only warmth but also kept small bits of grass from tearing into their skin. She noticed Sauntage watching the sky closely and asked, "Is there a storm brewing?"

He gave a vigorous nod as he answered, "I believe there is. It's still a ways off but we'll need some time to build a kaveta. See that stand of trees up ahead? We'll put up a kaveta there." Without waiting he prodded Dueby into action.

While they collected branches; the horses munched on grass just outside the tree line. Loud rumbles broke the quiet atmosphere causing them to move at a faster pace. To Maureen it seemed like they would have had plenty of material for even a crude shelter, but Sauntage kept pressing her to find more.

As she continued to use the hatchet on the lower branches of the surrounding trees he began to tie and weave a small structure. Although she could not tell exactly how it was put together Maureen knew it was done with a great deal of skill and knowledge.

Rain started to pelt them long before he had the kaveta finished. In a loud voice he called to her to drag all of their supplies under what protection she could. Answering him with her mouth was futile because of the thunder and torrential rain.

Once this was done he shouted at her to bring the horses into the trees where at least some relief could be found from the downpour. Dueby was the closest one so she quickly pulled up the stake holding his reigns in place and gently pulled him further into the trees. He seemed eager to follow her and nickered softly to clear water from his nose. Carefully pounding the stake back into the ground she gave him a gentle slap on the neck.

Lightning ripped the horizon not far from where they were when she pulled up the stake for Jeurku. There was a nervous whinny from him as his feet restlessly shifted on the ground. She drew close to him cooing softly in an effort to calm him. For a moment he shied away from her but then he appeared to relax so she started to lead him to the safer area.

When she had Jeurku nearly in place another flash momentarily brought daylight to their surroundings. It was immediately followed by a loud crack. From behind her Maureen heard Jeurku screech, but before she could respond an enormous weight thrust her forward with so much force that she landed face first near the base of a tree. Pain exploded in her cheek briefly and from a great distance she could hear Sauntage calling her. Then she knew nothing.

Feathers of awareness touched her mind briefly. Rain was still coming down and her face was pounding. Her soft moan brought a bitter taste to her mouth. Reality faded quickly after it.

Sometime later this memory played once more, only the rain was no longer falling.

Maureen lost count of the times she tried to open her eyes only to taste that bitterness and fall back to sleep. Each time, however, she was able to have a bit more clarity. What became most evident was deep throbbing pain on the right side of her face. Other things started to become clear as time passed.

The spoon touching her lips the moment she tried to move or make sound seemed to be the reason she kept falling asleep. So she determined to stay as still as possible to gather what information she could. With her eyes closed and pain radiating from her face it was hard, but she knew the horses were not far off because she heard them stamping their feet.

She also figured out that Sauntage was nearby from the sound of his breathing. From what she could tell he was asleep.

Cautiously, she lifted her right hand to her mouth. If she could keep that awful spoon away maybe she could find out what was going on around her. Her fingers trembled weakly, but did make it to her lips.

Once she felt certain that bitter concoction was not going to be administered, Maureen slowly lifted the lids of her eyes. Wherever she was it was dark. There was a skip in her heartbeat as she wondered if she might be blind.

With relief she noticed a break in the shadows and then heard a quiet whisper, "Maureen, Darling, I know it must be hard but you really need to get some sleep. This stuff tastes horrible and I'm sorry for that. Please, just rest a few more hours and it will make all the difference in the world I promise."

A soft moan left her lips as he gently removed her hand to administer the bitter medicine. Moments later all awareness was gone as she was swallowed up in dreamless slumber.

It was quieter when she came to the next time. Although she could hear Dueby and Jeurku softly munching and occasionally snorting they seemed to be farther away. Her ears strained for any noise coming from Sauntage, but nothing was discernable. Overhead the cry of a bird made her realize that it was likely daytime.

As carefully as she could Maureen cracked her eyelids. They immediately snapped shut at the bright light. Moisture trickled down the right side of her face.

After a moment of rest she attempted it once more. This time she was a bit more prepared for the blinding nature of her surroundings, so she forced her eyes to remain open for several seconds before allowing them to close.

By the time she had managed to open her eyes for the fourth time things began to take shape around her. There were large tree branches four feet above her head. Their deep green, almost black leaves were tightly woven together so that no light could be seen through them. From the spot directly over her head the ceiling of this kaveta arched much like the roof lines on the Trigguard's farm.

Several blinks brought clarity to the vision in her left eye, but her right remained blurry and ached terribly. To her left she was able to see all of their leather supply pouches lined up along the rounded wall. And on her right there did not appear to be much of anything except thick branches.

Taking a deep breath Maureen tried to lift her head off of the ground. Everything in her line of sight started to waver and roll so her head dropped with a moan. All she had been able to make out were the facts that her feet were barely inside the kaveta and its opening was wider than it was tall with one large stick in the center as a brace.

Seconds later Sauntage was kneeling on her right side talking softly, "Maureen? Can you hear me?"

"Yes." Her lips parted to speak but the sound that came out hardly sounded like her own voice.

"Here let me help you get a drink before you try to talk anymore." As tenderly as he could he slid his arm beneath her shoulders to lift her head and neck off the ground so she could take a sip from the water pouch without choking.

She savored the feel of the cool liquid on her dry throat and mouth. Until that moment she had not realized how thirsty she really was. After her shoulders were settled back on the dirt, Maureen said, "Thank you, Sau."

"You're welcome, Darling." He responded with a small smile and then seemed to hesitate before he finally ventured, "Do you remember what happened?"

Through her thick sticky tongue she answered, "The thunder and lightning freaked Jeurku. I think he ran me over trying to run away from it."

A heavy sigh of relief caused his entire frame to sag as he corrected, "You aren't far off actually. He was frightened by the storm and reared up because of it. When he came down he came close to hitting your back thankfully you tripped forward so far or he would have crushed you."

"He did hit me. I didn't trip. I was pushed." Her voice was raspy once more so he carefully held her by the shoulders so that she could drink again.

"Maureen, his hooves were the only part of his body close enough to touch you. I've checked your back several times. There isn't a mark on it." His eyes grew concerned that maybe she did not really remember what had happened.

She winced as the muscles over her right eye bunched in confusion. "I was pushed, Sau. Maybe his nose rammed me in the back."

"Jeurku's nose was straight up in the air when he came down and he swung it off to the right as you tripped to the left." Sauntage gently patted her right forearm in an effort to sooth her.

For a moment she thought through everything and then she stated simply, "Something pushed me, Sau. Really hard, in the middle of my back."

Silence fell between them for a full minute.

"It seems you have a guardian angel." Was all he could say as the wonder of that possibility washed over him.

"That's crazy isn't it?" She squinted up at him.

"I don't know. All I can tell you is what I saw and from where I stood there doesn't seem like there was anyway Jeurku could have touched you. He simply wasn't close enough to you at the time you went down." His shoulders lifted into a helpless shrug.

"And I'm telling you that I was shoved in the back and pushed forward. I remember it clearly." She licked her dry lips thoughtfully before she once more stated, "This is insane. Isn't it?"

He shook his head slowly as he replied, "No. At first I questioned what I saw. I was sure that horse must have hit you because of the way you hit the ground. When I couldn't find a mark or scratch on your back I told myself that you must have simply fallen." Sauntage tenderly brushed his fingertips down the left side of her face. "You need to rest. While you do I'll see what I can do about getting you something to eat."

There was a protest clearly rising on her lips when it was suddenly swallowed in a painful yawn. Without a word she gave him a nod of agreement and closed her eyes. She knew sleep was not about to come with the throbbing ache in her face but if she pretended well enough perhaps she could avoid that awful, bitter concoction he kept putting in her mouth.

Sunset was not far off when she woke up the next time. Dark

green-blue clouds were along the western sky and a brilliant emerald orb was sinking steadily behind the grassy hills. Because they had been so intent on their mission up to this point they had not stopped to notice much of the beauty around them.

Her right cheek was still aching, but not nearly so bad. Right now it was really her stomach that had her attention. Slowly licking her lips she called out as loudly as she could, "Sau? Sau, are you here?"

"Of course I'm here. I'll be right there, Darling." As he moved around outside the kaveta Sauntage made a bit of noise.

With confusion she listened to his actions trying to figure out what he was doing. "Is everything okay?"

"Yes, everything's fine. I was just finishing your dinner preparations just in case you woke up and wanted to eat." He said with a grunt as he crawled through the opening carrying something in his left hand. "So how about it? Are you hungry?"

Before she answered Maureen took a deep breath and smelled something delicious. "Oh, that smells wonderful."

"Good. Let me put this down and help you sit up. Then you can give this soup I made a try."

"Soup?" She said with a bit of a frown.

Reaching over to her left side Sauntage pulled one of the leather pouches closer. After gently lifting her shoulders off the ground he slid the bag filled with clothes underneath her back and then slowly released her weight onto it. "Yeah, you've got a nasty bruise along the right side of your face. I thought it might be a bit tough for you to chew on the meat I managed to catch so I made a broth for you."

"But I'll make a mess with it if I don't sit up more." With her hands on either side of her body to keep her balance Maureen started to move.

"Wait." He put his open hand just under her throat in an effort to hold her in place. "It's all right. There's a bowl and spoon here and I will feed it to you." When he saw her glare insisting that she could do it herself Sauntage went on to say, "Mo, it is possible that your cheekbone is broken and you haven't eaten in nearly two days so you have to take things slow. Just until we know how bad it is going to be."

"Fine." She responded with resignation as he lifted the first bite to her lips. Instantly she was grateful for his fore thought because pain stabbed through her upper jaw and eye socket. Tears rushed into her lower lids as she swallowed the first taste. Even though it was bland the warmth spread through her bringing comfort to the rest of her body. Slowly the warmth of the broth soothed the ache allowing her to focus on other things.

Sauntage was kneeling next to her holding a crude bowl in his left hand while he spooned the soup into her parted lips. His eyes appeared to be puffy as he intently focused on her mouth. As he brought the spoon to her lips his own mouth opened a bit.

After a few bites Maureen held up her hand for a break. Taking a deep breath she said, "I need a minute."

With a nod he pulled the bowl back so that he could sit more comfortably. "Sure. How's the pain?"

"I'll live." She gave him a lopsided grimace and then looked closely at his face. "Is there something wrong? Your eyes are all red and puffy."

He leaned forward with her dinner once again as he replied, "Yeah, I'm fine. No, really I mean it. After you went to sleep I started thinking about what happened. Mo, I know what I saw and there is no way that horse touched you. And I believe you did get pushed out the way." Sauntage pulled the bowl back to his lap as he said with conviction, "By an angel. He's real, Mo. God's real!"

"How can you be so sure?" There was no sarcasm in her voice, but there was doubt.

Pressing his lips together for a moment he then answered, "Because of what happened with that storm. Before I saw this stand of trees I was asking myself what we were going to do. I simply didn't have an answer so I found myself asking if there was a God out there like the one in the Bible then help us. Now before you start just hear me out. What better explanation do I have that we came to this place just moments after I asked for help? And how else can it be that you weren't crushed under Jeurku's feet? When I asked this God of Abraham, Isaac and Jacob for help finding us food earlier today I came across a mule deer. Maureen, I haven't seen any deer since we arrived in Liguesis, let alone one that stood still long enough for me to ready my makeshift spear." A sigh left him as he leaned forward with the spoon. "That's all I can tell you other than I just know He's real, deep down in my gut, I know God is real."

It was quiet as he finished his passionate response and she swallowed more soup. With her hand she asked him to hold off the soup for a moment while she asked, "He has a lot of rules and regulations. How are you ever going to figure them all out on your own? Some of those people in the Bible died because they didn't follow them correctly. If you say you believe in Him doesn't that mean you have to do what He says?"

"It says in Psalms that, 'The Lord is merciful and gracious, slow to anger and abounding in steadfast love.' If I can learn His rules quickly enough maybe I won't wear out His patience." He allowed her to nod but then pressed the spoon to her lips. "Come on you need to finish this soup and get some more rest. Maybe tomorrow you'll be able to sit by the fire for a bit." By the time he had managed to feed her the last of the soup her eyelids closed of their own accord.

Moving the next morning was not as bad as she had expected. Of course there was pain and throbbing in her face, but the rest of her body was feeling so much better that it hardly mattered. Overcast skies muted the light so that her eyes were not bothered as she sat on a log near the fire pit. Sauntage encouraged her to stay where she was for some time until they knew she would not get dizzy.

After sitting still for nearly an hour she got to her feet to wander around their campsite. Most of the trees bore some mark of their presence which saddened her. A few had been brought completely down while others had large gaping scars along the lower portion of their trunks.

Jeurku lifted his head to look at her as she drew closer. His warm chocolate eyes seemed to be offering an apology as he gazed at her steadily. With half a smile she reached out to rub his velvety nose. "You felt it too, didn't you, Boy?" She whispered softly. "What do you make of it? Do you think it was a ghost or perhaps an angel?" Shaking her head with a sigh Maureen admitted to him, "I'm not sure what to think."

As soon as she finished speaking he turned back to the grass near his hooves and left her to her thoughts. There were several things to consider. While she wanted to trust in the God described in the Bible, she was not sure she wanted to live up to His standard even if she thought some day she could; which honestly she did not.

Who could? Maureen thought quietly to herself. It would be impossible to remember all the rules they had been reading over the last few days. Let alone follow them. Why would a God set up a kingdom that His own rules would keep people from living in it?

Confusion knit her forehead in light creases as she turned back towards the fire pit to observe Sauntage. His dark head was bent over the Bible in his lap. He had been reading it for over an hour. There was a longing in her heart to have the same confidence that her husband now had. Once her boys were returned to her safely, then it would be easier to believe she decided.

# Chapter Ten

At her insistence they broke camp the next morning. According to Sauntage's calculations they were only three days hard riding from Shargaunal. She was more than anxious to reach her sons. It had now been three weeks since they had been kidnapped.

Maureen was apprehensive about riding once more. Outside of the jarring to her tender cheek she really had no desire to face the pain in her legs. Sauntage must have sensed her thoughts as they prepared to move out because he patted her left leg resting in the stirrup.

While he swung up on Dueby's back he looked back at her with a reassuring smile. "It won't be nearly so bad this time, Darling."

"Really?" She asked in disbelief with her eyebrows lifted. They quickly returned to their normal position when she felt the pressure on her bruised eye.

"You might feel a bit achy tomorrow morning but your body ought to be used to it now." He gave his full attention to Dueby and led the way out of the wide stand of trees.

Soon they were surrounded by the sea of grass. To distract herself from the discomfort she now felt in her face, Maureen began to ask more questions about Liguesis and her husband's childhood.

For quite a long time he shared story after story with her. When they stopped to rest he finally had to ask, "Why does this matter so much to you?" His words were not meant to be harsh but his tone said otherwise.

"If I don't put my mind on something else I'll go crazy thinking about Charlie, Ryan and Drew." She snapped at him and then went on snidely. "I learned three weeks ago that the man I married doesn't even exist! Excuse me for wanting to figure out who it was I did marry!" Getting to her feet Maureen stalked over to Jeurku and jerked his picket line from the ground.

The two of them walked in an easterly direction for more than fifteen minutes before she heard hooves pounding up behind her. With a great deal of will power she kept her back ramrod straight and refused to turn around no matter how much she wanted to do just that. Her husband's pace was so fast that she barely had time to think before the horse stopped and he dismounted several feet behind her.

"Maureen, please, forgive me." Sauntage said softly as he started walking next to her.

From a side long glance she could see that his eyes were red. It was not like him to cry so she was a little taken aback by the traces of moisture in his dark lashes. "Look, we're both tired and cranky..." She started to sigh but he cut her off.

"No, it has very little to do with that. For the last seventeen years I have buried most of my thoughts and memories of this land. My family is just a matter of days from here and they won't speak to me. All of your questions are bringing up things from the past that have long been buried." His voice trailed off momentarily and then he went on to say, "I think I knew deep down as soon as I saw that medallion that this would be my last trip here."

"But, what about your family?" Maureen gasped coming to a dead stop.

Sauntage did not halt as he responded, "Each time I go through The Gateway I put my family at risk. All of it. Watching you make this journey has made me really see how dangerous it is and how selfish I have been to all of you all these years." Finally, he paused to look back at her and he prepared to say something but his eyes rounded as his jaw lowered.

"Sau? What's the matter?" She asked glancing back over her shoulder. A choked cry broke off all thoughts as she observed a large cloud of dust billowing towards them from the west.

"Hurry!" He shouted as he bent to lace his fingers for her foot. "Come on! Go!"

No sooner had she managed to get her leg over the saddle when she heard a loud crack. Jeurku bolted faster than she thought possible from a complete standstill. She was grateful for that post in front of her once more because without it she knew she would have been thrown on the ground. There was a fleeting thought that she needed to learn what it was called.

Seconds later her husband was riding past her yelling at her to go faster. "That's the kings army. We can't let them spot us."

"How do you know?" She cried.

"Size of the cloud." He screamed back at her. "Too small for a storm. Too big for a hunting party. Have to find a place to hide."

His words barely reached her but Maureen got the gist of his message. They were in trouble. The horses must have sensed the impending danger because they galloped faster than she believed possible. With this speed came wind that stung her eyes and caused her bonnet to slip back on her head. Reaching up with her left hand she tried to pull it into place. Instead her fingers caught the lace at the top of her head loosening it.

When she brought her hand back down to grab the saddle Maureen felt the tie slide down over her face. It was not long before the leather strap was around her neck and the rest of the bonnet flapped against her back. The air blowing through her hair felt good at first but once she followed her husband's example of turning to look behind him, the tangled coils began to stick to her sweaty face.

After racing along for what seemed like an eternity Maureen could no longer feel her feet or hands. She had been using them to hold the saddle and Jeurku so tightly that all of the blood had rushed to other parts of her body. Breathing became difficult as well because every time her bottom hit the saddle all of the air was forced from her lungs and there was never time to draw enough oxygen to satisfy them.

Just when she thought this nightmare could not get any worse Maureen noticed the same kind of cloud rushing at them from the east. This one was not nearly so big, but she knew in her gut what it meant. They were trapped!

Panic seized her when she saw Sauntage begin to ease the pace of Dueby. What were they going to do? There was nowhere for them to hide. If they tried to run north or south there was not enough time to get out of sight. Her eyes darted from one direction to the other watching the horizons quickly changing color.

Tears slipped silently down her face; to be so close to reaching her sons and not make it. Suddenly, Sauntage stopped his horse and slid from his back. As her husband's knees dropped to the ground, Maureen lifted her face to the sky crying softly, "Oh, God, if you are up there in the heavens...please help us."

She then dragged her right leg over Jeurku's back and flopped to the grass at his feet. With her eyes closed and her face in the dirt she sobbed mindlessly. There was no more thought just pain. It was not long before a thunderous sound built all around them. Sauntage drew close to her and wrapped his body over hers in an effort to protect her from whatever might happen.

Time ceased to pass at a normal rate. On one hand it seemed to go on for an eternity with the continuous pounding of the king's army while on the other it rushed ahead as the noise grew louder by the second. In her ear Maureen heard her husband's voice, "I love you, Beautiful Carkna Slayer. Always know that I love you."

There was no time for her to respond because a dozen other men began shouting around them. The weight of her husband had no sooner left her than she was yanked to her feet by several hands. So many of the men were talking at once that the only words she was able to make out were, "We have them over here."

A few moments went by before her eyes adjusted to the sunlight once more. When she was able to see Maureen was startled by the silver helmets surrounding her. Sauntage was no longer in her line of sight but she knew he was only a few yards away because of a cluster of helmets to her left.

Behind the silver brace that stretched down each nose she saw triumphant dark eyes. They were celebrating a victory. Their movements were noisy due to the dingy metal plates covering their chests, arms and upper legs. This group of men looked like something right out of a history book.

She was glad to have the thick leather covering her arms because she was sure that the sharp edges of the gauntlets these men were wearing would have cut her flesh to ribbons. There were several questions being shouted at her by all of them. As each one spoke he leaned close to her face. From behind her Maureen felt a shove which forced her into the chest plate of the man directly in front of her. That man then pushed her back and slightly to her left.

For quite some time this went on with her growing disoriented and dizzy. Between the noise of their voices and armor she heard very little else. And with the constant motion they were forcing on her she could not see much either. Finally, her legs could no longer hold her up and she collapsed onto the ground. As she tried to hold her position on her hands and knees Maureen could feel her insides churning.

When she began to wretch the circle loosened around her briefly. It quickly tightened again when she was finished and they picked her up to move her to a different spot.

Through the knot of helmets around her she could see that Sauntage was suffering much the same fate. The group of men shoving her husband back and forth was much larger than the one dragging her. Along with the added numbers came more punishment. These men were severe.

Sauntage was not simply pushed into the metal plates of the soldiers circled about him. He was being thrown to the ground and then kicked by at least four men before others picked him up only to throw him down once again. She could not see his face but Maureen was sure it had to be a bloody mess. A choked cry left her as she watched this happening, "No!"

It was then that she began to realize just how many men had captured them. There were a dozen or so with her, at least twice that was surrounding Sauntage, and in a wide circle around all of them stood another group of men with their backs turned to them. These men held a variety of weapons and shields as they kept look out for a possible ambush.

Her guards were quieter now allowing her to hear and comprehend some of the things being shouted at Sauntage. "Traitor!" "Betrayer!" "Rebel!" "Enemy to the King!" Though he was never given the chance to respond to the charges Maureen doubted that he would have said anything anyway.

The gaps in the men allowing her to see him quickly closed. With the knowledge that there was nothing she could do for either of them she tried to grasp what the bigger picture was. What was going to happen to them? Were they to be tortured to death?

Nothing new was clear to her except there appeared to be another group of smaller men outside the line facing away from them. This group was apparently in charge of the horses belonging to the other men. It took her only a moment to realize that these were not really smaller men, but boys; most of them no larger than Charlie or Drew.

An excited shout from the outer circle caused all of the men to cease movement. As she turned her gaze to the west along with everyone else Maureen could not see very much. Silver helmets swayed back and forth as all of them sought to see what was happening. All she was able to see was the ever widening band of dust getting closer to them. She was, however, able to hear the familiar thunder drawing near.

With the halt in action she was able to get a brief look at the back of her husband's head. Pride rose up in her as she saw how straight and tall he stood amongst his accusers. Though he was not struggling against them she knew that they had not broken him.

More shouts were heard a few minutes later. This time they were coming from the riders approaching at breakneck speed. From that point on Maureen could not tell what was going on because so many things were yelled back and forth.

Suddenly, arms grabbed at her from behind to drag her further from Sauntage. Men in the outer circle slowly separated to form a horseshoe shape. Once a large enough gap had been created; the men all dropped to one knee.

When the soldiers went down she could feel her breath catch and eyes widen. There could easily have been a thousand or more men on horses now swarming in towards them. Only she and Sauntage were left standing so she kept flicking her eyes to his back in an effort to know what to do. He never moved a muscle. His hands were at his side and feet were planted shoulder width apart.

Large green flags came riding into view to announce the arrival of the king. Still Sauntage kept standing. Horns pierced the air bringing near silence to the area. Maureen licked her lips nervously. Why was Sauntage just standing there? Should he not at least bow down to the king as a sign of loyalty?

Through the narrow space between the colorful banners a single man rode on a magnificent horse. Two men rode behind him though not closely. His head was covered as his men were though his helmet had a solid piece of metal that wrapped under his chin. He scanned the field of his men until he saw the two prisoners standing boldly.

In one smooth gesture the chin plate came off and the silver covering was removed from his head. As soon as the eyes of the two men met, Sauntage slowly bowed his head and then lowered his knee to the ground.

Maureen was quick to follow her husband's example so she missed seeing what was going on around her for a little while. She heard the rattle of the armor as the men got to their feet. Some of them seemed to be moving away from her. A few quiet conversations went over her head as the soldiers went to gather their horses.

"Rise!" Was shouted in a loud booming voice some distance from her.

Afraid of what the consequences might be if she did not obey, Maureen rose to her feet. Almost all of the men that had been guarding them were now past the wide circle of men still facing outward for protection. Lifting her gaze cautiously toward the voice she stared in confusion and amazement.

Before she had time to react to what she saw there was a loud commotion coming from behind the flags. A single rider came pounding into the open area causing all of the soldiers to drop to one knee once more. Long flowing robes were swept out of the way as a tall woman dismounted. Deep green fabric billowed all around her as she stamped towards the two men in the middle of the field.

With a clenched jaw the king ground out loudly, "Mo! I told you I would handle this."

Resemblance between these men was astounding. It took Maureen several moments to add everything together in her mind. When she did she screeched at Sauntage, "You're a prince!"

He said nothing as he looked over his shoulder at her and then nodded.

Her astonishment was so great that Maureen did not notice the lightning fast movements of the queen. All she could do was gape at her husband. Somehow she ended up married to a prince. How was that possible? This was some wild dream. It had to be. When she realized that someone was standing right in front of her it was too late to prepare for the shout directed at her.

"Where is he? The boy with the red hair what have you done with him?" Using the palm of her hand the green clad queen indicated the boy's height.

"Ryan! You know Ryan? Please tell me he is all right..." In her excitement Maureen's brain had not registered everything happening so she had to gasp when she realized loudly, "You speak English!" No sooner had the words left her mouth than a strong leather clad hand took hold of her throat. Panic rounded her eyes as she gazed into the piercing eyes of the queen.

"I'll only ask you once more. Where is the boy?" If she was affected by the tears of the woman at her mercy she did not show it. Although she loosened her hold a bit it was only enough to allow air to pass over the redhead's vocal chords.

"Please, Your Highness, my sons have been kidnapped. We're trying to find them." Out of the corner of her eye Maureen saw Sauntage take several steps towards them with confusion knitting his forehead.

"Mother? How do you know English?" He asked at the same time six guards shouted at him to stop moving and pointed their weapons at him.

For a few moments Maureen did her best to answer the queen, but between the guards yelling and Sauntage badgering his mother it was too much. Words were flying around her so rapidly that she was lost as to what was happening. She was growing concerned about the soldiers that were slowly drawing close to them because their fingers were tensing and flexing on the weapons in their hands. These men were more than ready to defend their queen.

"Enough!" Bellowed the king.

Silence dropped over the field like a lead blanket. No one dared to defy the king; except the queen.

After releasing her hold on Maureen the queen marched with as long of a stride as her skirts and robe would allow; to stand before her husband with her hands on her hips. Quickly the two of them exchanged words and his hand came to rest gently on her shoulders.

As soon as they finished a few orders were issued in a much quieter tone that Maureen was not able to hear. All she knew was that men took hold of her arms behind her back and walked her to the far side of the guarded field. She was forced to turn her back to the activity and wait for whatever was to happen next. After a couple of attempts to locate Sauntage she had to give up because each time she moved her head a soldier poked her in the back or neck.

Time was hard to judge because of the number of clouds covering the sun. The activity behind her was difficult to grasp as well. There seemed to be a lot of horses coming and going at a regular interval, but they were not in a rush. Lots of pounding could be heard as well as some clanking. Not many words were spoken loud enough to understand.

This meant that Maureen was completely alone with her thoughts. Now that she had to absorb the reality that her husband was the son of a king, she considered several aspects of their life together. Sauntage had traded the chance to fill his father's position as king for the job of a garbage collector!

At first she was puzzled by this because as far as she had seen, other than technology, earth did not have any more to offer than this world. Then tears rushed into her eyes and her chest began to ache. A sob rose so suddenly that the guards all around her were visibly startled. Her knees buckled underneath her as her hands covered her face. It was her. He had exchanged his nobility for a life of menial labor for her.

No sooner had her knees touched the ground than two pair of hands lifted her carefully off the ground. Gently she was set on her feet and then she was told to walk. As she turned to comply with their instructions Maureen felt her head spinning. It was when two ungloved hands wrapped around the upper part of her arm that she realized that the guards were no longer dragging her along.

In fact she suddenly noticed that no one was walking directly in front of her. This meant that she was able to see a large tent made of a dingy gray material standing in the center of what was now a campsite. It was to this tent she was being directed.

With trembling over what she would meet inside Maureen tried to wipe the moisture from beneath her eyes, drew up her shoulders and took a deep breath. She had done nothing wrong except marry a man these people considered an enemy. If she met them with strength and confidence perhaps they would see that.

There appeared to be more than one door to this tent. When she approached the narrow opening she saw that it was not square as she had first thought, but rather two rectangles adjacent to each other in the shape of a tee. Four guards stood at the entrance with their tall spears next to them. One of them held up his hand for her to halt while another guard entered the tent.

Moments later that soldier came back with a nod and then she felt a gentle prod with a hand in the middle of her back. Licking her lips and wiping the rest of the moisture from her face with her fingertips, Maureen prepared to meet her fate. It was in the middle of the doorway that it occurred to her that she was facing her in-laws too. Her heart pounded even harder.

Once the tent material was over her head her eyes could make out nothing so she stopped moving. There were some dark shadows a few feet away but it was difficult to determine what things were. Straight ahead of her the fabric parted allowing daylight to fill the tent, or at least this part of it anyway. To her right was a long curtain wall that she knew from the outer dimensions of the temporary structure was not outer wall of the tent. The doorways appeared to be on the longer walls of the room in which she was standing.

"Come in." Was spoken from her left side in English.

Slowly Maureen stepped forward realizing for the first time that Sauntage was the one who had come through the other door. In the light their eyes met and she saw him close his eyelids for a long apologetic blink. There was no time for her to respond for suddenly the king was standing directly in front of her.

His intense, dark eyes stared at her as he spoke, "This interrogation will be simple. I will ask questions which my Lady, Queen Modeanna will translate and you will answer with all respect." Within these walls his voice was much quieter and reminded her of Sauntage, but from years of giving orders it had a gravely quality to it.

When the queen stepped closer he moved to stand at Maureen's side. Her face was tense as though this were the last thing she wanted to do. In a steady voice she repeated the king's words and then added, "Do you understand?"

"Yes, Your Highness, I understand." Maureen dipped her head slightly and then added quickly in Liguesian, "But that shouldn't be necessary because I can understand and speak your language if it is slow enough."

This seemed to upset the king momentarily but he quickly

recovered to ask, "What is your name?"

"Maureen Vadelum, Sire." She saw the queen's eyes flare before she looked on her son for confirmation. Out of the corner of her eye she noted the dip of her husband's chin.

"By what means did your husband put that bruise on your face?" There was barely controlled rage boiling in his near black eyes.

A loud gasp drew her back straighter and her jaw lowered without sound for several seconds. "Sauntage has never hurt me like that! I fell on a tree root during a thunderstorm. And he's the one that took care of me." All three of them were clearly shocked by her passionate response.

After a brief silence the king recovered enough to ask, "Where are you from, Maureen?"

To this she did not know how to respond so she glanced at her husband.

"Hide nothing." Sauntage responded with a sad sigh of resignation.

"I am from earth and I live in a place called The United States."

The queen stepped closer to ask, "What city and state do you live in?"

As she answered the question Maureen saw that the queen had removed her outer robe and now stood in a long flowing gown of deep jewel green. Her eyes were lighter in color than she had expected with the black hair only sprinkled with gray. This explained Sauntage and Ryan's eye color. They had this beautiful woman's eyes.

"How long have you been in Liguesis?" Came the kings voice once more.

"About three weeks." Hair on the back of her neck lifted as she heard an eerie guttural sound from the room behind them. She turned towards the sound of Sauntage's voice to listen as he quietly spoke.

"That's an aragaff. It won't hurt you; remember I told he was a symbol of my family." His brows lifted with encouragement for her to relax.

There was light glare in her eyes as she hissed, "Yes, you did. But you failed to mention that it was a pet or who your family was. What else have you left out, Prince Sau?"

A hearty chuckle from the king drew everyone's attention. "What is the old saying you brought with you, Modeanna? 'The apple doesn't fall far from the tree.'"

Color rose in the queen's face as a smile came to her lips. "I don't suppose there's any denying it now."

"No, my dear, there isn't. At least not to these two. You quite boldly proclaimed to them that you are of earth." With humor still in his eyes he turned to his son, "Do you think you are the only Liguesian to see the virtues of earth?"

Still reeling from this revelation Sauntage stammered, "I-I h-had th-thought so until Mother shouted at Maureen in English. At least the first in many generations."

"Well, you aren't. For now we'll leave it at that. We have other matters to discuss before I decide what to do with you." As he spoke the humor dropped from his eyes and he turned to Maureen. "What is your purpose for coming here? And how many times have you come here without our knowledge?"

"Sire, I didn't even know Liguesis existed until three weeks ago. I have never been here before. Our sons disappeared on their way home from school. A medallion with an aragaff on it was found outside our home. Whatever was written on the backside led Sauntage to believe the boys were brought here."

Heat smoldered in the king's eyes as he slowly stalked to his son. "Do you think me to be naïve? Or stupid? How many times have you traveled between worlds? And how many things have you brought here; things that could forever change the face of Liguesis?"

"You are the wisest man I have ever known, Father. It is I that is now proven beyond a shadow of a doubt to be without intelligence. I have come through The Gateway once a year since last you saw me. Three days is the longest I have ever remained except this journey to locate our sons. A pouch made on earth with a few things of earth in it is all I carried past The Gateway, besides my Fair Lady Maureen. She is no threat to our land, Father. Only to those who stand in her way of her children."

It was silent for a few seconds before the king bellowed towards the doorway next to Sauntage, "Bring me their things!"

Instantly, five guards came into the tent with the leather pouches and backpack. Once they had been placed on the ground at the king's feet he silently dismissed them. When the four of them were alone he nodded to Maureen saying, "Show me what you brought here."

Kneeling in front of the bag she pulled the zipper to open it. This bag had not been used much since they had left the Trigguard farm so it was nearly empty. First she pulled out the diamond pendant that had belonged to her mother. It had been the only thing of value the woman owned at the time of her death. With trembling fingers she held it up for the king to see.

He took the fine chain in his large hands to study it closely. "A lovely trinket." An appreciative nod went along with his widened eyes as he handed it to his wife.

"This is very valuable, Sauntago. It is a usually something a man gives to his wife after many years of marriage if he can afford it." Her eyes darted to her son and then to Maureen.

"Yes, Your Highness, it was. My Father gave that necklace to my Mother for their twenty-fifth wedding anniversary." As she watched the gold encased diamond swing gently from the queen's fingertips she wondered if she would ever see it again. Before she allowed herself to become too melancholy over the loss Maureen reached into the bag for the diary.

When she held the small book out she had to wonder why she had brought it with her. Years had passed since she had added anything to it and neither of them had even looked at it after it had been packed. An almost imperceptible lift to her shoulders caught the king's attention as he took it from her.

"A diary." Was the simple reaction from the queen when she saw the letters pressed into the hard cover. "It's a place to write private things."

"Can you still read English?" Sauntago asked his wife holding the book out to her.

"Given enough time yes I could. But I fear we do not have that luxury." She replied firmly passing it back to him.

His first reaction was a loud heavy sigh. "Of course you are right." Then he gazed at Maureen sternly as he asked, "Is there more in that pouch?"

"Oh, yes Sire there is just one more thing. It's a Bible; a book of stories about..."

"The Creator of the universe." Sauntage interjected firmly as his wife handed it over to his parents. "Please, Father, other than the bag could she keep these things? There is nothing amongst them that would threaten Liguesis in anyway. It's all she has left of earth right now." He was uncertain how his plea was received because his mother reached for the leather bound volume with moisture gathering in her eyes.

"Earth's record of Ewaris. My Grandmother had a Bible when I was a little girl. I went to church with her sometimes when we visited her." She took the Bible from her husband's large hands and held it reverently. A soft smile lit her face as memories obviously trailed through her mind. The pages fluttered passed her fingertips in rapid succession.

Suddenly, something between the pages brought her smile to an end. There was a look of horror in her eyes as she spread the covers apart laying the book into two even stacks. From between the pages she lifted a four inch by six inch piece of thick paper. "It's him!" She cried so loudly that the guards from both doorways came rushing into the tent with their spears ready.

They backed out when they saw the king's hand wave to them that all was well.

"Sauntago, it's the boy from my dreams." She held out the paper to her confused husband. "This is a photograph. A painting of sorts from a tool called a camera."

It was clear that the king had never seen anything like a picture. After gaping at it for a long moment he flipped the paper over to look at the back and then turned it back to the front. His fingertips traced along the faces as if he expected the images to move. "So real."

"Those are your Grandsons, Father." Sauntage said softly. "Ryan, Charles, and Andrew are..."

"Where is he, Sauntage? This one with the red hair." Queen Modeanna snatched the picture from the king and held it up so that her son could see at whom she was pointing.

"We don't know for sure." He replied with anguish. "Our story is long and all of it is yours to hear, but I beg you for a bit of food for

Maureen. She is not responsible for any of this."

With narrowed eyes the queen stepped around Maureen and then went to stand before her son. "For three weeks I have woken up because this little boy has entered my dreams. Until I know of him there will be nothing."

Maureen came to her feet behind the taller queen. In an excited voice she answered, "His name is Ryan and he is eight. He loves to build things with blocks and play with toys. School work is not his favorite thing but he is a pretty good student." Tears began to flow as her chin trembled. "Please, tell me what you have seen in your dreams."

Reluctantly, the older woman turned away from them and took a few steps. It was clear from the downward cast of her face that she was trying to decide how to answer. When she finally spoke her words were quiet and difficult to hear, "There is not much to tell I'm afraid. Every time the dream is pretty much the same. He is frightened and seems to be trapped in a cave. At the beginning of the dream he is crying out for help and there are other voices with him but I can see no one else. Then he becomes hoarse; his mouth opens but no sound is made. His hand goes to his throat as he starts to cough violently. After a bit he falls to the ground and I wake up." A shiver went up her spine as the images went through her mind. "The whole thing is terrible because I can't tell whether he is alive or not."

As she listened to the queen's dream, Maureen felt her breathing halt and her stomach tighten painfully. What else could it mean other than Ryan was seriously ill or even dead? And what of the older boys? Without conscious thought she walked into her husband's chest with loud sobs escaping.

Sauntage enfolded her tightly realizing that her strength was quickly fading. His own vision was disrupted at the moment as well as his ability to think clearly. The idea that the boys might have taken ill had never seriously crossed his mind. To keep the two of them from falling to the ground he slowly lowered his knees as he tenderly pulled her with him. He had no idea how long they sat in the middle of the tent. All that registered fully was the fact that after all of her effort and willingness to do all that was necessary he had failed her. The promise he made to her about returning their sons was beyond his grasp. "Oh, Mo, I'm so sorry. I've failed you once again."

In the back of her mind outside of her overwhelming grief she heard the sound of her husband's voice. Other noises registered after that but she did not really make any effort to understand them. Leaning into Sauntage's chest she found a small seed of hope growing. Against many odds they were still alive. Why could it not be the same for three strong boys? The queen had terrible dreams that did not necessarily make them true. Suddenly, she felt her lips moving to form the words, "God in heaven save us. You're the only one who can."

"Amen." He agreed firmly as he sensed her wave of grief had for the moment passed.

With slow deep breaths Maureen pulled back from his arms dragging her face across the top of her dark leather shirt. She felt his warm hands cover her cheeks and gently brush away the moisture. Their eyes met briefly and there was a definite rise in her confidence.

"Get up!" Barked the king.

In quick jerky motions the two of them rose to their full height. As they faced the king Maureen saw that a makeshift table had been placed towards the opposite end of the tent. On the other side of the low table were two wooden chairs that were intricately carved. So they were standing in a traveling throne room of sorts.

"Our time here is going to be short. You will be allowed to dine quickly as we hear your 'story'." He added sarcastic stress to his voice as he pointed to the small round table.

Two short logs were set on end for extra chairs and four matching place settings surrounded a platter with bread and roasted meat. Her breath suddenly caught in her throat as she stared at the lengths to which the king had gone in order to serve them. How could she explain to him that she appreciated the gesture but would rather get on with their sentencing? The last thing she wanted to do was tip the balance out of their favor.

"I know how very difficult it is, Maureen, but as I was always reminded, you must eat to keep your strength." There was a note of anger in the queen's voice as she sat in one of the carved seats. "In my grief over the loss of my eldest son, I allowed many meals to pass by me."

Wonder rounded her mouth and eyes as she stared at her husband's mother. She did understand. With a tiny nod she watched the flash of rage cross the older woman's face. It quickly fell away revealing the torn heart of the mother inside.

"Why did you betray us? How could you do this to us!" Flared Modeanna suddenly.

Before Sauntage could respond, his father laid a gentle hand on her shoulders as he sat next to her. "All in good time, Modeanna, we need to eat so that we can keep going."

"No, Father. I wish to answer Mother's questions. She has waited long enough to hear them." Using his hands he indicated that he did not want them to wait for him to eat, he continued, "When I discovered the writings about The Gateway I was overcome with boyish curiosity. For three years I looked for every bit of information I could find. After spending all that time I was determined to see it for myself, but I didn't say anything because I was afraid you would tell me I was wasting my time."

A heavy sigh left the king as his left eyebrow lifted. "You are right about that. I would not have allowed it."

"I made a number of trips to earth for nearly three years. Each time you were called away..."

"But how could you choose to leave your homeland and not at least leave a note?" Modeanna cried harshly before she cut a piece of stubborn meat with vengeance.

"Honestly, I never intended to stay on earth. Truthfully, I got lazy and made a mistake. The mountains and trees were so beautiful I got caught up in exploring them. Time got away from me and I fell asleep. Hunters found me, Mother, and to keep Liguesis safe I had to go with them. At first I was afraid these men would keep me prisoner, but they didn't. They took me to a hospital where I was looked after for a few days. Nothing could have prepared me for how to handle those people. Countless questions and tests. All I kept thinking about was how to keep them from finding out the truth. These men had powerful tools just for medicine I couldn't imagine what their armies might have.

"One group of doctors after another came to see me and I was shuffled from one hospital to another." He paused to gaze at Maureen with a tender smile and then he reached out to brush her bruised cheek with the back of his hand. "That was how I came face to face with the other half of my heart, Father. My Fair Lady Maureen came in to rescue me from my ignorance of earth."

The king leaned over the table to glare at his son, "But Fair Lady Maureen has said she learned of our land three weeks ago. How do you explain that?"

Pressing her lips tightly together Maureen put her bread back on her plate. With memories of that night running through her mind, she responded tersely, "Sauntage lied to me, Sire. He pretended to remember nothing about his past and wouldn't have said anything except for the boys disappearing."

"If he said nothing to you or your sons how could they possibly end up here?" His dark eyes drilled into her green ones waiting for her to crack.

"Several weeks after I met Maureen I had the chance to go back under the mountains to come home. I was so excited to tell you that I had met the lady of my dreams..."

"Then why didn't you?" Modeanna exclaimed loudly. "All I ever longed to know was whether or not you were alive! Instead I learn my son is a traitor to all that I raised him to be!"

Reluctantly, Sauntage answered, "Because on my way to see you I met with the one person that knew of my ventures. I was told how angry you were with me and thought it wise to let my messages be delivered by another's hand until you could forgive me."

"What messages?" Sauntago looked at him with a side long view which allowed him to see the puzzled disbelief in his wife as well. "We've had no word from you these seventeen years and only reports of your escapades over the last eight years."

"Each year I have lied to Maureen and the boys about going fishing for a week. Instead I have met my messenger and given him a letter for you which is then returned to me unopened the next year."

"Who is this messenger? I would have him brought here to speak on this matter!" Modeanna came to her feet in such a rage that the plates rattled and cups wobbled.

"Tagurah." Was all Sauntage could manage to choke past the tightening of his throat. He hated the thought of hurting his family more than he already had.

Like lightning the queen drew back her open hand and then threw it against Sauntage's face. "How dare you malign the name of my faithful son?"

Guards came rushing in from both entries ready to aid their queen. What they saw made it difficult not to smile. One of the prisoners was on the ground with his hand pressed to his left cheek. The other was frozen in fear with a fork full of meat halfway to her open mouth.

"Take them back to the outer ring and hold them separately. I want no chance for conversation between them. When we move out they will be bound on bare horseback until further notice. Do not allow them a chance to escape." His angry tones filled the tent and matched the deep red color flooding his face.

Maureen's fork clattered to the plate as she was roughly dragged from her log seat. While her eyes were still adjusting to the brighter sky she heard one of the two men behind her bark out orders to take her. Immediately, two more soldiers were at her sides with some kind of rope to make sure she could not escape.

For one hour she stood in the midst of six armored soldiers with her hands tied behind her back. Her legs had begun to hurt almost instantly from the physical strain she had endured earlier that day. At first she was grateful for it because she could not help but think things could have ended up much worse.

About the time that she was tempted to forget this fact Maureen received the command to move. With awkward steps she was guided to Jeurku. He was in fact without his saddle, but had a bridle for the guards to hold as they moved. Instead of using one of their hands to mount as she expected Maureen was hoisted roughly onto his back.

Once she was in place the rope around her wrists was untied and then re-tied in front of her. It was her guess that they did this to give her a way to hold on to the horse. Riding was still so new to her that she was nervous about doing it this way.

Much to her relief when they moved out from the camp it was at a very slow pace. Everyone was exhausted from the long hard ride earlier. Not much sound other than the horse's hooves could be heard above the clanking metal. For all intents and purposes she was alone.

A short time after their journey had been underway she turned to look back. Her jaw lowered in amazement at the number of riders following in her wake. She was by no means at the head of this traveling mass. This army was huge!

Sauntage was nowhere in sight nor were his parents. Not that she was really expecting to see any of them for the time being, but she had hoped. It would have been nice to know what was likely to happen to them.

As they plodded along the afternoon sun heated the large moving mass unmercifully. Maureen had to adjust her bonnet many times because she could not put it on properly with her wrists bound so tightly.

Hours later they finally stopped moving. That did not mean she was allowed to leave Jeurku's back, however. From the added height of his back she watched as a massive encampment was quickly created. The process had been repeated by this group so many times that it moved along like a well oiled machine. Horse after horse ridden by the youngest among them brought in pieces of the king's tent as well as other similar structures. As the parts were delivered several strong men assembled them rapidly. Looking around her she was also able to see groups of boys collecting firewood, caring for the tired horses and drawing buckets of water from a nearby river.

Without warning she was pulled from Jeurku's back and he was taken away for some much needed rest. A poke in the middle of her back told her it was time to walk forward. Wordlessly she was led to a remote area of this traveling city. The wide ring of guards was in place around three dozen small tents that were spread widely apart. Some of the tents had holes in the center of their tops which confused her until she saw ribbons of curling smoke rising through one. These were cooking tents.

Here and there on the ground were soldiers that had apparently finished their duties and were lying down for much needed rest. They had slipped off their armor to be more comfortable. Carefully she had to step around a few of these men.

When they stopped walking she looked around for the closest tent and group of sleeping men. More than fifty feet separated them from her.

There was a thick metal post nearby to which the soldier on her left directed her. Several inches off the ground there was a heavy metal chain attached to the post. Before she knew it Maureen felt a cold metal clamp wrap around her left ankle and then as soon as the rope was removed another went around her left wrist.

By the time she grasped her situation she had been left alone. A sad, weary and frustrated sigh left her as she looked around her. Her short experience with these men told her that it would do no good to shout for attention. They were trained to ignore her because she was a prisoner.

Even though she had no intention of trying to escape Maureen closely examined the post and chains holding her in place. It may have had a layer of rust just beginning to form but the post was very strong. The same, she soon observed, could be said for the chains at her foot and arm.

After a few minutes of walking in small circles around the post she finally sat on the grass she had trampled. Her back rested against the stake for a short while but soon grew too uncomfortable for her spine. She pulled her knees up to her chin so that she could lean forward to rest her chin on her knees.

It was not long before her thoughts turned to the dramatic turn her life had taken in just a few short hours. Technically she reasoned, with some disbelief, she was a princess imprisoned by her in-laws. This brought a smile to her lips because she felt it gave new meaning to the phrase 'being an outlaw with the in-laws'. Sighing sadly she wondered what was going to happen to them. Were they being dragged to a particular place for trial or execution? Was there some remote possibility that Tagurah was going to be found to be questioned?

Most importantly, she kept asking herself, what did this mean for the boys? Would they ever be able to free them now? Were they even alive after all this time? A tear traced slowly down her cheek.

"Maureen?" Said a voice in a soft whisper not far away.

She lifted her head only to realize that dusk had fallen and full darkness was only minutes away. With her eyes squinting in the darkness Maureen was able to make out the shape of the queen. Her eyes rounded and she quickly came to her feet to give an awkward bow. "Yes, Your Majesty?"

"Please, sit. I have some food for you and a blanket for the night." Carefully she set the items on the ground just inside the reach of the chains and then sat to face her prisoner.

"T-thank you, Your Highness." In shock she pulled the folded blanket closer only to discover the plate on top of it. It was difficult to make out what the food might be, but it smelled wonderful.

"Under the circumstances I know you probably aren't hungry, however, I urge you to eat. You will need the nourishment because our journey becomes harder for the next three days."

At first she only nodded and then it occurred to her that the queen probably could not see her movement in this fading light. "Thank you, Your Highness." The idea of eating in front of the queen made her feel awkward so she had decided to wait until she was alone.

"Go ahead and enjoy it while there is still warmth in it." As she watched Maureen take the plate into her hands she went on to say, "You really didn't know about my son's life here until a few weeks ago, did you?"

"No, Your Highness, I didn't." A sad note crept into her words as she picked up the fork she had discovered on the plate.

Modeanna waited politely to ask her next question. "Weren't you angry about it?"

"Furious. All those years he had lied to me." She stopped herself from thinking only about the night the boys disappeared and going on a mad ranting spree.

Though it could not be seen at this late hour, Modeanna frowned deeply. "But you are not angry now?"

"If I keep my thoughts on the moment he finally told me everything then yes I become angry. After all these weeks, however, I understand why he did it." It was hard to find the food on her plate she discovered as she moved the fork across the surface of her plate.

"And why do you believe Sauntage lied to you?" To keep warmer the queen changed her position to sit more like Maureen.

"Because he loves Liguesis almost as much as he loves me and the boys." She answered softly.

"Love?" The queen asked harshly. "What makes you think that

man knows anything about love? He turned his back on this land and scorned his family."

Tears suddenly rose in her eyes as she replied, "That man gave up the chance to lead this land to become a garbage collector to support me and our family..."

"And put a stake through the hearts of his Father and Mother." Modeanna sneered bitterly.

"Only he can answer for that. All I can tell you is that since we came through that Gateway he has been wrestling with himself about the way he has handled things. I think that is why he didn't tell me who his family was." It was as she spoke those words that the revelation fully came to her. He did not tell her that he was a prince because he was ashamed of himself and what he had done to his family.

"I will leave you to eat in peace now, Maureen." In one quick motion she was on her feet ready to leave.

Maureen was more than a bit awkward coming to her feet as she called softly, "Thank you, Your Highness." Although she was sure that the queen must have heard her there was no indication or reaction as she walked into the darkness.

"Maureen?"

A deep frown furrowed her brow as she sat.

"Maureen?" The voice repeated.

With a gasp of recognition she stumbled to her feet and tried to find the location of the voice as she acknowledged with a bow, "Yes, Sire."

"I thought perhaps you might need an extra blanket." His hands found hers in the blackness and turned over a bundle. "Be careful there is a plate on top."

A giggle escaped before she could stop it.

"What do you find so funny?" He demanded roughly.

Her lips rolled inward as she gained control of her laughter. "Please, Your Majesty, I meant no disrespect. But watch your step. I put the plate your wife brought me just inside my circle of reach." The loud rumbles from his chest startled her.

"I should have known she would have come here." Sauntago

sighed heavily and then said lightly, "For all of her toughness that woman has the softest of hearts."

"Sauntage told me she was not like other women in Liguesis." She recalled with lifted brows.

There was a moment of quiet before he slowly questioned, "I thought you said he had not told you about us."

Shaking her head Maureen clarified, "Oh, no, he told me lots of things about your family and life here in Liguesis. He even told me a bit of the history of your realm, Sire. What he didn't tell me was that he was the eldest son of the king and had been the next in line to take the throne."

"I see." He stated thoughtfully as he began to pace back and forth in front of her. "And what exactly did my son tell you?"

"That he was the second of four children, the eldest son. Sauntage explained a bit about the choosing of an occupation and how as the eldest son he was to take your place."

"Hmm. So he thinks to un-throne me after all these years and all the horrible things done in his name." There was a sneer on his lips and scowl in his eyes.

Because she was unable to make out the king's expression Maureen inserted boldly, "I don't know exactly what he is thinking, but I assure you it is not that. Yesterday morning he told me that this would be his last trip into Liguesis because he finally realized how dangerous the journey was. At the time I figured he meant that he would return to earth with me and our sons, but I think he knew we would be captured. Sauntage knows the punishment he deserves, Sire, and has decided to accept that responsibility." A moment later her own words sank into her heart causing a well to open behind her eyes.

"So now you would try to sway my judgment with your tears." The king snapped coldly.

After a deep breath she held her head high to respond, "If I plead for anything it is to see my sons safe. In regards to my husband I would ask two things. First, that he know I understand and forgive his secrets and second, that I could take his punishment for him."

"Do you think I could not order it so?" He asked sharply.

Her knees folded carefully beneath her as she looked up at him, "I have been told and now see that you are a man of great wisdom and are to be respected."

A wry grimace crossed his face as he admitted sarcastically, "And you, Maureen, are a lady of great persuasion not unlike your Mother-in-law."

With her jaw unhinged she heard him walk away into the night. It was a long time before she was able to settle her thoughts to sleep.

# Chapter Eleven

When she woke the next morning Maureen had trouble adjusting her eyes to the sunlight. She brought her hand to her mouth to stifle a yawn as she sat up and then stretched. A smile came to her lips as she saw that the two plates had been taken and in their place was an upturned log and a fresh plate. As she reached out to pick up the food she saw that a small leather pouch was sitting next to the log.

With curiosity she pulled the pouch closer. Wonder widened her eyes as she peeked inside to see the diary and Bible. Snatching the Bible she flipped through the pages to find the photograph of the boys. It was no longer tucked between the gold leaf pages. After searching the diary and bag Maureen discovered that the picture had not been given back nor had the diamond pendant.

A sad frown was on her lips as she leaned against the stake with her breakfast. In every direction there was bustling activity as soldiers ate and prepared to break camp. No one even looked her way which surprised and annoyed her because she really needed a few minutes of privacy.

Just before the call was given for the first group to mount a pair of soldiers came to help her. They said very little to each other and nothing at all to her. Instead of their voices these men worked with their hands and facial expressions.

Where she ended up being taken was not as secluded as she would have hoped. There was a tent to block all views from the rest of the camp except for the row of soldiers facing outwardly as camp protection. In order to be modest she had to sit as close to the side of the tent as possible and put her back to the men guarding her. That put the soldiers standing in the wide arc to her left side.

Maureen had just begun to lift her skirts when another guard came up behind her. This man spoke gruffly but was politely letting her know he was there and why. Gratefully she turned to say, "Thank you." Which she could tell surprised him very much because his movement to open a piece of fabric in his hands stalled.

"You're welcome..." He started to nod his head but then

awkwardly stopped.

Her cheeks lifted in a small smile. Now she knew at least part of the reason these men would not talk to her. They were unsure of how to address her. "My name is Maureen."

"Maureen." His lips tripped over the strange name and then he turned to go.

Twenty minutes later she had been placed on Jeurku's bare back as part of the first group of riders. Apparently they rode in separate battalions or regiments for safety and strategy. As the queen had warned the previous day this was a much faster pace. It was all she could do to hold the horse's mane and keep from bouncing off Jeurku. Thankfully the leather pouch she had been given had a long enough drawstring to go over her head to rest on her right shoulder and left hip.

Dust was soon billowing around her causing her eyes to water and her throat to feel chalky. Her cheek ached from the constant jarring motion. The thunderous sound of galloping horses soon made her ears throb painfully. Breathing began to get mixed with coughing fits. Because she did not have to worry about directing the horse Maureen was able to turn her face into her shoulder to act as a filter.

For what felt like hours they rode at this speed. She wondered many times where Sauntage was because she had not seen him among the riders of this battalion. The king she thought she might have seen earlier in the morning but as afternoon approached her eyes could focus on very little.

When they finally halted for a short rest Maureen was helped off the horse by the same soldier that had come to her rescue earlier and then led to a brook for a drink. Following the example being demonstrated all around her, she squatted at the water's edge. It felt so good on her sore throat to suck up handfuls of cold water. After she had relieved her initial thirst she went to work on removing the last several hours from her face. With so many others needing to reach the water her time at the brook was brief.

Once her guard brought her back to where their horses had been picketed he drove the metal stake into the ground. Soon she was leaning against it ready to fall asleep from exhaustion. He gave her a small chunk of bread, a piece of jerked meat and some kind of fruit that looked like an apple but it was very tangy.

Her afternoon passed exactly as the morning except it was longer. As the sun was dropping at her back she was having more and more trouble staying awake. Many yawns escaped her without cover because she was afraid that if she let go for even one second she would end up on the ground trampled by the troops behind her.

At long last she heard a long horn blast from further up the ranks. This sound had been made when they paused for lunch so she figured that this might be the dinner bell. Not that she cared to eat anything, but Maureen was so glad to be off the horse.

Within minutes of stopping she was again chained to the stake and left alone. Relief flooded through her that she had managed to make it to the end of the day. Two minutes later she was sound asleep.

Another two days went by in much the same way, however, the terrain made some drastic changes. Thick blonde brown grasses gave way to more trees and shaded areas. Though it was difficult to tell for sure she believed they were climbing in altitude by small increments. The air was several degrees cooler now even at mid day.

Many questions came to her mind as they went along, but with no one to answer them she soon grew frustrated. Fortunately by the third day she had begun to adjust to the demanding riding schedule so she was able to take a stick that had been charred in a campfire and write her wonderings in the diary. Some of them were answered by simple observance; however, most of them remained a mystery.

On that third day the army stopped much earlier in the day. She was able to tell that many of the soldiers were as confused as she was. As usual she was chained to the stake and left alone while the campsite was readied for the night.

Truthfully she did not mind too much though she was growing lonely. After Maureen had jotted down as many of her questions as she could remember, she pulled out the Bible and began to read. Knowing that something within these pages had changed Sauntage's mind about God spurred her on to learn more.

Soon the diary was out once again so that she could record even more thoughts and queries. Her confusion over a king that would keep people from coming into his kingdom unless they lived completely by his laws, knowing all along that no one could do it, slowly evaporated. From the book of Matthew she read the words of Jesus telling everyone that He came not to abolish the law, but to fulfill it. This was the beginning of clarity for her. Things all started to add together in her heart as she realized that God was not looking to keep the people He created away, He did everything to bring creation to Himself; through the death of his only Son.

Jesus came not just to invite mankind to come to the kingdom, but opened the gates wide for those who saw Him for who He was. Excitement built wildly as she now understood that God's standard had always been the same and that despite the fact that Adam and Eve had willfully disobeyed God's law bringing sin to all mankind He still wanted all people to know Him and love Him.

Tears flooded her eyes because she related to that kind of love. She would have given anything to have her boys with her safe and sound. Grasping fully the love God felt for her sent her to her knees with great sobs wracking her body.

A loud clearing throat brought her out of her cocoon of thankful prayers. Slowly pulling up from the ground she gazed up to see the tall soldier waiting for her attention. With a smile she stiffly got to her feet to face him.

Using his fingers he indicated that he wanted her to step closer to the stake to which she was clamped. This caused her smile to widen because she had learned that this was the only time he could openly speak to her. In a quiet whisper he said, "I'm sorry that I cannot treat you as a lady ought to be, but were I to do so it would be far worse for us both." When she was bound with the rope once more she was gently prodded in the middle of her back. Maureen sighed lightly because she knew now that her questions would go ignored and finally had some understanding as to why.

He took her to the king's tent which was again guarded by four soldiers. Her nerves suddenly jumped into over drive. Had the king decided what their fate was going to be? Before more questions could form the tent guard nodded for her to enter the temporary chamber.

Like the previous visit to this tent her sight diminished

immediately upon entering. The words spoken to her this time were not in English. "Come in. Both of you."

Sauntage pushed through the slit on the other side of the tent causing late afternoon sunshine to flood the dim room briefly. In that split second she saw his face lift slightly and then change as he saw her face. With her heart hammering in her chest she gave him a wide smile. Whatever they faced she hoped that he knew they were together.

"You may stand over here Maureen and Sauntage; you can stand in front of your Mother."

Not a sound was heard while they each found their own places. Sauntago and Modeanna Vadelum sat side by side in their carved seats. Their faces held no expression that she was able to read.

"After a great deal of thought and consideration I believe I have finally determined what should be done with you." Coming to his feet the king faced Maureen with a hard stare. "Do you recall our conversation of three nights ago?"

"Yes, Sire, I remember it." She saw Sauntage stiffen slightly.

"And did you mean what you said just before I left?" His eyes narrowed as he leaned over in an intimidating manner.

Not hesitating or breaking eye contact she replied firmly, "Yes, Sire, I meant every word."

For a moment he seemed speechless but then he said, "Good." Thoughtfully he put his hands behind his back and linked his fingers loosely. A few moments went by before he went on to say, "I have decided that per Maureen's request, she will be taking your punishment, Sauntage..."

"What!" He exploded loudly looking from his father to his wife. "No! It is mine to take not hers..."

"Silence!" Sauntago commanded. "She made the plea of her own will and I've come to realize that solves a few issues for me to accept."

In shock and amazement Sauntage cried, "Why? Maureen, why would you do such a thing?" His eyes were brimming with unshed tears.

"Because you are the best chance the boys have of ever being rescued. More than anything else I want our sons safe." She shouted back at him passionately and then added softly, "I read today, 'greater love has no man than he lay down his life for his friends'. For seventeen years now you have laid aside your life here for me, it's time I did the same for you."

"But Mo, I'm charged with treason." Two tears traveled down his dusty face.

"That is indeed the charge set on you Sauntage Vadelum. However, at the moment I am preparing to go to war with Galixtorn and don't have time for a trial. Nor do I have the extra men it would take to guard the two of you as prisoners, so you Sauntage are to be set free..."

Jumping up from her carved seat the queen flew at her husband in a panic, "Sauntago, how can you even think of doing such a thing?"

A slow smile built on his lips as he rested his hands upon her shoulders. "My Dear, you should know me better than that. There will be no escape attempts or she will be executed." With hardened eyes he went to his son and glared straight ahead at him. "You will serve in my army and if there is any hint of betrayal..."

"Maureen will be executed." He finished in a tight whisper. Then as he watched his father go back to his makeshift throne, he added, "Know this, King Vadelum, you needn't have kept my wife for this. It is my honor to serve you."

"I hope dear Lady that you can trust him. Your life is in his hands." A wry grimace crossed his face as he looked at his prisoner.

Sauntage cringed inside as his father used the word trust. Watching Maureen closely he looked for any sign of recoiling or angry stiffening, but amazingly there was none. As she boldly responded to the king's comment he felt his jaw lower in wonder.

"Sire, my life could be in no better hands." She could not help the grin that formed as she added, "Know this as well, King Vadelum, ropes and chains are not needed to keep me where you would like."

"Indeed?" Sauntago turned to her with lifted brow.

Modeanna puzzled about this aloud with deep creases on her tanned brow, "Why is that?"

"I like you and respect you, of course, but honestly, the more I see of you the less of a mystery your son is to me. Your actions explain who he is and why." The second the words left her mouth she knew that she had crossed a line of comfort for them. To compare a possible traitor to the king was clearly not acceptable.

Ignoring her comments he changed the subject as he sat back on his throne, "Now there are some additional guidelines to go over quickly before our dinner is served."

An hour later, Maureen was back at her stake alone. Apparently the king of Liguesis had spent a great deal of time on this arrangement considering the fact that he was marching his troops to a battlefield. He was quite a strategist to 'free' his son but force him into service in order to save her.

Once his rules had been stated the king ordered her to be returned to her 'cell' of sorts while Sauntage remained with his parents. So she had paced for a while and when her feet grew tired she lay on the ground not far from the post. Within minutes she was sound asleep.

When she woke up it was too dark to tell what time it was. Warmth was coming not from the blanket but from behind her back. With a gasp of surprise she sat up and turned around to look behind her. As she did a large hand brushed along the side of her neck.

"It's me, Darling." Sauntage whispered sleepily.

"Sau, what are you doing? What if you're caught?" She hissed at him angrily and tried to move away from his reach. It did not work as she felt the slack on her chains leave.

"My parents know where I am. I asked for their permission to be here and they granted it." There was lightheartedness in his tone that bordered on laughter.

"You're kidding?"

He could no longer hold back soft chuckles as he answered, "Now I'm just guessing but I think they want more grandchildren."

A frown tightened the muscles all over her face. "How did you come to that conclusion?"

"By the way you are being treated and the look in my Mother's eyes as you were taken from their tent. She was clearly upset at the sight of your hands tied behind your back. After you left I think she forgot that I was in the room with them because she asked Father if that was really necessary. He answered her in a tone I had never before heard in his voice. It was sort of sad and dejected."

Her eyes rounded and her mouth gaped momentarily. "So I'm expected to become pregnant!"

"No, no, it's a hope of theirs I think not an expectation." Sauntage tried to reassure her.

"In what way am I treated that tells you this?" There was no sleep left in her so she sat up facing him to listen for the answer.

"The amount of food you are given as a prisoner especially one who is believed to be aiding a traitor for one thing. And you are allowed to sleep instead of being woken up to eat right away."

Gasping softly she concluded, "That's why I haven't been sentenced to death. Because they think I could be pregnant."

"Part of it anyway. But honestly, they believe you. It's thrown off their entire perception of me and they don't know what to do. Father really likes you, too." Another chuckle escaped as he moved his hand to her face. "Now somewhere off to your left is a plate sitting on an up turned log with a cloth over it if you're hungry."

Without comment she pulled the food closer and ate quietly. She was not sure what everything was but it all tasted very good. As her husband's words echoed through her mind she had to wonder, "Do the soldiers get this fruit and the vegetables?"

"No, on a trip like this one fruit is usually sought after for only the queen. If it is found along the way the men will gladly take it, but after she has been given her portion."

The fork dropped back to her plate as she said, "Sau, this feels so wrong. These men need this food more than I do."

"Maybe so, but you'll never convince them otherwise. I told you that children are cherished here. That's the reason Mother is on this trip. To find Ryan and see him rescued." He felt a shiver run up her spine so he wrapped the blanket up around her shoulders.

"Sau, if children are so important here why didn't you want more than two? I wouldn't have minded a larger family." She puzzled hesitantly.

A heavy sigh dropped from his lungs and then he responded, "Mo, I would have loved to have more children, but I lack the ability to care for them. As it is we rely heavily on your income to make ends meet. And we don't live an extravagant lifestyle. In that respect things are different here. There's no little league, soccer, football, and boy scouts to pay for." His shoulders sagged forward a bit more and then he said quietly, "If you're done eating we should get some rest. I'm expected to train tomorrow."

"Train?" Maureen asked as she put the plate back on the end of the log.

"Yes, it has been years since I have handled a sword. I need all the practice I can get."

"A sword?" She felt the blood drain from her face.

Pulling her gently against his frame he reassured her, "Don't worry it's just practice stuff to begin with; made out of wood and not sharp at all. I'll be fine."

For a long time after his breathing became regular she was wide awake. Her lips moved in silent prayer to keep them all safe.

Sharp clacking noise woke her shortly after dawn. In the shadowy light Maureen saw two soldiers standing in front of Sauntage with long sticks held high. With her heart hammering in her chest she cringed as he tried to stay on his feet against these two.

Surprise caused her to slowly rise to her feet with her mouth gaping. After only a few moments one of the soldier's 'swords' went flying several feet behind Sauntage. Somehow he had managed to disarm the man completely. Doing this increased the intensity with which the other soldier attacked. First one had the advantage and then one quick motion tipped the balance the other direction.

This mock battle went on for quite some time drawing attention from others milling around. Eventually her view of them was obscured because of the number of people standing between her and the fight. With frustration she listened to cheers that were building for this soldier. Her foot stamped on the ground as her jaw clenched in a scowl.

Something tipped over drawing her attention. Excitement released in a quiet squeal as she picked up the log on which her food was normally delivered. She dragged it over to the metal stake and stepped up on top of it using the stake as a handhold.

For the most part this worked well as she was able to see a lot of the action and a good portion of the ground. As she continued to watch Maureen felt the color in her face leave. These men had judged her husband and wanted to pronounce sentencing in their own way.

Each clash of the sticks grew harder and it was clear that Sauntage was growing tired. His stick was not lifted quite as high nor was his swing as strong. At one point, he stumbled a little as they circled each other around their small arena.

Laughter filtered through the crowd and a few jeers were shouted above the noise. She was seething over this 'training' session. Had the king really ordered this?

Suddenly, the crowd on her left side quieted significantly. When she glanced over in that direction she saw the king and the queen moving towards the two men in the center. Their faces were difficult to see clearly but it was apparent that they disapproved of this scene.

Sauntage was breathing heavily as he met his opponent's weapon and then the tip of his stick hit the ground. Still heaving he only lifted his chin slightly as the soldier charged at him once more. This time instead of raising his stick in defense Sauntage poked it between the other man's legs with one hand and grabbed for his opponent's stick with the other. In a split second Sauntage had dropped his sparring partner and held both weapons securely.

The crowd went dead silent as the winner turned to the king and bowed his head briefly in respect.

Maureen clapped her hands and jumped up and down with loud cheers drawing the attention of everyone gathered. Much to her horror the log tipped beneath her feet sending her crashing to the ground. All the air was knocked from her lungs and her vision blurred. From a distance she could hear Sauntage yelling.

"Mo!" Within seconds he was kneeling at her side. "Mo, can you hear me?"

Tears trickled from her eyes as she tried to draw in a breath and found for a few moments that she could not do it. Finally, the barrier was broken and her lungs were able to function.

"Take it easy. Just breathe slowly. You've had the wind knocked out of you." The king said quietly near her feet.

"Does anything hurt, Maureen?" Modeanna asked anxiously searching the younger woman's face.

"Just my pride, Your Highness." Color flooded into her face.

Relief sagged Sauntage's shoulders as he sighed heavily, "Thank you, God."

Giggles rose in her throat as she recalled, "The Bible was right, pride does come before a fall." Wiping the moisture from her eyes she moved to sit.

With a shake of his head Sauntage rose to his full height. "Well, at least your sense of humor is still intact." His lip curled in a wry grin as he reached down to help her rise.

"Can you do that stuff with a sword, too?" Her eyes sparkled at him.

"Not quite as well probably, but yes I can handle a sword." He was puzzled by her adoring expression and the way she was leaning in towards him.

She batted her eyes at him with a widening smile and said softly in English, "If what you told me last night is true then kiss me."

"What?" His eyes flared at her.

Modeanna brought her hand over her mouth and hissed between her teeth, "Just listen to her, stupid."

Startled by his mother's use of English and maligning his intelligence it took Sauntage a moment to comply. As his lips met his wife's mouth he was shocked by her arms wrapping around the back of his neck and the passion in her response.

Confusion was still enveloping him when she reluctantly broke off the kiss to hug him tightly. "What was that about?"

"Those men were out to take you down and they didn't succeed so now they have all the more reason to hate you. If by my treatment as a prisoner they can guess the expectations and if as you say children are highly valued...then they are not going to risk the royal wrath that might come about if my heart is broken."

When they separated moments later he gaped at her and then glanced at the men now beginning to wander away from the area. "How did you come to that conclusion so fast?"

"I don't really know exactly. But why else would the king and queen come rushing over here if not for their hope?" She answered quietly.

"Why else indeed." His mother gave him a sarcastic roll of her eyes when he looked up at his parents.

"You must really think us stupid if you expect us to believe that you have not been in Liguesis all this time." Sauntago held his eyes steady and without emotion as he continued, "That captain you just brought down is one of my best swordsmen." Suddenly, the royal couple stalked back to their tent.

Three hours later the army met with a wide fast flowing river. Even as far back from the front of the battalion as she was Maureen knew this water was cause for concern. The thunderous sound was enough to make one think twice about crossing. Sauntage had left her side to get a better view of the situation. It never crossed either of their minds to have her join him because the guard set over her would never have agreed.

A few minutes later he came with a report. "Heavy rains from the north have raised the banks by a good two feet. There is no telling exactly how deep the water is. Father has decided to split the battalions and cross at different points." He grew quiet.

"Why would he do that?" She wondered suspiciously.

"We are two hours out from the Shargaunal mines; which is where Father is taking this army. I just learned that this army has been moved here because word had been sent out that Tagurah had been captured. That is why our story made my parents so angry and why they are having so much trouble believing us."

"Of course it is all starting to make sense now. Tagurah set you up all along because the idea of our boys being kidnapped to the very same place is just a little too coincidental." Her heart began to accelerate as she realized how close they were to reaching Charlie, Drew and Ryan. With tears swimming in her eyes she hoarsely asked, "Can you get to them, Sau?"

"It's hard to say, Darling, those mines are extensive. And we have no way of knowing exactly where they are being held." A heavy sigh left his shoulders slumped. "But given enough time to search I'm sure that I would reach them."

Letting go of Jeurku's mane Maureen grasped his forearm firmly. As she looked intently into his reluctant eyes she said softly, "Then when we get to the mines I want you to go after our sons."

"I can't, Maureen, he might love me, but he'll stick to his word. If I cross him he'll kill you."

While she understood his position she snapped, "It's all right, Sauntage Vadelum. This entire journey has been for our sons and I accepted the danger. They need you now. Whatever happens to me is in God's hands."

He was silent for a full minute and then turned to her with confidence, "Perhaps God will make a way for me to do both. Serve my Father and rescue our sons."

Before she could respond the command to move out was given. Her hands went quickly back to Jeurku's mane just as he jerked forward. With some pride she noticed that she hardly moved along his back.

Noise from the rushing water on their right side made conversation impossible so she was left to her own thoughts; which turned into desperate prayers for God's help and protection. Could he still do the kinds of things He did to all the armies that came against Israel? Like confusing the enemy so much that they killed each other instead of God's people.

Of all the times she had ridden Jeurku this one was the hardest. He seemed to know that north was not the direction they needed to go so he kept veering to the right. The terrain next to the river was hilly and muddy which slowed them down quite a bit.

An hour passed before the king called for another halt to test the waters. Two soldiers were sent across the wide span and once they safely made it to the other side a signal was sent to the king. This area was passable but dangerous. Word was quickly circulated to secure everything that was being carried and have a tight hold on the horses.

Maureen was not terribly frightened by this just anxious to have it all finished. When it was time for her to cross with her husband and guard, she was surprised to have the soldier pull her wrists close and slice the ropes.

"I cannot in good conscience let you do this bound. Should you fall or your horse flounder you deserve the chance to save yourself. But if you have any honor, Lady Maureen, you will remember that my life is at stake should you escape."

With a firm nod of understanding she replied, "Then know that if we are separated for any reason, I will be with the king demanding a search party for my guardian as he has been most kind to me and served his master well." Clearly her words rattled him a bit as they moved forward into the river.

Sauntage was on her right side while the guard was on her left. As they progressed slowly allowing the horses to pick their footing, she saw the king and queen upstream a few yards. Horses with riders were staggered throughout the water for a long stretch of shoreline.

Jeurku fidgeted sideways many times instead of going forward because the force of the water made it difficult to keep his footing. Even though she was sure he couldn't hear her, Maureen kept talking to Jeurku in an attempt to calm him. It was not even a quarter of the way across when the cold water frothed and foamed around her feet. Color left her face as she realized just how deep this was likely to be.

Once in a while a voice could be heard shouting, but words were impossible to decipher. A few times she spared a look to Sauntage who nodded at her encouragingly. His face was tight with determination.

Just as they passed the halfway point she felt Jeurku's feet leave the riverbed momentarily. Water was snorting out from his drenched nose. Fear crept over her in a great wave. If this huge horse could not handle this river how could she do it?

Loud cries drew her attention ahead of them and her heart dropped into the pit of her stomach. Queen Modeanna's horse had gone berserk and tried to rear up despite the deep water. In horror she watched as the queen lost her hold on the wild animal and fell into the roaring current.

Sauntage pushed Dueby to go faster and was able to catch a handful of his mother's clothing. His father had not had enough warning to do more than scream as she slipped from his reach. With the extra weight pressing against his body Dueby lost his footing for several seconds which kept Sauntage from pulling his mother above the waterline. Urging the struggling animal with his feet he strained with his left arm to lift his mother.

He could feel the fabric giving way so he let go of Dueby's mane to lean over to his left and get a better hold. It felt like hours before he was finally able to find part of her body to grasp and drag. As he got her pulled into his lap Sauntage could hear loud cheers erupting all around him. They still had a good distance to go before they reached the other shore. "Mother? Can you hear me?"

Nothing.

Cold fear crept up his spine. Had he been too slow? Flicking his eyes downward he saw no movement of her chest or mouth. Her bluish purple color frightened him. "Mother! Hold on! We're almost there!"

Maureen did her best to keep up with Sauntage but it was difficult. She knew by the tone of his voice that something was terribly wrong. By the look on the king's face he knew it as well. His ashen gaze never left his wife's face.

Thankfully the second half of the riverbed was much easier to cross. So when they left the water Dueby flew several feet before stopping. There were half a dozen men with lifted hands waiting to help their queen. Handing her down to them Sauntage scanned the sea of horses and soldiers. "Maureen!" He screamed as loud as he possibly could. "Maureen!"

The men gently laid her on a patch of ground and Sauntage dropped to his knees next to her. A light touch on her throat confirmed what he already knew. Her heart had stopped beating.

From the edge of the crowded river bank Maureen could hear Sauntage calling for her. She saw the king moving a few feet to her left and she rushed after him. Soldiers near their fallen queen had begun to block her way so she shouted back at him, "I'm here, Sau. I'm fine."

"She's not! Get over here!"

It took a bit of shoving but she finally made it to the middle to see Sauntago kneeling over his wife with great sobs wracking his frame while he held her limp body to his chest. Meeting her husband's eye she said, "That water is cold. Maybe there is a chance."

As his father lifted his grief stricken face to look at her Sauntage pulled his mother back to the ground. In English he cried, "You've taken CPR, Mo, what do we do?"

Dropping on the dirt next her father-in-law she yelled, "Roll her on her side towards me." Once this was accomplished she watched the water pour from the queen's mouth. With the palms of her hands she pressed on her abdomen and back which forced even more fluid from her lungs. "You need to loosen her dress. Tear it in the back. Hurry."

Although he could not see his father's face he knew the man had to be beyond shocked because he did nothing as his son tore her clothing. Anxiously he looked at his wife and asked, "What now?"

She pushed the queen's shoulder to press her onto her back and then placed one hand over the other on the middle of her chest to demonstrate. "Do this. No faster. No slower. And not too hard you'll break her ribs. I'll count. When I reach five pause; so I can breathe for her."

Other than her counting in English and the grunts of Sauntage as he worked to save his mother's life; nothing could be heard. Not even the horses made noise. Every minute or two she had him pause and check for signs of hope. Tears were streaming down both of their faces as they realized time was growing short.

Maureen did not have it in her to say so, but at best they had less than two minutes left before bringing her back meant certain brain damage. She held up her hand once more and put her cheek to the queen's lips. Just as she was preparing to cover her nose and mouth Maureen heard a gurgling deep in the queen's throat.

Without warning she pulled the queen's shoulder to roll her onto her side as she threw up all over the ground. Great shouts could be heard from all around as Modeanna Vadelum drew in air with great gasps. Sobs of relief and joy caused Maureen to tremble from head to toe. She fell into her husband's arm in exhaustion thinking he must have been ready to drop long ago.

Sauntago stared at his wife in amazement. He had been so sure that she was dead. Her searching eyes were dazed and unsure, but she managed to find her voice, "I fell off...how did you..."

"It wasn't me." His face lifted to look at Sauntage. In a whisper he acknowledged, "Our son and daughter saved you."

"What?" Modeanna shifted so that she could sit.

When Maureen realized what she was about to do, she pushed firmly on her shoulder. "No, Your Highness. Sauntage had to rip your gown so we need to get you something else to wear. Something dry; if it can be found." To say she was shocked when a dozen hands dropped items into the tight circle within thirty seconds would have been an understatement. "Your Majesty, it would be best for her to thoroughly dry and warm herself if the time can be spared."

Sauntago gave a strong nod saying, "Make camp. Send two men to meet Armok and tell him what has happened and that we will be delayed a day.

Men quickly scattered to follow his orders leaving only five of them in the circle. When Maureen saw who was standing over them she gave him a nod. "Where is my stake to be?" Before she could get to her feet a large hand went around her forearm causing her breath to catch.

"Modeanna was gone. There was no breath in her." His dark eyes begged her for something. "How did you do this? After the way you've been treated, why did you do this?"

Gently she told him, "Sau and I helped her breathe until she could do it on her own." Then a grin crossed her lips as she added, "There is nothing in my treatment that I don't understand, Sire. The truth is I have a question to ask Her Highness when she is able."

Loud rumbles leapt from Sauntage's throat for a few moments before he teased, "You aren't seriously going to ask her about that dance?"

"So what if I do?" She challenged with her arms crossed over her chest.

"There are a hundred other rituals and traditions of Liguesis that I've told you about and you want to latch onto a silly fishing tune." His head shook with humor as he went on to add, "Wait a minute. Let me help Father get Mother to a warmer place then I can go along with you. I'm tired I don't want to hunt all afternoon for that post." He was not aware of the look that went between his parents because he was unfolding a blanket. When his father spoke his actions froze.

"You are both free, Sauntage."

"Thank you, Father." A quick nod was all he could manage for a moment. "Mother, if you can roll towards me, Father can put this blanket underneath you and then carry you to a fire."

As soon as the king had his wife cradled in his arms Maureen held another blanket out to put over her. "Is there a way to make soup here? It would be easier on her stomach and help to warm her too."

Her former guard stepped forward to say, "I'll see to it if you like, Sire." At the nod of his king he raced to the cooking tent that was closest to being readied.

That night was unlike any other she had spent since entering the land of Liguesis. After Modeanna had been helped into dry clothing, allowed to warm herself by the fire and fed a bowl of hot broth; she fell asleep in her husband's arms. The king was clearly torn as he looked down at her because he knew she needed rest but he could not bring himself to let go.

Maureen sat across the fire studying the striking couple. Sauntago was a big man, probably an inch or two taller than his son and a good deal heavier. His dark almost black hair was graying only around his ears which made him seem younger than she knew him to be. She was surprised that it was cut and styled in a short fashion, being only a couple of inches in length all over his head.

Modeanna on the other hand had much longer hair than she would have expected given her age. It was braided into a thick rope that was draped over her shoulder to rest in her lap. Even though her eyes were closed Maureen did not have to imagine very hard what color they were because she had been looking at them for years. The queen was tall and well proportioned. She was not skinny, but giving birth to four children had not robbed her of her figure.

This fact made her cringe inside and look away. After only two children she had certainly lost hers. Sauntage must have felt her movement because his arm gently tightened around her waist. His warm breath pressed close to her ear causing chills to run up and down her spine.

"We really need to find you some more suitable clothing."

"Why? I mean other than it needing a really good washing it's worked very well. And it is designed for a woman." Her brow wrinkled in confusion. The way his eyes traveled over her outfit made her blush.

Light chuckles left him as he gave her a squeeze and placed a kiss at her temple. "Well, yes, it is made for a woman. A woman in a farming community. I meant that we need to find you appropriate clothing for a Liguesian Lady. You really have no idea how lovely you are, do you?" He grasped her chin and lifted it so that he could look into her eyes, "I'm not talking about your weight, Maureen, I'm talking about you. All of you. Inside and out." Once more he took a moment to study her frame before he added, "Though truthfully, Mo, if you were dissatisfied with how you looked you shouldn't be any longer."

With a gasp she stared at him and then shifted her eyes downward. It was not easy to visualize how everything had changed through the leather clothing, but it had. She felt her eyes widen and her mouth drop open as she realized for the first time that the excess fat on her body was gone.

"Is everything all right?" Sauntago asked quietly.

"Yes, Sir." Laughing heartily behind his hand Sauntage then added, "Everything is fine."

Before she stopped to think about it Maureen used the back of her hand to swat his chest. Then she saw the stiffening of the king's back and regretted it immediately.

"You sure?" Humor suddenly lifted his brows as he admitted, "I believe I recognize that gesture. I usually get that after I've made some remark my lady doesn't appreciate."

Maureen was sure the temperature rose ten degrees in as many seconds.

"Yes, I'm sure. She just doesn't want to believe me when I tell her how pretty she is." He gave his father a firm nod.

Laughter exploded from the king that startled them all. His entire body shook for nearly a full minute which gave his sleepy wife a chance to sit up and question everyone with her wide blue eyes. "Sorry, My Dear. I just couldn't help it."

"What is it? Sauntago, stop that. What is so funny?" All she received in answer from her son and daughter-in-law were deep shrugs.

When he finally regained control of his breathing he explained, "They are just like us."

Modeanna frowned at him, "Like us? We established that days ago; why is the fact that he is Liguesian and she is from earth funny now?"

"No, no, no. Not that. Our son is a great deal like his Father you've always said so. Well, I've just realized that he has chosen a woman very much like his Mother to be his wife. How many years did I spend convincing you that I love you no matter how you look? He even calls her by the same pet name."

"Mo was her nickname long before I met her." Sauntage defended strongly with his hands held in the air.

"It was your Mother's before I knew her as well. Perhaps it is a common earth name and it is simply that we are two Liguesian men with earthling wives."

There was a spark in Sauntage's eyes as he commented, "Your Majesty, after living on earth for so many years I can tell you with absolute certainty that there is nothing common about our chosen Ladies."

This opened hours of storytelling from both couples. Maureen was amazed by the openness of her in-laws and their many hurdles to being accepted by his parents. Since the deaths of his parents they had had no one with which they could confide. Only in secret journals meant for the next king were they able to share their story.

"It's Liguesian tradition." Sauntago explained to them. "When he reaches the age of ten the eldest prince is shown the ancient writings. In most cases curiosity takes its course and he ends up finding The Gateway. There have been a few that have questioned their father's about it; they would be our history's weaker monarchs."

"Then it's a test?" Sauntage asked incredulously.

Slowly a smile formed on the king's lips, "It is indeed a test."

For another two hours they listened to his parents share more traditions and stories from the past. Intermixed with this were questions that they answered about their life on earth. Yawns overtook Maureen somewhere in the middle of the king telling them of his discovery of The Gateway.

Sauntage was a bit surprised when his father stopped speaking in mid sentence and then looked at the two exhausted women. "Let's put these Ladies in our tent to rest more comfortably. You and I need to speak alone." His tone left no room for argument or discussion which disturbed him greatly.

# Chapter Twelve

When she woke the next morning Maureen was startled to find herself in a bed. Quickly glancing to her right she discovered that she had not spent the night alone even though she was the only one there at the moment. With long cat like stretches she got out of the bed and realized suddenly where she was. This was the royal bed chamber.

Of course it was nothing spectacular but it was far better than any other accommodations available at the moment. There were two small trunks with painted carvings on every side, the narrow mattress stuffed with grass and two candles on each of the trunks. A noisy yawn escaped as she came around the end of the mattress to leave the makeshift room.

The growl near her feet caused her to jump back onto the mattress with a loud screech. Her hair prickled all over her body as she heard a deep throated loud rumble. Great gold eyes blinked at her sleepily from the end of the bed. She allowed her eyes to dart around for another exit but much to her dismay there was none. What was she going to do?

Suddenly, the curtain wall separated and Sauntage came rushing in saying breathlessly, "What's wrong?"

Without a sound she pointed at the large creature now walking around his legs licking at his hands. Her panic started to subside as she now knew that this was the pet aragaff.

"I see you have met, Avix. Don't worry she's very impressive looking but she wouldn't know how to hurt a fly." By way of demonstration he knelt on the floor and rubbed the curly white fur along the aragaff's back.

It took a couple of deep breaths but she managed to draw close to the huge cat like creature. As she sat back on her haunches her head was taller than Maureen's waist. This made her nervous as she held out her trembling fingers. Before she knew it Avix was tickling her hand with long slurpy licks of excitement. "I'm very pleased to meet you, too, Avix."

"Come on. We haven't got much time before we head out for Shargaunal." He squeezed her fingers in his hand as he said, "Father and I talked until the wee hours of the morning. I believe I understand things a whole lot better, but for now I cannot explain. All that I am able to tell you is that the boys are in danger with this battle, however, the boys are the reason this army is assembled."

She held back her tears as long as she could and then as they slipped one by one down her cheeks she said, "Then let's go get our sons."

More than an hour went by before they were actually on the move. After breakfast had been eaten Maureen was given fresh clothing from the queen. The outfit was nothing grand or fancy but it was clean. Modeanna also showed her what the third section of their tent housed.

A loud cry of delight rose on her lips as she saw the tiny tub filled with fresh water. With a bemused smile she worked on the laces at her shoulders. Short though it was that bath made her feel like a new woman.

As they rode along the river's edge for a few miles she kept looking down at the bright blue fabric. Because she had been wearing the same thick leather outfit every day for nearly a month she felt a bit naked without it.

This material was soft like satin but not shiny. Yards and yards of fabric made up the long skirt and because she was a few inches shorter than the queen it had been hastily altered. Queen Modeanna had taken one of her husband's sharp blades to the hem and removed about four inches from it.

When she had looped the ties of the blue bodice Maureen found much to her surprise that the bust line fit a little loosely but not so much that it would fall away immodestly. However, the lower portion of the bodice was likely to be caught by the wind and fold upwards. Quick thinking on the queen's part saved this as well. Using the blade on the fabric cut from the bottom of the skirt she wrapped it around Maureen's waist as a belt. Another piece was cut to tie in her clean braided hair.

Sauntage had changed his clothes as well. Leather was still the material but it was cut more like a shirt and pair of pants found on earth. He had a sword strapped to his waist now and with his longer hair and grown out beard he looked like a pirate.

Many times she looked at him with her mouth opened to ask him to tell her what he had learned from his father. Each time she stopped herself saying that he had been right with nearly every decision on this journey she had to...trust him. Those words echoed through her mind. Smiling quietly to herself she realized that she did trust him. While they trudged along she asked God for a chance to be alone with him so that she could tell him.

Her chance did not come. Just a few minutes after her prayer they crested a treed hill that showed a wide valley with low mountains on the other side. From their position the king's army could see a battle being waged in the valley as well as the sides of the mountains. The trees around them provided a thick enough cover that they had not been discovered yet.

Maureen's eyes drifted shut. 'Dear God we need a miracle. Like one from the Old Testament. Help us. Save our sons, Jesus. You're the only one who can.' Her eyes flew open as Sauntage kissed her cheek.

"Stay with Mother. I'm going with Father to meet the second battalion's captain and decide where we go from here." He left without giving her a chance to respond.

For what seemed like hours they stood on the top of the hill. They did the best they could to remain hidden as the battle waged on below them. It grew more difficult by the minute for Maureen to stay where she was; knowing her boys might be right before her eyes.

Studying the fighters she could tell which ones were attacking the mountain and which were defending it. Those attacking were much better outfitted. Many of them had chain mail vests or plated armor suits. Almost all of them had a blue and silver insignia painted on the helmet, shield or clothing. Even though this was the case they were having difficulty taking out their enemies.

On that mountainous terrain with their troops spread between the mountains and valleys many men were being taken from behind. Each time a soldier fell from either army Maureen felt a chill go through her. This was not a movie. Men were dying right before her eyes and there was nothing she could do to stop it.

Sauntage came running up next to her breathing heavily. Carefully she slid from Jeurku's back so that she could talk to him without being overheard. His mother joined them and after taking a few deep breaths he said, "Father has decided to split our first and second battalions between the two major mine openings that are known to be here. We hope to draw as many men from the army holding the mines out of it as we can. If we are successful then perhaps our small third battalion can go in and recue any prisoners they may be holding. With any luck we will have the mines cleared out by nightfall."

Maureen nodded at him throughout his explanation. This plan seemed to be a good one. "Then you will be joining the third battalion and look for the boys?"

His hands came to rest gently on her shoulders as he said, "No, Maureen, I will be with the first battalion going into the main entrance of the mine. There are more troops holding this mine than Father could ever have imagined and he needs all the warriors he can get on those lines."

"Then I will search the mines." She tearfully straightened her spine letting him know that she was afraid but determined to do this.

A weight dropped onto his back, slumping his shoulders as he whispered, "I wish with all my heart that you wouldn't go, that the need for someone to go in there was not so great." He smiled at her suddenly and held her face in his hands as he stated, "But if there is anything I have learned about you on this journey, Lovely Carkna Slayer, it's not to underestimate you. God go with you." Sauntage pressed a kiss to her forehead and turned away at a jog.

Taking Jeurku's reigns she went in search of the third battalion's captain which was not hard to do. All the men of this group were giving their horses over to the boys. They would be going in on foot because there was not a safe place near the mines to leave them while they went through the caverns. Their leader was giving orders to small groups of four or five as they turned over their mounts.

No words were spoken between the women. Words were not really necessary. As they joined three other soldiers to hear the captain's direction they silently reached for each other's hands. His instructions were simple watch for entrances to clear of the enemy and get into as many of the tunnels as possible.

So along with about twenty young men they crouched in the trees at the crest of the hill. Slowly they maneuvered through the trees to draw as close as possible to the area in which they would be exposed. The sounds were overwhelming at times. Shields hammered by swords and even axes. Horses baying in fear and rage. Worst of all were men falling in agony.

There was a loud trumpet sound to the south of them that drew the attention of everyone on the battlefield. Much to her dismay Maureen saw Sauntage leading the charge through the valley on the back of Dueby the farm horse. Anxiously she watched as he engaged two men quickly disarming one and wounding the other. Other men around him were also having the same advantage. These armies were tired.

As she continued to watch the scene unfold she was confused to find the Liguesian army only engaging the troops pouring out from the mines. In fact it appeared that an unspoken agreement was reached with the blue and silver army. This excited her very much because rather quickly they were winning the battle. Very few Liguesian men were falling and the losses to the blue and silver were dropping off rapidly.

Her eyes kept flicking to their leader. How much longer did they have to wait? Not many were left in the mine troops. Shouldn't they move in now?

Just as she was about to draw closer to Modeanna and question this she heard loud cries emerging from the mine entrances. Dozens upon dozens of men on horseback came pouring from inside the small mountain. The Liguesian army followed the blue and silver troops in retreat through the valley.

Maureen's heart sank. A sick feeling settled in her gut. Her arm was tugged firmly drawing her attention to Modeanna.

"Be ready. It's almost time." She was intense and energized.

Before she could think about it she heard the call of their captain and charged furiously into the valley. Very few were left to bother them so after a three minute race they were standing in the dim light of a manmade cave. They were not allowed much time to recover before the captain was splitting them into smaller teams to conduct the searches.

Ten men led the way down the wide tunnel to which they had been assigned. Lanterns were hanging along the walls left burning presumably by the men waiting with their horses in these long corridors. Each of them silently took one as they ran ahead for what felt like miles to their burning lungs and tired legs.

Suddenly, the tunnel split into two sections. Without a word they divided evenly to continue their mission. It was not long before another split met them, so now Maureen was going with two soldiers and Modeanna was racing with two other men.

Ten minutes went by while they jogged slowly along a narrower corridor that had small chambers on either side. Tears pricked at Maureen's eyes as she saw only evidence of a military barracks here. This was not an area where prisoners would be kept. The moisture dripped over the rim of her lower lids as she heard the captain call out, "We've reached the end of this vein."

In dismay she held up her lamp to stare at the stone wall before them. There was a quiet thought building in her heart, 'I will never leave you nor forsake you.' She was not alone, God was with her and He knew where the boys were. Humbly she closed her eyes and asked, "Jesus, could you please show me where they are?"

Her eyes were still shimmering when she turned to follow the men. But this time they were filled with hope.

Getting back to the point where they had separated the women from each other did not take nearly as long. Within a minute of each other the groups met with similar reports. Soon all twelve of them were racing back to the mine entrance.

They were met by the captain who was quickly gathering reports from the teams as they returned. No one had yet to see any signs of other people left in the tunnels. Five tense minutes went by with very little conversation from the soldiers.

The captain counted each of the groups that had returned and found one missing. A few clipped orders had them organized to go in search of the missing team. Maureen and Modeanna found themselves in the middle of the troops trying to keep up with the longer steps of the men.

This tunnel was different from the one they had traveled in earlier because it had a stronger downward slope. High ceilings helped to keep the air from being too stale. With so many bodies though it quickly grew warm; especially when they were forced to slow down at narrower points in the tunnel.

Word came whispering back through the ranks during a temporary halt that they had located the missing team. Added to that a moment later was the fact that this tunnel met up with the other entrance somehow. Finally, they learned that the second half of their battalion had found enemies and were engaged in battle not far ahead. It was not long before new energy surged through this group and they pressed forward with passion.

When they reached the end of the long descending tunnel and entered a wide dome like chamber Maureen felt a hard tug on her right arm drawing her along the outside wall of the chamber. Modeanna pulled her low to the floor holding her finger to her lips for a moment as she scanned the area with her eyes.

"We must be careful. Without weapons we are useless in here." She continued to study the scene in front of them.

"What do we do? We can't go back the way we came." Her heart pounded painfully at the metallic clanking all around her.

Nodding decisively Modeanna answered, "There is another doorway leading out from here let's go see where it leads."

To Maureen that did not seem like a much better plan than staying right where they were, but she figured that there was safety in numbers so she followed. As soon as they stepped into this narrow tunnel the noise level dropped significantly. Stopping for a minute to catch their breath Maureen said, "Maybe we can find a place along here to wait it out a bit."

"Yes, let's hope so. Come on, we'd better put more distance between us and that battle." She did not wait for a response but picked up the hem of her dress and ran as quietly as she could down the winding corridor.

While she did her best Maureen found that keeping up with her mother-in-law was a challenge. At one point as they paused to rest and listen, she felt her knees drop to the floor. There was nothing left in them.

With tenderness Modeanna said, "We can rest here safely for a few minutes I think." Her eyes moved all around them to see if there was any information to be gained about where they were.

In long painful strokes Maureen massaged her legs begging them to carry her just a bit longer. As she gritted her teeth and scrunched up her face she looked upwards to a place her mother-in-law was studying. "What is it, Your Highness?"

"There seems to be another tunnel above us. I could almost swear I see light coming out of it. My eyes must be playing tricks on me." She pressed her dirty fingers over her dry eyes to sooth them.

"No, I see it too." A gasp escaped as she heard banging sounds echoing through the tunnel. "Come on. I think someone might be close by." Lacing her fingers together Maureen knelt to give the queen a boost.

Several kicks and scrapes later Modeanna was able to stand on Maureen's shoulder and pull herself up to the floor of the higher tunnel. As soon as the weight left her she turned to look for any cracks or ledges to use for climbing. Clearly she was not the first to want to do this because she found quite a few and managed to shimmy up the wall in no time flat.

They wasted no time moving away from the opening. Each of them held their breath as the pounding of metal covered bodies rushed beneath them to join the fray in the domed room. Once it fell quiet the two of them gasped loudly for breath. "Oh, that was far too close for comfort." Maureen acknowledged softly.

"Indeed it was. That tunnel is not safe. Even though this one is smaller we'll have to use it for the time being. Let's see if we can't figure out where it leads." Modeanna agreed with a firm nod.

Unfortunately they discovered that this tunnel was only about a third of the height of the other one so the two of them were forced to crawl. Long skirts made this very difficult so Maureen finally gripped two handfuls of the hem and held them while she moved her knees.

Modeanna paused to one side of the narrow tunnel and waited for her daughter-in-law to draw closer. In a soft whisper she said, "Look up ahead. There seems to be light coming from above us. What do you think it is?

Her lips twisted from side to side as she thought. "I don't know. Do you suppose there is another tunnel above us?"

With a shrug she answered back, "Could be. Let's go take a

peek." She did not have to add a caution to go quietly. Almost holding her breath the queen went forward keeping her eyes trained on the circle of light.

When she drew closer Maureen realized that it was unlikely that this opening in the tunnel lead to another floor. It was a round hole which went straight up for several dozen feet, but it was less than two feet in diameter. "This looks like an old air shaft. I wonder why it is here? What a strange place for it."

For a few moments it was silent as the two of them tried to think. "Wait. There's another hole up ahead." Unspoken curiosity drove them in unison to have a peek at what was at the end of this path. Most of the time, Modeanna lead the way. She was used to moving about in the long flowing skirt so this journey was much easier for her.

Suddenly, her right hand and arm dropped through the dark floor. In a panic she pushed with her left hand and toppled backward into Maureen's face. Her breath was coming in short gasps and her blue eyes were wide with fright.

"Are you all right?" Cried Maureen as she pulled the older woman close to her chest.

"Yes, I believe so." Modeanna nodded rapidly. "We'll need to be more careful. I never even saw that opening."

"Can you see anything down there?"

Frowning the queen leaned over for a quick peek. "No, not really. Just some dark shadows." Noise from below rose to her ears so she turned back to hiss, "Shh...someone's down there."

Although she did not reply Maureen moved so that she too could listen. Distant voices were drawing closer which caused panic to rise in her chest. Where could they go? Despite the fact that the hole in the floor was small, if they were found out it would not take long for soldiers to reach them.

Metal rattled loudly below just before a light was shining into the small space. "I'm telling you I heard something." Said a gruff voice as the tinkling of small pieces of metal was heard.

Both women closed their eyes willing whatever was to come to be over quickly. "Please, God, help us!" Silently screamed through Maureen's mind. Tears formed and dropped without notice.

"So what? We don't have time for this we still have to check the other two tunnels and be out of here before the whole mountain rattles apart. Come on. I for one want to make it out of here in one piece."

As quickly as the threat arrived it departed leaving the two ladies gasping with gratitude. The queen was the first to get a grip on her raging emotions. "This is the prison!"

Hope drove Maureen to take the lead at a pace double what they had been using. She stopped suddenly without warning looked to her right at her mother-in-law and hissed, "Wait! Do you hear that? Are we going the wrong way? There's a banging sound that is getting louder. And I could swear I just heard voices."

For nearly a full minute she tried to listen but all she could hear was her gasps to breathe. She was watching Modeanna turn her head this way and that when they heard it again. "Charlie!" Maureen screamed leaping forward as fast as she could. As she moved more sounds erupted causing her to cry out, "Drew!" Her vision blurred as tears of joy flooded her eyes. "Ryan!"

That light was getting closer at such a slow pace it frustrated her. When she finally reached the source of illumination she nearly fell through it. It was another hole that had been cut in the floor that looked down on a chamber below. Not much of it could be seen from their vantage point.

The queen crawled over the opening and lay flat to see as much as possible. "It's my dream!" She cried.

Below them; two figures darted across the chamber whispering to one another. Clearly they were afraid of something but it was difficult to tell what it might be. No more noise could be heard by the women.

"We've got to get down there." Maureen whispered finally staring at the fifteen foot drop with dismay.

Before Modeanna could respond a voice called up at them, "Hey, who's up there?"

Without hesitating Maureen sobbed happily in Liguesian, "It's Mom, Charlie." His dirty face looked up at them in confusion.

"How'd you know my name?" He demanded with his fists planted on his hips.

Laughing at her foolishness she switched to English, "Your Father and I gave you that name."

"Mom!" His jaw unhinged and he nearly fell over as his adopted brother bounced into view.

"Is that really you, Mom?"

"Yes, Drew it is..."

"How'd you get up there?" Drew frowned up at her voice not really able to see anything through the opening.

Quickly she answered, "It's a long story. We need to get you out of there first."

"There's this big iron door but you have to get the key." Drew said pointing behind him.

A heavy sigh left her as she tried to think.

"What's in the room with you?" Modeanna wondered.

Both boys startled and took a few steps back from the hole. "Who are you?"

"I'm Queen Modeanna." She answered somewhat sharply. "Now we haven't much time. What do you have in the room with you?"

"Just a couple of lanterns and buckets, three plates, three forks, three mattresses and three blankets, Mam." Drew replied respectfully.

"Not much to work with I'm afraid." Said the queen switching back to Liguesian.

"No." Maureen agreed quietly and then took a deep breath to ask, "Where's Ryan?"

"He's right over there, Mom. On one of the beds. He's really sick. We've been trying to take care of him as best as we can." Charlie responded emotionally.

Grasping each other's hands excitedly they cried in unison, "He's alive!"

Modeanna leaned further through the hole to try to see more of the room. "Let's see those blankets. How big are they?" When the boys each took an end to spread it out she continued, "Can you tie them together with a good strong knot at the corner?"

"Sure!" Running to get another blanket Drew worked quickly to do the queen's bidding. "How's that?"

"Perfect. Now do that with the other one." In quiet tones she told Maureen what her full plan was.

Although she was not sure it would work until they had a better idea she would give it a shot. So she quickly sat up to get ready for the next part of the plan.

"Now, toss it as high in the air as you can so we can try to catch it."

"Yes, Mam." Drew knew that Charlie had a much better chance of making it so he stepped out of the way to give his brother room.

With all three blankets tied together it was a heavy bundle to throw. Charlie's first throw fell about two feet short of the goal. His second managed to hit the ceiling but it was not close enough to the hole for Modeanna to catch it.

While her son repeatedly threw the knotted bedding, Maureen worked desperately to untie the fabric at her waist. With all the activity it had tightened down on itself and she could not seem to make it budge.

Each of his throws was becoming less accurate. He was panicking. Drew came closer and took over without much success. The blanket went to the ceiling every time but he could not make it close to the opening.

Little by little the knot was coming undone. Her breathing resumed its normal rhythm as she slipped the blue strip from her waist. "Here, Charlie, aim for the blue!" She allowed just enough of the material to drop through the hole for the boys to see. "Come on, you can do it, Charlie, I know you can."

Their loud cheers resounded in their ears as Modeanna pulled on the edge of the blanket. Soon it was in a heap next to the queen with just one corner in her hand. In quick jerky movements she added the blue material to their makeshift rope.

"Can you move those mattresses?" Maureen licked her lips as she waited for them to respond.

"Good idea. Here pull that end to make sure that knot is strong enough to hold them." Once it was tested the queen dropped it back through the hole saying, "There's a slip knot in that blue fabric help Ryan into it and tighten it around his chest. We'll hold this end so that he won't fall."

It was a challenge for the two young teenagers to lift their limp brother and get the rope securely fastened. The women were no less tested in their strength with having to hold onto it. As she watched her little boy flopping each time force was placed on any part of his body her fear over his life increased.

Seconds after the harness was in place they hauled in the rope. When he was close to the ceiling Modeanna braced her feet against one wall and her back against the other. "Reach down and carefully guide him through the hole while I pull him up."

Mixed emotions washed over her as she touched her Ryan for the first time in a month. He was alive and joy flooded over her in great waves, but his skin was unbelievably hot for the cool temperatures of the mines which made her ache with sorrow. After his head was clear of the hole she reached out to pull him to her chest. For a moment all she could do was sob against his hot cheek. Then taking a deep breath she gently set him on the floor so that she could take off the rope.

Not two minutes later she felt the glorious sensation of Charlie's arms around her shoulders. Helping him out of the slip knot; Maureen found herself sobbing and laughing at the same time.

Charlie took charge of getting the rope to his brother and did a fair share of the tugging to lift him out of their prison cell. He stared openly at his mother as she wrapped her bright blue arms around his brother. She looked so different. So thin compared to the last time he had seen her. "Mom? Is that really you?"

"Yeah, it's really me." She gave a tearful giggle as she posed for them.

Before they had a chance to respond, Modeanna broke in using English with tears on her face, "We must hurry. Something tells me we are in terrible danger here. Especially when they discover that their prisoners have escaped."

With a shake of his head Drew said, "Everybody else is gone. The last of the guards took off a few minutes ago. They're expecting some big earthquake or something I think. It's kinda hard to tell though 'cause their speaking in some weird language."

"That soldier we heard did say something about this mountain rattling apart." Maureen said thoughtfully and then looked up to meet her mother-in-law's gaze.

Together they cried, "They're planning to blow up the mines!"

"Then we need to move quickly." Modeanna stated firmly.

"How do we move Ryan?" Drew wondered. "He's totally out and we can't carry him in our arms here."

"I'll carry him on my back." Maureen said without hesitation.

Modeanna stopped her with a firm hand. "No, that won't work he can't hold on and you need to use both hands to crawl." It was silent for a few seconds while they looked at each other. "Wait." She quickly rattled off a series of instructions that were met with two blank stares. Rolling her eyes at her forgetfulness she repeated the plan in English.

Soon the five of them were making their way back to the main tunnel. Charlie and Drew were leading the way with Ryan draped face down over their backs. Maureen and Modeanna followed them making sure he did not roll off.

Suddenly, the boys stopped at the tunnel entrance. "What do we do? That's a ten foot drop easy."

"Here, set your brother down and we'll use the harness again. You first, Drew."

"But someone's going to be left up here." He protested loudly.

Clapping her hand on his shoulder she looked directly into his eyes she reassured him, "Trust me. It'll be all right. Just hurry." A few minutes later they were all staring up at her except Ryan who was cradled in his grandmother's arms. She scooted to the edge of the floor and stared at the wall looking for the best foot holds.

"No, Mom, you'll break your neck." Charlie cried with his arms stretched above his head. In amazement his hands slowly dropped to his sides as he watched his mother roll over onto her stomach and carefully make her way down the wall. He glanced at his brother to see if he was seeing the same thing or was this just his imagination. It was clear from Drew's gaping mouth that they were.

"Maureen, please hurry. Something's happened with the battle." Her eyes kept flicking to the large chamber to her left.

"Battle?" Echoed the boys. "What battle?"

With a deep breath she jumped the last few feet and answered, "The one straight up that tunnel."

"Take him, Maureen. I must try to reach Sauntago to warn him of what is happening. Perhaps there are enough survivors from the first and second battalions to help us." As their eyes met they shared an understanding smile.

"Thank you. Please, be careful, Your Highness." In shock she watched the queen race down the long corridor.

When she had disappeared from sight the boys turned to their mother excitedly, "How did you ever escape? We thought for sure he would have killed you."

"Escape?" She puzzled aloud. "From whom?"

"Dad." Charlie frowned at her wondering if she were all right. "He's the one who set this whole thing up. To steal us away from you."

"No, he didn't, Charles Vadelum..." Maureen caught herself using what was his middle name on earth and started to laugh. "Listen to me very carefully, young men, you must forget anything you've been told since you were taken from our house."

"You expect us to forget that we aren't in the US anymore. Heck I don't think we're on the planet earth anymore."

Charlie shook his brother's arm as he sarcastically snapped, "You've read way too many sci-fi books Drew. If we aren't on earth then where are we?"

"Liguesis." She interjected between them not just with her voice but her body as well. "Come on let's go, quietly." Her strides were short but quick as she pressed Ryan to her torso. As they drew near to the end of the tunnel she saw the queen standing next to a guard listening to him. Instantly she recognized him and rushed forward to listen in on the end of the conversation.

"It is over, My Lady." Her former guard gave a deep bow.

"What?" She hissed softly looking first at him and then at Modeanna. "How?"

"I must leave the details to others more informed than I, however, the king in his great wisdom has succeeded in trapping the leader of this treacherous band of rebels. He has sent out the orders to clear the mines of all Liguesians and Galixtorns while he takes care of him."

"This is not the way out of the mines and as I know you to have a very strong sense of direction you will tell me why you are here?" Modeanna straightened her shoulders regally demanding a truthful answer.

His eyes went to Maureen briefly and then he smiled as he looked at the boys. To his queen he said firmly, "It was my duty to guard, My Lady, and although I was forbidden to speak with her I learned what she was like by watching her. There was no way she was going to leave these mines without her sons and this was the closest tunnel when the king's order was given."

The queen nodded at him with satisfaction. "Then lead the way out of here, Captain Trigguard."

With an awkward bow he corrected, "I am only a guardsmen, Your Highness."

"Do you think after my years as queen that I cannot tell your rank, Captain?" She snapped harshly but her eyes sparkled with humor. "Now get me out of here."

Maureen had to bite her lip to keep from laughing out loud in the young man's face. But then his name struck a chord in her heart. "You are Arvou and Narmaka's son." She breathed softly with growing wonder. "That's why you treated me so well. You recognized your Father's horse."

"I am. At first I only wished to discover how you had come to have my Father's prized horses. And gain some assurance that my family was well. It took very little time to see that you really were only looking for your sons. We should go now, My Lady."

Shifting Ryan's weight she followed him into the chamber that she had never really had the chance to see. A quick look behind her assured her that Charlie and Drew were reluctantly following.

Only a few sharp clashes of metal could be heard now. As she looked around the practically empty room she was stunned by its size. Torches burning along the outer walls cast flickering shadows near at least six doorways. There were four tall columns standing in the middle of the room as supports for the twenty foot ceiling. Each of the columns was at least four feet in diameter at its base and did not appear to narrow until just before it reached the dome.

Other than a few boulders scattered about on the floor and several bodies there did not seem to be anything else here. So the clanking of metal confused her momentarily. Then she saw the tips of almost a half a dozen swords rising from the floor.

After taking a closer look Maureen realized that there was an opening in the floor from which several men were now emerging. Among the group she could see the blue and silver colors of the Galixtorn army as well as the Liguesian green. Her heart skipped a beat as she noted the colors she recognized as allies were outnumbered by a tight knot of black clothed enemies.

Their guard pulled his sword and held it at chest level in both hands. With his head he indicated that they should go to the right. Much to his dismay none of them moved.

"Holy Cow! Drew, do you see that?" Charlie did not really speak in a very loud voice but it echoed loudly as if he had used a megaphone.

"What's Dad doing with that sword?"

All of the men halted their assault and moved cautiously to view the disturbance. They split into two groups glaring at one another while they moved about the columns.

"It is over! You and your rebellion are at an end!" Shouted a shorter man with blue and silver paint on his helmet, sword, shield and armor. "Our people have had enough of your torment."

Her jaw lowered as her eyes widened. Tagurah was easy to spot due to his resemblance to his father and older brother. His hair was longer than Sauntage's and a few shades lighter, but his build and size were nearly identical. All of his movements were smooth and calculated. He knew exactly what he was doing as he carefully navigated between his father's men and the large pillars.

Modeanna gasped at the cold heartless laughter vibrating through the chamber. She knew that sound though not the evil tone of voice. Of their own accord her feet carried her further into the room. How could this be? Horror rounded her eyes as she met the malicious glare of her younger son. A cold chill went down her spine as he sneered at her.

"Welcome, to my home, Mother. Surprised?" His eyebrows lifted at her as he declared in perfect English, "Well, you shouldn't be. We all have our secrets don't we?" As he finished speaking he took a few steps in his mother's direction ignoring the sound of his father taking down his second in command.

Breathlessly she cried, "Tagurah, what have you done? Why would you do this?"

Pointing his sword tip at her he scowled, "All my life I've listened to you and Father spout the traditions of this land. How important they are and how vital it is to pass them on to future generations. And I accepted them until I found out what you are. Both of you. Hypocrites! Tradition should have seen me as next in line to the throne. But day after day year after year I was sent out on those ridiculous searches. My cowardly brother walked away from you and this land and I was still not good enough for Father to train."

"If you believe that, Tagurah, then you failed to read all of the ancient traditions. You were never in line for the throne." Sauntage clenched his teeth in rage as he sought to draw his brother's attention. With relief he felt the heat of Tagurah's blue eyes and then he began to lightly play with his grip on the sword. The last thing he needed was to have his fingers cramp in the middle of this duel.

Maureen felt her throat closing off. She could not breathe. Ryan was slipping from her arms as the strength left her arms. On either side of her the older boys pressed.

"Mom, what is Dad doing? I've seen that guy with a sword he'll kill Dad." Drew looked at her as the color drained from his face.

In a choked whisper she said, "Don't worry, Your Father knows exactly what he is doing." Although she could tell they were not convinced the boys remained quiet. Her lips parted quietly in a prayer. She begged God in a whisper to help Sauntage and his father win this battle quickly.

"You're a fool, Tagurah!" Sauntage yelled at him. "If all you wanted was the power you could have had that years ago. Idiot they sent you out to find proof of my life. All you had to do was find proof of my death and befriend Father's closest aide." His tipped slightly in the direction of Sauntago's advisor, Armok.

Rage boiled in Tagurah's eyes as he charged at his older brother. His sword was aimed at the center of the chest plate.

Sauntage swung his sword blade under his brother's and then did a subtle twist over the top knocking the younger man off balance. With a strong shove he sent Tagurah over the top of a boulder. Sparing a moment to look towards his mother he now saw for the first time Maureen and his sons. Time froze for that split second but resumed quickly when she shouted at him.

"Behind you, Sauntage!" She could feel the stares of the boys and said, "It's Liguesian. The language spoken here."

Sauntago found himself standing behind his younger son. Ready to draw him away from Sauntage and the others, but uncertain as to whether he could do what really needed to be done. Could he take the life of one son to save another? His gaze flicked to his wife. Swallowing hard he had to wonder if she could ever forgive him if he were forced to raise his blade to one of them.

His mind was racing. Something was not right with all of this. There was more going on here. It simply did not make sense. Why would his brother spend what had to have been years planning this kidnapping just to become king? Tagurah's rage was not over missing a fact from the history books. What was he not seeing?

To keep the royal family out of harm's way the newly dubbed captain pushed them to the left. He was hoping to take them to safety down that corridor because it was the closest he knew to lead out of the mines, but there was a rebel standing ten feet back with his sword and shield ready for action. Where had this man come from? Now he had to find a way to draw that man into the room and escort the royal family. Or could he push them back to the right to the other entrance? The clanging swords on that side of the chamber answered that question for the moment.

Licking his lips he prepared to take another hit. This time Tagurah was more in control of his emotions so his actions were well calculated. Muscles in his arms and back trembled from the speed and strength of his younger brother's attack. He could tell that he was being pushed closer to the rest of his family but for several moments he could not figure out why; driving him closer to their father and the king of Galixtorn only made the odds worse for Tagurah. The rest of his men seemed to be following his example with the soldiers they were engaging. All of them were being more or less pushed to the center of the dome.

Suddenly, Tagurah glanced back over his shoulder. A signal went between Tagurah and his servant. It was subtle, but the dip of his chin was clear. This was followed by a long evil chuckle. "You think me to be the stupid one?" He stepped calmly over a smoking object that rolled across the floor from the guarded corridor and landed at Sauntage's feet. "Taking out the two most powerful leaders of our world in one act leaves me to take not one throne but two. Having, you dear brother, and yours here as well assures me that no one will come along to threaten my throne. This really has worked out far better than I ever could have imagined because I already have the sympathy of the people and will have it all the more upon the death of the king and queen at the hand of their eldest son.  And with countless supporters already in the north I will soon control them as well."

Before Sauntage or his father could do anything to stop him he fled toward the tunnel entrance. His guard had turned to lead the way through the long corridor. At the threshold of the chamber he felt the hard steel blade jut between his feet causing him to drop face first to the floor.

The new captain guessed his fate before he even moved his sword. With his blade tangled in the other man's legs he knew he would be defenseless. "Run, Fair Lady Maureen! Run, My Queen!" Pride held his shoulders square. As he felt the agonizing pressure of Tagurah's weapon he saw his charges escaping with the good king of Galixtorn. By the time his knees hit the floor his attacker had fled and was quickly chased by a strange 'fiery' object that he had never before seen.

With all the strength he possessed Sauntage hurled sparking sticks of dynamite as far as he could into the tunnel. It managed to sail over Tagurah's head and drop four feet in front of him before the end of the fuse was reached.

Dust billowed up behind them swallowing them in a blinding cloud. Maureen was coughing loudly along with everyone else. The blast had left her momentarily unable to hear anything but the ringing in her ears. As they emerged into the fading afternoon light she looked around to find her family.

They were all there.

Sauntago, Modeanna and the Galixtorian king were kneeling beside the still form of Captain Trigguard. From their actions she could tell that he must still be alive so she asked God to please bless him.

Tears poured from her eyes as she watched Sauntage hug their sons. He was reluctant to let them go so with his arms still wrapped around both of them he rushed at her. Ryan was pressed between them as he leaned over to rest his head at the side of her neck.

"I love you, Beautiful Carkna Slayer." Sauntage whispered just before he broke down in loud sobs. Yes, he had managed to rescue his children, wife and parents, but he had been forced to take his brother's life to do it.

His grief broke off for the moment as the warmth of Ryan registered in his brain. Pulling back he brushed the hair from the little boy's brow and placed a kiss on his hot forehead. "Is he all right?"

"I don't know. There hasn't been time to really look at him." She allowed Sauntage to take him from her and kneel on the ground with Ryan across his lap. "He's got a high fever. The boys said he was sick." It suddenly dawned on her that Charlie and Drew could not understand what they were saying so she looked up at them. "How long has he been sick?"

"Pretty much since we got here. It started out with just a stuffy nose. He was almost over that when we got rained on outside and it came back." Charlie swallowed hard. "We tried to take care of him."

Sauntage reached up to grasp his sons' hands while Maureen listened to his breathing and heartbeat. "If he's been sick that long you two have done a remarkable job."

Her voice broke as she sat up to tell him. "His lungs sound congested. Sau, he needs antibiotics."

"We might find some herbs among the soldiers. Let's get him back to camp." Gently he lifted Ryan into his arms and rose to walk with him.

While he walked ahead with Ryan, Maureen took Charlie and

Drew by the hands to follow. Slowly they made their way off the battlefield. There only seemed to be fallen men belonging to Tagurah's army which surprised her. When she made a comment about it the answer she received in English shocked her.

"Much of this battle was staged for Tagurah's benefit. You see, Father had been dealing with these threats and horrific acts for years before my name started being used in junction with them. Tagurah used his band of rebels to manipulate my Father's actions..."

"Knowing that your Father would investigate these incidents." She nodded sadly with understanding.

"Yes, exactly. If Father was busy with official business then he was free to go wherever he wanted and do whatever he wanted."

"But that doesn't explain this battle being staged." Her brow wrinkled.

"What Tagurah never figured out was that the king of Galixtorn and Father had been in close contact over the matter for years, but they used only a few specifically chosen messengers that were sworn to secrecy about their missions. There were always rumors and speculation over the crimes committed and who was involved. Months ago Father started to put things together and realized that someone had been playing him for a fool."

"And all the evidence pointed to you as Tagurah planned all along."

"The kings arranged this little war less than three weeks ago when Father received word that Tagurah had been kidnapped by me. Galixtorn engaged Tagurah's men and many pretended to fall. Our men came in to draw out the second wave of men from the mines and lead them down through the valley. As they came after us Galixtorn rose up behind them before they could get away." A heavy sigh left him as he looked back over the valley. "So many men died today because I chose foolishly to confide in my brother. If he wouldn't have known about The Gateway or you and the kids he would not have had the means to do all of this."

At the base of the hill she too looked behind her at the soldiers working to find and care for the wounded. "Perhaps you are right, Sau. But I can't help thinking that if he hadn't known about you then he might have easily maneuvered his way to the throne of Liguesis years ago. How many more lives or nations could he have hurt then?"

# Chapter Thirteen

Hours later they were kneeling on either side of the king and queen's bed with Ryan between them. Sauntago and Modeanna were at the foot of the mattress with Charlie and Drew at the corners. A small supply of herbs used for fevers and infections was being shared throughout the wounded ranks; so the six of them were sitting vigil hoping for a change in Ryan's condition. Not a word had been uttered in a very long time.

Every now and then Sauntago left to check on his men and the progress of cleaning up the battlefield. Deep lines of concern were etched on the king's face. His lips were pressed together in a firm line. Despite the fact that his heart was breaking he had responsibilities that were his alone. As a man of honor he would see them through to the end. A heavy sigh left him but he cut it off when he heard footsteps coming up behind him.

Sauntage watched his father for a brief time before he drew closer. Knowing that the two dozen tents they were looking at housed men that were hurt from the battle made him reluctant to ask for advice. "Father, how are the men?"

"Most of the wounds will heal I believe. More than a hundred injuries have been reported and sadly three deaths. Tagurah's men did not fare well at all. Thankfully, King Jeraxial has had compassion on them and has the means to care for those men who have survived until they can be tried and tested."

Through a thick barrier in his throat Sauntage asked, "What of Captain Trigguard?"

"His wound is grave. But word of his courage has spread among the men and many are giving up their rations for him." Silence fell between them for nearly a minute. "You did not come out here for these questions."

"No, Sire, I didn't." He dropped his chin to his chest and then quietly admitted, "I came hoping for advice. Ryan is not getting any better. None of the medicines has made a difference. I don't know what to do now. I have spent this night asking Ewaris for mercy..."

His words halted when he felt the large hand grasp his shoulder.

"Son, my only advice to you is to follow your heart and gut. It has been clear all night that you have something on your mind. Whatever it is do it."

"Even if it means leaving the rest of my family in Liguesis?" Agony rent his voice and clenched his fists.

"Yes." Was all the king could say and then he turned to walk away.

At dawn all of the herbs had already been tried without success. Maureen had prayed softly throughout the night for another miracle. When she looked across the bed at her husband she knew he was wrestling with something. He must have sensed her questions because he suddenly got to his feet and left.

More than fifteen minutes went by and still he did not return. Puzzled by this she placed a kiss on Ryan's cheek and then went to find him. As she came out of the tent she nearly ran into Dueby who was tied to the tent stake. Sauntage was pulling things out of his leather pouch most of which he tossed on the ground next to the doorway of the tent.

"Sau?" Maureen said quietly with a deep furrow on her brow.

Heaving his shoulders he finally met her gaze with anguish. "Maureen..." His forehead rested on the horse's saddle briefly before he continued, "Darling, if Ryan doesn't get help soon he's going to die. You know that." Sauntage moved around the front of the horse to take her by the upper arms. "We've tried everything available here. He needs a doctor."

She could not help the gasp that escaped.

"Please, listen to me. I didn't tell you this before because it wasn't important or possible for our journey here, but The Gateway can be reached in four to five days time from here..." Her head began to shake with disbelief so he took hold of her face as he went on to say, "It is a straight shot from here through the heart of a desert. If I can ride at top speed without stopping I can reach The Gateway in four days. Remember the scuba tanks Tagurah left? I can use them to get him to a doctor."

Her heart was wrenching in two.

"I swear I will come back for you as soon as I can. I know you don't believe me. I know you can't trust me, but it's Ryan's life at risk." He forced himself to let go of her and when he did she ran back through his parents' tent and out the other side. With a heavy heart he went in to tell his sons and parents what he planned to do.

Charlie and Drew promised to care for their mother while he was gone, but were clearly not happy that their father would abandon them. Modeanna held him close while she cried into his shoulder. Sauntago nodded at his son with approval and offered to care for and protect his family until he came back. "We will wait for you at The Gateway." Was all he whispered into Sauntage's ear.

His father carried Ryan out to the horse until he could take him on his lap. With his foot in the stirrup he glanced up to see Maureen racing at him with her hands full. There were tears streaming down her cheeks as she came to a stop several feet from the horse. She did not want to startle him. Taking great gulps of air she handed him a dozen water pouches and a small bag of fruit.

"You'll need as much water as possible to cross a desert. Be sure to give Ryan a little bit every hour. Maybe the jarring ride will loosen what's trapped in his lungs." After he had strapped the pouches to the saddle she threw herself into his arms and said in his ear, "I do trust you Sauntage Vadelum." There had been more she wanted to say but his goodbye kiss left no more time or doubts between them. Swallowing the lump in her throat she watched them ride off in a south-westerly direction. When he was out of sight she dropped into a heap on the ground.

Long shadows of morning light were stretching across the huge encampment when she woke. After blinking a few times Maureen could see Charlie and Drew across the tent sleeping on pallets pushed together. Covering a yawn she twisted this way and that to awaken her muscles.

Both boys must have heard their mother because they too were getting out of bed. Concern caused tense lines around their lips and above their eyes. Drew was the first to find his voice, though he used it only to whisper, "Mom, are you all right?"

"We gotta hurry up and get out of here." Charlie jumped in before she could respond. Cautiously he peeked out of the curtain door only to come face to face with Avix. A loud yelp escaped him as he fell backward into the small sleeping chamber.

"Good morning, Avix. Come here." Maureen gently tapped her thigh to call the aragaff to her. While she scratched the animal behind the ears she explained in English, "Boys, I'd like to introduce you to Avix. She is an aragaff, an animal from Liguesis."

"Are you kidding, Mom?" Charlie hissed with wide eyes. "That thing is huge! It could take off your arm in one bite."

Her smile widened a bit as she answered, "According to your Father she wouldn't hurt a fly."

Drew's eyes flared with sarcasm as he wondered angrily, "And you would believe him after lying to us all these years? We don't even know what he's done with Ryan."

"As a matter of fact I do believe him and I do know where he has taken Ryan. Listen, let's go see what is happening with the rest of the camp and I'll do my best to tell you everything I can." Reluctantly, the young men followed her into a large grassy field with dozens of tents scattered around, smaller than the one they had just vacated.

"So what is this place, Mom? Some kind of gypsy village?" Charlie wondered as he observed the scurrying of several boys his own age as they delivered firewood and other supplies to the cooks.

"No, this is the army encampment. These men risked their lives to save you." At first she puzzled at the number of cooking fires out in the open, but then with sorrow she realized that the tents were needed for wounded men now. She swallowed a hard lump as she wondered which tent held Captain Trigguard, if he were even alive.

"Why? How did they even know we needed help?" In amazement Drew gaped at the sheer number of men moving in and around the tents.

"Truthfully, they didn't know for sure. You see the man that brought you here was..."

"Dad's brother! He lied to us about not remembering his past." Charlie exclaimed loudly.

A heavy sigh brought her chin to her chest before she said, "Yes, your Father lied to us. He lied to his family here as well. And trust me he had good reason to believe that was the only choice he had.

"Around the same time you were brought here three things happened. First, the queen began to have dreams of a little boy, Ryan, actually. Then the king of Liguesis was informed of a rebel army gathering in the mines as well as the kidnapping of your uncle."

"Okay, so Dad's brother lied about being kidnapped, but what has that got to do with the king and queen of this place?" Confusion was shaking more than Drew's head, though that was the only visible motion.

"Perhaps if we were properly introduced it would help."

At the sound of another voice from behind them the boys turned. When they saw the large man standing next to the woman the two of them stumbled back a few steps. It was not just their size or proximity that startled them, but the way the couple was dressed and stood.

Sauntago was still wearing leather pants though they were now clean. He also wore a vest made of animal hide under which he had a dark green shirt with long sleeves. Modeanna was wearing the gown that she wore when Maureen first saw her. Both of them were stiff and clearly uncomfortable with this situation; wondering how they would be received by their grandchildren.

Maureen stepped up between her sons and then gave the couple before her an awkward bow. "Your Majesties, may I present, Charles and Andrew Vadelum. Boys, this is Modeanna and Sauntago," She paused to smile at the two of them as she added, "Vadelum, your Grandparents."

"Grandparents!" They cried in unison.

Turning to look at his mother with his eyes blinking in disbelief, Charlie hissed softly, "I thought they were the king and queen here."

"They are." Maureen nodded at him and then lifted her gaze to smile at her in-laws.

"But that would mean Dad's a... prince." Drew breathed out softly as he openly stared at the tentative couple in front of him.

The smile would no longer stay contained as she wrapped an arm around each of their shoulders and giggled softly. "Yes, your Father was a prince, but he gave up his crown to marry me." With hope she felt some of the tension leave the young men as they considered the information they were receiving.

"Wow." Was the only word that Drew could get past his lips. His eyes blinked several times as he tried to figure out what all of the information he had just received from his adopted mother meant.

"No way." Charlie whispered under his breath. As he stared at the man before him he realized how much he was reminded of his father.

Modeanna could wait no longer to touch them so as she reached out to hug Drew she said, "Forgive me I know this is so very hard. But I have waited so long for this day." Once her arms went around him Modeanna let her tears freely flow.

Sauntago pulled Charlie into an embrace at the same time. "I never even dared to dream about a moment like this." As he pulled back from his grandson his hands took either side of Charlie's face and he smiled with pride, "No, Grandfather could be prouder than I am right now."

Because the boys were not able to understand Sauntago their eyes stared blankly at him while their lips held stiff smiles. Modeanna translated her husband's words for him and she saw the light of understanding and blush of humility cover their faces.

Each of them mumbled their thanks and then turned to look at their mother for direction.

"Don't worry. You two will be speaking Liguesian in no time." She quietly reassured them.

Around the small family campfire that night Maureen watched the humorous interaction between grandfather and grandsons. Modeanna like Maureen observed with quiet smiles and occasional comments. Much of their conversation was made up of finger pointing, hand gestures and charades. Charlie and Drew learned the Liguesian language even faster than she had. By the time she ordered them to bed that night, Drew and Charlie had already learned two dozen words and phrases.

As the two of them shuffled away from the fire Maureen felt a momentary twinge of guilt. The last thing she wanted to do was to stifle the desire the boys had to learn their father's language. With a sigh she soon followed them knowing that however much she might not like it she had to do her best to protect them. In this case she knew they were in desperate need of sleep. If they didn't get rest soon she was concerned that they too would become sick.

When she prepared to turn down the wick on the lamp a few minutes later, Charlie stopped her with a question. "Mom?"

"Yes." A soft smile came to her lips at the sound of his voice calling to her. It felt so good.

"What if Dad doesn't come back?" His eyes shifted rapidly over her face to read every movement of the muscles.

"He'll be back." Gently she pulled the blanket up around his neck and tucked it over his shoulders. "It may take him some time, but he'll be back."

Drew sat up next to his brother to look her in the eyes as he asked, "How can you be so sure? I mean he's lied to you for...what...seventeen years?"

"You're right. He hid his identity from me...us all this time. But somehow in a strange way that is all he did. Everything else about him...his personality...his character is still the same. Who he is really never changed."

The boys gave her confused nods just before she turned the wick on the lantern down and the light slowly faded.


At times it was difficult for Maureen to keep her mind focused on what was happening before her. During the first few days after Sauntage had left there was a great deal of work to be done among the wounded. This was difficult for Maureen because she did not know how to care for many of the injuries. With patience Modeanna showed her how to address some of the medical needs of the men and the two of them worked throughout the tents.

Many of the men were reluctant to have the women treat them, which Maureen found puzzling until her mother-in-law pulled her aside to explain what was happening. As they walked some distance away from the tents she lowered her guard with a sad sigh. "I know this is hard to understand coming from where we do, but you must be careful when going in to help these men. According to the social structure here the only women that are to serve them like this are their wives or at their ages perhaps a mother. It will be especially hard for them because I am their queen. Now that the battle is over and Sauntage has proven to most of them he is worthy of their respect, this will likely be so for you as well."

A gasp parted her lips as she suddenly said, "So that's why he made such a big deal about me killing that snake and taking care of him. Of course I did it because I love him, but truthfully I would have cared for a stranger if I were in the same position."

"Of course, anyone here would as well, but it is how that is done of which you must be cautious. Any touch that you give must be for the injury only. You cannot give that squeeze of encouragement or pat of sympathy. To them this would be dishonoring to your husband. They will do their best to protect you from this by refusing your offer of help. It took me a long time to realize that it is not really a matter of pride for these men, but respect." Her eyes traveled over her daughter-in-law's face to see if she understood. In the moments that followed she saw the slight nodding of Maureen's head and knew that she did grasp what they were up against.

"I would assume then that this would be the case for the words we speak as well?" When she saw Modeanna's movement, she took a deep breath. "Well, then I think I will stick close to you for a while. At least until I have a handle on how this is done."

With a grim smile Modeanna agreed, "That's a good idea. We'll begin with those men whose injuries have left them unconscious."

She observed Modeanna for several hours as she went in to treat the men. As time went by it was easy to see that it was not so much the wounds themselves that bothered the queen, but the separation. The inability to express how sorry she was for the pain each of these men were facing clearly grieved her.

This was easier for Maureen to relate to as she went to the first young man on her own. After seeing her mother-in-law do this many times she thought that she was ready to try this on her own. While she was pouring water over the bandage on his leg he startled awake. It was the first time he had apparently woken up since the battle and he was clearly confused. In a matter of fact voice she said to him, "Be still. All will be well. You have a cut that needs to be cleaned."

His eyes darted around him for a moment or two and then he lifted his head off of the ground to see what she doing. He frowned deeply at his limb for a moment before he lowered his head once more with his eyes closed. Muscles along his throat worked to keep his emotions under control because he knew from that quick glance that this wound was serious and could mean the loss of his leg were infection to develop. Stiffly he lay there as he accepted her help and fought back the tears. Those were for later when he was alone.

Even though she had never seen this young man before Maureen knew that he was frightened about his future and in terrible pain. Social guidelines demanded that she not speak to him more than to tell him what she was doing medically for his leg. She was sure that when she finished his bandage her face now had the same lines of distress she had seen on her mother-in-law. Before she could go to the next patient, Maureen had to take a break.

Quietly she moved away from the tents looking around her for a place of solitude. There really wasn't a place to be completely alone because the ring surrounding the camp was still in place though not in so large a number. If she were to pass outside their circle of protection the guards would raise an alarm. In the end she went back to the throne room where their bags were kept.

Tears slipped from her eyes as she knelt on the ground. Her cries were silent, but her mind screamed against the suffering she was witnessing. How could she do this?

As the tears subsided she lifted her face from the ground and found that her cap had fallen from her head. For a few seconds she stared at it remembering the woman that had given it to her. Gathering her hair at the back of her head she quickly twisted it into a coil on top of her scalp. A smile formed on her lips as she reached down to pick up the cap and put it back on her head.

Narmaka's words drifted through her mind, 'Two of my sons have gone to serve the king in this battle as have many of our neighbors and their sons. Arvou and I hear the horrible stories coming from the border. From here there is not much we can do to stop what is happening. But what we can do we will do in the name of our Lord, Ewaris and the king of the land, to hopefully save your sons. Perhaps there are enough Liguesians who feel as we do and can make a real difference in this war.'

Suddenly, Maureen knew where she would find the strength to care for these men. In the knowledge that she could not fix all of their hurts, but could make a difference. What she was able to do she would do in the name of Ewaris hoping that they would know what she did. He loved them. With a firm resolve she got up from the ground, wiped the tears from her face and then went back to the tents to serve the king's men.

She learned with great joy that Captain Trigguard was still alive though his condition was not good. He was battling an infection in his wounds for which they did not have enough medicine. For hours Maureen took turns with her mother-in-law bathing his face, chest and arms in an effort to cool him. Their efforts were not rewarded with anything other than the fact that he still drew breath.

Naturally her thoughts wandered to Ryan and Sauntage as she helped treat the wounds of the men. Each time she changed a bandage or helped a soldier eat a meal Maureen thought of Ryan and prayed for him and Sauntage. Despite the knowledge of how serious Ryan's condition was Maureen had a deep sense that God was in control and He knew what they all needed.

Four days after Sauntage had left with Ryan; Maureen kept finding herself staring off to the southwest wondering if they had made it to The Gateway. Many times she wished they could have sent a soldier along so that she might know how her son and husband fared on the journey. As much as she wanted to ask if she and the boys could travel to The Gateway with a couple of the men, Maureen knew that was not possible. They could not risk anyone else learning about the passage to earth.

Once a prayer for her husband and son was lifted she quickly added on pleas for comfort on behalf of Sauntago and Modeanna. Their commitment to their nation was revealed in everything that they did, but it was clear to Maureen how deeply they were hurting over what had happened to their family. Every now and then one of them would turn to face the direction of the mines. After staring for several minutes they would square their shoulders or wipe their hands across their cheeks, and turn to whatever work was at hand.

When the battle had been over for one week, Sauntago surprised them at the campfire by saying, "Rest well tonight because we will begin the journey back in the morning."

The fire popped between them sending a shower of sparks upward into the black sky. "But what about the wounded men?" Maureen asked looking briefly at the other family members gathered with them.

"Most of them are well enough to travel without much difficulty. And those that are not quite strong enough have requested that we begin." He answered slowly.

"Why would they want to do that?" Wondered Charlie with a frown.

"Captain Trigguard needs more medicine and the men wish to do this for him." Sauntago lowered his gaze to the dirt before him. "That young man needs a miracle at this point."

Quietly the five of them left the fire pit and went into the royal tent. Maureen and the boys curled up on pallets in the throne area while the king and queen slept in the small bed chamber.

Sleep was a long time in coming for Maureen as she turned her thoughts into prayers. So many things weighed heavily in her mind and there really was no one other than God to whom she felt she could go. Sauntage was of course not there, his parents had worries of their own and the boys were too young to carry her burdens.

As the days went slowly by she felt a deeper connection and understanding of God and His love for them all. The Bible was a place where she found courage as well as connection to Sauntage. Just thinking that perhaps he had read a particular part of scripture gave her comfort. Even though their days were long and filled with things to learn, see and do Maureen could not help staring off into the distance and thinking of her husband and son. Her prayers for them never ceased.

Pride swelled in her heart as she watched her boys. They quickly embraced the challenges of traveling across the wide open country. Each of them was assigned tasks to help with the smooth passage of the large moving city. At first it was difficult for them to remain awake once they sat down before the evening fire, but gradually they were able to fully enjoy stories shared by their mother and grandparents.

During the day Maureen followed in the wake of Captain

Trigguard. A few of the men had worked to build a skiff that dragged behind one of the horses. It was uncanny how that horse seemed to know without being told where to walk so that his burden would not feel more discomfort. Maureen often wondered if the young man was aware of anything because he rarely stirred much more than a deep throated moan.

Because the rains in the north had been so heavy the river in which Modeanna had nearly drowned was still over flowing. The king ordered his troops to travel further south before crossing. This allowed them to bathe Captain Trigguard often in hopes of keeping his fever from going out of control. Much to everyone's relief this worked quite well so that by the time the army reached a point of safe crossing he appeared to be resting more comfortably.

Sauntago took this crossing much slower; sending small groups instead of a steady stream. With each group he rode along as a rear guard ready to assist if the need arose. Every time a new group went he escorted one of his family members on a fresh or rested horse. When the time came for Captain Trigguard to be brought over the raging flow, Sauntago chose three of his highest ranking men to assist him on the corners of the skiff.

Once everyone was safely across with no incidents an audible sigh went through the crowd. This along with the stable, if not improving, condition of the Captain helped the men to relax. On the whole the moral of the group was rising so evenings brought a great deal of celebrating in many forms. There were many stories told around the campfires, a few new victory songs written, and when the soldiers found it, too much alcohol consumed. This was all done with consideration of the royal family and the losses it had suffered so it never got terribly loud late at night nor were there many things shared within their hearing.

As the large army worked its way west just a couple of miles north of the Garak Desert, it began to thin out tremendously. Sauntago began to release the men from their duties as they came to various streams or rivers that led north towards their homes or villages. He made an effort to speak to each one or at least groups of them to thank them for their faithful service.

It was a difficult trip for the king. While he had led this fine group of men and they had rooted out a great evil from the land, many of them now carried scars. If not physical ones then emotional. In the middle of the night Sauntago often heard the cries of his men as they relived moments of the battle in their dreams. His heart ached for these young men because most of them were not meant to be soldiers. All of them had, of course, gone through the initial military training as teenagers, but they had gone on to other occupations. Now he felt a deep sense of responsibility to these men. They left their families, homes and livelihood to help him. Other than a few words of praise or thanks what could he offer them that would equal their sacrifice? With humility Sauntago Vadelum realized there was no greater gift.

So each time the army reached a waterway the king called for a halt long enough to gather the men who lived north of where they stood. Sometimes there were only a handful and other times there were dozens of men standing before him. His speech was never the same, but it always ended with Sauntago lowering one knee to the ground, his helmet in hand and his head bowed to them.

Maureen stood between her mother-in-law and sons during these ceremonies. She was often amazed by the tears visible in the eyes of the men. Having their king bow to them meant a great deal to them apparently. Although she was curious about this reaction Maureen never asked Modeanna about it because she always turned away with quiet sobs and it did not cross her mind to ask Sauntago.

Charlie and Drew did not understand much at the first few rivers so they stood respectfully at their mother's side. After getting to know this man whom they now knew as grandfather, however, they would turn at the end of the ceremony and wipe streams from their cheeks. "Man, Drew, every one of them would have died for him. You can see it on their faces." Whispered Charlie after a particularly large group had turned northward.

"And even though they didn't know about us to begin with, I'd bet any of them would have died for us too." Drew brushed away two fresh tears and then turned his eyes toward the group preparing to head further west. "One almost did."

"Sure wish there was something we could do for Captain Trigguard." Charlie fell in step with his brother both of them were deep in thought.

When they had circumvented the desert the king gathered what troops remained for the final and largest ceremony. It was clearly a surprise to all of the men that the king and his family were no longer going to be traveling with them. Many of the soldiers openly shook their heads as if to defy Sauntago's orders for them to return home. When he saw this the king announced his intentions, "It is my wish to see Captain Trigguard home personally. To tell his Father and Mother of his selfless bravery." This seemed to appease most of them. A few offered to stand with the king to guard and protect Captain Trigguard. To this the king firmly answered, "Your loyalty and bravery are to be commended. But as I believe you have completed your task to make Liguesis safe once more you are all ordered home to your families while I proceed with mine." His voice left no room for argument so reluctantly the men turned away each to the direction he needed to go.

Once he was certain that none of the men were within hearing distance Sauntago said quietly to his family, "We will travel in a north easterly direction as they all expect. After I am certain that no one is following us we can head south for The Gateway."

For a full day the six of them moved slowly in the direction of Captain Trigguard's home. Every couple of hours they paused to check the captain's condition. It was now more critical that they keep watch over his fever as water was harder to find and carry. This was very difficult for Maureen and her eyes kept turning to her left wondering if they had possibly gone too far west and would have to back track to reach The Gateway.

Much to her relief the king announced as they ate dinner next to a small creek, "We will rest here for the night. As long as the Captain fairs no worse in the morning we will head south." He paused to sip water from a wooden cup. "This will not be easy."

"How come?" Charlie wondered with a puckered brow. "Don't we just go south?"

Sauntago turned to his wife to help him explain the situation in

English. Modeanna smiled softly at him and squeezed his forearm firmly, "They understand more than you realize."

With a tender smile for his wife Sauntago took a deep breath and then turned to the boys. "We have all seen how dangerous it is for our worlds to be breached. There can be no trace of our journey to The Gateway. No one can be allowed to do that. So for a distance; a long one we will have to travel single file through this stream..."

"What about the Captain?" Maureen interjected with a frown.

"I will have to walk behind the skiff and hold the end up as we go." His voice sounded tired as if he had already spent the day doing what he was describing. "One of you will have to keep the reins on my mount to make sure he does not leave the riverbed."

"How long do you think we need to follow the stream?" Modeanna wondered quietly.

Sauntago pressed his lips together thoughtfully for a long moment and then responded, "Until it meets with the river flowing on the eastern edge of the Garak Desert. After that it should be safe for a group our size to travel beside the water. If I have estimated correctly we should be able to reach that river before nightfall tomorrow."

Licking her lips lightly to hold back her growing excitement, Maureen asked, "And The Gateway?"

"Less than three days." A nod and smile went to his daughter-in-law as he understood her anxiousness. For her sake he hoped his son had been successful in reaching the help Ryan needed.

Morning could not come soon enough for Maureen. Many times throughout that night she found herself awake listening to the creatures of darkness to try to determine the hour. Before she could do this, however, she would drift off to sleep once more.

Finally, her eyes were able to detect the barest of change in the color of the sky. Deep black velvet was giving way to dark green. As she watched the lifting of night Maureen quietly talked to the Lord about the fear she was experiencing. What if Sau was not at The Gateway or did not return quickly? There was no way for her to go through those caves alone; not with two boys. Sauntago and Modeanna could not be expected to wait indefinitely so if he was not there soon what should she do? These issues weighed heavily in her mind, but strangely when they turned into prayers, there was a comfort that Someone was listening; Someone that cared even more than she did.

Everyone woke early that morning anxious to break their camp. Breakfast was eaten quickly in silence which was unusual for them after so many days traveling in much larger numbers. Sauntago swallowed his last bite and rose to his feet, saying, "It occurred to me last night that we need to have a trail leading away from this creek. If there is no trace of us on the other side then anyone following would know we went through the water. So we are going to keep moving westward until this water is well out of sight and then we will very carefully turn back to retrace our steps to this point. Because there are no roads in this area nor are there many that pass through here I believe anyone trying to follow us won't pay very close attention to our tracks until they end. By that time hopefully they would have trampled our tracks leading back here." He started to walk away but then paused as he thought of something else. "Perhaps we should leave something here where we camped."

"Why?" Charlie wondered with a puckered brow.

"If someone is trying to follow us and they are close we will either see them along the trek back or find what we leave behind moved."

Modeanna came to her feet abruptly as she added, "I agree. And if by chance we do meet anyone we will have a perfectly reasonable explanation for the direction we are going."

Drew visibly shivered as he said to his brother under his breath in English, "I don't know what was scarier. Being kidnapped or going home."

"Yeah, I know what you mean. It's like being in the middle of a spy movie." Whispered Charlie with his eyes trained on his grandfather. "Something tells me that our new Grandpa is the one to follow around here though. We're safe with him."

"I think you're right. At least I sure hope so." With a lopsided smile Drew rose to his feet to get ready.

Despite all of the concerns carried by all of them they returned to the creek without incident nearly two hours later. Everything was just how they left it so Sauntago gave the instructions for the next leg of the journey. Maureen led the way with Jeurku through the center of the small trail of water. As Sauntago directed she went slow choosing their steps carefully for several miles. Charlie followed her on a huge war horse that his grandfather said would instinctively follow the pair in front of him. Modeanna also rode a well trained war horse for this part of the journey. Her job was a bit tedious, however, because she had to pay more mind to the animal behind her than the one she rode. Sitting nearly backward in the saddle she held the reigns of her husband's horse to direct him as they went. Although he was an intelligent creature and well trained they could not risk him deciding he did not need to follow simply because he had no rider.

Sauntago solemnly put his head and arms through the makeshift harness he had created the night before. It was fashioned from the rope Sauntage had made when they first arrived in Liguesis. He had taken several strips and wove them in a lattice work pattern which rested against his spine and then wrapped around in front of his body to form a large knotted loop on each side. To these loops he tied ropes that were woven through the end of Captain Trigguard's skiff. As long as the water did not rise higher than the kings mid thigh the injured man would remain dry.

At first Drew was nervous about bringing up the rear of their group. But as the day went on he found himself grateful for his job. His horse was a bit smaller than the one his mother rode and was not trained in quite the same way so Drew had to pay close attention to the direction he gave to the animal. It was his responsibility to check the banks of the shallow creek to make sure there were no signs of their passage. This allowed him to study the landscape as they went.

Most of the plants that were more than ten feet from the water's edge were a golden brown color. He imagined that it was a lot like the prairies of the Midwest. Closer to the stream bed there were a few trees with exposed knotted roots and low scraggly bushes in a variety of shapes and shades of green. Peace enveloped him as they went along despite the knowledge of possible danger at any moment.

Charlie was having a bit harder time than his brother. The thought that his brother had such an important job all of a sudden and he had to just sit bothered him. Why hadn't Grandfather picked him to bring up the rear? Had he done something that displeased the king? These questions went through his mind a few times and then more followed. Everyone else had a job to do, so why didn't he? What was wrong with him? Mother's job was a cinch he could have done it in his sleep. Was his grandfather judging him based on his father? Had his Dad's lies caused his Grandpa to think less of him? How could he change the king's mind? Could he do something that would show his grandfather that he was not like his father?

Modeanna resisted the urge to complain even in her thoughts as she lost the feeling in her backside and arms. Compared to her husband's position she had it very easy. From where she sat Modeanna could see Sauntago's chest and head. Her heart ached for him as she watched the sweat pour from his brow. Every now and then a grimace would pull his mouth and eyes closer together making him appear much older than he was.

After several miles had passed; the stream bed widened by almost two feet. This gave them a chance to relax just a bit in their saddles. Each of them took the opportunity to munch on nuts, berries and leftover grass cakes. It had taken a good dose of hunger for Maureen to taste the fried cookie sized discs. When supplies had begun to run out two days before; she had watched her mother-in-law gather handfuls of certain weeds. She had shown Maureen what to look for so the two of them collected a large supply of the tall stalks with seed heads still intact. Once they stopped for the night she was taught how to grind the seeds in a bowl with a rock. There was an art to this process as too little force only rolled the hard nuggets around the sides of the bowl and too much tended to make them bounce over the rim.

Now as the sun moved to her right side Maureen was grateful for the lesson. The small brown cakes were crispy on the outside like a chip but a thin layer of moist flour remained in the middle to keep one's mouth from becoming too dry. They had a sweet somewhat nutty flavor which surprised her.

As the afternoon wore on she found her eyes lifting to the horizon more often. So far she had not seen an end to the small river they were using. All that was in front of her was a sea of grasses split in two by the 'road' they were following. More times than she would have liked to admit Maureen raised her hand to cover a yawn.

When the clouds overhead began to change color she grew concerned. No other river was in sight. In fact the one they were walking through was reducing in size. Her eyes lifted nervously to the sky and a soft pleading prayer formed on her lips. Dear God they needed help! To insure the safety of both worlds they had to stay in the water, but they couldn't go on in the dark because they didn't have enough lanterns. Not to mention how tired they all were.

Her pleas grew stronger when the first cooler breeze hit her warm cheek. She was having a difficult time keeping her eyes focused so she could not even imagine the suffering of Sauntago. Countless miles he had trudged through water and muck without stopping.

Because there was some distance between all of them, they were walking through water and except for Modeanna their backs were to each other they didn't speak much the entire day. The rhythmic steps of the horses set a pace and combined with the water to overtake their sense of hearing. After so many hours of the same noise it took Maureen some time to realize that there was another sound breaking through the monotony. Her breath caught in her chest as she realized how close they were to their goal.

Less than a quarter mile ahead there was a sudden drop which led into the other riverbed. A joyous cry broke through her dry throat and lips, "We've made it! The other river is just ahead!" Their quiet rejoicing made her smile as she led them for the final minutes of that journey. As Sauntago had instructed her Maureen watched the river carefully to see how quickly it was flowing. Much to her relief it was larger than the one they were standing in but not so big that they couldn't cross it.

With careful steps she urged Jeurku down the slope into the river. He went obediently to the bank on the far side where she pulled up the reigns and told him to stop.

All of them cried out in pain as they changed positions for the first time since that morning. It hurt more to stand than Maureen thought possible. Her head was spinning as she leaned her forehead against Jeurku and she heard Sauntago speak for the first time in hours.

"Well done, Family!" He slowly shrugged the harness from his shoulders as he went on to say, "Our day is not yet over though. There is still much we must do." Sauntago lowered the skiff to the ground as gently as he could and then turned to Charlie, "I know you are tired and sore but I have a job of great importance for you."

Charlie's eyes brightened, "You do?"

"Yes, I need someone with fresh eyes to search these banks for a plant. Well, actually the leaves of this plant; lots of them. Let's get a lantern for you and I'll show you what to look for."

Walking along the water's edge Charlie studied each plant carefully. His heart had risen back to its place and swollen by several degrees. This job was critical to his family and Captain Trigguard. Grandfather had said so. A feeling of guilt had niggled in his heart briefly when he heard his grandfather explain how he had saved this job just for Charlie; knowing he would be the best suited for it after such a difficult day.

While Charlie gathered leaves for a pain relieving tea the rest of them took care of the horses and made camp for the night.

Captain Trigguard fared better than any of them expected after so many hours without water. His fever had risen a few degrees but it was not raging out of control. As soon as they had a fire built Modeanna and Maureen set about bathing the injured man with cool water.

Drew looked for more wood to keep the fire going late into the night. It was not easy to chop at even the smaller trees because he was so tired. Each time he brought a branch back to chop and put in a pile he swore the pile got smaller.

Sauntago went in the opposite direction of his grandsons in hopes of securing a meal for his family. Darkness was rapidly settling in around him as he sat on the lower branches of the largest tree he could find. In his right hand he held his wife's small sword. To keep his muscles from locking he tensed and loosened his grip every couple of minutes. He did not hold much hope of landing a grand meal, but he had hoped to get something they could use to flavor a soup.

An hour later he returned triumphantly to their camp with a medium sized orfizda draped across his shoulders. With its thin legs, round body, long neck and small rack of antlers; an orfizda resembled a deer. It was gray with black spots along the spine and sides, but the belly was a soft cream color. This young buck would provide them with several meals if they were careful.

Excitement went through their small group giving them each just enough energy to finish the day. Drew and Charlie received a lesson in gutting an animal while Modeanna and Maureen brewed the leaves for tea. As much as all of them wanted to sip the tea as they waited for the orfizda to roast over the low flames they resisted. Sauntago warned them that the brew had to be downed quickly because it had sleeping properties as well as pain relief.

Maureen was not sure she believed him until her eyes opened to bright sunshine. In amazement she looked around her to find everyone else still sleeping though they were beginning to stir. She kept as still as possible for fear of the pain that was likely to overwhelm her body. Everyone else must have had the same feeling because other than their eyes no one moved a muscle.

Sauntago was the first to bravely shift his frame to a sitting position. Many groans escaped his mouth before he was upright. A heavy sigh left him as he confessed, "We will have to stay here an extra day. That trip was far more difficult than I imagined. Our horses deserve a day of rest too. Give me a moment or two and I will serve everyone a dose of tea. This day will be best passed in slumber."

Maureen was awakened by noise though for a few moments she was not certain what it was. Late afternoon had fallen which surprised her. Slowly she moved one leg thinking to herself that she needed to find the seed of that plant to take home with her. Though she was terribly sore as when she learned to ride a horse; the pain was now bearable.

With a start she realized that Drew and Charlie were not next to the makeshift fire pit. A frown formed above her eyes and around her lips. The king and queen had yet to stir which caused panic to wash over her in huge waves. "Drew! Charlie!" She cried over and over as loudly as she possibly could.

Sauntago and Modeanna were startled awake by her frantic screams. Before they had enough of their faculties to react there was a loud reply off in the distance.

"Mom, we're over here!" First one and then the other yelled as the two teens made their way back to the fire. In their arms was wood for another fire and bunches of leaves for more tea.

"What are you doing? You scared me half to death!" Maureen shouted with tears threatening in her eyes. "Don't wonder off like that again." Her trembling hand rose and pressed against her mouth as she realized how harsh she sounded when it was clear that all they were doing was trying to help.

Calmly Sauntago came to his daughter-in-law and gently rested his hand on her shoulder as he faced his grandsons. "Good work, Men. You have us well on our way for supplies, but your Mother is right. It is not safe for you to go off on your own without telling anyone."

Charlie placed the leaves next to the pan they had used the previous night and then responded, "We were just trying to help; didn't mean to scare anybody."

"Of course you didn't." Modeanna rose quickly to her feet with a deep grimace. "It's just so soon after your kidnapping that we are still jittery."

Drew emptied his arms and then went to his Mother. With his arms wrapped around her shoulders he lowered his face to the side of her neck and said, "I'm sorry, Mom, next time we'll wake you up first."

The toe of Charlie's leather boot etched circles in the dirt as he watched intently. His voice was full of regret as he admitted, "We never even thought about it. Guess we should have."

Maureen managed a bright smile for them as she responded, "Just give me a little more time to adjust to the fact that you really are here and the danger is past." When the words left her mouth she wished them back with all of her heart because there was a slight twitch in the king at the same moment the queen flinched. But once they had escaped it was impossible to erase them. Deep down she knew that her in-laws did not blame her though it was difficult not to feel responsible for the painful quiet which then settled on their camp.

# Chapter Fourteen

Once they resumed their journey it went at a slower pace. All of them were still feeling the effects of the long trek through the stream. None of the horses objected to the more leisurely movement. They traveled at such a rate that they took turns walking beside their mounts to give them a break.

This meant an extra day of travel before they reached The Gateway which bothered Maureen a bit. She was so anxious to find some sign of her husband's passage it often chafed her internally to walk so slowly. To the best of her ability she tried to hide it because she had already noticed the looks of concern Modeanna had for her.

It was on the fourth day of following the second river that the landscape and water started to change. Large trees rose up along the far bank that spread quite a distance away from the water's edge. There were lots of trees and bushes along their side as well, which forced them to travel several yards from the riverbed, but the concentration of plants and trees was considerably lower. In fact to her left Maureen could see large patches of dry ground with only short clumps of grass all around.

As the horses maneuvered around the trees Maureen realized that they were headed a bit southward. This fact excited her as she knew it meant they were drawing closer to the next river and the wall of rock along the border. Her breath caught audibly in her chest when she saw a dark peak against the late morning sky.

"It won't be long until we reach the next waterway and turn southward." Sauntago encouraged her quietly. "We could still have a long wait once we reach The Gateway, however."

"Yes, I know, but there will be signs that they have been there. Sau might have thought to tell us when they arrived or left." She felt the weight of his large hand on her shoulder and lifted her eyes to his face. By the expression in his eyes Maureen knew that he was just as anxious as she was.

"We will keep the boys with us after we cross the next river." He said firmly with a nod and then moved ahead to speak with his wife.

A spark of pride rose in her chest as she realized that the king had full confidence in her ability to handle whatever she met at The Gateway. Not knowing what she would find once she got there though made her edgy. At least when the boys were missing she had had Sauntage to help her through it. His parents were wonderful and their boys great, but they were not her husband. And she missed him so much.

Shortly after the sun reached its highest point they reached the large river that they had first followed upon arriving in Liguesis. She could not help spurring Jeurku into a faster gait. It should only be a few more hours given the fact that they could have walked the distance in less than two days had it not been for the carkna. Without looking back Maureen sped along the river bank she recalled so well.

Something told her that Sauntage had left something there for her. Her hair slowly fell from the tight braid she had made that morning. The bright blue fabric of her borrowed dress billowed out behind her.

Soon the top of the water fall came into view which made her want to ride even faster. It quickly grew larger and as it did she scanned to the right a short distance to find the cave entrance leading to The Gateway. Something was moving along the edge of the waterfall's pool. She had trouble making it out at first but with joy she realized it was a person.

Jeurku must have sensed her desire to go faster or simply knew if he reached that rock wall this torturous ride would be over. Tears spilled out from her eyes when he heard her coming and turned to wave excitedly at her. Finally, she pulled up the reigns to halt the exhausted horse.

Sliding off his back her eyes never left him for fear she was imagining him. Seconds later his little arms were clinging to her neck while he cried over and over, "Mommy! Mommy!"

After taking in his being alive she held him at arm's length to look him over. Ryan's skin was still pale but not hot. His cheeks were sunken and his limbs much too thin. The red in his hair like hers was diminished in the sunlight as were his freckles. A wide grin filled his entire face. "I love you."

"Me too, Mom. Boy did I miss you!" Ryan's voice was muffled as she crushed him against her heaving chest, but he did not resist.

Several moments went by without either of them saying anything. Reluctantly, Maureen released her little boy and smiled at him through a waterfall of tears. She had knelt on the ground in front of him so she had to stand up before she could move when she asked, "Where's your Father?"

"Oh, he's sleeping in the cave. He's been so busy helping me get better I think he got worn out." Ryan shrugged. "Where's Charlie and Drew?" His eyes dimmed with concern as he waited for her to answer.

"They're coming. I just had to race ahead and see you." She kissed his head.

Slowly they walked towards the cave arms tightly wrapped around each other. "Great! I can't wait to thank 'em. They did everything for me when those guys took us. You shoulda seen 'em, Mom. Charlie and Drew are like real heroes."

"I know. And they have told me how brave you were through everything that happened. I'm so proud of you, Ryan." She smiled tearfully at him still not sure she could trust her eyes.

"Dad's been telling me about all the stuff you did to find us. He said you killed a gigantic snake and rode a horse for hundreds of miles. And he said that the king and queen here took you as a prisoner, but they let you go after you saved the queen's life."

Maureen licked her lips slowly and then lowered her knees to the ground. "Do you understand where we are? Or anything that has happened?"

His eyes went to the ground and his leather covered foot scuffed through the grass. "Yeah, sort of. I mean I know we aren't in America anymore and that Daddy never really forgot who he was." Ryan lifted his blue eyes to her as he asked, "Did you know that Daddy has family here? And he said maybe I could meet some of them before we go home. Wouldn't that be cool?" Before Maureen could react he shifted his body to look behind her as he cried, "Hey, here they come! Be right back, Mom."

With a grateful smile she watched him run to his brothers; who were still a long distance off. Then she turned to go into the cave. It took her eyes a long time to adjust to the dark interior so she used her hands along the wall and her memory to reach the domed room with The Gateway pool off in one corner. If he were sleeping she reasoned, Sauntage would likely be off in the side room that Tagurah and he had built.

There was a dim light coming from the door as she drew closer. A smile spread on her face as she saw him lying in slumber. Licking her dry lips she called softly, "Sauntage?"

He did not stir.

With lifted brows she came closer saying a little louder, "Prince Vadelum?" Her grin widened as she saw him waken, realize she was there and leap to his feet.

Pulling her to his chest he kissed her tear streaked cheeks saying hoarsely, "Maureen, I love you." His voice broke as he went on to add, "I missed you so much over these last few weeks."

"Oh, me too. I can hardly believe that we're finally all together." She pressed the side of her face into his chest as her arms wrapped around his waist.

Suddenly, Sauntage pulled back to look into her eyes as he asked, "Did you see Ryan?"

"Yes, I saw him as I rode up here. He looks wonderful, Sau. How did you get him medicine so quickly? And then get back here?" Her eyes scanned over his clean face with the full beard and long hair.

"It was absolutely incredible, Darling. I think you were right about that ride through the desert. About halfway across it all the junk in Ryan's chest started to break up and he started coughing. Since we've been here I have found all the plants I could think of to help with the infection and fever. Between those and The Gateway pool he's recovered so quickly. He's got a long way to go, but I believe the danger is over."

"Yes, I think so too." Maureen pressed her lips together and then in a wavering voice she said, "Do you really think there is something special about that water?"

"Well, I can't say for sure, but it certainly would seem to have healing properties. Why?" He puzzled aloud as he sensed something bothering her.

Swallowing back the lump in her throat Maureen managed to answer, "Captain Trigguard is with us. He is doing better though he hasn't actually regained consciousness. We can tell that he is still in quite a bit of pain and his fever comes and goes."

With determination he placed his hands on her shoulders, "Let's get him in here right away." Sauntage snatched a pouch off of the bunk and then tried to pull her along behind him as he headed for the entrance of the cave. When he sensed her resistance he puzzled aloud, "What is it, Darling?"

A slow smile spread across her lips, "Well, he isn't actually here just yet. Your Father's men built a skiff that is pulled behind his horse so he has to keep a much slower pace than I had to. Drew and Charlie were just coming into view when I came in here."

The lift of his eyebrows as he grasped what she was saying was comical. Suddenly, the pouch hit the floor and she was in his arms.

That night they dined on fish and berries that Sauntage and Ryan had found earlier that morning. As they gathered around the fire after the meal Maureen suddenly felt tears prick her eyes. Her boys were across from her teasing each other and Sauntage's left arm was wrapped around her waist holding her tightly to his side. Sauntago and Modeanna sat in a similar posture watching their Grandsons with smiles. She blinked several times to keep back the flow of water because she didn't want to miss a thing in this memory.

Ryan sat between his brothers and as they talked he was jostled back and forth once in a while. He didn't seem to mind in the slightest. In fact there appeared to be a great deal of respect amongst the three of them because of what they had faced together.

Sauntage broke the silence of the adults as he said, "Your Mother tells me that none of you have explained what happened."

Charlie looked at his father with a solemn nod. "Yeah, we just couldn't talk about it. Not knowing how Ryan was and all." His head dropped to his little brothers briefly.

"There isn't much we can tell you, Dad." Drew explained with a sigh. "All I can remember is standing on the porch waiting for Charlie to unlock the front door and then this funny smelling rag was jammed over my mouth..."

"Same here. Except I heard Drew make this weird noise so I turned around to see what he was doing. Just before that rag hit my face I saw some guy that looked like Dad shoving Ryan into the backseat of a pickup truck." He studied the ground for a moment before he added, "Next thing I know we're sitting in some dark cold cave with our hands and feet all tied up."

"Those guys were so scary." Ryan recalled with a shutter. "They were all dirty and 'cept for the guy that looked like Dad nobody talked to us. Just sat and stared at us real mean like."

"Where did you get the idea to leave us messages in the candy wrappers?" Maureen broke in softly.

"You got those?" Cried Drew as he and Charlie shared a high five over their brother's head. "I saw something like it in an old movie once. Can't believe it actually worked though. How'd you figure it out?"

Giving his wife a proud squeeze Sauntage answered, "Your Mother caught on to what you did."

"I didn't really think it would do anything honestly. But Ryan was so scared we figured it might distract him a bit from what was happening."

With energy Ryan nodded to let everyone know his brother was right. "That place was cold and scary. All those bats and those mean guys. About the only thing good there was the candy. At least 'til Charlie thought it might be poisoned."

"Yeah, and we were all so hungry we just inhaled it." Drew admitted with a hand over his stomach remembering the terrible ache.

"How did you get through the caves?" Maureen wondered gently. "My entire body aches just thinking about how bad that was."

There was a deep frown on Charlie's face before he looked at his mother to respond, "I don't know. Can't remember much of anything about the cave after we ate the candy. One of the guys used that rag on us and the next thing I know we're sitting in this huge room with a high ceiling and all these spikes hanging from it."

"Seems like a weird dream. Everything was so hazy and dark. And just when we thought we were awake a rag would show up." For a moment he stopped to search his memory for any thoughts he might have forgotten. "Once we got here they stopped using the rag on us."

"Yeah, then they tied us to horses and forced us to ride for hours on end." Charlie snarled bitterly. "It was bad enough for Drew and me, but we've played baseball and football we're used to that kind of stuff. I don't know how Ryan did it. He didn't even cry."

"Sure wanted to though." The little boy admitted with his arms wrapped around his knees. "'Specially when my throat started hurting in that dessert."

Modeanna gasped suddenly, "You were taken through the Garak Dessert?"

"Yes. We got water from this river and rode on horses due east for five or six days I think. Nighttime wasn't so bad it was pretty cool. Daytime, though, that was like an oven."

"And one of the men would dig up these plants so we could all get water and a bit of food." A brief glance went to his young brother before Drew added, "That's when Ryan started sniffling."

"Yeah, and you guys gave me some of your food and water to make me feel better." Ryan bumped lightly into each of his brothers by way of saying thanks.

"He seemed a lot better by the time we got to the place where you found us." Drew leaned back to his left to return his affection and then went on to add, "Most of the men in the mines treated us pretty decent. One even helped us learn a couple of words."

"We had plenty to eat and drink. And they even took us outside for walks 'til Ryan got wet in this huge storm and then got sick. Those guys still came to take Drew and I, but we wouldn't go without Ryan."

For a few moments it was quiet. Then Drew spared a quick glance for his Grandparents before he added, "Uncle Tagurah came to talk to us quite a few times. Especially after Ryan got sick. At first he seemed nice enough; you know, acted like he wanted to be our friend and all. He even brought some medicine that worked 'til we ran out."

"Then about a week before you showed up he stopped coming. The whole place seemed edgy and we could hear metal clashing all the time. A couple of days after that the guy that taught us some words brought our dinner and told us they were getting ready to fight."

"Everything else you pretty much know." Drew ended with a heavy sigh, obviously glad to have the telling behind him.

All of the adults sensed that the boys needed to leave the subject alone for the time being. So for quite a long time the only noise was the crackling fire. Sauntago hated to break up their first family evening, but his responsibility called to him. His eyes traveled from his Grandsons to his son as he cleared his throat to speak. "We should see to the Captain."

"You're right, we should, Sire." Without further words he rose with a lantern to find his way to the cave where Captain Trigguard had been stretched out on a bunk to rest after his first soak in The Gateway pool.

Captain Trigguard was moved to the skiff and then carried to the water's edge where his clothes were gently removed. Only a couple of low moans were heard throughout this process which concerned both men helping him, though neither of them spoke of it. Sauntage stepped into the pool carefully staying as close to the edge as possible because the slope of the rock floor was so great he would easily have gone in over his head.

When he was ready he gave a nod to his father and they worked together to submerge all but the injured man's head into the water. As Sauntage held Captain Trigguard's head against his shoulder, Sauntago held the lantern above him to look closely at the angry wound across his stomach. "I don't see how this will help him. His skin has healed together fairly well. It's his insides that are infected."

"I don't understand how it works either. At least it worked for Ryan and he didn't have any wounds on his skin. Maybe we should give him some of this water to drink."

Giving his son a nod he rose to get a cup to help them administer the water without drowning him in it. In the end, however, the two of them decided to wait until they had finished bathing the Captain before helping him sip. Most of the water ran down his chin as Sauntago tipped the small vessel to his still lips. As he dabbed a soft cloth from his wife's wardrobe along the Captain's chin Sauntago whispered, "May Ewaris have mercy on you and make you whole."

"Amen." Sauntage agreed as he finished lacing the last of the ties on his shirt. "Let's get him back to the povout bed. Perhaps morning will bring the change we pray for."

Sauntago and Modeanna shared the second bunk In the povout

room while Sauntage and his family slept around the dwindling fire. With her husband's warm arm around her and the knowledge that her son's were only a few feet away Maureen slept better than she had in two months. The sun was well on its daily journey when she finally opened her eyes. In the distance she could hear the voices of her husband and sons. A content smile spread across her face as she listened to them.

Curiosity finally got the better of her so she rolled over to see what the four of them were doing. Her grin widened when she saw them looking under rocks for the worms needed for fishing. It was clear that Ryan had learned to do this already and was thoroughly enjoying the lesson he was teaching his brothers.

Sauntage must have sensed her gaze because he turned in her direction with questioning eyes. As he walked toward her she rose to meet him with laughter bubbling involuntarily through her lips. After drawing her close for a long kiss he said, "We're working on breakfast."

"I can see that." She giggled at the frowns on Charlie and Drew's faces. "Shall I build a fire or help with the fish?"

His brows lifted suddenly as he realized, "Either one would come natural to you now, wouldn't it?"

"Hmm, I hadn't thought about it. Of the two I believe the fire would be easier." Maureen's nose wrinkled as she admitted, "I don't have to dig up or tie on worms."

He laughed heartily as she turned to use their makeshift bathroom and then went back to help the boys catch breakfast.

Sauntago and Modeanna appeared just minutes before the meal was ready to eat. They were well rested and the most relaxed Maureen had ever seen them. Captain Trigguard still had not come to consciousness but he rested more peacefully according to the king and queen which they took as a good sign.

While they slowly enjoyed their fish Sauntage grew quiet and thoughtful. His eyes often went to his mother's face and then dropped back to the dying fire.

Sauntago allowed this to go on until his meal was over and he set aside his plate, saying, "Ask what you will, Son. There may never be another time to do so."

This fact seemed to startle Sauntage but also made him bold as he turned his eyes to his mother and asked pointedly in English, "How on earth did you end up here?"

Her laughter rang loud and long before she answered. "In exactly the same way you have gone back and forth all these years." The smile on her lips lessoned and her eyes glaze over as time rolled back in her mind. "Truthfully I am here because of Ewaris' grace. God's mercy and grace. I am not ashamed of where I came from, but I do not like going back even in my thoughts." With a heavy sigh she went at length back to her childhood and the pain it held.

Time passed almost unnoticed as Modeanna shared details that she had clearly not even allowed her mind to think on in years. As she talked about her family Maureen could not help but think of her husband. Sauntage could relate to her better than anyone about holding secrets from his family, but that was where the similarities ended. His secret held two parts of a wonderful family that loved him.

The family that Modeanna separated from did not hold her in high regard. In fact she suffered abuses at the hands of more than one family member before Sauntago discovered her hiding in a cave. Tears filled her eyes as she ended her tale and looked to her rescuer with tender eyes. "All of that was the life of someone I no longer know. This is who I am now." She placed a gentle kiss beside his lips then rose to be alone.

After watching her walk away Sauntage looked at his father to ask emotionally, "Shouldn't you go with her? Mother shouldn't be alone after what she just went through." He lowered his eyes almost ashamed that he had wanted to know.

"My Fair Lady Modeanna is not alone. She is walking with Ewaris asking Him to once again take those memories from her. Do not hold your head guilty in any of this. You were not responsible for that pain and it does neither of you any good." Once his words were done Sauntago got up to check on The Captain.

Much to everyone's joy Captain Trigguard opened his eyes with comprehension that afternoon as he was bathed. His awareness was brief but he clearly reacted to Sauntago's presence. After the Captain was tucked back into the bunk they had a celebration of sorts with whooping, shouting, laughter and hugging. The king was the one to reign in the festivities as he considered Captain Trigguard's situation. "We must have eyes on him more often. He could wake up at anytime and because we don't know yet if he has suffered any injury to his mind we need to be sure he can't hurt himself."

"Shall we take turns sitting with him then?" Modeanna questioned with her hands held out as if they held the solution instead of her words.

It took them some time to arrange a schedule because all of them wanted to be the first to stay with him. In the end it was decided that they would go by birth order which caused a dark shadow to cross Sauntage's face.

"I just realized. I don't even know you're true birthday or age!" Maureen gasped loudly at her husband.

There was a frown on his lips as he responded, "It doesn't really matter all that much does it?"

Her eyes narrowed on him as she tried to understand his hesitation. "Of course it does. How can we determine which one of us sits with him if we don't know who is older?"

Quietly he answered, "You may sit with him first, Mo." Color touched his face as his eyes lifted above her head.

"I was right! All these years I knew I was older than you." She watched the muscles tense along his jaw and neck. "And it bothers you, Sau." Giggling Maureen poked at his ribs as she demanded, "By how much?"

"Almost three years." He admitted between clenched teeth and turned to walk away.

The realization of what that meant settled on her slowly. If that were true then he would have been under the legal age when they married. Although he most likely didn't know that at the time Sauntage would have become aware of that fact over the passing years. As she watched him striding towards the river she couldn't help but smile at him. Maureen followed him at a rapid pace and then stopped several feet behind him.

"Do you think this bothers me, Sau?"

"You know what bothers me, Mo." He sighed heavily.

"No one else has to know." She came around to face him with her hands on her hips.

His eyes blazed at her as he shouted back at her, "I know, Maureen."

"Why does it make a difference now, all of a sudden, after all of these years?" Her eyes pleaded with him as her fingers reached out to do the same.

"Because I know God now. I didn't know...didn't believe in Him back then. At the time I told myself I wasn't hurting anyone I was simply protecting Liguesis." He shook his head with bitter remorse.

"Sau," Maureen took a step closer to him and then tenderly cupped the side of his face to make him look at her. "I have forgiven you for the past. Let it go. You were young..."

Looking at her smiling eyes briefly he lowered his gaze to the water. "Selfish. The truth is I wanted the best of both worlds." A heavy sigh left him as he went on to add, "And I caused a great deal of suffering and pain because of it."

"Yes, that is true. We have all been affected by those deceptions, but we can correct this one." Her brows lifted with intensity.

"How?" Sauntage gazed at her with disbelief.

"When we get back marry me. If it matters all that much to you we can go change all of your information with the government too."

"Doesn't it bother you that legally we're not married?" He felt his jaw open wide as she shook her head at him.

Laughter bubbled up as she explained, "Honestly I don't really care about what the law says. My heart tells me what matters. And it is saying to me that in God's eyes we are joined together as one."

Without words he pulled her to his chest. It was a long time before he loosened his arms from around her back. "I love you, Mo." Was all he said as he turned to go back towards the family. When they reached the fire pit Sauntago had already left to sit with Captain Trigguard.

Each of them sat for a couple of hours during the day. During her turn Maureen used a lantern and read from the Bible. The Captain's breathing was regular and even as though he were in a deep sleep.

Once in a while she would look up at the poor young man and cringe. He had not been a very big man to begin with, but due to his injury and the infections he had lost a great deal of weight. His pale skin was loose over his arms and legs where the muscles had faded away. It sagged over his thin face like a cloth molding to every angle.

One such time she looked up to see his eyes darting around over his head. Sauntago and Modeanna had also reported seeing this so she grew excited as she closed the Bible and drew close to him. In a soft voice she said to him, "Hello Captain. Can you hear me?"

The young man jolted slightly at the sound of her voice and then moved his eyes about to locate her. As soon as he did a well of tears rose in his eyes.

"Let me help you sip some water." She put her arm gently beneath his head as she lifted the cup to his lips.

Water dribbled down his chin and around his neck as he tried to work the muscles in his throat. There was disappointment when the cup disappeared but it was only momentary as sleep claimed him.

Maureen was fortunate to see his eyes open once more before Sauntage came in to relieve her. After they had shared a long kiss she left the povout room to join the rest of the family. While she sensed joy as she shared her interactions with the Captain, Maureen also felt an undercurrent of sorrow developing in the queen. At first this confused her but as time went on she realized what it was and began to pray for comfort for her mother-in-law.

While one family member was keeping watch the others carried out the business of camp. Sauntago had gone hunting with his wife's sword and came back with an animal Maureen didn't recognize slung around his neck. Sauntage helped his father prepare the meat for roasting over the fire as Modeanna and Maureen made sure the fire was ready. Not much in the way of conversation took place until after they had eaten their dinner.

Each time they changed shifts they found his condition improving rapidly. Captain Trigguard was finally able to tell them that his given name was Narvakoa. Words drained his strength quickly so after they learned his name they encouraged him to remain silent while broth was spooned into his mouth. As long as he didn't use energy to talk or move Narvakoa managed to eat an entire bowl of soup every few hours. This seemed to bring a healthier color to his skin which brought hope to them all.

Within two days he was able to chew small bits of fish or meat that were floating in the broth. His determination to get well was noted by everyone as he worked to sit up against the walls to eat, but submitted to orders when told to stop. Sauntago and Sauntage carried him to the pool at least three times each day allowing him to soak for several minutes. Narvakoa moved his legs and arms about carefully as either the king or Sauntage held his head above the water's surface. This activity helped increase his strength and endurance which soon became noticeable on his frame. Muscle started to fill in the loose skin of his body faster than any of them thought possible.

Four days after he had spoken the men carried him outside to enjoy some time by the evening fire. For a few minutes he sat propped against Sauntage's back to eat a plate of food and then Narvakoa rested on the skiff next to the fire.

By the week's end he was taking a few dozen steps on his own. Maureen watched him in amazement. It was almost impossible to believe that this was the same man that they had literally dragged across the countryside. She also paid attention to the reaction of the king and queen.

They cheered Narvakoa on in each of his accomplishments, but when his therapy sessions were over the two of them often grew quiet. When their son was occupied with Narvakoa, the two of them would take long walks out of sight.

On a cool morning nearly two weeks after reaching The Gateway Pool, Narvakoa sat with the family around the campfire. Energy had returned to him so he was now interested in learning all that had taken place while he had been ill. He listened to the answers of his questions with awe and humility.

Maureen offered a few responses as did everyone else, but she became distracted by the tight lines forming around the queen's mouth. Modeanna had grown quiet; completely lost in her own thoughts which caused her to drop her guard over her countenance. The pain reflected in her features made Maureen's throat swell to the point of not being able to swallow.

Her eyes darted to Sauntage and she caught a look that passed between he and his father. With a deep sigh he nodded to the king in agreement.

Clearing his throat awkwardly, Sauntago said, "I believe Narvakoa is strong enough now to manage the journey to his home." His gaze moved to the young man with a slight smile of pride. "But Captain Trigguard there is a matter of our nation's security at stake here."

Narvakoa jolted visibly with these words and quickly looked around at the faces no longer meeting his eyes. "Sire, I don't understand?"

"Yes, I realize that this is rather confusing to you. But the truth is that where we are sitting is sacred ground of sorts. This is a place where Ewaris has left his handprint you might say..." Sauntago was taken aback when his voice was interrupted.

"Then I am alive and well by His hand." Captain Trigguard whispered in shock.

"Yes." Replied the king not ready to be interrupted a second time.

"This place must be protected, Sire. Were the whole realm to learn of it, they would come and eventually destroy it."

"Very astute. You are wise beyond your years." His eyes studied the young Captain before he went on to say, "And you will understand the measures we must take with you to keep this ground sacred?"

Without hesitation Narvakoa rose to his feet and then knelt to the ground. "I am yours to command, Your Majesty."

"After our mid-day meal you will again take to your skiff. I will then ask you to take doses of sleeping juice until we reach your home."

At this, the young man flinched his displeasure, but refrained from making any comment.

For two hours not many words were spoken. None were needed. They all knew what would take place after the Captain slept.

When his food was gone Narvakoa quietly thanked them all for their care and then moved silently to the skiff. He could tell by the silence of this otherwise noisy family that something was amiss. While he was curious Narvakoa had learned in his short term of military service that one often avoided more trouble by simply obeying orders.

The last time he had stretched the meaning of his directions it nearly cost him his life. No such danger seemed to be present for the royal family so he willingly waited for his medicine.

Modeanna handed the cup of brewed leaves to her husband with trembling fingers. She watched closely for the change of sleep to settle over the Captain's body. As soon as she was sure that he was no longer aware of his surroundings, tears slipped unchecked from her eyes.

Sauntage pressed his lips together as he faced his father. "It's time." After receiving a nod of agreement he turned to his sons. "We must say goodbye."

Wordlessly the boys threw themselves into the open arms of their grandparents. Several minutes went by before they stepped back to seemingly memorize one another. Tender touches went to each of the boys with whispered prayers of blessing.

Maureen was next to be folded against her father-in-law's chest. For a long time words failed to even enter her mind let alone move in her lumpy throat. As his arms pulled her closer to his heart her eyes opened widely. The left could see nothing as it was too close to his body, but out of the corner of her right Maureen saw that the queen had run to stand near the bank of the river. Her head and shoulders were slumped forward with violent tremors wracking the proud woman's frame.

Suddenly, she moved her palms to the king's chest. With as much strength as she could muster, Maureen pushed away from him. Meeting his pained eyes she demanded with quiet intensity, "Could he ever be forgiven by the people of Liguesis? For the true betrayal of leaving and the lies of his brother?"

Confusion knit his brow for a brief moment before he responded, "It would take time and much effort on his part, but yes the people would eventually welcome him."

Her fingers wrapped around several inches of his clothing and wrinkled the material in her tight grip. "Would he cause harm to your reign?"

When he realized what her questions were leading to new tears washed into his eyes. "It would not matter. He is my son."

A smile spread to her lips as she released his clothing and turned to follow her husband's slow steps. He had dejectedly begun the long walk to his mother's side. Maureen's feet raced to catch up to him and she succeeded in reaching him when he was still out of hearing distance from the queen.

Sauntage heard the rustle of her long skirt and the deep breaths she was pulling into her lungs. When he turned to face her he was not prepared for the speed at which she hit him. His feet stumbled backwards several paces and he caught a glimpse of his father and sons standing quietly by the skiff. It was impossible to read what she was thinking because her head was shaking back and forth so quickly. There was no choice for him but to wait until she caught her breath to speak.

"No, Sauntage, we can't do this." She grabbed the sides of his face firmly. "You can't do this to her. She lost one son right before her eyes; she can't lose you again, too."

"Maureen," He whispered harshly with a pained look over his shoulder at his weeping mother. "I have no choice. I have to..."

"Why?"

Pressing his lips together he gathered the strength to answer, "Earth is our home. It's your home; the boys' home."

"No, Sau. There is nothing on earth that I care about more than what is here. Everything else pales in comparison to what is here. That lady is your Mother our sons' Grandmother and they are standing with their Grandfather. All of that is lost to them on earth."

A cry tore from his lips as he shouted back at her, "You don't think I've thought about those things? Agonized over them! It's not that simple, Maureen." He turned away from her and paced in an arc before her.

"Well, what on earth makes it so hard?" She shouted back at him.

His feet stopped in front of her as he explained in a slightly calmer tone, "Maureen, I can't come back here and pick up where I left off. I am a betrayer to the crown. I'd be lucky if I didn't end up in a prison cell."

"For the joy it would bring the queen I have no doubt you could get the king's pardon." She could not hold the smile that pulled on her lips.

"Darling, I think you have some misunderstanding here. Even if I am pardoned I am no longer in line to be king. There would be no royal life for us here."

Her eyes narrowed on him as she spat back, "Do you really think I care about that? Are there no jobs here for you that equal or are better a garbage collector? A very respectable position and necessary for the health and well being of our earthly community to be sure; but you are much more than that to our sons now. And to me."

In a much softer voice he responded, "Life here with a career I would be allowed to take would not be much better than you have already experienced. There would be no better future for our sons. As much as it hurts to leave Mother and Father for you and the boys I have no choice."

Anger rose in her. Through clenched teeth she challenged him, "Your Mother and Father risked their very lives for us. We watched the men of his army go to back to their families reluctantly in many cases. Liguesis has lessons and gifts our children could never get on earth. Most importantly would be their Father should he choose to be the man he was raised to be." Without waiting for him to answer she stalked back to where their sons were waiting next to their grandfather.

They did not dare to say a word to her for the heat in her eyes. Ryan drew close to her and cautiously placed his small hand in hers.

"He must choose his own way." Sauntago said gently then bowed his knee to the ground in front of her as he added, "Thank you, Fair Lady Maureen, for making that decision as hard as possible."

Something in the glint of his eye caused her to laugh brightly.

"Know this, all of you," He added as he rose to his feet looking at each of them in turn, "You will always have a home here should you wish it."

"Thank you, Your Majesty." She returned the bow from her waist and then whispered, "For everything." When she came to her full height she looked towards the cave entrance. "I'm going to prepare what we need for the journey." Her feet moved as though they had lead weights attached.

With a heavy hand the king brought a halt to her steps. "Wait. Look." His other fingers indicated the direction her husband had continued to walk.

Fresh tears had washed into her eyes robbing her of her vision. Maureen used the sleeves and shoulders of the gown to wipe away the moisture. When she could finally see clearly she held her breath.

Sauntage was at the river's edge with his knee bent before the queen. For a moment she stiffened, but then she quickly turned around to look at them waiting by Captain Trigguard. Modeanna's mouth slowly opened and as her son came to his feet she threw herself into his embrace. There was joy radiating from her as Sauntage swung her in a couple of circles.

"Does that mean we get to stay?" Ryan cried excitedly.

Drew looked down at his brother to say, "Man, I hope so."

Charlie spared a few seconds to gaze at the cave entrance longingly and then moved his head so that he could see his grandfather. Though he lacked the same level of enthusiasm he nodded with determination. "Yeah, this place is amazing." He admitted with a grin to his grandfather.

Maureen did hear what her sons said and knew that Charlie would likely struggle at times. As she ran to meet her husband walking back towards them, however, it was the last thing on which her mind dwelt. Laughter bubbled up as she met his wide embrace and felt her feet leave the ground.

# Epilogue

The trek north took longer even though they had horses because they had to stop every few hours to prepare a fresh batch of tea for Captain Trigguard. Sauntago wanted to drag out the journey in hopes that the length of the trip would be beyond the young man's grasp should temptation ever arise. He soon realized that his concerns were unfounded as Narvakoa refused to open his eyes when he woke. Instead he quietly spoke to let them know he was conscious.

When Sauntage informed his father that they were just a couple of miles from the Trigguard farm, the king called for a halt. Once everyone had dismounted their horses Sauntage and his sons took the reins to care for the animals. Knowing he was not worthy to take his father's place he had asked to serve in the royal stables so they could be close. Without hesitation Sauntago had agreed much to Modeanna's dismay. She felt that her son had earned a better position than stable boy, but the look she had received from her husband told her not to argue the point.

While they waited for Narvakoa to awaken the king solemnly gave them instructions for their arrival at the Trigguard farm. Confusion knit everyone's brow as they tried to understand why this occasion had to be so formal.

It was when Narvakoa received his directions that Modeanna finally spoke on the matter. "Oh, Sauntago, his family probably thinks he's dead. How can you ask him to wait so long on that skiff?"

"I expect you all to trust me." He gave each of them a firm look of warning.

"My Queen?" Captain Trigguard bowed to her before he added with a smile, "I am the second son of a farmer. A great man, but not overly taken by his title. With his blessing I came to serve our king. Never did I imagine that I would ever have the chance to speak to you, Sire, let alone be cared for by your hand. My Father taught me to respect your position, but you have earned my devotion. As long as it does not go against Ewaris, I will follow your every command." Once his speech ended Narvakoa gave a short bow and then moved to take his place on the skiff.

Maureen felt excitement rise in her as the familiar farm came into view. It was difficult to hold back the smile on her face, but to follow the king's orders she did her best. Like before it was clear when they had been spotted because of the activity in the yard in front of the house. For a brief moment Maureen was puzzled by the number of older males and then she realized that the third son would have already returned home from the battlefield.

By the time they drew near to the house the large family had assembled around a single chair that had been brought from inside. This confused Maureen as much as seeing Maruti sitting in it. Shouldn't Narmaka have been the one seated? With a quick glance to her husband she saw his hand gesture in front of his stomach and gained understanding.

At first the family had not known that the group was the royal family. But as soon as they drew closer the Trigguards stiffened. Color left some of the faces only to be found in others. They collectively bowed on the ground before the horses and waited to be spoken to.

"Rise, please." Sauntago said gently. After the large group had gone back to their original position he went on to ask, "Is Farmer Master Trigguard here amongst you?"

"I am, Sire." Arvou stepped forward to bow at his waist.

An emotionless mask fell on the king's face as he demanded quietly, "Did this man and woman come to you for help?"

Arvou hesitated as he looked briefly towards Sauntage and Maureen. "They came to our home, Sire. We welcomed them. And yes, Your Majesty, I gave them aid."

Narmaka quickly joined her husband boldly proclaiming, "We all did, Sire. We had no idea they were traitors to the crown."

The king seemed to ignore her as he continued his interrogation, "And why did you give them the best of your animals?"

He was startled by the question but quickly answered, "Sire, we knew the sorrow of surrendering our sons for the greater good, we had no reason to doubt the story of their sons being taken. We did what we hoped someone else would do for our sons if they were in need."

"I see." Sauntago replied quietly. After a moment of silence he swung down from his horse. To the amazement and shock of the Trigguard family he dropped to his knee in front of Arvou. "Then I have you to thank for the lives of my grandsons."

"Sire?" Whispered Arvou awkwardly.

Coming to his feet Sauntago pointed to the boys and called, "Drew, Charlie and Ryan were indeed taken and you made their safe return possible." His eyes shifted to the young man standing ramrod straight next to his mother. "Where did you serve?"

"Arms man Rouva Trigguard at your service, Your Majesty." Lifting his eyes after a respectful bow he answered, "I was sent with the northern troops when it was discovered that my brother served as well." His head lowered with pain as his hand went to his mother's shoulder in comfort.

"Then you have heard of Narvakoa's story?"

"Yes, Sire, we know our son gave himself in service to the crown. We are pleased that he was able to serve you." Narmaka said tearfully.

"Are you aware that Narvakoa sacrificed himself to save my family?" Asked the king with his eyes traveling over the large group of faces.

"But those stories were of a Captain, Sire, our son was an Arms man." Arvou spoke breathlessly.

"He was indeed. But in the midst of battle My Fair Lady Modeanna saw fit to promote him. Her insights are rarely wrong. His wounds were grave and he suffered much..."

Narmaka could no longer contain her grief. Loud sobs escaped though she attempted to stifle them with her hand.

"Please, allow me to finish, my dear lady." When he knew he had her attention he added, "And I wish to make it up to him." Suddenly, he turned around and shouted, "Captain Narvakoa Trigguard!"

With a smile Narvakoa rose from the skiff to face his family and king. He was not able to answer the king's call right away because he was swarmed by his family.

Sauntage laughed heartily as he dismounted and helped his mother to do the same. As he held out the reigns for Drew and Charlie, he reached up to take Maureen by the waist. "Let's tie them by the fence in front of the barn; there is a trough for them there.

From where she stood next to Jeurku Maureen could see the Captain shyly sharing his experience with his family. Her husband's arm draped around her shoulders, as he leaned down to place a kiss on her temple.

In a few minutes the Captain was finished telling what little he could remember. Narvakoa was careful to leave out the details of the time they had spent at the healing pool. He seemed to want the moment of everyone's attention on him to be over.

A few more minutes went by as Sauntage and his family waited off to the side. There was so much noise and activity that he knew it would be some time before he could give his thanks to the Trigguards. This did not bother him as he enjoyed watching the love shared by this large group.

Maureen smiled up at her husband and noted the thoughtful look in his eyes. In wonder she said, "You really would have a dozen children wouldn't you?" Although he responded with a chuckle she could sense a level of sadness in his answer.

"No, need to worry about that, Mo. Our needs will be met by my work in the royal stables, but there won't be enough to support more than we have. You must keep in mind that my rank is that of a young man Drew or Charlie's age."

His words were meant to encourage her she knew, but for some strange reason this knowledge left her feeling hollow inside.

Sauntago waited for the celebration to die down a bit before he called out in a loud voice, "Captain Trigguard!"

"Yes, Your Majesty?" Narvakoa gave an immediate bow and then stood at attention.

"As I said before, I wish to make this up to you. You are hereby given one month leave to spend with your family. After this you will report to the castle in Wiaurk to begin your new duties."

"New duties, Sire?" Narvakoa wondered with his eyes darting to his parents who were standing tensely near him.

"Yes, specifically you are to report to the throne room." It was hard for him to remain silent but for affect and understanding of everyone listening he waited some time before turning to Arvou. "With your permission, Farmer Master Trigguard, I wish to break with tradition. Your son has proven himself to be loyal, brave, self-sacrificing and wise beyond his years. And though it is much later than any king would like to begin; I wish him to be trained as the next king's advisor with your blessing, of course."

An audible gasp went through the entire family. All of them simply stared at the king with disbelief.

Humor lifted the corners of the king's mouth as he looked at Narvakoa and asked, "That is if you think you can serve him with the same integrity you have shown me."

When Sauntago turned to look over his shoulder at his son, Maureen felt him stiffen. A moment later the significance hit her. He was restoring Sauntage to his place as crowned prince. She could see the glittering tears in his eyes as he lowered his knees to the ground.

"It is I that should serve him, Father." Sauntage admitted weakly.

The king gave a firm nod to him as he stated, "As long as you bear that in mind, you will be a king long remembered as wise and worthy."

His eyes lifted at his father's words and he discovered everyone had taken a knee before him. Taking hold of his wife's hand he gave it a squeeze, as he arose saying, "By the grace of Ewaris I will always remember."

Modeanna threw herself into her husband's chest and grasped his face to kiss him repeatedly. Giggling at this, Maureen decided to follow her mother-in-law's lead. After several kisses though she pulled back slightly to tease, "Something tells me I should be worried now since your rank has just risen significantly."

Sauntage grinned at her and then chuckled against her lips as he agreed, "Well, we really ought to have at least one princess in the family."

Tenderly she rubbed her palms against his cheeks. Tears shimmered in her eyes as she smiled at him. "Only one? Prince Sau, I thought for sure you would have asked for a dozen."

Also Available By

# Clarissa L. Ross

## *The Power of the Truth*

ISBN  978-1-4116-7296-3

It came as no surprise to Caroline that her estranged husband was angry. In her mind he had every right to be. But when everything she believed about the past is suddenly challenged, can she learn to accept his forgiveness?

When Johnathan is forced to face his wife he takes a leap of faith never dreaming where it could lead. In the midst of the journey he cannot help but wonder if they can ever really be free from the painful past.

As they unravel the web of assumptions and lies, Johnathan and Caroline discover they have the chance for a future. But the mystery of the past threatens to steal, kill and destroy. Can they withstand the present dangers long enough to see...The Power of the Truth?

Available at Amazon.com
**http://www.amazon.com/gp/product/1411672968**

www.ingramcontent.com/pod-product-compliance
Lightning Source LLC
Chambersburg PA
CBHW030346020726
47493CB00003B/706